THE WOMEN

Also by Kristin Hannah

The Four Winds

The Great Alone

The Nightingale

Fly Away

Home Front

Night Road

Winter Garden

True Colors

Firefly Lane

Magic Hour

Comfort & Joy

The Things We Do for Love

Between Sisters

Distant Shores

Summer Island

Angel Falls

On Mystic Lake

Home Again

Waiting for the Moon

When Lightning Strikes

If You Believe

Once in Every Life

The Enchantment

A Handful of Heaven

THE
WOMEN

KRISTIN
HANNAH

ST. MARTIN'S PRESS
NEW YORK

First published in the United States by St. Martin's Press, an imprint of St. Martin's Publishing Group

THE WOMEN. Copyright © 2024 by Kristin Hannah.
All rights reserved. Printed in the United States of America. For information, address St. Martin's Publishing Group, 120 Broadway, New York, NY 10271.

www.stmartins.com

Interior and endpapers designed by Donna Sinisgalli Noetzel

Photograph credits: title page by EchoArt / Shutterstock.com (dog tags), Militarist / Shutterstock.com (background); page 1 by Keith Tarrier / Shutterstock.com; page 281 by Bettmann / Contributor / Getty Images

Photograph of Vietnam Women's Memorial on page 465: Vietnam Women's Memorial, Washington, D.C. © 1993, Eastern National, Glenna Goodacre, Sculptor. Photo Credit: Greg Staley.
Use of this image does not imply endorsement of Eastern National or the National Park Service.

Library of Congress Cataloging-in-Publication Data

Names: Hannah, Kristin, author.
Title: The women / Kristin Hannah.
Description: First edition. | New York : St. Martin's Press, 2024.
Identifiers: LCCN 2023026802 | ISBN 9781250178633 (hardcover) |
    ISBN 9781250348838 (international) | ISBN 9781250178657
    (ebook)
Subjects: LCGFT: Novels.
Classification: LCC PS3558.A4763 W66 2024 | DDC 813/.54—
    dc23/eng/20230615
LC record available at https://lccn.loc.gov/2023026802

Our books may be purchased in bulk for promotional, educational, or business use. Please contact your local bookseller or the Macmillan Corporate and Premium Sales Department at 1-800-221-7945, extension 5442, or by email at MacmillanSpecialMarkets@macmillan.com.

First Edition: 2024
First International Edition: 2024

This edition was printed by Lakeside Book Company.

10 9 8 7 6 5 4 3 2 1

This novel is dedicated to the courageous women who served in Vietnam. These women, most of them nurses and many of them raised on proudly told family stories of World War II heroism, heeded their country's call to arms and went to war. In too many instances, they came home to a country that didn't care about their service and a world that didn't want to hear about their experiences; their post-war struggles and their stories were too often forgotten or marginalized. I am proud to have this opportunity to shine a light on their strength, resilience, and grit.

And to all veterans and POW/MIA and their families, who have sacrificed so much.

And finally, to the medical personnel who fought the pandemic and gave so much of themselves to help others.

Thank you.

PART ONE

*This war has . . . stretched the generation gap so
wide that it threatens to pull the country apart.*

—FRANK CHURCH

One

The walled and gated McGrath estate was a world unto itself, protected and private. On this twilit evening, the Tudor-style home's mullioned windows glowed jewel-like amid the lush, landscaped grounds. Palm fronds swayed overhead; candles floated on the surface of the pool and golden lanterns hung from the branches of a large California live oak. Black-clad servers moved among the well-dressed crowd, carrying silver trays full of champagne, while a jazz trio played softly in the corner.

Twenty-year-old Frances Grace McGrath knew what was expected of her tonight. She was to be the very portrait of a well-bred young lady, smiling and serene; any untoward emotions were to be contained and concealed, borne in silence. The lessons Frankie had been taught at home and at church and at St. Bernadette's Academy for Girls had instilled in her a rigorous sense of propriety. The unrest going on across the country these days, erupting on city streets and college campuses, was a distant and alien world to her, as incomprehensible as the conflict in faraway Vietnam.

She circulated among the guests, sipping an ice-cold Coca-Cola, trying to smile, stopping now and then to make small talk with her parents' friends, hoping her worry didn't show. All the while, her gaze searched the crowd for her brother, who was late to his own party.

Frankie idolized her older brother, Finley. They'd always been inseparable, a pair of black-haired, blue-eyed kids, less than two years apart in age, who'd spent the long California summers unsupervised by adults, riding their bikes from one end of sleepy Coronado Island to the other, rarely coming home before nightfall.

But now he was going where she couldn't follow.

The roar of a car engine disturbed the quiet party; car horns honked loudly, in succession.

Frankie saw how her mother flinched at the noise. Bette McGrath hated anything showy or vulgar, and she certainly didn't believe in announcing one's presence by honking a horn.

Moments later, Finley banged through the back gate, his handsome face flushed, a lock of curly black hair fallen across his forehead. His best friend, Rye Walsh, had an arm around him, but neither looked too steady on his feet. They laughed drunkenly, held each other up, as more of their friends stumbled into the party behind them.

Dressed impeccably in a black sheath, with her hair in a regal updo, Mom moved toward the group of laughing young men and women. She wore the pearls her grandmother had bequeathed her, a subtle reminder that Bette McGrath had once been Bette Alexander, of the Newport Beach Alexanders. "Boys," she said in her modulated charm-school voice. "How nice that you are finally here."

Finley stumbled away from Rye, tried to straighten.

Dad motioned to the band and the music stopped. Suddenly the sounds of Coronado Island on a late spring night—the throaty purr of the ocean, the whisper of the palm fronds overhead, a dog barking down the street or on the beach—took over. Dad strode forward in his custom-made black suit, crisp white shirt, and black tie, holding a cigarette in one hand and a Manhattan in his other. With his close-cropped black hair and square jaw, he looked a little like an ex-boxer who'd hit the big time and learned how to dress well, which wasn't too far off. Even among this handsome, well-dressed crowd, he and Mom stood out, radiated success. She was old money and had always been at the top of the social ladder; he had climbed his way up to stand confidently beside her.

"Friends, family, recent academy graduates," Dad said in his booming voice. When Frankie was young, he'd still had a hint of an Irish accent, which he'd worked hard to eliminate. He often touted his own immigrant mythology, a story of bootstrapping and hard work. He rarely mentioned the good fortune and opportunity that had come with marrying the boss's daughter, but everyone knew. They also knew that after the death of Mom's parents, Dad had more than tripled their wealth with his zeal for developing California real estate.

He put an arm around his slender wife, drew her as close as she would allow in public. "We are grateful that you have come to help us say bon voyage to our son, Finley." Dad smiled. "No more bailing him out of the Coronado police station at two A.M. after some ridiculous drag race."

There was a smattering of laughter. Everyone at this party knew the circuitous track Finley had taken to adulthood. From earliest memory, he had been a golden boy, a wild child who could make the hardest heart soften. People laughed at his jokes; girls followed him everywhere. Everyone loved Finley, but most agreed that he was a handful. He had been held back in fourth grade, more for constant mischievousness than anything else. He was sometimes disrespectful in church, and he liked the kind of girl who wore short skirts and carried cigarettes in her purse.

When the laughter ended, Dad went on: "A toast to Finley and his grand adventure. We are proud of you, son!"

Servers appeared with bottles of Dom Pérignon and poured more champagne; the tinkling sound of glass on glass filled the air. Guests surrounded Finley; men clapped him on the back in congratulations. Young women pressed forward, vying for his attention.

Dad motioned to the band, and music started up again.

Feeling left out, Frankie headed into the house, past the large kitchen, where the caterers were busily putting canapés on trays.

She ducked into her father's office. It had been her favorite place as a child. Big tufted leather chairs, footstools, two walls of books, a massive desk. She flicked on the light. The room smelled of old leather and cigars, with a hint of expensive aftershave. Neatly organized stacks of building permits and architectural plans lay atop the desk.

One entire wall of the office was devoted to their family history. Framed photographs Mom had inherited from her parents and even a few Dad had brought with him from Ireland. There was a photo of Great-Grandfather McGrath, in his soldier's uniform, saluting the camera. Alongside that photograph was a framed war medal that her Grandpa Francis had been awarded in the First World War. The photograph of her parents' wedding was positioned between her grandfather Alexander's framed Purple Heart and a newspaper clipping with a photo of the ship he'd served on coming into harbor at the end of the war. There were no photographs of her father in uniform. To his great shame, he had been labeled 4-F and disqualified for military service. It was something he lamented in private, only to family, and only when he'd been drinking. After the war, he'd convinced Grandpa Alexander to begin building affordable housing in San Diego for returning veterans. Dad called it his contribution to the war effort, and it had been spectacularly successful. In conversation, he was always so "military-proud" that, in time, everyone on Coronado seemed to forget he hadn't served. There were no photographs of his children, not yet. Her father believed that one had to earn their way onto this wall.

Frankie heard the door open quietly behind her, and someone said, "Oh. I'm sorry. I don't mean to intrude."

She turned and saw Rye Walsh standing in the doorway. He held a cocktail in one hand and a pack of Old Gold cigarettes in the other. No doubt he'd been looking for a quiet place to smoke.

"I'm hiding from the party," she said. "I don't feel much like celebrating, it seems."

He left the door open behind him. "I was doing the same thing, I guess. You probably don't remember me—"

"Joseph Ryerson Walsh; goes by Rye. Like the whiskey," Frankie said, trying to smile. It was how he'd introduced himself to her last summer. "Why are you hiding out? You and Fin are thick as thieves. You both love a good party."

As he neared, her heart did a queer little stutter. He'd had that effect on her from their first meeting, but they'd never really spoken. She didn't know what to say to him now, when she felt a little bereft. Lonely.

"I'm going to miss him," he said quietly.

She felt the sting of tears and turned quickly away, faced the wall of memorabilia; he moved in beside her. They stared up at the family photos and mementos. Men in uniforms, women in wedding dresses, medals for valor and injury, a triangle-folded and framed American flag that had been given to her paternal grandmother.

"How come there are no pictures of women up here, except for the wedding pictures?" Rye asked.

"It's a heroes' wall. To honor the sacrifices our family has made in service of the country."

He lit a cigarette. "Women can be heroes."

Frankie laughed.

"What's funny about that?"

She turned to him, wiped the tears from her eyes. "I . . . well . . . you don't mean . . ."

"Yeah," he said, looking down at her. She couldn't remember a man ever looking at her in such a way, so intensely. It made her catch her breath. "I mean it, Frankie. It's 1966. The whole world is changing."

———

Hours later, when the guests had begun to make their polite exits, Frankie found herself still thinking about Rye, and what he'd said.

Women can be heroes.

No one had ever said such a thing to her. Not her teachers at St. Bernadette's, not her parents. Not even Finley. Why had it never occurred to Frankie that a girl, a woman, could have a place on her father's office wall for doing something heroic or important, that a woman could invent something or discover something or be a nurse on the battlefield, could literally save lives?

The idea of it was like an earthquake, an upending of her sheltered view of the world, of herself. She'd been told for years, by the nuns, by her teachers, by her mother, that nursing was an excellent profession for a woman.

Teacher. Nurse. Secretary. These were acceptable futures for a girl like her. Only last week her mother had listened to Frankie talk about her struggles in upper-level biology and said gently, *Who cares about frogs, Frances? You're only going to be a nurse until you get married. And by the way, it's time you start thinking about that. Quit rushing through your classes and slow down. Who cares if you graduate early? You need to date more.* Frankie had been taught to believe that her job was to be a good housewife, to raise well-mannered children and keep a lovely home. In her Catholic high school, they'd spent days learning how to iron buttonholes to perfection, how to precisely fold a napkin, how to set an elegant table. At the San Diego College for Women, there wasn't much rebellion among her classmates and friends. Girls laughed about working for their MRS degree. Even her own choice of nursing as a degree hadn't required much introspection; all she'd really focused on was getting good grades and making her parents proud.

As the musicians packed up their instruments and the waiters began clearing away the empty glasses, Frankie flipped off her sandals and left the yard and wandered across empty Ocean Boulevard, the wide, paved street that separated her parents' house from the beach.

The golden sand of Coronado Beach stretched out in front of her. Off to the left was the famous Hotel del Coronado and to the right was the large Naval Air Station North Island, which had recently been recognized as the Birthplace of Naval Aviation.

A cool night breeze plucked at her bouffant chin-length bob, but it was no match for the layer of Aqua Net that kept every strand in place.

She sat down in the cool sand, looped her arms around her bent knees, and stared out at the waves. A full moon hung overhead. Not far away, a beach bonfire glowed orange; the smell of smoke drifted on the night air.

How did a woman go about opening up her world? How did one begin a journey when no invitation had been issued? It was easy for Finley; the path had been laid out for him. He was to do what all the McGrath and Alexander men did: serve his country with honor and then take over the family real estate business. No one had ever suggested any future for Frankie beyond marriage and motherhood.

She heard laughter behind her, the sound of running feet. A young blond woman took off her shoes at the water's edge and splashed into the surf. Rye followed her, laughing, not even bothering to take off his shoes. Someone sang "Walk Like a Man" off-key.

Finley plopped down beside Frankie, fell drunkenly into her. "Where have you been all night, doll? I missed you."

"Hey, Fin," she said quietly. Leaning into him, she remembered their lives on this beach; as children, they'd built elaborate sandcastles and bought Creamsicles from the jangling ice-cream truck that drove up and down Ocean Boulevard in the summer. They'd spent long hours on their surfboards, feet dangling over the sides, talking beneath the hot sun as they waited for the right wave, sharing their deepest secrets.

Together, always. Best friends.

She knew what he needed from her now; she should tell Fin she was proud of him and send him off with a smile, but she couldn't do it. They'd never lied to each other. It didn't seem like the time to start. "Fin, are you sure you should go to Vietnam?"

"Ask not what your country can do for you; ask what you can do for your country."

Frankie sighed. She and Finley had idolized President Kennedy. His words meant something to them, so how could she argue? "I know, but—"

"It isn't dangerous, Frankie. Trust me. I'm a Naval Academy graduate, an officer with a cushy assignment on a ship. I'll be back in no time. You'll hardly have time to miss me."

Everyone said the same thing: Communism was an evil that had to be stopped; these were the Cold War years. Dangerous times. If a great man like President Kennedy could be shot in broad daylight by a Red in Dallas, how could any American feel safe? Everyone agreed that communism couldn't be allowed to flourish in Asia, and Vietnam was the place to stop it.

The nightly news showed smiling soldiers marching in packs through the Vietnamese jungle and giving newsmen the thumbs-up. No bloodshed.

Finley put an arm around her.

"I'll miss you, Peanut," he said. She heard the catch in his voice and knew he was scared to go.

Had he been hiding it from her all along, or hiding it from himself?

And there it was, the fear and worry she'd been trying to suppress all night, to ignore. Suddenly it was too big to bear. No looking away now.

Her brother was going to war.

Two

For the next six months, Frankie wrote to her brother every Sunday after church. In return, she received funny letters about his life on board the ship and the antics of his fellow sailors. He sent postcard pictures of lush green jungles and aqua seas and beaches with sand the color of salt. He told her about parties at the O Club and rooftop bars in Saigon and celebrities who came to entertain the troops.

In his absence, Frankie increased her course load and graduated early, with honors. As a newly registered nurse, she landed her first-ever job, working the night shift at a small hospital in nearby San Diego. She had recently begun to think about moving out of her parents' home and getting an apartment of her own, a dream she'd shared with Finley in a letter only last week. *Think of it, Fin. Us living in a little place near the beach. Maybe in Santa Monica. What fun we could have . . .*

Now, on this cool night in the last week of November, the corridors of the hospital were quiet. Dressed in her starched white uniform, with a nurse cap pinned on her sprayed, bouffant bob, Frankie walked behind the night charge nurse, who led the way into a private room devoid of flowers or visitors, where a young woman lay sleeping. Frankie was being told—yet again—how to do her job.

"High school girl from St. Anne's," the night charge nurse said, then mouthed, *Baby,* as if the word itself were a sin. Frankie knew that St. Anne's was the local home for unwed mothers, but it was a thing no one ever talked about: the girls who left school suddenly and came back months later, quieter and lonely looking.

"Her IV is low. I could—"

"For goodness' sake, Miss McGrath, you know you're not ready for that. How long have you been here? A week?"

"Two, ma'am. And I'm a registered nurse. My grades—"

"Don't matter. It's clinical skills I care about, and you have little of those. You are to check bedpans, refill water pitchers, help patients to the toilet. When you're ready to do more, I'll let you know."

Frankie sighed quietly. She hadn't put in all those long, exhausting hours in study carrels, getting her nursing degree early, so that she could change bedpans and fluff pillows. How was she going to acquire the clinical skills she needed to land a job at a first-rate hospital?

"So please record and monitor all IV meds. I'll need the information promptly. Go."

Frankie nodded and began her nightly rounds, going from room to room.

It was almost three in the morning when she came to Room 107.

She opened the door gently, hating to waken the patient if she could help it.

"Have you come to see the freak show?"

Frankie paused, uncertain of what to do. "I could come back . . ."

"Stay. Please."

Frankie closed the door behind her and moved toward the bed. The patient was a young man, with long, shaggy blond hair and a pale, narrow face. A weedy patch of blond and brown hair tufted above his upper lip. He looked like a kid you'd find surfing the break at Trestles, except for the wheelchair in the corner.

She could see the outline of his legs, or his one leg, beneath the white blanket.

"You can look," he said. "It's impossible not to. Who wouldn't look at a car wreck?"

"I'm bothering you," she said, taking a step back, starting to turn.

"Don't go. They're sending me to a psych ward for trying to kill myself. Involuntary hold, or some bullshit. Like they would know what I was thinking. Anyway, you might be the last sane person I see for a while."

Frankie moved forward cautiously, checked his IV, made a notation on his chart.

"I should have used my gun," he said.

Frankie didn't know how to respond. She had never met anyone who had tried to commit suicide. It seemed impolite to ask why, but equally impolite to remain silent.

"I made it three hundred and forty days in-country. Thought I was home free. That ain't good. Bein' a short-timer."

At Frankie's obvious confusion, he said: "Vietnam." He sighed. "My girl—Jilly—she hung with me, wrote me love letters, right up until I stepped on that damn Bouncing Betty and lost a leg." He looked down. "She told me I'd adjust and to give it time. I'm trying . . ."

"Your girl told you that?"

"Hardly. A nurse at the Twelfth Evac Hospital. She got me through, man. Sat with me while I lost my shit." He looked at Frankie, reached out for her hand. "Will you stay till I fall asleep, ma'am? I have these nightmares . . ."

"Sure, soldier. I won't go anywhere."

Frankie was still holding his hand when he fell asleep. She couldn't help thinking of Finley, and the letters he wrote to her each week, full of funny stories and the beauty of the countryside. *You should see the silk and gems over here, doll. Mom would never stop shopping. And boy, do sailors know how to party.* He told her repeatedly that the war was coming to an end. Walter Cronkite said the same thing on the nightly news.

But it was still going on.

And men were dying. Losing their legs, apparently.

A nurse at the Twelfth Evac Hospital. She got me through, man.

Frankie had never thought about nurses in Vietnam; the newspapers never mentioned any women. Certainly no one talked about any women at war.

Women can be heroes.

At that, Frankie felt a kind of reawakening, the emergence of a bold new ambition.

"I could serve my country," she said to the man whose hand she held. It was a revolutionary, frightening, exhilarating thought.

But could she? Really?

How did you know if you had the strength and courage for a thing like that? Especially as a woman, raised to be a lady, whose courage had been untested.

She let the idea soar, closed her eyes, imagined telling her parents that she'd joined the Navy and would be going to Vietnam, writing a letter to Finley: *Drumroll, please, I've joined the Navy and will be shipping out to Vietnam! See you soon!*

If she did it now, they could be over there together. In-country.

She could earn her place on the heroes' wall, and not for marrying well. For saving lives in wartime.

Her parents would be so proud of her, as proud as they'd been of Finley. All her life she'd been taught that military service was a family duty.

Wait.

Think about it, Frankie. It could be dangerous.

But the danger didn't resonate. She'd be on a hospital ship, far from the fighting.

By the time she let go of the soldier's hand, she had decided.

In the past week, Frankie had planned her day off obsessively, saying nothing to anyone about her intentions, seeking no counsel. She'd repeatedly told herself to slow down, think it through, and she'd tried to do it, but the truth was that she knew what she wanted to do and she didn't want anyone to dissuade her.

After a quick shower, she returned to her bedroom, which had been designed for a young girl years ago, with its frilly canopy bed and shag rug and striped, cabbage-rose-print wallpaper. She chose one of the conservative dresses her mother so often purchased for her. *Quality pieces, Frances; that's how a woman distinguishes herself at first glance.*

As expected, this time of day, the house was empty. Mom was playing bridge at the country club and Dad was at work.

At 1:25, Frankie drove to the nearest Navy recruitment office, where a small clot of war protesters stood outside, yelling slogans and holding up signs that read WAR IS NOT HEALTHY FOR CHILDREN AND OTHER LIVING THINGS and BOMBING FOR PEACE IS LIKE SCREWING FOR VIRGINITY.

Two men with long hair were burning their draft cards—which was illegal—while the crowd cheered them on. Frankie had never understood these protests. Did they really think that a few posters would convince LBJ to stop the war? Did they not understand that if Vietnam fell to communism, so would all of Southeast Asia? Did they not read about how vicious such regimes could be?

Frankie felt acutely conspicuous as she got out of her car. She clutched her expensive navy calfskin purse close to her side as she approached the crowd, who chanted, "Hell, no, we won't go."

The crowd turned toward her, stilled for a moment.

"It's a damn Young Republican!" someone shouted.

Frankie forced herself to keep walking.

"Oh man," someone else said. "This chick is crazy."

"Don't go in there, man!"

Frankie opened the recruiting station's doors. Inside she saw a desk beneath a sign that read: BE A PATRIOT. JOIN THE NAVY. A sailor in uniform stood at the end of the table.

Frankie closed the door behind her and went to the recruiting desk.

Protesters banged on the window. Frankie tried not to flinch or appear nervous or afraid.

"I'm a nurse," she said, ignoring the sounds coming from outside. "I'd like to join the Navy and volunteer for Vietnam."

The sailor glanced nervously at the crowd outside. "How old are you?"

"Twenty, sir. Twenty-one next week."

"The Navy requires two years of service before they send you to Vietnam, ma'am. You'll need to do two years stateside, in a hospital, before you ship out."

Two years. The war would be over by then. "You don't need nurses in Vietnam?"

"Oh, we need them."

"My brother is in Vietnam. I . . . want to help."

"I'm sorry, ma'am. Rules are rules. It's for your own safety, believe me."

Dispirited but not discouraged, Frankie left the recruiting office—hurried past the protesters, who yelled obscenities at her—and found a nearby phone booth, where she consulted the Los Angeles yellow pages and found the address for the nearest Air Force recruiting station.

Once there, she was told the same thing, that she needed more stateside experience before shipping out to Vietnam.

At the Army recruiting station, she finally heard what she wanted to hear: *Sure, ma'am. The Army Nurse Corps needs nurses. We could ship you right out after Basic.*

Frankie signed her name on the dotted line, and just like that, she was Second Lieutenant Frances McGrath.

Three

By the time Frankie got back on island, the streetlamps were coming on. Downtown Coronado was dressed for the holidays with streamers and lights; white-bearded, red-coated Santas stood in front of several shops, ringing bells. Illuminated snowflakes hung from lines strung above the street.

At home, Frankie found her parents in the living room, dressed for dinner. Dad stood at the bar, flipping through the newspaper, while Mom sat in her favorite chair by the fire, smoking a cigarette and reading a Graham Greene novel. The house was decked out for the holidays, with an extravagance of lights and a ten-foot tree.

At Frankie's entrance, Dad closed the newspaper and smiled at her. "Heya, Peanut."

"I have news," Frankie said, practically bursting with excitement.

"You've met a boy you like," Mom said, putting down her novel. "Finally."

Frankie came to a stop. "A boy? No."

Mom frowned. "Frances, most of the girls your age—"

"Mom," Frankie said impatiently, "I'm trying to tell you something important." She took a deep breath and said, "I joined the Army Nurse

Corps. The ANC. I'm now Second Lieutenant McGrath. I'm going to Vietnam. I'll get to be with Finley for part of his tour!"

"That's hardly funny, Frances," Mom said.

Dad stared at Frankie, unsmiling. "I don't think she's joking, Bette."

"You joined the Army?" Mom said slowly, as if the words were a foreign language that she was trying to sound out.

"I'd salute but I don't know how. Basic Training starts in three weeks. Fort Sam Houston."

Frankie frowned. Why weren't they congratulating her? "McGraths and Alexanders always serve," she said. "You were thrilled when Finley volunteered."

"The men serve," Dad said sharply. "The *men*." He paused. "Wait. Did you say the Army? We're a Navy family, always have been. Coronado is a Navy island."

"I know, but the Navy wouldn't let me go to Vietnam until I'd served two years in a hospital stateside," she said. "Same with the Air Force. They said I didn't have enough experience. Only the Army would let me go right after Basic Training."

"Sweet Jesus, Frankie," Dad said, running a hand through his hair. "There's a reason for rules like that."

"Take it back. Unvolunteer." Mom looked at Dad. She got to her feet slowly. "Good Lord, what will we tell people?"

"What will you . . ." Frankie didn't understand. They were acting as if they were ashamed of her. But . . . that made no sense. "How many times have you gathered us in your office to talk about this family's record of service, Dad? You told us how much you wanted to fight for your country. I thought—"

"He's a man," Mom said. "And it was Hitler. And Europe. Not some country no one can find on a map. It is not patriotic to do something stupid, Frances." Tears filled her eyes. She dashed them away impatiently. "Well, Connor, she's what you taught her to be. A believer. A *patriot*."

At Mom's rebuke, Dad left the room, trailing smoke behind him.

Frankie went to her mom, tried to hold her hand, but Mom stepped adroitly aside, not letting Frankie touch her. "Mom?"

"I shouldn't have let your father fill your head with all that history. He made it sound so . . . epic, those family war stories. Although none of them were his, were they? *He* couldn't serve, so it became . . . oh, for God's sake, none of it matters now." She looked away. "I remember when my father came home from the war. Broken. Stitches holding him together. He had nightmares. I swear it's what killed him early." Her voice broke. "And you think you'll go over there and see your brother and have an adventure? How could you be so stupid?"

"I'm a nurse, Mom, not a soldier. The recruiter said I'll be stationed at a big hospital, far from the front. He promised I would get to see Finley."

"And you believed him?" Mom took a long drag off of her cigarette. Frankie saw how her hand was shaking. "It's done?"

"It's done. I report to Basic Training in January and then I ship out for my tour in March. I'll be home for my birthday next week and for Christmas. I made sure. I know how much that matters to you."

Mom bit her lip, nodding slowly. Frankie could see that her mother was trying to corral her emotions, trying to look calm. Suddenly she reached out, pulled Frankie into her arms, hugged her so tightly she couldn't breathe.

Frankie clung to her, buried her face in the teased, sprayed hair. "I love you, Mom," she said.

Mom drew back, wiped her eyes, and looked hard at Frankie. "Don't you be a hero, Frances Grace. I don't care what you've been taught or what stories men like your father have told you. You keep your head down and stay back and stay safe. You hear me?"

"I promise. I'll be fine."

The doorbell rang.

It was a distant sound, barely audible above the combination of

their breathing and the unspoken words swirling in the silence between them.

Mom glanced sideways, toward the foyer. "Who on earth could
that be?"

"I'll go," Frankie said.

She left her mother standing in the living room, alone. In the foyer,
Frankie stepped around the gleaming rosewood table that held a large
potted white orchid, and opened the door.

Two naval officers in dress uniforms stood there at attention.

Frankie had lived on Coronado Island all of her life, watched jets
and helicopters roar overhead and sailors run in lines along the beach.
At every party or gathering, someone told a World War II or Korea
story. The town cemetery was full of men Coronado had lost in wars.

She knew what officers at the front door meant. "Please," she whispered, wanting to back up and close the door.

She heard footsteps behind her, heels on hardwood. "Frances?"
Mom said, coming up beside her. "What—"

Mom saw the two officers and let out a quiet gasp.

"I'm sorry, ma'am," one of the officers said, taking off his hat, tuck-
ing it under his arm.

Frankie reached for her mother's hand, but Mom pulled away.
"Come in," Mom said in a husky voice. "You'll want to speak to my
husband . . ."

———

*Sorry to inform you, ma'am, that Ensign Finley McGrath has been killed
in action.*

Shot down . . . in a helicopter . . .

No remains . . . all hands lost.

No answers to their questions, just a quietly spoken, *It's war, sir,* as
if that said it all. *Answers are hard to come by.*

Frankie knew she would remember this evening in startling, scalding images: Dad, standing tall, his hands shaking, showing no emotion until one of the officers called his son a hero, his voice quiet as he asked for details—as if they mattered—Where, when, how? Her mom, usually so elegant and cool, curling into herself on the chair, her carefully coiffed hair falling slowly apart, saying again and again, *How can it be, Connor, you said it was barely a war.*

Frankie didn't think either of her parents noticed when she slipped out of the house and crossed Ocean Boulevard to sit in the cool sand.

How had he been shot down? What was an officer's aide doing in a helicopter? And what did it mean that there were no remains? What were they supposed to bury?

She felt tears well again, and closed her eyes, recalled images of Finley on this beach, running into the surf, holding her hand, teaching her how to float on her back, how to swim, taking her to see *Psycho* when Mom had specifically forbidden it, sneaking her a bottle of beer on the Fourth of July. She closed her eyes and let the memories flow; she remembered him and their life together, their fights and squabbles. Going to Disneyland for the first time, riding their bikes in the summer, and racing to the tree on Christmas morning, him letting her win. Her big brother.

Gone.

How often had she and Fin been out here at night together, running on the beach, riding their bikes home at night, guided by streetlamps, laughing, poking each other, holding their arms outstretched and thinking that riding a bicycle without holding on was taking a risk?

How free they had felt. Invincible.

She felt a presence on the beach behind her, heard footfalls.

Mom sat down in the sand beside her, half falling the last few inches. "They say we should bury another man's boots and helmet in my son's casket," she said at last. Her lower lip was bleeding a little, where she'd bitten it. She scratched at a red spot on her neck.

"A funeral," Frankie said, thinking about it for the first time.

Mourners in black, perched on pews, Father Michael droning on, telling funny stories about Finley, about his days as a rebellious altar boy, how he'd washed his toy soldiers in the baptismal font. How could any of them stand it?

An empty coffin. *No remains.*

"Don't go," Mom said quietly.

"I'm right here, Mom."

Mom turned. "I mean . . . to Vietnam."

Vietnam. A car crash of a word now.

"I have to," Frankie said. It was all she'd thought about since learning about her brother's death. How to get out of her commitment to the Army, how to stay here with her parents and grieve and be safe.

But it was too late for that. She'd signed on, made a promise.

"I don't have a choice, Mom. I can't undo it." She turned, said, "Give me your blessing. Please. I need you to say you're proud of me."

For a split second, Frankie saw her mother's pain. It pulled the life from her cheeks and the color from her skin. She was pale, washed-out. She stared at Frankie, her blue eyes dull, lifeless. "Proud of you?"

"You don't have to worry about me, Mom. I'll come home. I promise."

"Those were your brother's last words to me." Mom's voice broke. She paused for a second, looked like she was going to speak. Instead, she got slowly to her feet, turned away from Frankie, and walked back across the sand.

"I'm sorry," Frankie whispered, too softly for her mother to hear, but what did it matter?

It was too late for words.

Too late to take any of it back.

Four

Frankie excelled in Basic Training. Along with learning to march in formation (teamwork) and put on combat boots and a gas mask quickly (you never knew when you might be wakened at midnight for an emergency; you needed to move fast in a war zone), she'd learned how to apply a splint, debride a wound, carry a stretcher, and start an IV. She could roll bandages faster than any other recruit.

By March, she was more than ready to put her new skills to the test. She had packed and checked her large Army-issued duffel bag, which she'd crammed full with her flak jacket, steel pot helmet, combat boots, GI kit, white nursing uniform, and field jacket.

And now, at last, she was on her way. Hours after landing in Honolulu, she boarded a jet bound for Vietnam, the lone woman at the front of a line of 257 uniformed soldiers.

Unlike the men, dressed in their comfortable olive-drab fatigues, neatly bloused inside black boots, Frankie was required to travel in her class A uniform: a green jacket, slim skirt, nylons, polished black pumps, and flat garrison hat. And beneath all of that, a regulation panty girdle to keep her nylon stockings up. It had been uncomfortable when she'd left Texas and boarded the plane bound for Vietnam. Now, twenty-two hours later, it was downright painful. It seemed ridiculous to her that in this day and age she couldn't wear pantyhose.

She tucked her new soft-sided overnight travel bag into the overhead bin and took a seat next to the window. As she sat down, a garter on her panty girdle snapped and popped her thigh like a rubber band. She struggled to get it fixed sitting down.

Soldiers filed past her, laughing and talking, shoving each other. Many of them looked to be her age or even younger. Eighteen, nineteen years old, most of them.

A captain in stained, wrinkled fatigues paused at the end of her row. "Mind if I join you, Lieutenant?"

"Of course, Captain."

He sat down in the aisle seat. Even in fatigues, she could see how thin he was. Heavy lines creased his cheeks. His clothes had the vague, unpleasant odor of mildew.

"Norm Bronson," he said with a tired smile.

"Frankie. McGrath. Nurse."

"Bless your heart, Frankie. We need nurses."

The plane rolled forward, lifted off from the runway, and rose into the clouds.

"What's it like?" she asked. "Vietnam, I mean."

"Words won't help, ma'am. I could talk all day about what it's like and you still won't be ready. But you'll learn fast. Just keep your head down." He leaned back and closed his eyes.

Frankie had never seen anyone fall asleep so quickly.

She reached into her black regulation handbag, pulled out her information packet, and reread it for the thousandth time. Repetition and knowledge had always calmed her, and she was determined to be as exemplary a soldier as she'd been a student. It was the only way to prove to her parents that she'd been smart to enlist, courageous even; success mattered to them.

She had memorized all of the military command and hospital locations, had underlined them in yellow on her map of Vietnam. She had also taken the behavioral guidelines to heart. Rules for personal conduct, for security on base, for what to wear and how to deal with firearms, for always taking pride in being a soldier.

Everything made sense to her in the Army. Rules existed for a reason and you followed them to maintain order and help each other. The system was designed to force soldiers—men and women—into conformity. To build teams. It could save your life, apparently. Fitting in, being part of something larger, knowing your job, and doing it without question. She was comfortable with all of it.

As she'd told her mother repeatedly, she was going off to war, but not really, not like the men on this plane. She wouldn't be on the front lines, wouldn't get shot at. She was going to Vietnam to save men's lives, not to risk her own. Military nurses worked in big bright buildings, like the huge Third Field Hospital in Saigon, which was protected by high fencing and was far from the fighting.

Frankie leaned back and closed her eyes, letting the rumble of the engines lull and calm her. She heard the buzz of men talking, laughing, the snap-hiss of colas being opened, the smell of sandwiches being handed out. She imagined Finley on the plane with her, holding her hand; for a split second, she forgot that he was gone and she smiled. *Coming to meet you,* she thought, and then her smile faded.

As she drifted off to sleep, she thought she heard Captain Bronson mumble quietly, "Sending goddamn babies . . ."

When Frankie woke, the airplane cabin was quiet except for the hum of the jet engines. Most of the window shades were drawn. A few overhead lights cast a gloomy glow over the men packed into the jet.

The loud razzing, the laughter, the horseplay that had marked most of this flight from Honolulu to Saigon was gone. The air seemed heavier, harder to draw into her lungs, harder to expel in an exhalation. The new recruits—recognizable by their still-creased, green fatigues—were restless. Unsettled. Frankie saw the way they looked at each other, their smiles bright and brittle. The other soldiers, those weary-looking men in their worn fatigues, men like Captain Bronson, sat almost too still.

Beside Frankie, the captain opened his eyes; it was the only change in him from sleeping to awake, just an opening of his eyes.

Suddenly the plane lurched, or bucked, seemed to turn onto its side. Frankie smacked her head on the tray on the back of the seat in front of her as the plane nose-dived. The overhead bins opened; dozens of bags fell out into the aisle, including Frankie's.

Captain Bronson put his rough, gnarled hand on hers as she clutched the armrest. "It'll be okay, Lieutenant."

The plane stalled, steadied, lurched upward into a steep climb. Frankie heard a *pop* and something cracked beside her.

"Is someone *shooting* at us?" Frankie said. "Oh my *God*."

Captain Bronson chuckled. "Yeah. They love to do that. Don't worry. We'll just circle around for a while and try again."

"Here? Shouldn't we go somewhere else to land?"

"In this big bird? Nope. It's Tan Son Nhut for us, ma'am. They'll be waiting on the FNGs we got on board."

"FNGs?"

"Fucking new guys." He smiled. "And one beautiful young nurse. Our boys'll clear the airport in no time. Not to fret."

The plane circled until Frankie's fingers ached from the pain of her grip on the armrests. Outside, she saw orange and red explosions and streaks of red across the dark sky.

Finally, the plane evened out, and the pilot came on the loudspeaker to say, "Okay, sports fans, let's try this shit again. Buckle up."

As if Frankie had ever unbuckled her seat belt.

The jet descended. Frankie's ears popped, and the next thing she knew, they were thumping onto the runway and powering down, rolling to a stop.

"Senior officers and women disembark first," sounded over the loudspeaker.

The officers waited for Frankie to exit first. She wished they hadn't. She didn't want to be first. Still, she grabbed her travel bag from the aisle and slung it—and her purse—over her left shoulder, leaving her right hand free to salute.

When she exited the aircraft, heat enveloped her. And the *smell*. Good Lord, what was it? Jet fuel . . . smoke . . . fish . . . and honestly there was a stench of something like excrement. A headache started to pulse behind her eyes. She made her way down the stairs, where a lone soldier stood in the darkness, backlit by ambient light from a distant building. She could barely make out his face.

Off to the distant left, something exploded in orange flames.

"Lieutenant McGrath?"

She could only nod. Sweat crawled down her back. Were they *bombing* over there?

The soldier said, "Follow me," and led her across the bumpy, pockmarked runway, past the terminal, and to a school bus that had been painted black, even the windows, which were covered in some kind of chicken-wire mesh. "You're the only nurse arriving today. Take a seat and wait. Don't exit the bus, ma'am."

The heat in the bus was sauna-like, and that smell—shit and fish—made her gag. She took a seat in the middle row of seats, by a black-painted window. It felt like being entombed.

Moments later, a Black soldier in fatigues, carrying an M16, climbed into the driver's seat. The doors whooshed shut and the headlights came on, carving a golden wedge out of the darkness ahead.

"Not too close to the window, ma'am," he said, and hit the gas. "Grenades."

Grenades?

Frankie inched sideways on the bench seat. In the fetid dark, she sat perfectly upright, was bounced up and down in her seat until she thought she might vomit.

At last the bus slowed; in the headlights' glare, she saw a set of gates manned by American MPs. One of the guards spoke to the driver, then backed away. The gates opened and they drove through.

Not much later, the bus stopped again. "Here you go, ma'am."

Frankie was sweating so profusely she had to wipe her eyes. "Huh?"

"You get out here, ma'am."

"What? Oh."

She realized suddenly that she hadn't gone to baggage claim, hadn't retrieved her duffel. "My bag—"

"It will be delivered, ma'am."

Frankie gathered up her purse and travel bag and went to the door.

A nurse stood in the mud, dressed in a white uniform, cap to shoes, waiting for her. How on earth could that uniform be kept clean? Behind her was the entrance to a huge hospital.

"You need to exit the bus, ma'am," the driver said.

"Oh yes." Frankie stepped down into the thick mud and started to salute.

The nurse grabbed her wrist, stopped the salute. "Not here. Charlie loves to kill officers." She pointed to a waiting jeep. "He'll take you to your temporary quarters. Report to admin for in-processing tomorrow at oh-seven-hundred."

Frankie had too many questions to pick just one, and her throat hurt. Clutching her travel bag and purse, she walked over to the jeep and climbed up into the backseat.

The driver hit the gas so hard Frankie was thrown back in her seat; a jagged metal spring poked her in the butt. The nighttime traffic on base was stop-and-go. In snatches of light, she saw barbed wire and sandbags built up around wooden buildings, armed guards standing on towers. Soldiers walking the streets in fatigues, holding guns. A large water-tank truck pulled up next to them, rumbling, and rolled past. Horns honked constantly, and men shouted at one another.

Another checkpoint—this one looked haphazardly thrown together with metal drums and coils of barbed wire and a tall chain-link fence. The guard waved them through.

Finally, they came to another fence, this one topped in coils of concertina wire.

The jeep braked to a stop. The driver leaned over, shoved the door open. "Your stop, ma'am."

Frankie frowned. It took time to maneuver out of the jeep in her tight skirt. "In that building, ma'am. Second floor, 8A."

Behind the tall ironwork fence, she saw what looked like an abandoned prison. Windows were boarded up with plywood and big chunks of the walls were missing. Before Frankie could ask where to go, the jeep was backing up, honking at something, and speeding away.

Frankie went to the gate, which creaked loudly upon opening, and stepped into a weedy front yard, where scrawny children played with a half-deflated ball. An old Vietnamese woman squatted by the side of the fence, tending to something cooking over an open fire.

Frankie followed a broken path to the front door and entered the building. Inside, a few gas lanterns flickered light against the walls. There was a woman in fatigues waiting for her in the shadowy entry. "Lieutenant McGrath?"

Thank God. "Yes."

"I'll show you to your room. Follow me." The woman led the way past a hallway filled with cots, and up a set of sagging stairs to a second-floor room—cubicle, really. A room barely big enough to hold the set of bunk beds in it, with a single dresser. Maybe the building had once been a convent or a school. "In-processing tomorrow at oh-seven-hundred hours. Report to admin."

"But—"

The soldier walked away, shut the door behind her.

Darkness.

Frankie felt around for a light switch, found and flipped it.

Nothing.

She opened the door again, grateful for the bit of ambient light coming from gas lanterns in the hallway. She went in search of a bathroom, found one with a rust-stained sink and toilet. She turned on the faucet, got a weak flow of tepid water, and washed her face, then took a drink.

A woman in an Army-green T-shirt and shorts walked in, saw Frankie, and frowned. "You'll be sorry about that, Lieutenant. Never drink the water."

"Oh. I'm new . . . in-country."

"Yeah," the woman said, eyeing Frankie in her skirt uniform. "No shit."

Frankie woke in the middle of the night with cramping in her stomach. She ran down the hall to the toilet and slammed the door shut behind her. She'd never had diarrhea like this in her life. It felt as if everything she'd eaten in the past month came rushing out of her, and when there was nothing left, the cramping went on.

Dawn brought no relief from the pain. She checked the time, rolled into a ball, and went back to sleep. At 0630 hours, she got up, stood on shaky legs, barely able to button her uniform. The panty girdle was torture.

Outside, the weedy yard was full of skinny-armed Vietnamese children, who eyed her silently. A laundry line held dozens of green fatigues.

She pushed past the gate and walked through the huge, busy base, which was a haphazard collection of buildings and tents and shacks and roads, without a tree anywhere that she could see. They'd obviously created the place with bulldozers. There were pedicycles with whole families on them, old cars pulled by water buffalo, and dozens of Army vehicles vying to get somewhere fast. A jeep splashed past her, the driver honking at the children on the side of the road, at the water buffalo roaming alongside.

No one looked twice at the woman in her Class As, walking carefully, hoping not to vomit.

It took Frankie nearly an hour to find the administration building, which was situated near Ward A of the sprawling Third Field Hospital, where nurses in starched white moved in groups, sometimes running, and announcements blared through black speakers.

She knocked on the closed admin door, heard, "Come in," and did as she was told.

Inside the office, she saluted to the thin female colonel seated at the desk in front of her.

The woman looked up, lifted her chin in a sharp, birdlike motion that upset the perfect perch of her cat's-eye glasses. The way she sighed at Frankie's entrance was hardly encouraging. "And you are?"

"Second Lieutenant Frances McGrath, Colonel."

The colonel rifled through the paperwork. "You're assigned to the Thirty-Sixth Evac Hospital. Follow me." She rose sharply and walked past Frankie to the door.

Frankie struggled to keep up, hoping she wasn't going to have another bout of diarrhea.

The colonel led the way through the throng of personnel toward a round white helipad with a red cross painted on it, where a helicopter waited. The colonel gave a thumbs-up to the pilot, who immediately started the engine. The huge rotors rotated slowly, became a blur that blasted hot air at her.

"I have . . . questions, Colonel," Frankie stuttered.

"Not for me, Lieutenant. Go. He doesn't have all day."

The colonel forced Frankie to bend forward and pushed her toward the whirring helicopter.

At the open side, a soldier grabbed her by the hand and swung her inside and then shoved her toward a canvas seat in the back of the aircraft.

"Hang on, ma'am," the soldier yelled as the helicopter immediately lifted into the air, dipped its nose, and then soared forward, flying over the huge American base, and then above the chaos of Saigon.

Frankie's stomach rebelled at the movement.

This did not seem safe. And where were their guns? How could they shoot back at the enemy if necessary? She heard an explosion somewhere; it rattled the helicopter, which swooped sideways. She clamped a hand over her mouth and prayed that she wouldn't vomit.

Another explosion. A rattle of gunfire. The helicopter shook hard, clattered like a thousand bolts in a metal box.

Frankie survived the terrifying flight one breath at a time. It was often all she could do not to scream. And then, miraculously, they were descending, lowering toward a helipad.

When they touched down, the copilot looked back at Frankie. "Ma'am?"

"What?" Frankie yelled.

"You gotta get out."

"Oh. Right."

She couldn't make herself move.

The soldier who'd helped her aboard—a medic—yanked her out of her seat and hauled her toward the open door. A female first lieutenant in stained fatigues stood nearby, holding on to her canvas hat, staring up.

The medic threw Frankie's bag out of the helicopter. It landed at the first lieutenant's feet.

"Ma'am?" he said impatiently.

Jump, Frankie.

In heels.

She hit the ground hard enough to buckle her knees. She dropped her purse and bent quickly to pick it up. Taking a deep breath, ignoring the pain, she slowly straightened and started to salute. "Lieutenant McGrath, reporting for duty."

"Not here," the first lieutenant said. "I like being alive. I'm Patty Perkins. Surgical nurse." She held on to Frankie for just a moment, steadying her, and then abruptly let go and started walking.

"Welcome to the Thirty-Sixth. We are a four-hundred-bed evac hospital on the coast about sixty miles from Saigon. You are one of nine female nurses on staff, in addition to male nurses and medics. We keep this place running," the first lieutenant yelled back at her. "It's considered one of the safer posts. The DMZ is up north, so fighting here is minimal. We provide care for the VSI who are medevaced—"

Frankie struggled to keep up. "VSI?"

"Very seriously injured. Here you'll see everything from leprosy to amputations to rat bites to what's left of a soldier after a land mine. Most wounds require delayed primary closures—DPCs—which means we clear and debride wounds but don't close. That will be your biggest job. Most casualties are here three days or less. From here, the lucky ones go to the Third Field Hospital in Saigon, for more specialized treatment; the unlucky ones go back to their units; and the really unlucky ones go home in a box. Keep up, Lieutenant." The woman led the way past a series of Quonset huts. "That's the ER, Pre-Op, the two ORs, Post-Op, the ICU, and Neuro." She kept going. "That's the mess hall. Officers on the right side. Report to Major Goldstein in admin tomorrow at oh-eight-hundred. She's chief nurse." She came to an abrupt halt in front of a row of identical wooden buildings whose lower halves were protected by stacked sandbags. "This is your hooch. Showers and latrines are over there. Shower quickly, the flyboys like to hover over and watch." Patty smiled, then offered two bottles of pills.

"Malaria and diarrhea. Take them religiously. Don't drink the water unless it's out of a Lister bag or jerry can. If you want, I'll show you—"

Patty stopped midsentence, cocked her head, listening. A moment later, Frankie heard the sound of helicopters.

"Crap," Patty said. "Incoming. I guess you're on your own, Mc-Grath. Get settled in." With an encouraging smile, she patted Frankie's shoulder and hurried away. Frankie heard the thud of dozens of booted feet running on the wooden ramps throughout the camp.

Frankie felt abandoned.

"Buck up, McGrath," she said aloud. Reaching for the door to her hooch, she stepped up the single step and entered a dark, musty, buggy room, about fifteen feet by thirty feet, that was divided into three separate cubicle-like spaces, each with its own green canvas-and-metal cot, a makeshift bedside table, and a lamp. Olive-green netting hung in swoops over the ugly plywood walls. Above one cot, color photographs were tacked to the wall: a couple, standing in front of a red horse barn, a man with close-cropped hair, leaning against the hood of a Chevrolet truck, that same man standing between a little red-haired girl and a huge black horse. Above the other cot were posters of Malcolm X and Muhammad Ali and Martin Luther King, Jr. The third cot—hers, presumably—had nothing tacked onto the wall, but the plywood was full of tack holes and torn bits of paper from posters that had been put up and ripped down. Her duffel bag was on the floor.

There was a small fridge in one corner, and someone had built a bookcase out of old slats and filled the shelves with worn paperbacks. It was stiflingly hot and there was neither a fan nor a window. A layer of red dirt coated the floor.

Closing the door behind her, she sat down on the narrow cot and opened her overnight bag. A brand-new Polaroid camera lay on top of the carefully wrapped stack of framed photographs she'd brought from home. She reached for the top one, unwrapped it, held it on her lap. The picture had been taken at Disneyland. In it, Frankie and Finley stood in front of Sleeping Beauty Castle, holding hands. A split second before the camera lens clicked, Finley had grabbed the ticket booklet from Mom and ripped out the E tickets, saying, *Me and Frankie are goin' straight to the Rocket to the Moon. And then to the Submarine.* And Mom had said quietly, *I hope they serve drinks at one of those kiosks, Connor.*

Frankie felt the sting of tears. There was no one here to see, or to care, so she didn't bother dashing them away. She stared at the image of her brother, with his protruding teeth and spit-shined hair and freckled face, and thought: *What have I done?*

Next, she unwrapped a picture of her parents, taken at one of their famous Fourth of July parties, both of them smiling, a table draped in patriotic bunting behind them.

They had been right. She had no business being so far away from home—at war—without Finley. How would she last a year?

At that, her stomach roiled again.

She ran for the latrines.

Five

Hours later, Frankie was still lying on her cot, trying not to cry or vomit, wishing she'd never joined the Army, when the door to the hooch banged open. In walked a pair of women in blood-splattered clothes: a Black woman with closely cropped hair who wore shorts, a T-shirt, and combat boots, and a tall, Olive Oyl–thin redhead in stained fatigues. Frankie figured they were both older than she was, but not by much.

"Look at that, Babs. New blood," Olive Oyl said, unbuttoning her olive-green blouse, tossing it aside.

There was blood on the woman's bra. She walked forward, clomping her boots, unconcerned about her state of undress. "I'm Ethel Flint from Virginia. ER nurse." She reached for Frankie's hand, shook it aggressively, like cocking a rifle. "This here is Barb Johnson, surgical nurse, from some one-stoplight town in Georgia. She's mean as a dang snake. She made the last girl cry on a regular basis."

"That isn't true, Ethel, and you know it," the Black woman said, pulling the damp T-shirt away from her chest. "Good God, it's hot."

Frankie stared at Barb. Honestly, she didn't know many Black people. Something about the way Barb stared back, her eyes narrowed and assessing, made Frankie feel like a kid who'd wandered into the wrong classroom.

"I'm Frankie McGrath," she said. Her voice gave out halfway through the introduction and she had to start over.

"Well, Frankie, ditch the uniform," Ethel said, stripping off her bra and putting on a V-necked olive-drab T-shirt that revealed the silver beaded chain of dog tags around her neck. "There's a turtle party in your honor—"

Barb snorted. "Hardly, Ethel. Don't give the kid a false impression."

"Well, maybe that's a bit of a stretch, but we have two turtles in today and one guy going home."

"What's a turtle?" Frankie asked.

"You are, kid," Ethel said, sounding old and tired and worn-out. "Now move your behind. I'm thirsty as hell. It's been a long day, and I surely could use a Coca-Cola."

Frankie wasn't used to stripping in front of strangers, but she didn't want her roommates to think she was a prude, so she began to undress.

It wasn't until she was down to her undergarments that she realized she had nothing in her duffel or overnight bag to put on except her crisply folded, new green fatigues, which she'd been told to wear for work, or her pajamas, or a pale blue summer dress that her mother had convinced her would be perfect for her days off, or her white nurse uniform.

"A girdle," Ethel said with a sigh. She opened a drawer and rifled through it, pulling out a pair of cutoff shorts and an Army T-shirt, and tossed them to Frankie. "Don't worry, it's not just you. They don't tell us the truth about what to wear over here."

"Or anything else," Barb said.

Frankie peeled off the girdle and rolled down her cinnamon-hued stockings. She stood there for a second, feeling her roommates' scrutiny, then quickly put on the borrowed clothes. The T-shirt was huge and hung to the top of her thighs, almost covering the cutoff jean shorts once Frankie rolled over the waistband to make them fit.

Opening her duffel, she found her flak jacket and Army-issued steel pot helmet and slipped into the sleeveless jacket, immediately felt its weight. The helmet fell down and covered her eyes.

"It's a party," Barb said. "Not a John Wayne movie. Take that shit off."

"But—" Frankie turned too fast; the helmet clanked hard onto the bridge of her nose, hurt. "Regulations state—"

Barb walked out of the hooch. The door banged shut behind her.

Ethel gently took Frankie's helmet off, tossed it on the bed. "Look, I know today is a lot. We will help you fit in, I promise. But not now, okay? And as for the flak jacket, just no, okay?"

Frankie undid the flak jacket and tossed it aside. It landed on the helmet on her cot. She felt exposed and ridiculous in an oversized T-shirt that hid her shorts and showed her bare legs and shiny, brand-new combat boots that she'd polished obsessively. Why hadn't she packed sneakers? Had the men who wrote the "What to Bring" section of the information packet even *been* to Vietnam? She'd had her hair cut in a Twiggy-inspired pixie for her tour, and now, after thirty-eight hours of travel and this hellish humidity, God knew she must look like she was wearing a black swim cap. Or like she was twelve years old.

Ethel walked fast, talking as she went. "Welcome to the Thirty-Sixth, Frank. Can I call you Frank? This is technically a mobile hospital, but we haven't gone anywhere in a while; instead, we keep getting bigger. We have several doctors and four surgeons—you'll know them instantly. They think they're gods. There are nine of us women nurses and a couple of male nurses and lots of medics. In most wards, the hours are oh-seven-hundred to nineteen hundred hours, six days a week, but we are short-staffed right now, so really, we go until the last casualty is taken care of. If it sounds like a lot, it is, but you'll get used to it. Hurry up. You're lagging."

In the falling darkness, Frankie couldn't see much of the place: a
row of shacks—the hooches—a large wooden building that housed
the mess, the nurses' latrines, a chapel, a row of Quonset huts that
were weakly illuminated, the hospital insignia painted on their exterior
walls.

Ethel rounded the corner of a Quonset hut and suddenly they
were in a wide-open space, a patch of red dirt surrounded by shadowy
structures. All of it looked hastily constructed, temporary. Not far
away—close enough to hear the whoosh of the tides—lay the South
China Sea.

Pale light glazed a coil of concertina wire that created a perimeter
for the camp. Off to the left was a sandbagged bunker, its entrance a
gaping black square beneath a wooden arch, upon which someone had
spray-painted OFFICERS' CLUB on the crossbeam. A curtain of multicolored beads shielded the interior from view.

Ethel pushed through the curtains. The beads made a soft clattering sound.

The place was bigger inside than it looked. Against the back there
was a plywood bar, with stools in front. A bartender stood behind
it, busily making drinks. A Vietnamese woman in pajama-like pants
and a long tunic top carried a tray from table to table. A stereo system boasted huge speakers; beside it, there were hundreds of eight
track tapes. "Like a Rolling Stone" blared into the space, so loud
people had to shout in conversation. A trio of men threw darts at a
dartboard on the wall.

Smoke filled the air, stung Frankie's eyes.

Men and a few women filled the room—sitting at tables, standing
along the walls. One guy was standing on his head with his bare legs
crossed. Most were smoking and drinking.

When the song ended, there was a beat of silence. In it, Frankie
heard snippets of conversation, bits of laughter, someone yelling, *No
love lost there, man.*

Ethel clapped her hands to get attention. "Hey, all, this is Frankie McGrath. She's from . . ." Ethel turned. "Where are you from?"

"California."

"Sunny California!" Ethel said. She pulled Frankie forward, introducing her to the other officers. Patty was near the bar, smoking a cigarette, playing cards with a captain. She smiled and waved.

Suddenly the music changed. Out came "East Coast girls are hip . . ."

People clapped, yelled out, "Welcome, Frankie!"

A man pulled her into his arms, started dancing with her.

He was tall and lanky, good-looking, in a white T-shirt and worn Levi's. His beach-sand-blond hair was regulation short, but the smile on his face—and the marijuana cigarette in his mouth—told her that he was the kind of guy her father had told her to stay away from. Well, really, that was all men. ("War bachelors, Frankie. Married men who think love's a free-for-all when bombs are falling. Don't you go all that way and shame us.")

He exhaled the sweet smoke in a rush and offered her the joint. "You want a hit?"

Frankie's eyes widened. It wasn't the first time she'd been offered marijuana (she *had* gone to college, albeit a Catholic one), but this was Vietnam. War. Serious times. She hadn't smoked marijuana at the San Diego College for Women and she sure as heck wouldn't do drugs here.

"No, thanks, but I'll take a—"

Before she could say *Coke*, an explosion rocked the O Club. The walls rattled, dirt rained down from the ceiling, a footlocker crashed to the floor, someone shouted, *Not now, Charlie! I'm drinking*—

Another explosion. Red light flashed through the beaded curtain. A red-alert siren blared across camp.

A voice came out over the loudspeaker: *Attention all personnel, take cover. Security Alert condition red. We are under rocket attack. Repeat: condition red. Take cover.*

Rocket attack?

Another explosion. Closer. The beads swayed and clattered.

Frankie wrenched out of whoever-he-was's arms and headed for the door.

He grabbed her, pulled her back.

She panicked, screamed, tried to wrench free. He held her close.

Someone cranked up the music as dirt rained down on them all.

"You're safe, McGrath," the man whispered in her ear. She felt his breath on her neck. "At least as safe as anywhere in the damned country. Just breathe. I've got you."

She heard the rockets flare and explode, felt the ground shimmy under her feet.

Frankie flinched at every explosion. *Oh God. What have I done?* She thought of Finley.

Regret to inform you . . .

No remains.

"I've got you," the man said again as her breathing sped up. He tightened his hold. "Don't worry."

The siren sounded again.

She felt the man's hold on her ease, felt his tension soften.

"That's the all clear," he said. And when another explosion sounded, he laughed and said, "That's us. Giving it back to them."

She looked up, embarrassed by her fear. What kind of soldier was she? Standing here, shaking and ready to cry on her first day? "But . . . the bunkers . . . shouldn't we go . . ."

"What kind of host would I be if I shoved you out of your own party because of a little mortar attack? I'm Jamie Callahan. Chest cutter. From Jackson Hole. Just look at me, McGrath. Close out the rest."

Frankie tried to focus on her breathing, on his kind, sad blue eyes, tried to pretend she wasn't terrified. "You're a d-doctor?" she made herself say.

He smiled, and it showed her at last that he was young, or at least not old. Maybe thirty. "Yep. Ward Five. Surgical." He leaned close. "Maybe you'll work under me."

She heard the sexy slur of his voice and smelled the alcohol and marijuana on his breath and the strange, shifting, exploding world righted for a moment, became as familiar as a doctor hitting on a nurse. "My dad warned me about guys like you."

The explosions stopped.

"That's it," Jamie said with a smile, but something about it was wrong, as if maybe he'd been scared, too.

Someone cranked up the music. "These boots are made for walkin' . . ."

The crowd joined in, sang along, paired up and started dancing.

Just like that, the party was back in full swing, with people smoking and drinking and laughing as if they hadn't just been bombed.

Jamie smiled. "How about a shot of whiskey, California girl?"

Frankie had trouble finding her voice. "I don't know . . ." She'd turned twenty-one a few months before, but she'd never drunk hard alcohol.

He leaned close. "It'll stop the trembling."

Frankie doubted that. "Will it?"

He gave her a sad look. "For tonight, it will."

Six

The next morning, Frankie woke disoriented, uncertain where she was.

Then the smell hit: shit and fish and rotting vegetation. And the heat. She was drenched in sweat. Her sheets smelled sour.

She was in her sauna-hot hooch, in Vietnam. With a pounding headache.

She sat up and swung her legs over the side of the cot.

For a terrible minute, she thought she might vomit.

She'd had two shots of whiskey last night. *Two.*

And nothing to eat.

The last thing she remembered was dancing with Ethel to "Monday, Monday." Had Frankie's shorts fallen down at one point, pooled around her shiny new combat boots? She thought so, thought she remembered someone saying, *Nice gams, Frank!* and Ethel laughing as Frankie struggled to pull the shorts back up.

Oh God. Way to make a good first impression.

Where were Barb and Ethel?

Feeling shaky, dehydrated, she scratched her short hair and looked around. A large gray rat sat on the dirty wooden floor, holding a half-eaten candy bar in his pointy pink paws; at her look, he stopped nibbling and stared back at Frankie through black, oil-drop eyes.

Tomorrow morning, she'd throw something at him. Now she felt too weak to expend the effort.

Frankie got out of bed, ignoring the rat, who was now ignoring her, too, and dressed in her creased olive-green fatigues, taking care to tuck her pants into her spit-shined new boots.

The rat scurried across the wooden floor and disappeared behind the dresser.

"Okay," Frankie said, standing in the small, crowded space. "You can do this."

She'd eat something and drink plenty of water and report for duty. She would drink water only from the Lister bag and take her malaria and diarrhea medications on time.

Outside, she saw that the compound was a sprawling complex of buildings, all set on a mostly treeless patch of rich red earth. There were buildings and shacks and huts and tents. The Quonset huts that housed the wards looked like giant tin cans cut in half vertically and pressed into the dirt, with their entrances protected by sandbags.

She followed the center aisle, which was flanked on either side by a long covered area and rows of buildings. She passed the men's quarters, the pharmacy, a small chapel, and the Red Cross station, the PX. In the center of the aisle, below a tall water tower, was a raised stage. Empty now.

The mess hall ran perpendicular to the stage. She paused at the open door of the long wooden building. Inside, it was divided in half; one side for officers, one side for enlisted.

She found a table set with bread, muffins, a vat of American peanut butter, and a tub of butter. She poured a cup of coffee and gulped it down, hoping it would quell her pounding headache. When she emptied the first cup, she put peanut butter on a piece of toast and downed it with eight ounces of milk.

She instantly felt sick and ran for the latrines, but made it only halfway there before she vomited at the side of the PX.

When there was nothing left to vomit, she moved cautiously back onto the walkway, made her way to Major Wendy Goldstein's office. Inside, the chief nurse sat at a desk behind a mound of paperwork, dressed in faded, pressed fatigues.

Frankie stepped inside the office and saluted. "Second Lieutenant McGrath reporting as ordered," she said clearly.

Major Goldstein looked up. Her face and hair were both pale and could have given the impression of fragility, but somehow the opposite felt true. "What time is it, Lieutenant McGrath?"

Frankie glanced at the black wall clock, which was protected by a black wire cage. "Oh-eight-oh-three hours, Major Goldstein."

The major pursed her lips. "Oh good. I was afraid you couldn't tell time. When you are told to report to me at oh-eight-hundred, I expect to see you precisely at oh-eight-hundred. Are we clear?"

"Yes, Major," Frankie said. "I was . . . sick."

"Don't drink the water or you'll spend your whole tour either vomiting or crapping. Didn't someone tell you that? I think—" She stopped midsentence, drew in a sharp breath. She cocked her head to the left, listening. Then said, "Damn."

Frankie heard the distant *thwop-thwop-thwop* of incoming helicopters. "Are we under attack?"

"Not in the way you think." She closed a manila folder. "Let's see what you're made of, McGrath. I'll assign you tomorrow. Be here at oh-eight-hundred sharp. For now, it's all hands on deck. Report to Lieutenant Flint in the ER."

"The emergency room? I'm not—"

"It's not a cocktail party invitation, McGrath. *Move.*"

Frankie was so confused, she forgot to salute. She couldn't even remember if she was supposed to salute. She turned and rushed out of the admin building, followed the covered walkway to the set of

Quonset huts that made up the wards. Her new boots started to hurt her feet.

At the helipad, marked by a red cross on a white circle on the ground, she saw three helicopters, each emblazoned with the Red Cross insignia, buzzing overhead. None had manned gunners at the doors. So these were the Dust Offs she'd read about. Unarmed medevac helicopters that transported injured men off the field. Two of them hovered as the third lowered.

A medic and two nurses appeared almost instantly and began off-loading men on litters.

Moments after that chopper lifted up, another lowered onto the pad. More corpsmen showed up to offload the wounded. An ambulance drove up to Pre-Op.

Frankie found the Quonset hut that housed the emergency room.

Medics ran in and out, carrying men on litters: one lay screaming, his own severed leg on his chest; another had no legs at all. Their uniforms were bloody; some of their faces were still smoking from burns the medics—or their friends—had put out. There were gaping chest wounds—one guy she could see had a broken rib sticking up. Ethel stood in the midst of the chaos like an Amazon goddess, directing traffic, positioning the casualties, pointing out what to do with the wounded. She seemed unaffected by the chaos. More men followed her commands. There were so many wounded that some had to be left outside, their litters set on sawhorses, waiting for space in the ER.

Frankie was overwhelmed by the horror of it. The screaming, the smoke, the shouting.

A medic saw Frankie standing there and shoved a boot into her arms.

She stared down at it, saw that a foot was still inside.

Frankie dropped the boot, stumbled just out of the way, and vomited. She was about to vomit a second time when she heard, "Frank. *Frank* McGrath." Ethel grabbed her by the arm.

Frankie wanted to run. "I'm not trained for this."

"We need your help."

Frankie shook her head.

Ethel touched Frankie's chin, made her look up. "I know," she said, pushing her hair back with a bloody hand. "I know."

"In Basic, they taught us how to wrap bandages and shave a man for an operation. I shouldn't be here. I—"

"You can hold a man's head. You can do that."

Frankie nodded numbly.

Ethel took her by the hand and led her to the staging area in the ER. "This is triage," Ethel said. "We assess here. We decide who gets seen and when. We treat the ones we can save first. That screen over there in the back? We put the expectants there—men who probably aren't going to make it. We see them last. We can treat five gutshot wounds or amputations in the time it takes to handle one head injury. You understand? The walking wounded—those men over there." She pointed to a group of soldiers who stood beside the screen with their fellow soldiers, talking, smoking, doing what they could to comfort the expectants. "They'll be seen when we have time."

Ethel led Frankie to a soldier lying on a litter. He was drenched in blood and one arm was just . . . gone. She looked quickly away.

"Keep breathing, Frank," Ethel said calmly. "Hold his hand."

Frankie positioned herself at the patient's side and forced herself to look down. At first all she saw was the horror, the devastating amount of blood, the arm that had been severed at the elbow, revealing the white of bone and pink gristle and dripping blood.

Focus, Frankie.

She closed her eyes for a second, exhaled, and then opened her eyes. She saw the soldier this time, a young Black man wearing a dirty green bandanna, who looked barely old enough to shave. Very carefully, she took hold of his hand.

"Hey, ma'am," he said in a slurred voice, "have you seen my buddy Stevo? We were together . . ."

Ethel snipped the uniform off of the young man, revealing a massive abdominal wound.

Ethel looked up. Her eyes were tired. "Expectant," she yelled out.

Two medics appeared and picked up the litter and carried it to the staging area behind the screen.

Frankie looked up at Ethel. "He's going to die."

"Probably."

Was this what Frankie had joined the Army for, to watch young men die?

"We will save plenty of lives today, Frank. But not all of them. Never all of them."

"He shouldn't die alone."

"No," Ethel said, and gave her a tired smile. "Go, Frank. Be his sister, his wife, his mother."

"But—"

"Just hold his hand. Sometimes that's all we can do. And then . . . come back here."

When he was dead; that was what Ethel meant. Frankie felt as if a giant weight were suddenly pressing down on her as she stepped around the screen. The soldier—kid—was off by himself. She saw that he was crying.

She approached him carefully, looked down, saw his name and rank. "Private Fournette," she said. It seemed to get quiet suddenly. She couldn't hear the screaming of the helicopters coming and going or the nurses yelling at one another. All she could hear was this man's labored, bubbly breathing.

She kept her gaze averted from the horrible gaping wound that showed his glossy intestines and dripping blood.

She moved in close, reached down, took hold of his cold hand.

"Private Fournette," she said again. "I'm Frankie McGrath."

He blinked slowly. Tears slid down his face, mixing with dirt and blood. "Have you seen Stevo? Private Grand. It was my job to keep him safe. He just got in-country two days ago. His mama and mine work at the same salon. In Baton Rouge."

"I saw him," Frankie said, finding it hard to speak past the lump in her throat. "He's fine. He was asking about you."

Private Fournette smiled, a little sloppily. "My . . . something hurts, ma'am. I figure that shot is wearin' off. Man, I surely could use a cold beer." He started to shake. His hand in hers went limp, grew colder. "Ma'am," he said.

"Yes?"

It was a long time before he spoke, a shivering silence. "I wish I'd a told . . ." He wheezed hard. Blood bubbled up from his mouth. "Loved her."

"You'll tell her after surgery," Frankie said. "Right after they fix you up. I'll help you write a letter."

"I . . ." He paused, shuddered, and closed his eyes.

His hold on her hand loosened. One minute he was there, holding her hand, whispering his regret, and the next moment, he was gone.

Mass casualty. That was what they called tonight, or actually MASCAL. Apparently, since the recent influx of troops, it was beginning to happen so often that they didn't have time to call it by its full name.

Frankie stood in the back corner of the Quonset hut that housed the ER. After nine hours on duty, she was beyond exhausted and her feet burned with blisters, but it wasn't the ache in her bones and muscles and feet that mattered. It was shame.

How on earth had she thought she belonged here? That she had something to offer men who were grievously wounded? She'd been as much help as a candy striper.

Tonight she'd held scissors in hands that never quite stopped shaking and cut off T-shirts and flak jackets and pants, revealing wounds that she couldn't have imagined before today. She still heard patients' screams inside her head, even though the ward had emptied a while ago.

Casualties, she reminded herself. Back in the world, they were patients; here, they were casualties. The Army was full of terms like *back in the world.* That was how everyone referred to the life that they'd left behind.

Frankie sighed heavily, heard footsteps, and knew it was Ethel, coming to check up on her.

"Well, that was an ass-kicker," Ethel said, lighting up a cigarette. "And no, not every day is like this, thank God."

In her mind, Frankie nodded. She was pretty sure that in fact she just stood there, staring at nothing.

Ethel put an arm around her. "How are you, Frank?"

"Useless," was all she could say.

"No one is ever ready for this. The worst part is that you'll get used to it. Come on."

Ethel kept her hold on Frankie, led her through the camp. Frankie felt every one of the new blisters on her feet. Outside, the night air smelled heavy, like blood on metal; there was no moon to light the way.

In the mess, she saw a few men sitting in the enlisted section, drinking coffee, and as they approached the O Club, she smelled smoke wafting through the beaded curtain. Music followed the smoke, infused it with memories of home. *"I wanna hold your ha-aa-aa-and."*

In the distance, she heard the whoosh of waves rolling in and out. The sound called to her like a siren song, reinflated her youth. Nights on bicycles with Finley, riding free, their arms outstretched, stars overhead.

Finley. She'd felt his ghost beside her all night, seen his eyes in the face of every soldier whose hand she'd held.

She pulled away from Ethel and walked alongside a coil of concertina wire, a barrier of razor-sharp spikes.

In front of her: the sea. It was a glow of silver, a sense of movement, and the comforting familiarity of it, the salty tang in the air, called out to her, reminded her of home. On the beach, she sat down in the sand and closed her eyes.

She felt the salt, tasted it. The sea—

No. Not the sea.

She was crying.

"You can't be out here alone, Frank. Not all soldiers are gentlemen." Ethel sat down beside her.

"I'll add that to my list of mistakes."

"Yeah. You gotta be careful. Over here, the men lie and they die."

Frankie had no idea what to say to that.

"So. Which is it?" Ethel finally said.

Frankie wiped her eyes and looked sideways. "What?"

"Are you out here grieving the boys we lost or your own piss-poor set of nursing skills?"

"Both."

"That means you've got what it takes, Frank. We all went through it. Nurses back in the world are second-class citizens. And, big surprise— they're mostly women. Men keep us in boxes, make us wear starched virgin white, and tell us that docs are gods. And the worst part is, we believe them."

"Doctors aren't gods here?"

"Of course they are. Just ask them." Ethel pulled a pack of cigarettes out of her pocket, tapped one out, offered it.

Frankie took the cigarette. She didn't smoke—never had—but just now, it gave her something to do with her unsteady hands and blocked out the smell of blood.

"Why did you join the Army?" Ethel asked.

"It doesn't matter anymore. It was a stupid, childish thing to do." She turned to Ethel. "Why did you join?"

"We all have a long-story and a short-story answer to that, I guess. Long story, after I got my nursing degree, I decided I wanted to follow in my dad's footsteps and become a veterinarian. I was headed that way when the man I loved shipped out. Short story: I followed him." Her voice softened. "His name was George. He had a laugh that fixed everything."

"And he—"

"Died. And you?"

"My brother died over here, too. And . . . I wanted to make a difference." Frankie stopped, hearing the naivete in her words.

"Yeah. That's why I re-upped for a second tour. We all want that, Frank."

Back in the world, when Frankie had told her friends that she'd hoped to make a difference over here, hoped to make her family proud, they'd rolled their eyes and acted impatient with patriotism; but out here, sitting beside this woman she barely knew, Frankie remembered the pride she'd felt on joining the Army.

"I'm sorry about your guy," Frankie said. "George."

"He was a real looker, my Georgie," Ethel said with a sigh. "And for a while, I hated that I'd followed him here and lost him anyway, but I stuck it out, and now I'm glad I stayed. That's what I've learned, Frank. I am better and stronger than I ever thought, and when I go back to my daddy's farm in Virginia and get back into vet school, I know there's nothing that can stop me. I want it all, Frank. A husband, a kid, a career. A big ole life that ends when I can barely get out of my rocker, with kids and animals and friends all around me. You'll find out what you want over here, too. I promise."

"Thanks, Ethel."

"Now, enough seaside weeping. Do you drink, Frank?"

Frankie didn't know how to answer that. She'd gone to fraternity mixers in college, and she'd had a few beers, and she'd had two shots of whiskey on her first night in Vietnam, but really, she was a good girl who followed the rules. She'd turned twenty-one in December—the age drinking was legal in California—but with Finley's death and the terrible holidays last year, she hadn't celebrated her birthday. "I have."

"There's plenty of it over here," Ethel said. "Watch out. Take care of yourself. That's my advice. I don't drink, but I don't judge, either. Over here it's live and let live. Whatever gets you through the night." She got to her feet, put a hand down for Frankie. "Get up, Lieutenant, brush yourself off, and let's clean up and fill our bellies and then head to the O Club to blow off some steam. You just survived your first MASCAL in 'Nam."

Frankie had never seen any human eat as fast as Ethel did. It was like watching a hyena gulp down a kill as predators closed in.

Finally, Ethel pushed her empty plate aside and said, "I feel like dancing. You?"

Frankie looked down at her barely eaten Salisbury steak covered in brown gravy, and the overcooked green beans. Why had she taken so many mashed potatoes? "Dance?"

How could she dance? Her stomach kept roiling and cramping. She couldn't shake the horror of what she'd witnessed tonight, nor could she accept her ineptitude. She was nauseated and ashamed. She pushed her chair back and stood up.

The mess hall was full of soldiers in bloody fatigues. She was surprised at how loudly they talked and how often they laughed. Frankie wondered how anyone who'd lived through a MASCAL could get over it so quickly.

She followed Ethel out of the mess. As they walked past the empty stage, Ethel told a story about the Christmas show at Di An when

Bob Hope had entertained the troops. "I sent a picture of me and Bob Hope home to my dad. He said he hung it up on the bulletin board in the barn, told everyone that his girl was saving lives . . ."

Frankie wasn't listening. She had never felt less like being around people. She started veering to the left, eager to escape back to her hooch.

Ethel took hold of Frankie's arm, as if she'd read her thoughts. "Steady, Frank."

At the O Club, Ethel pushed the beaded curtain aside; the clattering sound filled in the beat of silence between songs.

Inside, there was barely room to sit or stand. Men stood in groups, talking, smoking, drinking. A *Stars and Stripes* newspaper lay on the floor with the headline MCNAMARA'S LINE FORTIFIED ALONG DMZ. The air was gray with smoke.

How could they be here, as if nothing had happened, some still with blood in their hair, drinking alcohol and smoking?

"Whoa, Frank. You're breathing like a racehorse. You don't want to dance, I get it. Hang on." Ethel grabbed two cold Cokes and maneuvered back through the crowd, toward the doorway.

"Hey, pretty mamas, don't leave us!" someone yelled out.

"Was it something we said?"

"I'll put my pants back on. Come back!"

The two women walked past the latrines and the empty shower stalls and came to the row of hooches.

Opening the door, Ethel pretty much pushed Frankie up the steps from the wood-slatted walkway and into the dank, dark, foul-smelling hooch.

She turned on the light and took Frankie by the shoulders and forced her to sit on her cot.

"I smell like blood," Frankie said.

"And you look like hell. It's a groovy combination."

"I should shower."

Ethel handed Frankie a Coca-Cola and they sat down on Frankie's cot, side by side, shoulder to shoulder.

Frankie looked up at the horse and barn pictures tacked above Ethel's cot and felt a pang of grief. "My brother and I rode horses a few times. I loved it."

"I got my first horse when I was four. Chester the chestnut," Ethel said. "Mom used to saddle him and set me on his back and garden. I still have that dream of us sometimes."

"She's—"

"Gone. Breast cancer. Please don't say you're sorry. I know it's true. How old are you, Frank?"

"Twenty-one."

Ethel shook her head, made a whistling sound. "Twenty-one. Hell, I barely remember that age anymore. I'm twenty-five."

"Wow," Frankie said.

"You thought I was older, right? We age in dog years over here, Frank. And it's my second tour. By the time I leave I'll have chin hairs and need bifocals, you watch."

Ethel lit up a cigarette. The gray smoke wreathed them, made Frankie suddenly homesick for her mother. She found herself softening just a little.

"Where's Barb?"

"A kid from her hometown was brought in tonight with the crispy critters. Not good. She's sitting with him, I bet."

"Crispy critters?"

"Burn victims. I know, I know, we shouldn't call them that. You'll learn fast, Frank. We laugh so we don't cry."

Frankie could hardly grasp such a thing.

"I don't think Barb likes me," Frankie said. "Can't say I blame her."

"It's not you, Frank. Barb has had a tough road."

"Why?"

Ethel gave her a look. "You have noticed the color of Barb's skin, I take it?"

Frankie felt her cheeks burn. There had been no Black girls at St. Bernadette's, no Black families at St. Michael's Church or on Ocean Boulevard. None in her sorority or her nursing program. Why was that? "Of course. But—"

"But nothing, Frank. Let's just say Barb is sick and tired, and leave it at that. She's also one of the best surgical nurses you'll ever meet." Ethel put an arm around Frankie. "Look, Frank. I know how you feel right now. We all do. We've been there. You're thinking you screwed up by signing up for 'Nam, thinking you don't belong. But let me tell you, kid, it doesn't matter where you're from or how you grew up or what god you believe in, if you're here, you're among friends. We've got you."

Frankie lay on her cot, her hair still damp from a lukewarm shower, and stared up at the ceiling. Hours had passed this way; she couldn't sleep.

Her feet throbbed with the pain of new blisters. Barb's snores filled the small hooch, sounded like the ocean rolling in. Far away, there was the sound of gunfire popping. Ethel tossed and turned, her cot squeaking at every movement.

Images from tonight's MASCAL ran through Frankie's mind, a kaleidoscope of horror. Torn limbs, blank stares, gushing bleeds, sucking chest wounds. One young man screaming for his mother.

She needed to use the restroom. Should she waken one of her roommates to go with her?

No. Not after the night they'd had.

She threw the covers off and got out of bed, stood there in the dark.

She heard something scurry across the floor and already she didn't care. What were rats to her after tonight?

She dressed in her fatigues and slipped her stockinged feet into her boots, immediately feeling the raw blisters that had formed.

Outside, the compound was relatively quiet. Some distant gunfire, an engine humming—a generator, maybe—a faraway beat of music. Someone somewhere was listening to a transistor radio.

She shouldn't go out. She knew that. It could be dangerous. *Not all soldiers are gentlemen,* Ethel had said, reminding Frankie that the Army at war wasn't so different from the world.

Still. She couldn't breathe in here, couldn't sleep, and her bladder ached with the need to be emptied. The horrible images she'd seen wouldn't let her go and the heat was giving her a headache.

She stepped down onto the hard-packed dirt and walked toward the latrines. Off to the left, a shadowy figure stood at a burn barrel, throwing things into the fire. The stench wafted this way.

A narrow walkway spread over a ditch, with coils of spiked wire on either side. She walked cautiously over the makeshift bridge and ducked into the women's latrines.

When she exited the building, she smelled cigarette smoke and stopped.

A lone orange-gold light shone down from a post overhead, revealing a man standing not far away, smoking.

She turned away quickly, stepped on something that cracked.

He turned.

The chest cutter. Jamie.

In the ghoulish light, his handsome face looked drawn, even as he tried to smile at her.

"I'm sorry. You want to be alone," she said. "I'll go—"

"Don't," he said. "Please."

Frankie bit her lip, remembered Ethel's warning about men. This was a lonely place, hidden. She glanced back toward the relative safety of her hooch.

"You're safe with me, McGrath." He held out a hand. She saw that it was shaking. "Hell of a thing, for a surgeon's hand to shake," he said.

Frankie moved toward him but remained out of reach.

"You caught me on a bad night," he said.

Frankie didn't know how to respond.

"A friend from high school came through today. We played football together. He said, *Save me, JC*." His voice broke. "I haven't been JC in a long time. And I couldn't save him."

Frankie could have said the kind of thing she'd heard at Finley's funeral, the empty, shiny words of a stranger. Instead, she said, "You were with him when he died. You can tell his family that he wasn't alone. That will mean a lot to them. I know, believe me. My brother died over here and all we got back was another man's boots."

Jamie looked at her for a long time, as if her words had surprised him. Then he tossed down his cigarette, ground it out with his heel. "Come on, McGrath. It's late. I'll walk you back to your hooch."

He moved toward her. She fell into step beside him. On the makeshift bridge, he let her go first, and at the closed door of her hooch, he stopped.

"Thanks," he said.

"For what?"

"Just being here, I guess. Sometimes it doesn't take much to save a man in 'Nam."

On that, he gave her a false, fleeting smile, and walked away.

Seven

The next morning, when Frankie woke up, she was alone in the hooch. She dressed quickly and presented herself at admin at precisely 0800.

She saluted. "Lieutenant McGrath, Major."

"I heard you were as much help in the ER as a tiara," the major said, and opened a manila folder. "A nursing degree from some small Catholic women's college and almost no clinical experience. And you're young." She peered at Frankie through black horn-rimmed glasses. "What on earth brought you here, Lieutenant?"

"My brother—"

"Never mind. I don't care. But I hope to God you aren't here to say hi to a brother." Major Goldstein pushed her glasses higher up on her nose. "The Navy and Air Force won't even let a girl like you in 'Nam. They require *training*." She closed the folder, sighed. "Anyway. You're here. Unready, unprepared, but here. I'm assigning you to Neuro. Night shift. How much damage can you do there?"

"I'll do my best."

"Uh-huh. Welcome to the Thirty-Sixth Evac Hospital, McGrath. Be the best version of yourself."

Housed in a Quonset hut near the OR, the Neuro ward was a brightly
lit, domed space filled with Stryker frame beds. Frankie had never seen
the specialized beds before, but she'd learned about them in school and
in Basic Training: beds for paraplegics, for patients with pelvic fractures,
burn patients, or others who couldn't handle much manipulation. Two
rows of beds were separated by a wide aisle. Metal tubing ran the length
of each wall for hanging IVs. The amount of equipment at each bed
was staggering: ventilators, cooling blankets, monitors, IVs. Frankie
didn't even recognize most of the machines. The overhead lights were
blaringly bright. She heard the *whooh-thunk* of ventilators, the buzz of
EKG monitors.

In the front left corner, an older man in faded fatigues sat at a desk,
writing. The only other soldier she saw (standing) was a corpsman at
the far end of the ward; he was checking on a patient.

Frankie straightened her posture and tried to look more confident
than she felt as she walked over to the man at the desk. "Second Lieutenant McGrath, reporting as ordered, sir."

The man looked up. He had the tiredest eyes she'd ever seen and a
face that showed a history of acne. Heavily jowled cheeks blurred his
jawline. "Frances, right?"

"Frankie, sir."

"Captain Ted Smith. Doctor. How much nursing experience do
you have, Frankie?"

"My RN, sir. And . . . some time on the night shift at my local hospital."

"Uh-huh." He stood up. "Walk with me." He strode forward. At
the first bed, he paused. Beside him lay a young Vietnamese man, his
head wrapped in bandages, through which blood had seeped in a red-
brown burst.

"He's Vietnamese," Frankie said, surprised.

"We treat the villagers who are brought in," Captain Smith said. "Anyway, Frankie, every patient in here is brain-damaged. Most have no pupillary response. You know what that means?"

Before she could answer, he took a slim flashlight out of his breast pocket and shone it into the patient's eyes. "See that? No reaction. Fixed and dilated. You'd note that in his chart, along with the time and date."

He showed her where and how to make the notation and then handed her the flashlight and walked on, took her past one young American soldier after another who lay naked beneath pale sheets, staring at nothing; most were on ventilators. There were several Vietnamese patients. "This one walked into a rotor," he said at the bed of a man with half his head bandaged and one arm gone. The last bed was occupied by a Black man covered in bandages. He writhed, babbled unintelligibly. Then he screamed as if in pain.

"He's not comatose but not fully conscious, either. He has a chance at some kind of recovery. Most don't, honestly. We've developed the skills to save their bodies, but not their lives," Captain Smith said.

Frankie looked out over the many beds, a split sea of white and metal and men and machines. Each one someone's son or brother or husband.

"We monitor and change dressings and keep them breathing until they can see a neurologist at the Third Field Hospital. You'll learn to see subtle changes in their conditions. But this is an evac hospital. They won't be here long."

"Can they hear me?"

"Good question. Yeah, Frankie. I think they can. I hope so, anyway. You can start an IV?"

"In theory, sir." She felt her own incompetence like a scarlet letter on her fatigues.

"Don't worry, Frankie. You've got heart, I can tell. Skills, I can teach."

———

April 14, 1967

Dear Mom and Dad,

Hello from the 36th Evacuation Hospital! I'm sorry it's taken me so long to write. It's hard to express the speed of life over here. I'm either terrified or exhausted most of the time. When my head hits the pillow, I'm out. Turns out you can learn to sleep through anything if you're tired enough. I've been focusing on improving my nursing skills, which were, to put it kindly, subpar. I work long hours on the Neuro ward, where I've been assigned.

I'm learning so much! I spend my shift shining bright lights into my patients' eyes, marking down any pupil dilation, or lack thereof, changing surgical dressings, suctioning wounds, monitoring ventilators, changing IVs, turning paralyzed patients every few hours, pinching or poking places on the bodies to see if they can feel pain. It is every bit as glamorous as it sounds, and Mom, you would definitely have something to say about how I look these days, but my skills are improving. Slowly.

I've made two friends over here. Ethel Flint, an ER nurse from Virginia, and Barb Johnson, a surgical nurse from Georgia. They're keeping me sane. My superior, Captain Smith, is great, too. He's from a small town near Kansas City. You would love him, Dad. He collects watches and loves backgammon.

I miss you. Send me news of the real world. All we get for news-papers over here is the Stars and Stripes, *and the only radio is Armed Forces Radio. Suffice it to say that we don't get news about the latest Burton-Taylor brawl. Please write back soon!*

Love you,

Frankie

The relative quiet of the Neuro ward was the perfect place for Frankie to improve her nursing skills. She was able to breathe here, to concentrate, to ask questions of Captain Smith, and with practice came the start of confidence. There were few emergencies on this ward; the patients' wounds had already been cared for in the OR. The patients were comatose, but most had other wounds that needed care, too. The quiet gave her time to think, to process, to read the detailed care notes she wrote after checking each patient. The job at the Thirty-Sixth Evac was to get the patients stable enough to go to a field hospital for treatment. Pain management was the task Frankie took the most seriously. Because her patients couldn't speak, she took extra care with each one to assess—and assume—their pain levels.

From a distance, the ward seemed to be full of young men stuck in the hinterland between life and death. Most had little or no reaction to any stimulus, but as Frankie learned the skills it took to care for these men, she began to see them not merely as bodies in pain, but as men hoping for something more. Each soldier made her think of Finley. She spoke to them softly, touched their hands. She imagined each patient lying here, locked in the black void of a coma, dreaming of home.

Now she stood at the bedside of nineteen-year-old Private Jorge Ruiz, a radio operator who had saved most of his platoon. Captain Smith had placed him in the back of the ward, which meant that he wasn't expected to live long enough for transfer.

"Hey, Private," Frankie said, leaning down close, whispering directly into his ear. "I'm Frankie McGrath. I'm one of your nurses."

She pulled a stainless steel cart closer. It was stocked with sterile gauze, peroxide, and adhesive tape. She'd need to replenish it all for the shift change. The overhead lights blared down on her, making her eyes ache.

She reached gently for his leg, wondering if he had any sensation of being touched as she unwrapped the bloodstained gauze.

"This might hurt," she said gently as she began to pick at the crusty, dried gauze, pulling it out of the pink, jagged wound. She wished she could dampen the gauze to make it free easier, but this way the wound bled, and bleeding was good.

Beneath the gauze, she looked for blackened bits of tissue or green pockets of pus. She leaned forward to smell the wound.

All normal. No infection.

"Looking good, Private Ruiz. A lot of the boys in this room would be envious of a healing like that," she said as she re-bandaged the wound.

Beside her, the ventilator rose and fell, whooshed and thunked, inflating and deflating his sunken chest.

A commotion at the doors interrupted the quiet. Two bloodied soldiers in dirty, ripped fatigues walked into the ward, shoulder to shoulder.

"Ma'am?" one of them said, stepping close to Private Ruiz. "How is he?"

"He's in a coma," she said.

"Will he wake up?"

"I don't know."

The other soldier stepped in beside his friend. "He saved our lives."

"He wanted to go home and be a fireman. Some shit-ass border town in West Texas. I told him he'd never pass the test." He looked at Frankie. "I gotta tell him I was just yankin' his chain."

"He's hanging on," she said. It was all the hope she could offer. And it was true. With life, there had to be hope.

"Thank you, ma'am, for taking care of him. Could we take a picture of you with him? For his mama?"

"Of course," she said quietly, thinking how much a picture of Finley would have meant to her family. She moved closer to the young man, held his limp hand in hers.

The soldier snapped the shot.

"He's lucky to have friends like you," Frankie said. "Tell his mother he wasn't alone."

The soldiers nodded solemnly. One of them took a pin off of his pocket—an insignia of some kind—and handed it to Frankie. "Thanks, ma'am." He stared at Ruiz for a moment longer, then left.

Frankie pocketed the pin and looked down at her patient. "You have some good buddies," she said, replenishing his IV.

By the end of her long night shift, it was all she could do to stand upright. With barely a glance at Debbie John, the nurse who'd come in to replace her, Frankie stumbled out of the ward. It was early in the morning and already the sun beat down on her. She bypassed the mess hall—not hungry—and the O Club—no desire to party—and headed to her hooch. She could tell by the sound of small arms fire and helicopters in the distance that there would be patients incoming soon. She'd better sleep while she could. Thankfully, the hooch was empty. Barb and Ethel worked days, mostly. For weeks she'd barely seen her roommates.

Grateful for the relative quiet, Frankie untied her boots, put them in her locker, and lay down on her cot. She was asleep in minutes.

———

"Rise and shine, princess."

"Go away, Ethel. I'm sleeping." Frankie rolled onto her side.

"Nope. Babs and I have talked about it and we are taking you under our wing. Wings?" She looked at Barb, who shrugged.

Frankie groaned and put the pillow over her head. "Cool. Starting tomorrow."

"Starting today, Frank. You've been hiding out with the gorks for six weeks. We haven't seen you in the O Club in weeks. Who comes to 'Nam and plays with no one?"

"I'm learning to be a competent nurse."

"That's what today's all about. Now get up before I pour cold water on you. Put on your fatigues. We're going on a field trip. Bring your camera." Ethel yanked the blanket off of Frankie, revealing her bare legs.

Grumbling, Frankie stumbled out of bed and dressed in a T-shirt and fatigue pants that were still new-looking, unmarred by bloodstains. There weren't a lot of bloody emergencies in Neuro.

Ethel and Barb waited for her outside the mess hall. "We're off to see the wizard. Word is that no wounded are incoming," Barb said, smiling. She handed Frankie an olive-green canvas boonie hat. "You'll need this."

Outside, the camp was blissfully quiet, no helicopters delivering wounded, no mortars exploding in the distance. Men were throwing a football back and forth as a water truck rolled past.

Ethel and Barbara led the way to a two-and-a-half-ton truck—a deuce and a half—that was parked near the gates of the hospital. They climbed up into the back, along with Captain Smith. Several men from an infantry unit stood among them, carrying rifles.

"Climb in," Barb said to Frankie. "They're not gonna wait forever."

Frankie climbed up into the truck's bed and took a seat on the metal floor, beside the gunner. The big truck rumbled to life, shook, started to roll forward.

"Where are we going?" Frankie asked.

"MEDCAP," Ethel said as the deuce and a half rumbled past the guarded gates and out into the countryside. Was it safe out here? "The Medical Civic Action Program. We provide medical care to locals. I'm sure you've seen them in the wards. Captain Smith organizes these outings whenever he can, says they remind him of his practice back home."

They drove through a village that was not far from the hospital compound, saw fatigues and uniforms and olive-green T-shirts hanging from laundry lines. And then they were out in the country, jungle to the left, dirty brown river to the right. A bunch of kids floated downstream on a tire, laughing and shoving each other.

Frankie used her Polaroid and snapped a photograph of a young boy herding a black water buffalo along the water, and one of an old woman dressed traditionally in a long, split tunic over slim pants, which Frankie had learned was called an *ao dai*, carrying a woven basket full of fruit.

The soldiers standing in the back of the truck straightened, their guns aimed at the lush jungle in the distance. "Stay sharp," one of them said, adding: "Snipers."

Frankie stared out at the jungle, lowering her Polaroid camera to her lap. A team of enemy shooters could be hiding out there. She imagined men squatted behind stands of elephant grass, their guns pointed at the truck. She scrunched down, held the hat on her head, started to sweat.

The truck rumbled down a muddy, potholed road and through the green countryside. Evidence of war was everywhere—burn scars on the land, sandbags, rows of concertina wire, explosions sounding in the distance, choppers flying overhead. In a huge patch of jungle, leaves were dying and had turned orange; Frankie knew it meant that the U.S. had sprayed the area with an herbicide, Agent Orange, to kill the vegetation and limit the enemy's ability to hide.

She saw Vietnamese women moving through the rice paddies or walking in the tall grass, wearing their flowing *ao dais* and conical straw hats, carrying babies and toddlers as they worked beneath the hot sun.

They drove upward onto a mountain and, at last, came to a village tucked on a small, flat plain cut into the lush hillside. Neat gardens were carefully fenced and homes built of bamboo stood on stilts. In this remote village, the people lived as their ancestors had—hunting with crossbows and rice-farming.

The village appeared to have been built around a beautiful, but decaying, stone building, a relic of Vietnam's contentious French-occupation past. The villagers—mostly small, hunched-over old men and women with thin necks and narrow wrists, their teeth blackened by constant chewing of betel seeds—came out from their huts to stand in front of the deuce and a half in a straight line, their hands clasped, their heads bowed respectfully.

Ethel started to rise.

"Be careful," one of the armed infantrymen said. "The VC are everywhere. They plant bombs on kids and old women. They could be in the bush."

Frankie looked around. Bombs . . . on kids? How would you know? How could you tell these people from the Viet Cong, whose hidden bombs had blown up so many soldiers? How did you know who was an enemy and who was an ally?

She took a hard look at the line of villagers, in their flimsy black clothes, noticing there were no young people, male or female; only the very old and the young children. Were there swords hidden in sleeves, guns tucked in waistbands?

"Come on, guys," Barb said. "No use worrying."

"Let's get to work," Captain Smith said. The medical team jumped down from the truck.

Frankie was the last to step down into the red dirt. How were you supposed to protect yourself from invisible enemies?

Captain Smith moved in close, patted her arm. "You're a good nurse, Frankie. Go show them."

She nodded as he walked toward an elderly man, who was no taller than a ten-year-old American boy, with dark skin and black teeth. He smiled at the medical team; deep lines crinkled his face. He drew them toward him with a crooked finger, then turned and led them up into the broken-down French villa. The stone walls were riddled with bullet holes; in several rooms the walls had crumbled. Woven grasslike mats lay on the floor. A fire glowed in a large fireplace. In it, a black pot bubbled and popped, sending a rich scent of spices into the dank room.

The old man picked up a large earthenware jug and held it up to Captain Smith. He said something that sounded like, "*Bac-si, Ca mon*," in a rickety voice. He took a long drink and handed the jug to the doctor.

He wasn't going to drink it, was he? What was it?

"It means 'thank you, Doctors,' I think," Barb said. She was the second to take the jug after the doctor, and drank deeply, then handed the jug to Frankie, who took it slowly.

She eyed the crockery lip and slowly lifted it to her mouth. She took a small sip, surprised to find that it tasted sweet and sharp, a kind of wine.

The old man smiled at her, nodding, said something in his language.

Frankie smiled back uncertainly, took another sip.

After the welcoming ritual, the team set up stations to help the villagers. Everything was communicated by hand signals. None of the villagers spoke a word of English. The medical team set up a makeshift clinic with a portable exam table in a bare hut with a thatched roof; another table was set up outside with a tub full of soapy water for scrubbing lice out of children's hair and washing sores on their skin. Flies landed on everything, on hair, on lips, on hands. The driver of the truck handed out candy to the children, who gathered around him, clamoring for more.

For the next several hours, Frankie administered to the villagers in the living area of the old villa. The villagers, young and old, waited patiently to be seen for a variety of ailments. Frankie dispensed worming pills, antacids, aspirin, laxatives, and malaria tablets. She checked teeth and looked in ear canals and listened to heartbeats. She was nearly at the end of her line of villagers when a small boy, not more than five, sneaked in to stand beside her. He wore a short-sleeved shirt and shorts, and had dirty feet and unevenly cut black hair that he'd plastered back from his face with red mud. He didn't speak or tug on her sleeve; neither did he leave her side.

"What do you need, little one?" she asked when the last in her line of patients had been treated.

He smiled up at her in a way that melted her heart.

She lifted him up into her arms. He wrapped his arms and legs around her and gazed at her questioningly, said something in his language.

"I don't—"

The boy slipped out of her arms and took hold of her hand, pulling at her.

He wanted her to follow. Frankie glanced back. No one was watching her. Outside, Ethel was giving out shots and Barb was cleaning an old woman's machete wound.

Frankie hesitated; she'd been warned to be careful. The VC could be hiding anywhere.

The boy tugged harder. He looked so innocent, so young. Not someone to fear.

"Okay," she said.

He led her down a cracked stone hallway, through which vines crawled between the crumbling stone tiles and spread out, tentacle-like, across the mold-blackened floor. At a closed wooden door that hung half off its hinges he paused, looked up at her, and asked a question in his language.

She nodded.

He opened the door.

Frankie smelled something rotten and foul . . .

Inside, a candle flame illuminated a child lying on a grass mat, covered in dirty blankets, with a chamber pot not far away. Frankie covered her mouth and nose with a handkerchief and moved closer.

The girl was adolescent, thirteen maybe, with tangled black hair and sallow skin. Her left hand was wrapped in a dirty, bloody bandage.

Frankie knelt beside the girl, who eyed her warily. "I won't hurt you," she said, lifting the bandaged hand and slowly unwrapping it. The smell of rot assailed her. The hand had been mangled beyond recognition. Green pus oozed out of the open sores. In one finger, a bone stuck up through ripped black flesh.

Black flesh. Gangrene. She'd read about this, but had never seen it.

The boy said something in his language. The girl shook her head violently.

"Stay here," Frankie told the boy, carefully releasing the girl's ruined hand.

She went through the doorway and down the hall, out to the sweet, fresh outside air. "Captain Smith! Over here! Bring your bag."

She led the doctor back to the dark, fetid room. He crossed the stones quietly, his footfalls matching the rapid beats of Frankie's heart.

He knelt by the girl, examined her injuries, and then sighed heavily. "She must work in one of the sugarcane mills. This is a roller injury."

"What can we do?"

"We could send her to the Third Field Hospital. They have a Vietnamese ward, but these villagers are a self-reliant people. They won't want to let her go, and we can't guarantee her we'll come back. Amputation and antibiotics are the best chance she has to live. If we do nothing, the gangrene will spread and she'll die from the infection."

They looked at each other, but neither thought there was a question. They had to try to save this girl's life.

"I'll call for Ethel—"

"No. I want you, Frankie. Tell the boy to leave."

Frankie felt a surge of panic, but Captain Smith was already kneeling, opening his bag. He took out a syringe and administered a sedative. When the girl closed her eyes and went limp, Captain Smith said, "Hold her down, Frankie," and pulled out a saw.

The young Vietnamese boy ran.

Dr. Smith administered morphine.

"Hold her by the forearm," Captain Smith said. "Hard."

Frankie held on to the girl and did her best to help; the amputation was so brutal she had to look away several times, but when the surgery was over and the girl lay still, Frankie carefully treated the stump and wrapped it in clean white gauze. When Frankie finished treating the amputation, she turned and saw a slim, elderly South Vietnamese woman standing against the wall, with tears in her eyes. "Maybe that's her grandmother," Frankie said softly.

"Give the antibiotics to her and try to explain," Captain Smith said. "Show her how to wrap the bandage."

Frankie nodded. She went to the silent woman in the back of the room and did her best to explain what care the girl needed.

The woman gazed up at her steadily, nodded in understanding, and then bowed deeply.

Frankie gave the woman the antibiotics and gauze, and then followed Captain Smith out of the building. As she moved toward the truck bed, she felt a tug on her sleeve.

The little boy held out his small hand, unfurled his fingers. In his palm lay a smooth gray stone. He said something in his language, pushed it toward her. She had a feeling it was a precious possession. "Is she your sister?" Frankie asked.

He smiled, pushed his hand at her again. She took the stone gently, not wanting to offend. Then she reached behind her neck to unclasp the Saint Christopher medal she'd worn since her confirmation at thirteen. She handed the necklace to the boy, whose eyes widened in joy.

She dropped the smooth stone into her blouse pocket and climbed into the back of the truck. As they drove away, the very old and very young villagers standing silently in a row, Frankie pulled the stone out of her pocket.

A nothing little rock, something she'd ordinarily ignore.

In her palm, it became a talisman. A reminder that, hopefully, a girl would grow to adulthood because of their work on this day. Yes, the girl would join a generation of amputees who had survived war, but she could run and play and marry and hold a child in her arms.

"You did well today, Frankie," Barb said. "There might be hope for you after all."

Ethel took out a pack of smokes. "This is step one toward getting our girl out of Neuro."

Frankie took a cigarette and lit it up. "What's step two?"

Barb smiled. "Well, honey, we're still working on that."

Eight

April 21, 1967

Dear Frances Grace,

I can hardly believe you've been there for more than a month.

In your absence, the country has gone mad.

Sit-ins. Protests. Raised fists. Believe you me, more than a few of these free love girls are going to wake up in trouble, and where will their dirty-footed lovers be then? In prison or long gone, I'd say. The world changes for men, Frances. For women, it stays pretty much the same.

The President says the protests are prolonging the war.

Your father and I watch the news every night, hoping for a glimpse of you, however silly that is. The soldiers seem to be in good spirits.

With love,
Your mother

PS. I saw an old friend of yours, I can't recall her name, the frizzy-haired girl from St. Bernadette's that played volleyball so poorly—

anyway, I saw her in a televised picket line in San Francisco. Her breasts were moving so fast they looked like Sonny Liston's boxing gloves doing battle under a dirty T-shirt. Can someone please explain to me how bouncing breasts advance the cause of freedom?

⁓

As her shift neared its end and night began to fall, Frankie sat in a chair beside one of her patients, a young man from Oklahoma. She'd been promoted to the day shift two weeks ago.

She closed the book from which she'd been reading aloud. *Sometimes a Great Notion.*

"Well, Trevor," she said to her patient, "I'm beat. Gotta hit the showers and mess and then bed. It was so dang hot today that the water might be lukewarm." She touched his hand. "You're heading out to the Third tomorrow. I'll miss you."

She gave his hand a squeeze and then went from bed to bed, saying good night to each of her patients with a touch and a whispered, "You're safe now. We will get you home." It was all she could think of to say to men so broken. Then she grabbed her warm can of TaB and headed for her hooch.

It was a hot, dry day in May. The blistering sun had baked the dirt to hardpan and dried out her skin and hair. She was constantly scratching and sweating.

In the hooch, she found Ethel and Barb dressed in civilian clothes—Ethel in a summery dress she'd had made by a Vietnamese woman in Saigon, and Barb in a custom-made black silk *ao dai.*

Frankie saw her dress laid out on her bed, the one she'd bought at Bullock's: a pretty blue sheath with a Peter Pan collar and matching belt. Something out of the last decade. Her mother had insisted she take it to war "for parties."

Frankie pushed the dress aside and plopped onto her bed. "I'm exhausted."

Ethel looked at Barb. "Are you tired?"

"Dead on my feet."

"Are you going to sleep or go to Captain Smith's goodbye party?"

"That's tonight?" Frankie said, her shoulders slumping. "Darn."

"Move it, Frank," Ethel said.

There was no argument to be made. Captain Smith had been an amazing teacher and superior officer. He'd shown Frankie kindness and patience in teaching her the skills needed to care for the patients in Neuro. She had spent countless hours with him in the ward, even shared a Coke with him a time or two in the O Club. She'd oohed and aahed over pictures of his kids back in the world. No way she would miss a chance to say goodbye.

"That's our ride?" Frankie said, frowning as they approached the helipad. Choppers might be big and maneuverable, but they were targets, too. The enemy loved to shoot them out of the sky, and when a chopper exploded midair, there were often no remains to be found. She knew that too well.

Hot air whooshed from the rotors, whipped up dirt, stung her eyes.

Ethel shoved Frankie forward; a soldier swung her into the chopper. Frankie scrambled for the back, took a seat, and pressed herself against the wall.

Barb and Ethel each sat in one of the open doorframes, their feet swinging over the edge, laughing as the helicopter rose into the air and shot forward, nose down, tail up.

The noise inside the chopper was earsplitting.

As they banked left, Frankie saw Vietnam through the open doorway: The flat green swath of jungle, a brown ribbon of water, dotted with boats. White sand beaches bordered the turquoise waters of the

South China Sea. Verdant mountains in the distance reached up into the blue cloud-strewn sky.

There was destruction, too. Concertina wire that caught the light and sent it back in a thousand glints of color. Giant red holes in the earth, trees fallen or cut down. Scrap metal heaps strewn along roads. Helicopters swooping across the landscape, firing at the ground, being fired on. The constant whir of their rotors, the *pop-pop-pop* of mortar attacks. Tanks rolling on dirt roads, throwing up red clouds of dust. These days, the U.S. constantly bombed the Ho Chi Minh Trail. Up in the mountains near a village called Pleiku, there was fighting.

"That's Long Binh," one of the gunners yelled.

Long Binh, Frankie knew, was one of the largest bases in-country. Tens of thousands of people lived and worked there. She'd heard that the PX on base was bigger than any department store back home. From above, it was a sprawling city carved out of the jungle, built on a flat red rectangle of dirt. Bulldozers bit at the edges, constantly making more room. There wasn't a blade of grass or a tree to be seen, nothing green, no patch of shade left from the jungle they'd torn down to build their temporary city.

They touched down on the helipad just as sunset turned the sky a brilliant, blazing red.

Frankie angled cautiously forward, edged out of the chopper, and followed Ethel and Barb, who knew exactly where they were going in the dirty, smelly confusion of roads and people and tanks and bulldozers. The place was a hive of activity; a huge hospital was being built to house the rising number of wounded.

The Officers' Club at Long Binh was legendary. Frankie had heard stories of epic parties and fall-down-drunk fests, even of the MPs being called on occasion. Captain Smith—who'd been in Long Binh for most of his first tour—still spoke often of the club, and said he wouldn't want a going-away party to be held anywhere else.

Barb reached the O Club first and opened the door. Frankie moved in beside her. She felt conspicuous in her ridiculously conservative blue dress, with her nails bitten down to the quick and her black pixie cut grown so shaggy she looked like one of the Beatles. The headscarf she'd tied over it did little to help. At least she had sneakers now, instead of just her boots.

The Officers' Club was not what she'd expected. But what had she expected? White linen tablecloths and waiters in black, like the country club on Coronado Island?

In fact, it was just a dark, seedy bar. The stifling-hot air smelled of cigarette smoke and spilled booze and sweat.

A wooden bar ran the length of the building; a line of men were bellied up to it. More sat clustered around wooden tables in mismatched chairs. There weren't many women here, but the few that were here were on the dance floor. She saw Kathy Mohr, one of the surgical nurses from the Thirty-Sixth, dancing with Captain Smith. A banner had been strung above the bar. It read BON VOYAGE, CPT SMITH.

Frankie was reminded suddenly of the catered party her parents had thrown to celebrate Finley going to war.

It felt like another world ago, another time.

Appallingly naive.

Barb dragged Frankie through the clot of men, elbowing her way. At the bar, she ordered a gin and tonic and two sodas, yelling to be heard over the din of voices and music. A soldier stood beside her, smiling wolfishly, thrilled to see two American women. Frankie saw the Big Red One patch on his sleeve, for the First Infantry.

Barb ignored the man and carried the three drinks toward an empty table. The music changed, became sexy. A song Frankie hadn't heard before. *"Come on, baby, light my fire."*

Frankie was about to make her way to the table when someone touched her arm.

Dr. Jamie Callahan stood there, smiling. She remembered how

he'd helped her through her first red alert, how steadying his voice had been, the kindness he'd shown her, and the night they'd talked by the latrines. She'd seen him once or twice in the mess hall or the O Club since she'd been promoted to days, but they'd not talked much.

Tonight, in his white T-shirt and fatigues and combat boots, he was Robert Redford in *This Property Is Condemned* good-looking. And he knew it. Dirty-blond hair, grown longer than regulation allowed, blue eyes, square jaw. Anyone would have called him the American boy next door, and yet there was sadness in his eyes, a slight sag to his shoulders. She sensed a despair in him that lay just below the surface. Grief. Perhaps he saw it in her, too.

"It's a party now that the nurses have arrived," he said, giving her a strained smile.

She met his gaze. The weeks she'd spent studying comatose patients had sharpened her observation skills. "Are you okay?"

The music changed. Percy Sledge's soulful "When a Man Loves a Woman" filled the room.

"Dance with me, McGrath," he said. It wasn't a cocky, I'm-so-cool-and-you'll-be-swept-away request, not what she would have expected. That kind of thing she would have laughed at.

This was a man's plea, tinged with desperation and loneliness.

She knew that feeling well. She felt it during every shift as she moved among her comatose patients, hoping for miracles.

She reached for his hand. He led her out onto the dance floor. She fit up against him, felt the solid strength of him, and realized suddenly, sharply, how lonely she was, too. And not just here in Vietnam, but ever since Finley's death.

She rested her cheek on his collarbone. They moved in an easy, familiar rhythm, changing their steps only when the music changed.

Finally, she looked up, found him looking down at her. She reached up slowly, eased the hair out of his eyes. "You look tired."

"Rough day."

He tried to smile, and the effort touched her. She knew how hard that particular camouflage could be.

"They're so young," he said.

"Tell me something good," she said.

He thought for a minute, smiled. "My seven-year-old niece, Kaylee, lost a tooth. The tooth fairy left her fifty cents and she bought a goldfish. Her brother, Braden, made the soccer team."

Frankie smiled at the sweetness of it. She was about to ask him something about his life back in the world when the door to the O Club burst open, letting in the sound of a distant mortar attack. A trio of men walked in.

Strode, really. They were noticeable, loud, laughing. They didn't look military, let alone like officers. All three had hair that was too long to be regulation. Two had mustaches. One wore a cowboy hat and a Warlocks T-shirt. Only one wore the blue fatigues of the Navy. They had their arms around each other's shoulders and were singing what sounded like a fight song.

They pushed through the crowd and sat at a table that bore a RE-SERVED sign. One of them raised a hand and a Vietnamese waitress wearing an *ao dai* rushed over with a bottle of Jack Daniel's and three shot glasses on a tray. A smaller guy with reddish hair and a sparse mustache threw his head back and howled like a wolf.

"Who are they?" Frankie asked. They looked more like Berkeley students or cowboys than naval officers.

"New squadron. The Seawolves. Naval helicopter combat support. The Navy needed bird pilots, so last year they chose a few jet jockeys, asked for volunteers, and taught them to fly choppers. They may look arrogant and unchecked with their hair and clothing, but they're workhorses. They've flown a lot of medevacs for us in their off-hours. You call on one of the Seawolves, and if they aren't fighting Victor Charlie, they show up." He fell silent for a moment, then said, "I've been thinking about you, McGrath."

Now he sounded and looked like any other on-the-make surgeon. This man she could laugh at. "Really?"

"You've been hiding long enough."

"Hiding?"

"In Neuro. Your girl squad—Ethel and Barb—tell me you're ready to move up."

"Oh."

"Captain Smith says you did exceptional work. Fastest learner he's ever had, he said."

Frankie didn't quite know how to respond. Captain Smith had never said that to her.

"He also says you are compassionate, which I already knew."

"Well . . ."

"The point is this. Did you come to this hellhole to change bandages or to save lives?"

"Well. I don't think that's quite fair, sir."

"Jamie," he said. "For God's sake, McGrath. *Jamie.*"

"So. Jamie. I don't think that's quite fair. An opportunistic infection can—"

"Come work in surgery with me. Patty Perkins is a short-timer. I need someone good to replace her."

"I'm not good enough," she said. "Take Sara from the burn unit."

"I want you, McGrath."

She heard more in that sentence than belonged there, enough heat to set off warning bells. "If this is just a way to sleep with me—"

He gave her an easy smile. "Oh, I'd love to sleep with you, McGrath, but that's not what this is about."

"I'm not good enough. Honestly."

"You will be when I get done with you. Scout's honor."

"Were you ever a Scout?"

"Hell, no. I still can't figure out what I'm doing here. Too much debt and too many war stories, I think. My dad told me I was a fool. But here I am and here I'll be for another seven months. I need a kick-ass nurse at my side."

Frankie was afraid of all of it—mass casualties, failing at her job, keeping Jamie at bay—but she'd been here almost two months and, as bad as it was, time was moving fast. She'd learned what she could from Neuro. If she really loved nursing and wanted to be even better, it was time to take the next step.

"Okay, Captain Callahan. I'll put in for a transfer to surgery."

"Excellent." He looked very pleased with himself. There was a glimmer in his eyes that Frankie assumed had seduced plenty of women. She did not intend to fall prey; but the truth was that he tempted her. And she was pretty sure he knew it.

On the day of her first shift in the OR, Frankie paused at the stacked sandbags outside the door, took a deep breath, and walked into the Quonset hut.

Chaos.

Bright lights, music blaring, doctors and medics and nurses shouting instructions, casualties screaming. She saw Jamie, dressed in a bloody gown and masked up, coming toward her. There was blood everywhere, on walls, the floor, faces—dripping, geysering, pooling. Patty Perkins, in bloody fatigues, yelled, "You're in the way, McGrath," and pushed Frankie aside; she stumbled and hit the wall as two medics carried a litter into the OR. On it, a soldier—a kid—was sitting up, yelling, "Where are my legs?"

"Just breathe, McGrath," Jamie said, touching her shoulder gently with his gowned elbow. She looked up at him, saw his tired eyes above his mask.

A gurney wheeled past them, a young man with his guts hanging out. Barb was running alongside the gurney. "Coming in from Pre-Op."

Frankie stared at the trail of blood behind the gurney, feeling sickness rise into her throat.

"Okay, McGrath. You know what a DPC is, yes?" Jamie said.

She couldn't remember.

"*McGrath.* Focus."

She knew, of course she did. She'd been tending to them for weeks. "Delayed primary closure. Dirty wounds need to be cleaned. We close them later to prevent infection."

"Right. Come with me."

Frankie moved through the OR, realizing halfway across that Jamie was close enough to keep her moving forward. He led her to a young man who lay on a gurney.

"This is a D and I. Debride and irrigate. That's a frag wound. We need to stop the bleeding and remove the metal fragments and cut away the dead skin. Then we irrigate with saline. We make little holes out of big ones. Can you help me?"

She shook her head.

He stared down at her, said softly, "Look at me."

She exhaled slowly and looked up at him.

"No fear, McGrath. You can do this."

No fear.

"Right. Yes," she lied. "Yes, of course."

———

For the next six hours, the doors to Ward Six banged open repeatedly, with medics and corpsmen bringing in the wounded from Pre-Op. Frankie learned that it was called a push.

Now she stood across an operating table from Jamie, both of them capped, gowned, and gloved. Between them lay a young sergeant, whose chest had taken a close-range gunshot. To Frankie's right was the tray of surgical instruments and supplies.

"Hemostat," Jamie said. He gave Frankie a moment to study the tray of instruments, and then, "It's next to the retractor. See it?"

Frankie nodded, picked up the forceps, and handed them to him. She watched, mesmerized, as he repaired the wound, stitched a vein deep inside the man's chest.

"Allen clamp." He took the clamp she handed him and went back to work.

By 2200 hours, Frankie was dead on her feet and covered in blood.

"All done," Jamie said at last, stepping back.

"Last patient!" Barb said, cranking up the radio on a Van Morrison song. Singing along, she crossed the OR and approached Frankie and Jamie. "How did my girl do?" Barb asked Jamie.

Jamie looked at Frankie. "She was great."

"I told you you could cut it," Barb said to Frankie, giving her a hip bump.

Patty skidded into place beside Barb. "Good job, Frankie. You'll be a star in no time." She slung an arm around Barb. "O Club?"

Barb pulled down her mask. "You got it. See you there, Frankie?"

Frankie was so tired she could barely nod.

Barb and Patty put arms around each other's shoulders, kept each other standing as they headed for the doors.

Jamie pulled off his surgical cap and called for a medic to take the patient to Post-Op. When the gurney was wheeled away, Jamie and Frankie were left alone in the OR, facing each other.

"Well?" he said, giving her a steady look. She knew somehow that it mattered to him, how she felt about tonight.

"I have a long way to go," she said. Then she smiled at him. "But, yeah."

"There are men going home to their families because of us. That's about all we can hope for." He moved closer. "Come on, I'll buy you a drink."

"I don't really drink."

"Then you can buy me one."

After they discarded their scrubs and caps and gloves, he took her hand and led her out of the OR.

She found herself leaning into him as they walked. She'd never had a serious boyfriend, never made love. Back in the world, it had seemed important to be a good girl, to make her parents proud, but honestly, the horror she saw here every day made the rules of polite society seem unimportant.

Not surprisingly, the O Club was packed with people, all of whom looked exhausted and beaten up after tonight's push. But they were done now and needed to unwind. Ethel was seated at a table alone, smoking a cigarette; Barb was on the makeshift dance floor in some man's arms, barely moving to the music. It looked more like they were holding each other upright than dancing. Some guy in the corner was strumming a ukulele.

Jamie led Frankie to Ethel's table and pulled out a chair for her. Frankie practically fell into it. Then he headed to the bar for drinks. "Well?" Ethel asked, offering Frankie a cigarette.

Frankie took it, lit it off of Ethel's. "I didn't kill anyone."

"Hell, Frank, that's a great first day in the OR." She sighed. "Triage was brutal. Charlie really tore the shit out of those boys. Every single expectant died."

Ethel held Frankie's hand for a moment, both giving and receiving comfort. Then she stood up. "I can't stand it in here tonight. I'm going to the hooch for quiet, maybe write my dad a letter. You?"

Frankie glanced at Jamie, who was headed back from the bar. "Jamie's—"

"Married."

Frankie looked up at Ethel. "Married? What? He never said . . ."

Ethel touched her shoulder. "Be careful, Frank. Not everything the world teaches women is a lie. You don't want to get a reputation over here. I know I'm a good Baptist girl and far from cool, but some things are simply true, no matter how much the world changes. Think carefully who you climb into a cot with."

Frankie watched Ethel walk out of the O Club.

Moments later, Jamie sat down beside Frankie, scooted in close, offered her a Fresca. "I got you this, but I seriously recommend the whiskey."

"Do you?" She sipped the lukewarm soda.

"There's a hotel in Saigon," he said. "The Caravelle. It has a great rooftop bar. You'd love it. Soft beds. Clean sheets."

Frankie turned to him. "You should wear a ring, you know."

His smile faded. "McGrath—"

"When were you going to tell me?"

"I figured you knew. Everyone knows."

"What's your wife's name?"

He sighed. "Sarah."

"Do you have children?"

"One," he said after a pause. "Davy."

Frankie closed her eyes for a moment, then opened them. "Do you have a picture?"

He took out his wallet, pulled out a photograph of a tall, slender woman with bouffant hair, holding a towheaded boy with plump cheeks and marshmallow arms and legs.

He put the photograph away. There was a silence between them now, a quiet steeped in Frankie's disappointment. "It . . . doesn't have to have anything to do with . . . this. Us. Here."

"You disappoint me," she said.

"I . . ."

"Don't tell me lies, Jamie. Respect me, *please*. I believe in old-fashioned things. Like love and honesty. And vows." She downed her soda so fast it burned her throat. Then she stood up. "Good night."

"Don't run off, McGrath. I'll be a gentleman. Scout's honor."

"I believe we've already determined that you were never a Scout."

"Yeah," he said. "But I could use a friend tonight."

She knew how that felt. She wondered if it had been the photograph of his child that stole his smile and made him sad. Slowly, she sat down beside him. The truth was she liked him; too much, maybe, and she needed a friend tonight as much as he did. "How long have you been married?"

"Four years." He looked down at his drink. "But . . ."

"But what?" she asked, knowing it was a dangerous question. They were a long way from home here, in a world that felt impossibly fragile. Lonely.

"Sarah got pregnant the first time we had sex. At a dorm party in her senior year. I was in med school. It never occurred to either one of us not to get married."

"And . . ."

"I'm a good guy, McGrath."

She stared at him, feeling strangely bereft. As if a chance had been lost before she'd even known of its existence. "And I'm a good girl."

"I know that."

Between them, a silence fell. Then Frankie forced a smile.

"Sarah must be a saint to put up with your sorry ass."

"That she is, McGrath," he said, looking at her sadly. "That she is."

———

May 16, 1967

Dear Mom and Dad,
I am training to be a surgical nurse now.

I want to be good at this more than I've ever wanted anything.
It's a good feeling to love what you do.

The countryside is beautiful here. A kind of green I've never seen before, and the water is a stunning turquoise. We are in the monsoon season now, but so far that just means flashes of hard rain that come and go, leaving sunshine behind. No wonder everything is so green.

I'm taking lots of pictures and can't wait to share this all with you. Then you'll understand.

How's life back in the world?

Love you,
F

PS. Please send hand lotion and crème rinse and perfume. And a new St. Christopher medal.

———

May 31, 1967

Dear Frances Grace,
I think about you all the time. I light a candle for you every Sunday, and I know your father sometimes sits in your Bug, with his hands on the steering wheel, staring at the garage wall. What he is thinking, I can only guess.

It is a strange world we are all in. Volatile and uncertain. We—Americans, I mean—can't seem to talk to each other anymore, our disagreements seem insurmountable.

I imagine it would feel wonderful to be good at something that mattered. That is something that too many of the women of my generation didn't consider.

With love,
Your mother

Nine

Frankie had stopped being afraid every time she walked into the OR. She was still often uncertain, but, like the turtle they'd called her on her first night, she'd developed a hard shell to protect her heart from what she saw and the confidence to move past her own fear in order to help the men—and women, and children—who ended up in the OR. It was the only way to survive.

Patty, in her last weeks at the Thirty-Sixth, made it her mission to give Frankie every skill she'd learned during her tour, and of course Barb was always ready to lend a hand in the OR, regardless of how little sleep she'd had the night before. And Ethel was there for emotional support.

Now, on a hot, rainy June day, as she assisted Jamie in surgery, she heard the whirring of choppers overhead. More than one. It didn't even surprise her anymore, the escalating number of wounded coming through the OR, the growing number of pushes. The U.S. and ARVN, the Army of the Republic of Vietnam, had pushed into the Demilitarized Zone that separated the Communist North from the American-aided South, and the fighting was brutal. She wished Patty were still here, but she'd gone home last week. With a hell of a send-off.

"Shit," Jamie said, through his mask. He was elbow-deep in the kid's abdomen. "His spleen's ruptured."

Frankie picked up a clamp and handed it to him.

Moments later, the OR doors banged open. Barb, masked and gowned, wheeled in another casualty from Pre-Op. "Doc, sucking chest wound. It's bad."

Jamie cursed under his breath. "I'll get to it . . . we gotta get this spleen out . . ." He reached out, took instruments from Frankie, and handed them back, working quickly. Sweat appeared on his brow; droplets slid down to his mask. Finally, he stepped away from the table. "That's it. You're on your own now, McGrath."

"Me?"

Jamie took off his gloves and reached for a new pair. As he started on the chest wound, he said, "You can close, McGrath. You've watched me do it enough. Just take nice, wide bites of fascia, put in all of the stitches, tag them, and tie the sutures with five square knots. Count 'em. Five."

She shook her head. "I can't."

"Damn it, McGrath. We don't have time for fear. You're good enough. Do it."

Frankie nodded, swallowed hard, moving in closer to the patient's draped, sliced-open abdomen.

"It's just like sewing, McGrath. Don't all you nice sorority girls know how to sew? You can stitch."

Frankie took a deep breath and released it. *You can do this.*

She took another moment to focus, to tune out the noise and mayhem, the sound of the rain hitting the roof; when she'd calmed, she gently began to close the kid's fascia, one stitch at a time. She counted each knot, kept careful track of them.

"Good," Jamie said, glancing over at her. "I knew you could do it."

Frankie had never focused on anything so intently in her life. The din in the OR faded away. She felt her own heartbeat, the flicker of her pulse, the air moving through her lungs. The whole world compressed into the bloody space in this kid's belly. By the time she'd closed the fascia, she was sweating profusely, but she kept working. Finally, she let out a long breath and closed the wound and stared down at her work: the sutures were perfect. She had never felt so proud.

This, she thought. *This is who I came here to be.*

"I'm done here," Jamie said to Frankie.

"Me, too," she said.

They both looked up at the same time. Even though he was masked, she could tell that he was smiling.

"Told you, McGrath."

She could only nod.

"Now move," he said. "I just heard another Dust Off land."

In late June, monsoon season hit with a vengeance; the weather was like nothing Frankie had ever seen.

Howling winds ripped off roofs, tore away signs. Rain fell in sheets, blown sideways by the wind. The red dirt turned to a viscous, clinging mud that oozed into the OR from outside, mingling with blood on the concrete floor. It was a constant job to shovel it away. Frankie and the other nurses and the medics, and anyone else they could wrangle into picking up a shovel, spent time trying to push the mud outside.

And it was *cold*.

Frankie stared down at the patient in front of her, his guts split wide open, his chest covered in frag wounds. Tonight's storm battered the Quonset like a kid continuously hitting a toy barn with a hammer.

"He's gone," Jamie said, then cursed under his breath.

She looked at the clock for time of death, reported it in a quiet voice.

She had been on her feet for twelve hours. Monsoon season made every part of life more difficult. Or maybe it wasn't the weather that was bad; maybe it was the increased number of wounded that came through these doors. Last week had been mostly quiet, with lots of downtime for the nurses; not so this week. LBJ kept sending more and more troops into the fray, hoping manpower would turn the tide, while the *Stars and Stripes* published rah-rah-America-is-winning-the-war articles every week.

She shivered hard, her stained, faded fatigues damp beneath her surgical gown. Her pockets bulged with cigarettes and lighters. (She always kept them on hand to give to her boys. That was how she thought of the casualties now: as her boys.) In her breast pocket she had a small flashlight and bandage scissors. A length of stretchy rubber tubing hung limply from one epaulet, just in case she needed to draw blood on the fly. A Kelly clamp hung from one belt loop. A blue surgical cap covered her shaggy hair and a mask covered her nose and mouth. All anyone could see of her was her tired eyes.

Jamie looked at her over the dead body of a kid who had probably been playing high school football six months ago. "You okay, McGrath?"

"Fine. You?"

He nodded, but she saw the truth in his eyes. He was as exhausted and dispirited as she was.

They knew each other so well now. In the past month, they'd spent more hours together than some married couples spent together in a year. All of this hardship—the rain, the damp, the cold, the mud, the wounds, the hours spent trying to save men's lives—had bound them together, made them into more than friends. Sometimes, over here, the only way to handle the emotional pain was to laugh—or cry. Frankie rarely cried anymore, but when she did, she was probably in Jamie's arms. He was always there for her and she was there for him. He could make her laugh in the harshest of moments.

They stood together for hours, she and Jamie, working in tandem.

She knew every nuance of emotion on his face: the way he gritted his teeth in anger when he saw a child burned beyond recognition by napalm or a soldier who worried about his friends even as he was bleeding out. She knew he missed his beloved Wyoming ranch, with its cool nights and hot days, and its horses in the barn, and a field full of flowers just beyond his front porch. He missed fly-fishing and horseback riding and floating down the Snake River on an inner tube, a six-pack of beer floating with him. She knew that Sarah was a kindergarten teacher who sent him baked goods every week and worried that he didn't write back often enough, and repeatedly asked if he was okay, and that he couldn't write anything in answer to that question except *Yes.*

She fought her feelings for him, but at night, alone in her cot, she thought of him, thought, *What if.* It might all be a mirage, this connection between them, brought on by proximity and the horror of what they saw every day, but it felt real.

He touched her whenever he could, as casually as possible, and with a forced smile. Sometimes they found themselves standing together, or sitting side by side, just staring at each other, saying nothing, both of them feeling too much for the other and knowing that words wouldn't ease their longing.

She peeled her gloves off and lowered her mask. Both of them had red mud in the corners of their eyes, dripping down in tears, and in their teeth. "What a day."

"I need a drink. Maybe ten. Join me?"

Tonight, her longing for him was too sharp to hide. She needed to be away from him. "I am too tired for the O Club," she said.

"Is that possible?" he said.

Frankie meant to smile. "Tonight it is."

They pulled off their gowns and caps and put on their Army-issued green ponchos and walked out of the OR and into a raging rainstorm.

"Just when you thought it couldn't get any worse," Jamie said.

Rain clattered on the walkway's roof and fell in sheets on either side of them, riveting the thick red mud.

They walked past the mess hall, and Frankie realized with a shock that it was lunchtime. Time lost all meaning during a MASCAL, and when they were understaffed, as they were now, shifts seemed to go on forever. She hadn't eaten since, when? Dinner last night? Her stomach grumbled. She didn't signal her intention, just stumbled sideways, bumping into Jamie, pushing him aside without meaning to. Bypassing the urn of hot coffee (*Shower* was all she could think), she grabbed two donuts and stumbled back out of the mess, where Jamie stood waiting for her.

"Glazed," she said, handing him one.

"My favorite."

"I know."

They crossed behind the stage, where a sign—MARTHA RAYE COMING NEXT WEEK—had been torn down by the wind and lay twisted and ruined in the mud. Frankie tucked her donut inside her poncho to protect it.

Jamie stopped in front of the sandbagged entrance to the O Club. Wind shoved the beads sideways, made them clatter against the wall. She smelled cigarette smoke. Music rose above the din. "Happy Together" by the Turtles.

Imagine me and you, I do . . .

"I do, you know," he said.

"Do what?"

"Imagine me and you. I dream of you, McGrath."

Frankie's breath caught. Just now, as exhausted as she was, the will it took to pretend to feel only friendship for him was hard to summon. She couldn't smile. All she could think of was that she loved him. God help her. "Jamie, don't . . ."

"If only I'd met you first," he said.

"You wouldn't have looked twice at me. Big college football star and soon-to-be surgeon."

He touched her cheek in a swift caress. Her skin felt colder without his touch. "You have no idea how beautiful you are, McGrath."

Frankie was afraid that in one more second of standing here looking at him, in this secret world where rain fell all around them, they—she—would lose this battle. If one leaned forward, the other might, too. She had never wanted to kiss a man more. The love she felt for him caused a physical ache in her chest. She had to force herself to step back. She wanted to say something clever, but nothing came to her. Flipping up her hood, she angled forward to keep the rain from sluicing down her back and ran for the nurses' showers.

They were empty, probably because of the storm. Rain battered the elevated four-hundred-gallon water trailer, called a Water Buffalo, that fed the showers. Frankie stripped and hung up her fatigues and poncho. In the cold air, the shower water felt warm. She didn't need to look down to see red water coming off—red blood, red mud, red sweat. Geckos climbed the wooden walls of the shower, hid behind the crossbeams.

She washed her hair and body. Without even bothering to dry off, she stepped back into her damp, dirty clothes and boots, flung the slick wet poncho back over her body, and ducked back into the rain. At the plank bridge that ran over a gushing river of mud and water, she paused, slowed enough to check her balance so she didn't fall into the coiled concertina wire on either side, and then she was back under the covered walkway.

The hooch was rattled by the rain; water sluiced down the wooden sides, created an ankle-deep puddle of red mud outside the door. She opened it slowly, stepped inside, bringing the mud and rain with her. There was no way to avoid it. In this season of wind and rain, the hooch always smelled of mildew and mold and the floor was always muddy.

On the small dresser by her bed, Frankie saw a brown-paper-wrapped, multi-stamped box beneath a blue airmail letter. Mail!

She hung up her wet poncho, made herself a cup of coffee, peeled out of her damp fatigues, and stored her boots in her footlocker. Dry boots made a world of difference over here. She put on the pajamas her mother had sent her last week, dabbed some perfume on her throat, and climbed into bed.

She opened the box, saw a bag of homemade cookies, a box of See's chocolates, and some Twinkies inside, and smiled. When she tore open the envelope, a newspaper clipping fell out. In it, a crowd of protesters were burning the American flag.

July 5, 1967

Dearest Frances Grace,
I only want to write with good news, but the world has gone insane. The hippies aren't so peaceful anymore, I can tell you.

Thousands of war protesters. Boys burning their draft cards and women burning their bras. Race riots. Good Lord. Our annual party was a rather diminished affair, I must say. All anyone talks about is the war. You remember Donna Van Dorn, from Sunday school? At bridge club last week, I heard that she started dropping the acid and left college to join a folk band. Supposedly, she is living in some commune and making candles. For goodness' sake, she's a DAR member and a sorority girl.

People at the club are starting to wonder if the war in Vietnam is wrong. Apparently, some International War Crimes Tribunal found the U.S. guilty of bombing civilian targets, including schools—SCHOOLS, Frankie!—and churches and even a leper colony. Who knew there were even lepers left in the world?

Stay safe, Frances, and write soon. I miss you.
Love,
Your mother

Frankie found an almost-dry sheet of thin blue airmail stationery so she could write back. In this humidity, the ink smeared through to the other side.

July 18, 1967

Dear Mom,
Thank you so much for the treats. I can't tell you how much they lift everyone's spirits in this terrible monsoon season.

The weather is tough to describe and tougher to endure. The only thing worse than the rain is that my friend Ethel's DEROS came in. That's Army-speak for the date eligible to return overseas. In other words, her date for going home.

(You remember me telling you about Ethel—the one who plays the violin and wants to be a big-animal veterinarian?) Anyway, in September, she'll be leaving Vietnam. Going home.

I can't imagine doing this without her.
But I will, I guess.
Over here

Frankie heard the sound of incoming choppers and put down her pen.

Sighing, she stowed the unfinished letter and most of the treats in her makeshift nightstand and dressed in her still-damp fatigues and put her boots back on.

Her shift was over, but what did that matter, as understaffed as they were? There were wounded incoming and nurses would be needed. Slipping the still-wet poncho over her clothes, she headed for the OR and saw a pair of ambulances drive up to the Pre-Op door, just off the helipad.

Jamie was already in the OR, in his surgical cap and gown. "No rest for the wicked, eh, McGrath?"

She handed him a Twinkie. "None at all."

———

In late July, on a day with no incoming casualties expected, Barb organized a MEDCAP trip and the three nurses and Jamie headed for the helipad, where a stripped-down Huey waited for them. Today they were catching a ride to St. Elizabeth's Orphanage, which was housed in an old stone church not far away.

Holding her olive-green boonie hat on her head, Frankie angled forward and ran for the helicopter and jumped aboard. For the first time, she didn't move to the back. She didn't want to be afraid anymore, didn't want to think of Finley every time she climbed into a helicopter.

Instead, she sat carefully on the floor near one of the gunners, whose machine gun pointed down at the land below. She cautiously swung one leg over the edge, then the other. Barb sat in the other open door. Ethel and Jamie sat in the back. When the chopper lifted, Frankie's breath caught.

And then they were up, flying over the countryside.

Frankie had never felt so free, so fearless. Wind whipped across her face. The green landscape below was stunningly beautiful; she saw the thread of sand along the turquoise South China Sea.

The helicopter banked hard, turned inland, and swooped low over some rice paddies. Frankie saw a red dirt road that sliced through a dense swath of elephant grass; there, the chopper paused, hovered, the rotors thwopping loudly, the grass flattened by the wash. Slowly, the bird lowered to the ground and touched down just long enough to let the MEDCAP team get out, and then flew away, headed north.

As the medical team approached the orphanage, the doors banged open and children in ragged clothing surged forward, waving their hands, jostling each other in excitement. They knew the Americans brought candy to hand out to the children. Behind them, Vietnamese nuns, dressed in black habits, wearing conical straw hats, looked on wearily.

The nurses were swarmed by a group of young girls, all reaching out, wanting to touch them. Beside Frankie, Barb dropped to her knees, let the children touch her hair as she handed out suckers. Then she lined the kids up for vaccinations.

For the next four hours, the nurses administered vaccines and gave out vitamins, tended to rat bites and treated malaria. Jamie stitched up wounds and even pulled a few rotten teeth.

They were packing up to go when a petite, pretty young Vietnamese nun came forward. She walked up to Frankie, looking hesitant. "Uh . . . *madame?*" she said in French-accented English.

"Yes?" Frankie said, wiping the sweat from her brow, resettling the bag of her medical supplies over her shoulder.

"You could please follow me?"

Frankie followed the nun into the cool interior of the orphanage. Each room had been turned into a dormitory, with straw mats on the floor for sleeping. One room held a dozen or more cribs, where babies slept and cried. It broke Frankie's heart to think of how many orphans were being made by this war. Who would care for these children and babies when it ended?

At last, they turned a corner and stepped into an oblong room. Burned-down candles sat on windowsills and along the floor—so, no electricity.

There was only one child in here, a toddler, a girl, on a mat with her knees tucked up to her chest and her arms wrapped around her bent legs. She seemed to be making herself as small as physically possible. Frankie looked questioningly at the nun.

"A heat in her forehead," the nun said, touching her own forehead to communicate clearly.

Frankie knelt on the hard stone floor beside the mat. Up close, she could see that the girl was a little older than she'd thought, but her body had been pared down by malnutrition.

"She will not eat," the nun said.

"Hey, little one," Frankie said, stroking the girl's messy black hair.

The girl didn't move or respond, just gazed at Frankie through sad brown eyes. Her snarled hair obscured an ugly burn that puckered the skin along her jaw.

"What's your name?" Frankie asked, touching the child's forehead, studying the burn, which didn't look to be infected.

Fever, but not a bad one.

"We do not know her name," the nun said quietly, kneeling down to stroke the girl's back. "Her village was bombed. She was found by one of your medics, hiding in a ditch." She paused. "In her dead mother's arms."

Frankie felt a heaviness in her heart, a sorrow that she knew would stay with her. There was no defense against a thing like this. No matter how hard a shell she'd built up to protect herself, some pains couldn't be forgotten. This girl would be one of them, one of the faces she would see in her sleep. Or on the nights she couldn't sleep.

"We are calling her Mai. We do not know if she understands us. Some . . . of them . . . are too broken . . ."

Frankie wanted to take the child in her arms and tell her that it would be all right, but would it be all right for a girl like this?

Frankie dug in her bag for some baby aspirin and antibiotics. "These should control her fever. And I'll give you an ointment for her burn. It will help with scarring."

Then Frankie reached back into her medical bag and pulled out a cherry sucker, which she offered to the girl.

The girl just stared at it.

Frankie unwrapped the sucker, licked it and smiled, then offered it again.

The girl reached out slowly, took hold of the slim white stick. Staring at Frankie, she brought the sucker to her mouth, licked it.

And licked it again.

And again.

Frankie waited for a smile that never appeared. She wished she were surprised, but she understood this child's trauma all too well. More and more villages were being burned or bombed. More Vietnamese were dying, leaving their children alone in the world. The tragedy of it all was overwhelming.

She started to get to her feet.

The girl reached out, touched her ankle.

Frankie sat back down.

Tears glistened in the girl's eyes.

Frankie took the child in her arms, rocked her gently, hummed "Puff the Magic Dragon," until the girl fell asleep. Frankie stared down at the wounded child in her arms, this girl who was too small for her age and scarred for life and probably all alone in the world, and her heart ached for Mai and the children like her, devastated by this war. She stroked the girl's hot forehead and kept singing, holding back tears one breath at a time.

"McGrath? The chopper's on its way back. We need to go."

Frankie turned, saw Jamie standing in the doorway.

She put the sleeping child on her mat and leaned down to kiss her scarred cheek. "Sleep well, Mai," she said in a taut voice.

Her balance felt off as she stood up. Her feet were tingling.

Jamie was there instantly, holding her steady. She reached for his hand, held it, not daring to look at him.

"Frankie—"

She couldn't help herself. She turned to him, and he took her in his arms and held her. She felt the tears gather in her eyes, burn, and fall; they were lost in the cotton field of his T-shirt.

He didn't say anything, just held her until she was strong enough to pull away.

"Thanks," she said at last, not looking at him, wiping away her tears.

"She'll remember your kindness," he said. "That little girl. Probably for all of her life. And she will run and play and grow up."

The words meant so much to Frankie that she could only nod. How had he known exactly what she needed to hear?

They walked out into the sunshine. In the ratty yard, the children were playing with a ball the team had brought them, were kicking it back and forth and laughing. Not far away, the helicopter landed on the dirt road, its rotors flattening the elephant grass and stirring up the red dirt.

The medical team ran for the chopper and jumped aboard. Frankie sat in the open door, her legs hanging over the side. Every now and then, she pulled her Polaroid camera out of her bag and snapped a picture and pulled the ghostly print from the camera, waving it to dry until the image appeared, but her heart wasn't really in it.

In the distance, another helicopter flew low over the jungle, spraying herbicide.

They landed back at the Thirty-Sixth with ease, where it was quiet.

Amazingly, there were no people running from the ER to Pre-Op to the OR, no patients in triage, no ambulances rumbling into the compound, no rain falling in sheets, no lakes of mud to wade through. She and Ethel and Barb and Jamie walked to the mess hall, where the women grabbed some sandwiches and TaBs and Jamie got a beer.

On the beach, a dozen shirtless men played volleyball. Music blared out from a set of speakers, and the sound of hammering rang out—more buildings being erected. In the distant hills, mortar rounds exploded, made a sound like popping corn. Jamie wrenched off his shirt and kicked off his shoes and joined the men at the volleyball net.

The women dragged three beach chairs out onto the sand and sat there, eating their sandwiches, staring at the white sand and blue water. And at the bare-chested men. Tonight, a movie screen would be set up out here. Rumor was that someone had gotten a print of *The Great Escape*.

Behind them, someone cranked up the music as loud as it would go. "Leaving on a Jet Plane" got people singing along. A pair of female Red Cross volunteers—called Donut Dollies—dressed in their skirted uniforms, pushed a cart full of drinks and cookies out to the beach. Their nickname might sound soft, but those girls were tough as nails. They traveled all over Vietnam, by whatever transport was necessary, to boost morale among the troops.

"What's wrong?" Barb asked Frankie.

Frankie wasn't surprised by the question. They were more than best friends, she and Barb and Ethel. The radical, the farm girl, and the good girl; back in the world they might never have met each other, might never have become friends, but this war had made them sisters. "There was this little girl at the orphanage," Frankie said. "She'd been burned. Our medics found her by the side of the road—in her dead mother's arms."

Ethel gave a tired sigh.

Frankie couldn't stop thinking about Mai, lying in a ditch, burned, still held in her dead mother's arms. "Her village had been bombed."

War was one thing; bombing villages full of women and children was something else. God knew there were no stories about it in the *Stars and Stripes*. Why weren't they reporting that truth?

A silence fell between them; in it lay the ugly truth that none of them wanted to face. The village was in South Vietnam.

And only the Americans had bombs.

Ten

August passed in a series of hot, rain-drenched days; sometimes the air was so humid it was hard to breathe. Everything Frankie put on and took off in this monsoon season smelled like mildew and was splattered with mud. There was no way to fully clean or dry clothes. Like everyone in camp, Frankie had learned not to care.

In September, the rain finally stopped and a soul-sucking heat took its place. At the end of every shift, when she took off her mask and surgical cap, they were soaked through with sweat. The Quonset huts and hooches became oven-like. After some relaxation at the O Club, or a movie under the stars on the beach, or maybe a game of gin rummy with Ethel and Barb, she collapsed onto her cot, praying for sleep.

"Wake up, Frank."

"No." Frankie rolled over on her cot, taking her damp sheet with her.

A sharp jab in her shoulder came next. "Wake up. It's thirteen hundred hours."

Frankie groaned and rolled over. Her eyes opened slowly, painfully. Last night's mortar attack had gone on for hours; the explosions had rattled the hooches so hard that drops of red mud splatted down from the flat ceiling and landed in blotches on Frankie's cheeks.

Frankie threw an arm over her eyes. "Go away, Ethel. We only went to bed an hour ago."

"Two, actually," Barb said. "Think for a moment about what day it is."

Frankie pushed herself to a half sit, anchored up on her elbows. She saw the calendar tacked up on the wall above Ethel's bed, with all the days Xed off. "Ethel's DEROS."

"That's right, sports fans," Ethel said, pulling the pink curlers out of her hair. "'Nam is losing the best nurse ever to serve in this man's Army. I'm going back to the world. And I am not leaving this hellhole after two tours of duty with a pizza party at the O Club. Get your swimsuit on, Sleeping Beauty. I have a bird waiting for us."

"Swimsuit?"

Frankie could hardly believe it. Yesterday, they'd worked for fourteen straight hours, on their feet for all of it; she'd spent most of those hours in surgery. Her back and knees hurt. And now . . . She glanced at her wristwatch. They were going to go swimming at some Officers' Club . . . at 1300 hours on their only day off in two weeks?

Ethel yanked the covers back, revealing Frankie in her T-shirt and panties. She wore socks to bed, even in this heat, to save her toes from bugs and other creepy crawlers. Truth be told, it was why she wore panties, too.

Frankie climbed out of bed. (It took effort; her legs felt like jelly and her feet felt as if wild dogs had chewed on them while she slept.) She put on her two-piece belted red swimsuit, stepped into her sneakers, and headed to the latrines.

The smell hit her halfway there. Human shit and smoke. Some poor FNG was on shit duty. Literally. His job was to empty the latrines and burn the waste in fifty-five-gallon metal barrels.

She followed the plank walkway to the showers. This time of day, the water was almost warm, heated as it was by the sun. Still, she showered quickly and towel-dried her body. Not that she needed to in this heat.

"Finally," Ethel said when Frankie strolled back into the hooch. "A damn debutante takes less time to get ready."

"What do you know about debs?" Frankie said, buttoning her cut-offs and bending over to lace up her sneakers. Then she grabbed a pair of scissors and hacked at the hair around her face. There was no mirror in the hooch, which Frankie figured was just as well.

Barb covered her short Afro with a bandanna, tied it in the back, and then took the scissors from Frankie. Without a word, she took over cutting Frankie's hair. Frankie let her do it, completely trusting. Such was the nature of the friendships Frankie had formed over here. It wasn't hyperbole to say that she trusted Barb and Ethel with her life.

"Come on, country club deb," Barb said to Frankie, tossing the scissors on the dresser. "The boys'll be waiting."

"Boys?" Frankie crammed some clothes into her pack and the trio left the hooch.

The Thirty-Sixth was surprisingly quiet today. Oh, there was mortaring going on—explosions in the jungle past the concertina wire— but no red alert siren yet. She could hear men shouting. They were playing football in the open space in front of the empty stage.

At the helipad, an armed helicopter waited—one of the Seawolves' choppers. The nurses bent forward and ran toward it. The gunner reached out, helped them all aboard. At the last moment before take-off, Jamie appeared, in gym shorts and a faded Warlocks T-shirt, and jumped into the chopper.

The pilot gave them a thumbs-up and up they went, the rotors picking up speed. The *thwop-thwop* became a blur of sound. The bird's nose did a sharp dive, the tail lifted, and they sped forward, flying low. Gunners stood at fixed machine guns at the open doors.

Frankie sat in a canvas seat in the back of the chopper with Jamie beside her.

Through the open doors, she saw the world flash by: white beaches, turquoise water, red dirt roads that cut like veins through it all as they sped south, toward Saigon. As they neared the capital city, Frankie saw a verdant green landscape, shot through with silver strands; the Mekong Delta appeared like a lace overlay. Far away, flashes of orange flared in the jungle, explosions in the bush.

A few minutes later, the chopper touched down in a flat, treeless field.

The pilot powered down, then took off his flight helmet and turned around. "Another perfect landing for the Seawolves. Ladies, please note it in your diaries."

Ethel laughed. "Frankie, meet Slim. Smile, but don't believe a word he says. He thinks he's James Bond. That's what happens when a guy can fly jets and choppers. He thinks he's a god."

Slim was tall and lanky, with broad shoulders. A bushy mustache and ragged beard somehow enhanced the pretty-boy face underneath, giving him a rakish look. He immediately put on a battered cowboy hat to go with his camo T-shirt and short swim trunks.

"James Bond *wishes* he was me," Slim said, touching up his non-regulation mustache. He was a good-looking man. Beyond good-looking, actually, and he knew it. "Howdy, ma'am," he said to Frankie, who couldn't help smiling at his southern charm.

"And Slim wishes he was me," said the copilot, a thin, sinewy guy with red hair and a scraggly mustache. He grinned at Frankie and the other women, showing off a set of crooked teeth. "Call me Coyote," he said, and let out a wolf howl to go along with his introduction.

He helped the ladies out of the chopper and held on to Frankie's hand a moment longer than was necessary. She felt him staring at her as he said, in a slow Texas drawl, "Ladies, welcome to Seawolves' summer camp."

It was so ridiculous, so back-home, that Frankie couldn't help laughing.

In front of them, a wide brown river arced lazily past, lapping against a reedy, marshy shore. The skyscape of Saigon rose in the distance, across the opposite shore. A banged-up speedboat hugged the bank, empty but for a man with a machine gun, sitting in the back, eyeing every movement on land and water and in the air.

The land between the helicopter and the river had been turned into Beach Party Central. A banner that read WE WILL MISS YOU, ETHEL, was strung between two bamboo poles. Beneath it, a stocky man in a Rolling Stones T-shirt stood at a barbecue, grilling burgers. A portable generator powered a stereo and "Purple Haze" blared through the speakers, loud enough to drown out the distant whine of the war.

At least thirty people were here—nurses from the Thirty-Sixth and Long Binh and Vung Tau, medics and doctors and corpsmen. Frankie recognized several Dust Off pilots, as well as several Seawolves, and more than a few of the Donut Dollies from the Thirty-Sixth. They all stopped what they were doing at Ethel's arrival and turned to face the nurse and began clapping and whooping.

"Speech, speech!" someone cried out.

Ethel grinned. "Nurses don't give speeches," she said. "We party!"

A roar of approval rose through the crowd. The music changed to "Good Lovin'" and several people started dancing.

Ethel looked up at Slim. "Cool flying, cowboy."

He put an arm around her, drew her close. Frankie knew that Slim and Ethel had developed a solid friendship over here; they'd bonded over their shared love of southern barbecue and western dancing and horses.

"My boys will miss you," Slim said.

"I'm one of many, Slim. Barb and Frankie put me to shame."

He kissed her cheek. "Glad you're leaving this shithole, pissed you're leaving us behind."

"Ha. Like you Seawolves didn't claw all over each other to join the unit. You'd rather be here than on that farm you grew up on."

"Some days," he said.

"Yeah," Ethel said. "Ain't that the God's truth. Best of times, worst of times."

"If you two get any more philosophical or mushy, I'm gonna puke right on your boots," Barb said. "We didn't haul our asses here to watch you *feel* things. We're here to say bon voyage to the best damn nurse at the Thirty-Sixth. So, where's the booze?"

Coyote ducked over to a pyramid of coolers and opened the top one, pulling out four cold beers and bringing them back.

Frankie snapped the cap and took a hesitant sip. Almost before she'd swallowed, Ethel grabbed her hand and said, "Come on, California girl," and dragged her across the party and onto the speedboat moored at the river bank. How in the hell had they come up with a speedboat?

A tall man with a shaggy mustache and a Rainier Beer T-shirt stood at the wheel. He tipped his ratty straw cowboy hat at her. "Howdy, ma'am."

Coyote jumped on board, gave another howl, and put an arm around Frankie. "What d'ya say, Frankie McGrath? You game?"

"You know it." She took a sip of the ice-cold beer. It tasted surprisingly good on this hot day. How long had it been since she'd felt this free and young?

"We got a taker!" Coyote said, untying the mooring line. "Take us out, Renegade."

The guy at the controls grinned and hit the gas. Frankie stumbled into Ethel, who gave her a raised eyebrow. "What is the most important rule in 'Nam, Frank?"

"Don't drink the water?"

"That's number one. Number two: never volunteer."

The boat sped through the water, a thrilling, heart-stopping ride.

Suddenly they slowed. The boat stopped in the middle of a wide expanse of the river and rolled from side to side.

Coyote tented a hand over his eyes, his gaze scouring both shores. "Don't see anything to worry about."

"What, us worry?" Renegade said. Leaning sideways, he pulled up a pair of old, battered wooden water skis.

Frankie laughed.

Then he produced a ratty flotation belt, upon which someone had written KEEP IT UP, BOYS. He tossed the belt to Frankie.

She stopped laughing. "When I said I was game—"

"I knew you were my kind of girl." Coyote lit a cigarette and gave her a wicked smile.

"I . . . I've never skied before."

"You will dig it, trust me. Put on the belt."

Frankie glanced out at the river. She'd heard about bodies floating in this brown water, swollen from death and rigged with explosives. And this was the tropics. Were there poisonous snakes and alligators? What about the VC? Could Charlie be underwater with a plant on his head for camouflage, waiting for an American stupid enough to water-ski in the Saigon River?

Frankie took a deep breath and remembered Jamie's words.

No fear, McGrath.

She exhaled and stripped down to her two-piece bathing suit and fastened the belt around her waist.

"So," Ethel said, touching her shoulder. "I started water-skiing when I was a kid at Bible camp. A fun life story for another time. Anyway, hold on and lean back and keep the skis perpendicular to the boat. Let us pull you up, just like getting out of a chair. The rope goes between the skis. If—when—you fall, let go immediately."

"In case I die, I'll say goodbye now."

Ethel laughed. "Goodbye, Frank. It's been great knowing you."

Frankie slipped over the side of the boat into the brown, murky river water. Clutching the skis in one hand, she swam out behind the boat and spent more than five minutes trying to put her bare feet into the rubber bindings. At least three times she got the skis on and immediately flipped onto her face and had to fight to right herself, all the while keeping her mouth clamped shut. The idea of drinking this water scared her more than getting bit by a snake.

Finally, she got herself into position. She sat back, put the rope between her skis, held on to the bar, and nodded.

The boat started, dragged her. She fought to keep her skis steady.

They hit the gas, sped up.

Frankie got halfway up and face-planted.

The boat turned sharply, swung back around.

Ethel threw her the rope. "Let us drag you. We'll hit it when you look steady."

Frankie nodded, her mouth squeezed shut, trying not to think of the water getting into her eyes and nose.

It took four more tries, and by then Frankie was too tired to fight the rope or the speed. She just leaned back and held on and thought, *How many times do I have to try?*, and then, quick as an indrawn breath, she was up, skiing behind the boat, struggling to keep her skis steady and her weight equally distributed.

She saw the people on the boat clapping for her. She held herself in the calmer water between the white vee of the wake, her skis thumping and falling on the water. Wind lifted her hair and the hot sun shone down on her, and for a beautiful, heart-stopping moment she was just a girl at a beach party with her friends. She thought of Finley, teaching her to surf in the rolling waves. *Catching a wave, Fin. Look at me.*

She was overcome by a joy so strong and sweet and pure that there was only one thing to do.

She let out a wolf howl.

That evening, sunset turned the world purple and red. In the distance, across the ribbon of river, the lights of downtown Saigon shimmered.

The group on the beach had faded along with the daylight. Stuffed with cheeseburgers and potato chips and American beer, half-drunk, they sat around a roaring campfire.

Frankie, pleasantly buzzed on three beers, leaned against Ethel. Holding hands seemed like the most natural thing in the world. "Tell me about it again," she murmured.

"The grass is so green it hurts your eyes," Ethel said. "My grandfather found the land and saved every dollar he made blacksmithing to buy it. There's nothing I love better than riding on autumn roads at a full gallop. You'll come someday, you and Barb. We'll eat barbecue and ride horses and forget everything we saw over here."

Frankie loved Ethel's stories about Virginia: the county fairs, the 4-H competitions, the church socials. It sounded like a world that didn't exist anymore.

"I won't let you go back without me," Frankie said. Before Ethel could answer, Jamie stumbled over and stood in front of Frankie.

She was afraid to look up at him. She'd kept her distance all day because her defenses felt weakened by the beer she'd drunk and today's camaraderie and the strange sense that these were good days, maybe—impossibly—the best of their lives.

Jamie was now officially a short-timer. His DEROS had come in and he had less than three months left on his tour. Like all short-timers, as his leave date neared, he'd begun to worry that nothing would work out for him, that Vietnam had somehow ruined him and he wouldn't get out alive. And every day Frankie confronted the reality that he was one day closer to leaving.

"Dance with me," he said, holding out his hand.

He wouldn't have done it sober, not here in front of everyone, on a night when the longing in his eyes was obvious, and she wouldn't have agreed on another night, either. But just now, with three beers in her system and Ethel leaving, Frankie didn't have the strength to say no to him. She let him pull her to her feet.

He led her away, took her in his arms.

His hand slipped down her back, past the curve of her waist. She felt his fingers slip under the waistband of her baggy shorts.

She reached back, moved his hand to the small of her back. "Be a good Scout."

"You want me, McGrath," he said. "And God knows I want you."

She looked up at him. "It doesn't matter what either one of us wants."

"Come to Maui for R and R with me tomorrow."

"Sarah would not appreciate that," Frankie said. She knew Jamie was meeting his wife for R and R. "Once you see her, you'll forget all about me."

He leaned forward so slowly she knew he expected her to stop him, but she couldn't. He kissed the side of her neck.

She let it go on longer than was smart and then pushed him away, immediately missing the feel of him. "Don't. Please."

"Why not?"

"You know why," she said in a quiet voice.

"Could you have loved me?" he asked quietly.

She wanted to say *I already do* so badly it took every bit of will-power she possessed to smile. She touched his face, let her hand linger on his skin for a moment, letting it be the words she didn't dare say. Then she walked away from him while she still had the strength to do so, and sat back down by Ethel.

"That man loves you," Ethel said quietly.

Her feelings for Jamie were not something Frankie could talk about, even with Ethel. She leaned against her friend. "How can I do this without you?"

"I love you, too, Frank. And you're going to be okay without me."

Without me.

Maybe it was the three beers she'd drunk, or the eerie, falling darkness, pocked by the sounds of a distant war, but a wave of homesickness assailed her, made her think of Finley. *No remains.* She was tired of losing people.

"I must be cuckoo for Cocoa Puffs," Ethel said. "Certifiable. Because I don't want to leave."

"I'm crazy, too, because I don't want to see you go."

The fire crackled and popped. Slim roasted a marshmallow over one of the licking red flames. The music had been turned down.

Suddenly the night erupted in noise and color. Red explosions, tracers through the dark sky. A machine gun's *ra-ta-ta-tat* not far away.

The gunner from the bird ran over. "Sorry, gang. Riot just called in. The Seawolves are needed at Rocket City. Party's over."

Frankie looked at Ethel. "Rocket City?"

"Pleiku. It's up in the Highlands. Dangerous place."

The party dispersed; people ran for the chopper, for the boat, for the three jeeps hidden in the brush. Frankie and her friends boarded the helicopter, which lifted up into the air quickly.

The land below was pocked by explosions. In the Huey, up in the air, bombs and rockets and gunfire burst all around them, bright orange stars in the dark. The smell of smoke.

The chopper veered sharply, climbed fast.

"They're shooting at us," Slim yelled into the comm headset. "Damn rude on a beach day."

The bird veered so sharply that Frankie cried out. Jamie put an arm around her, held her close. "It's okay, McGrath," he whispered into her ear. "I've got you."

Frankie let it be, just for a moment, then pulled away.

The gunner shot back. *Pop-pop-pop.*

Another sharp turn, an evasion. A fighter jet streaked past; below, a piece of the jungle exploded in red flames. Frankie felt the heat of it on her face.

Pop-pop-pop.

The machine gun at the door rattled in response, spent casings clattered to the floor.

All it would take was one good hit and the bird would go up in flames. She couldn't help but think of Finley. Was this what it had been like for him?

It was over as quickly as it began. The helicopter swooped sideways, lowered over the smoldering canopy of the jungle, and dropped down onto the helipad at the Thirty-Sixth.

———

At 0300 hours, a red alert siren blared through camp. Then came the sound of incoming choppers. A swarm of them. One Dust Off after another landed in the pouring rain, full of wounded. Frankie and Barb and Ethel stumbled out of bed and ran to the helipad, helping to offload them. Frankie spent the next eight hours at Jamie's side, going from one surgery to the next, until she was so tired she could barely stand.

At 1100 hours, when the last patient was rolled out of the OR, Frankie reached numbly for a mop and began cleaning the floor until Jamie stopped her. "We're done," he said. "Someone else can mop up the blood. Let's go."

Nodding, she put on her green poncho, flipped up her hood, and followed Jamie out of the OR. The wooden walkway was underwater. Rain pounded the roof overhead. He put an arm around her, steadied her as they walked through the compound.

At Jamie's quarters, he came to a stop; Frankie realized suddenly that she was too close to him, touching his body with her own as they stood beneath the overhang, barely out of the rain. A tiny drizzle of someone else's blood streaked down Jamie's neck. She reached up to wipe it away.

Jamie almost smiled, but not quite. "You want to kiss me before I go," he said. "I knew it."

"Have fun in Maui," she said, embarrassed by the jealousy she felt at the idea of him being with his wife. "Bring me back something fun."

There was more love in his eyes than should be there, and probably too much in hers. "I love you, McGrath. I know I'm not supposed to . . ."

She longed to say it in return, but how could she? Words were creators of worlds; you had to be careful with them. He was going to meet his wife, see pictures of his son. "I'll miss you," she said instead.

He stepped back. "See you in a week."

As she watched him leave, the moment played over in her mind: *I love you, McGrath.*

Maybe she should have said it, too. But what good could come of her love for him? He wasn't hers to love. When she couldn't stand the regret anymore, she flipped her hood up and headed for her hooch.

She opened the door and realized instantly what she'd forgotten during the push.

Barb sat on Ethel's empty cot. "She's gone."

Frankie sat down beside Barb, not even bothering to pull off her wet poncho. "We didn't get to say goodbye."

"She didn't want us to. Probably slipped out while we were looking the other way. Bitch."

It was the way of Vietnam; people came, they did their tour, and they left. The lucky ones, like Ethel, flew home in one piece. Some wanted parties for their send-off and some wanted to slip away in silence. Some wanted both. Either way, you woke up one day and your friend was just gone.

War was full of goodbyes, and most of them never really happened; you were always too early or too late.

Like with Finley.

She had said goodbye to her brother long after the words could have mattered to him. That was one thing this war had taught her; there was never enough time with the people who mattered.

<hr />

It rained for the next week. Not a drenching, monsoon rain, just a thumping, ever-present *drip-drip-drip* that demoralized everyone. Even gatherings at the O Club had all but ended. No one felt like partying in this weather.

Now, as midnight neared, Frankie stood in the OR, in mask and cap and gloves and gown, closing an incision. Not far away, the new doctor, Rob Aldean, from Kentucky, was trying to save a young Vietnamese woman's leg. While Jamie was on R and R in Maui with his wife, they were down to two surgeons, and that wasn't enough to keep up with the casualties. To make matters worse, they hadn't replaced Ethel yet, so they were understaffed in nurses, too. Four patients lay on tables awaiting surgery, with more in triage and Pre-Op.

A bright light shone down on the patch of brown-washed skin of the soldier who lay anesthetized before Frankie.

After her last stitch, she dropped her bloody instruments on her tray and peeled off her gloves. "I'll get Sammy to take you to Post-Op, Private Morrison," she said aloud, even though the patient couldn't hear her.

She heard the distant sound of a helicopter coming in. Dr. Rob looked up, his worried gaze meeting Frankie's. They were at their ragged end.

Just one chopper. "Thank God," Frankie said.

Rob went back to work.

The OR doors banged open and a gowned and masked Barb came in with a pair of medics carrying a bloody patient on a litter. "We need a surgeon. And you, Frankie. Stat."

Frankie could tell it was bad by the look in Barb's eyes.

Frankie washed her hands and picked up a new pair of gloves, snapping them on.

The soldier on the litter wore a blood-soaked T-shirt and fatigues that had been cut off at the thigh. He'd lost his left leg at the knee, a medic had field-wrapped the bloody stump, but that injury was nothing compared to his chest wound.

A thick layer of black-red blood covered his face. She picked up his dog tags. "Hey, Captain C—"

Callahan.

Jamie.

She looked up at Barb, saw the grief in her friend's eyes. *I'm sorry,* Barb mouthed.

"His bird was shot down, ma'am," one of the medics said.

Frankie wiped the blood from Jamie's face and saw the grievous injury to his skull.

"Rob!" she shouted. "Get over here. Now!"

The doctor came over, looked down at Jamie, and then at Frankie. "He won't make it, Frankie, you know that, and we have—"

"Save him, Doc. At least try." She reached for Jamie's cold, limp hand, held it. "Please. *Please.*"

Eleven

Jamie lay in a Stryker bed in Neuro, naked beneath a sheet, his face bandaged so completely that only one closed eye could be seen. A tube snaked into his nostril. A ventilator kept him breathing. *Whoosh-thunk.* Another machine monitored his heartbeat. Rob, the surgeon, had done what he could, and then stepped back, shaking his head, saying, "I'm sorry, Frankie. I'll write to his wife tomorrow. You should say goodbye."

Now Frankie sat by Jamie's bed, held his hand. The heat of his skin indicated that an infection was already taking hold. "We'll get you to the Third, Jamie. You hang on. You hear me?"

Frankie's mind played and replayed the last thing Jamie had said to her. *I love you, McGrath.*

And she'd said nothing.

God, she wished she'd told him the truth, wished they'd kissed, just once, so she could have that memory.

"I should have . . ." What? What should she have done? What could she have done? Love mattered in this ruined world, but so did honor. What was one without the other? He was married and Frankie knew he loved his wife. "You're strong," she said, her voice strained. The nurse in her knew no one was strong enough for some injuries; the woman in her longed to believe in an impossible recovery.

"Lieutenant? Lieutenant?"

The voice seemed to come from far away. Scratching, irritating, a thing to brush off.

She realized a pair of medics were standing beside her. She noticed belatedly that one had laid his hand on her shoulder.

She looked up at him. How long had she been here? Her back ached and a headache throbbed behind her eyes. It felt like hours, but it hadn't been long at all.

"The bird's here. He's being medevaced to the Third. A neuro team is standing by."

Frankie nodded, pushed her chair back, and stood. For a second, she was shaky on her feet.

The medic steadied her.

She saw the duffel bag at his feet. "Those are Jamie—Captain Callahan's things?"

"Yes, ma'am."

Frankie reached into her pocket and pulled out a felt-tipped marker and the small gray stone she'd been given by the young Vietnamese boy. It seemed like a lifetime ago that he'd pressed it into her palm. It had become a talisman for her. She wrote *You fight* on one side of the stone and *McGrath* on the other. She slipped it into his duffel bag.

She leaned over and kissed his bandaged cheek, felt the heat of his fever, and whispered, "I love you, Jamie."

Slowly, she drew back, straightened. It took every scrap of strength she possessed to step back while they prepped him to leave and then rushed him out of the OR and toward the helipad.

Halfway to the helipad, Frankie heard the medic yell, "Code," and saw him begin chest compressions.

Jamie's heart had stopped.

Frankie screamed, "Save him!"

They lifted Jamie onto the waiting helicopter; the medic jumped aboard, continued chest compressions as the helicopter lifted up slowly.

Frankie stood there, staring up into the Dust Off.

She saw the medic stop compressions, pull his hands back, shake his head.

"Don't stop! He has a strong heart!" she screamed, but her voice was drowned out by the whir of the rotors. "Don't stop!"

The helicopter flew up and away, merged into the darkness of the night, and became a distant whir of sound, and then even that was gone.

Gone.

How could his heart stop? His beautiful, beautiful heart . . .

She closed her eyes, felt tears streak down her cheeks. "Jamie," she said in a cracked voice. All she wanted was one more minute, just a look, a second to tell him that he hadn't been alone in what he felt, that in a different world, a different time, they could have come together.

The pounding thud of outgoing mortar shells and rockets was all that remained, steady as the beat of her heart. When she turned away, Barb was there, waiting. She opened her arms wide.

Frankie walked into her friend's embrace, let herself be held for as long as she dared.

Arms around each other, they headed to the O Club. As always, the smell of smoke wafted outside. Inside, music. "We Gotta Get Out of This Place." Their newest anthem.

Barb pushed the beaded curtain aside.

Inside, there were probably a dozen people gathered in small groups. No one was laughing or singing or dancing, not on this night, not in the wake of what had happened to Jamie. Some things could be partied away, pushed aside by booze and drugs and momentarily forgotten. Not this.

Barb snagged a bottle of gin from the bar and then led the way to a ratty sofa and sat down. "I imagine you're ready for a real drink now."

Frankie sat down next to her friend, leaned against her.

Barb took a big chug of gin and handed Frankie the bottle.

Frankie stared at it for a moment, almost said, *No thanks,* and then thought: *What the hell?* She reached for the bottle, took a long, fiery swig, and almost gagged. It tasted like isopropyl alcohol. It was even worse than the whiskey she'd drunk—with Jamie—on her first night here.

You're safe, McGrath . . . I've got you.

Barb took a drink. "To Jamie," she said quietly. "He's tough, Frankie. He could make it."

To Jamie, Frankie thought, forcing herself to take another drink. She needed something to dull this pain. She closed her eyes, but in the darkness of her mind, all she saw was the medic stopping compressions.

Frankie wanted, just for a moment, not to be a nurse, not to be serving in a war, not to have worked in Neuro, not to know what Jamie's injuries and stopped compressions meant.

"There's something else," Barb said. "I hate to bring it up now . . ."

"What?" Frankie said tiredly.

"My DEROS came today. I'm outta here on December twenty-sixth."

Frankie had known this was coming, but still it hurt. "Good for you."

"I can't do another tour."

"I know."

Finley. Ethel. Jamie. Barb.

"I'm so tired of goodbyes," Frankie said quietly, squeezing her eyes shut to keep from crying. What good were tears? Gone was gone. Crying didn't change it. "To Jamie," she said again, more to herself than to Barb, reaching for the bottle of gin.

—⁓—

September 30, 1967

Dear Ethel,

I don't know how to write this letter, but if I don't say the words to someone, I'll keep lying to myself. Jamie is gone.

I can't seem to breathe when I think about losing him. I want to believe he will survive, will make it home to his family, but how can I believe that with what we've seen? His wounds were . . . well, you know what it looks like. And I did my time in Neuro. Anyway, I am tired of losing people.

It's been three days since he was hurt and it's all I can do to get out of bed. I'm not crying, not sick to my stomach. I'm just . . . numb, I guess. Grief tears me apart when I stand.

They need me in the OR. I know that's what you'll say. It's what Barb says. I am trying like hell to care about that. But how can I walk into the OR and know he won't be there? I'll reach for him, call out to him, and someone else will answer.

You'd think, after losing my brother, I'd be a little more durable.

He wasn't even mine. I keep thinking of his wife and his son. I want to reach out to them, ask if he made it, but it wouldn't be right. It's not my place. And he'll reach out to me if he can, won't he? Maybe not . . . Like I said, he was never mine.

I miss you, girl. I could use your steadiness now, maybe one of your stories about galloping your horse through autumn leaves . . . or even one of your lectures on barbecue as a noun.

Hope all is well back in the world.

Love,

F

—⁓—

October 9, 1967

Dear Frank,

My heart breaks. For Jamie, for his son and his wife, and for you and all of the men he would have saved.

Damn war. I remember how I felt when I lost Georgie. I don't think there's a word for that kind of grief. But you know what I'm going to say. It's 'Nam.

You meet people, you form these bonds that tighten around you, and some of the people you love die. All of them go away, one way or another. You don't carry them around with you over there, you can't. There isn't time, and the memories are too heavy. You'll always have the piece of him that was yours and your time together. And you can pray for him. One way or another, Frank, he's gone for you, and you know that. As you said, he was never your guy, no matter how much you loved him.

For now, just keep on keepin' on, Frank.

Sending peace and love, girlfriend.

E

October 13, 1967

Dear Ethel,

Today it's hot enough to roast meat on the hooch floor, I swear to God. I'm sweating so much I have to keep wiping my eyes.

Thanks for your letter about Jamie.

You're right. I know you're right.

I can't keep thinking about him. Wishing, remembering, replaying the choices we both made over and over. Fortunately for me, the 36th has been quiet for the past week. But maybe that's not good. Too much time to think.

I guess I have to feel lucky to have known him, and to have learned from him. Too damn many lessons to learn over here, but the one that's for sure is this: life is short. I'm not sure I ever really believed that before.

I do, now.

Thanks for being there for me, even from half a world away. I sure would love another picture from home. I miss you.

Luv ya,

F

Frankie put down her pen, took a sip of warm TaB, and folded up the piece of thin blue stationery. Leaning sideways, she put the letter on her bedside chest, beside the stack of letters from home she'd been rereading.

She should write to her parents, too. She hadn't written in days, unable to find the words to put a pretty spin on her life over here.

She could write and say she was safe, she supposed. That was what they wanted to hear. Although, in truth, that was what her mom wanted to hear. She had no idea what her dad wanted from her anymore. He hadn't written a single letter.

According to her mother's frequent letters, everyone back in the world was talking about music and hippies and the so-called Summer of Love. The Summer of Love. (There wasn't so much as a mention of it in the *Stars and Stripes*.) It was vaguely obscene. As if boys weren't dying by the boatload over here.

She leaned back against the wall and closed her eyes, hoping to fall asleep. She wanted to dream about Jamie—it had become comforting in a sick kind of way, obsessively remembering him—but now, instead, she thought about Barb's DEROS, coming up in December.

How could she survive over here without her best friend?

A knock at the hooch door woke her up.

"Come in."

The door opened. A young private stood there, looking nervous, his knobby Adam's apple bobbing up and down. "Lieutenant McGrath?"

"Yeah?"

"Major Goldstein would like to see you."

"When?"

"Now."

Frankie nodded and got slowly to her feet. She reached down for her shoes and put them on.

At the admin building, she knocked on the chief nurse's office door, heard a mumbled, "Come in," and opened the door.

The major looked up. Frankie saw exhaustion in the slant of her shoulders and the lavender bags under her eyes.

"Are you okay, Major?" Frankie asked.

"Rough few days," the major said.

Frankie knew the major wouldn't elaborate. Major Goldstein was old-school. There was a chain of command for a reason. Fraternization was out of the question. In a world where there were very few women to start with, and most were of lower rank and experience, it had to be lonely as hell. Certainly, the men who were of her rank considered themselves superior.

"You're being transferred to the Seventy-First Evac."

Frankie's stomach dropped. "Pleiku?"

"Yep. It's near the Cambodian border. Central Highlands. Deep jungle." She paused. "Heavy fighting."

"I know."

Major Goldstein sighed heavily. "Losing you is pure shit from my end. I'll get some newbie nurse to replace you, no doubt, but orders are orders. You're a hell of a combat nurse." She sighed again. "So, naturally, I lose you. It's the Army way. Make sure your will is up-to-date. And write your parents a nice letter before you go."

Frankie was too stunned—too scared—to say anything except, "Thank you, Major."

"Believe me, Lieutenant McGrath, you will not thank me for this."

Frankie left the admin building in a daze.

Pleiku.

Rocket City.

She walked past a group of men playing football on the beach and a pair of uniformed Red Cross workers sitting in portable beach chairs, watching the game. More shirtless men sat in chairs, getting some sun. Someone was setting up the screen and projector for tonight's movie.

She found Barb in a beach chair, reading a letter from home.

Frankie sat down beside her. "I've been transferred to the Seventy-First."

Barb took a long drink of her gin and tonic. "Man. No one screws a woman like this man's Army."

"Yep."

"So, when do we go?"

Frankie must have misheard. "We?"

"Honey, you know I love to travel. I can get transferred with you. No sweat. God knows they need us both up there."

"But Barb—"

"No talking, Frankie. For as long as I'm in this godforsaken place, I'm with you."

———

The hooch door banged open. No knocking. A swatch of hot yellow sunlight blasted into the dim interior.

Barb stood there, still dressed in the khaki shorts and T-shirt and combat boots she'd worn to the ER this morning. Her Afro was bigger now; in the past weeks, she'd let it go, called it her private rebellion.

A young woman stood beside Barb, wearing her Class A uniform and carrying her Army-issue handbag and a soft-sided travel bag.

Electric-blue eye shadow drew attention to her wide, frightened eyes. Frankie could see how the poor girl was shaking.

"I'm Wilma Cottington from Boise, Idaho," she said, trying to iron the stutter out of her voice.

Barb said, "Land of potatoes."

"My husband is in Da Nang," Wilma said. "I followed him."

"A husband in-country. How lucky." Frankie made brief eye contact with Barb. They both knew a husband in-country was potentially lucky. Or extremely unlucky.

"I'm Frankie." She stood up. "Why don't you unpack? We'll show you around when you're done."

Wilma looked around the hooch.

Frankie knew exactly what she was thinking and feeling.

They'd all been turtles once, and the Thirty-Sixth was a carousel of people coming and going. Wilma would make it—become a more-than-competent nurse—or she wouldn't. Most likely she would, even without Frankie or Barb to train her. Major Goldstein would start her in Neuro.

The circle of life in the Thirty-Sixth.

A rat scurried across the floor; Wilma screamed.

Frankie barely noticed the rodent. "That isn't the worst of what you'll see, kid."

Kid.

They were probably the same age, but Frankie felt ancient by comparison.

"Don't drink water unless it comes from a Lister bag, Wilma," Frankie said. "That's as good a place to start as any."

October 20, 1967

Dear Mom and Dad,
Hello from hot and humid Vietnam.

I never told you about our beach party. I went waterskiing for the first time. Then we had a mini-American Bandstand dance party on the beach. There are these Naval helicopter pilots—the Seawolves—who really know how to have a good time.

My friend Ethel went home and Barb and I surely miss her. I never knew how intense wartime friendships could be.

I've been at the 36th Evac Hospital for six months, and it seems that the brass wants me to move up north, into the Central Highlands, to the 71st. I'll send you my address when I know what it is. Barb is going, too.

Until then, could you please send some hand lotion, tampons (they sell out in the PX because the men out in the bush use them to clean their rifles), shampoo, crème rinse, and I sure would love some more See's. And I'm almost out of perfume. The boys love it when I smell like the girls back in the world.

I'll write again as soon as I'm settled. I'm nervous about the transfer, but excited, too. This will really sharpen my nursing skills.

I'm sorry I haven't written for a while. I lost a good friend recently, and I've been in a bit of a funk. But I'm getting better now. Not much time here for grief, even though there's plenty of cause. Life isn't always easy, as you can imagine. People come and go. But I love nursing. It's important you know that, and that you know I'm happy I came here. Even on bad days, even on the worst days, I believe this is what I'm meant to do and where I'm meant to be. Finley told me once that he'd found himself over here, that his men were important to him, and I know how he felt.

Love to you both,

F

Frankie's first sight of Pleiku was from the air, in a supply helicopter, looking down at the dense green jungle below. Barb sat on the other side of the chopper, peering down, too.

A flat pad had been cut into the lush green mountainside—a huge square of red dirt held a ramshackle collection of tents and Quonset huts and temporary buildings. Looking at it, Frankie remembered—or finally understood—that the Seventy-First was a mobile Army surgical hospital. It struck her suddenly what that meant. Mobile. Temporary. In the jungle, near the Cambodian border, where the Viet Cong knew every footpath and clearing, where they planted bombs to blow up their American enemies. Coils of concertina wire protected the compound from the jungle that encroached on all sides.

The chopper dropped down to the helipad. Barb and Frankie jumped down as several soldiers moved in to unload supplies, including the nurses' footlockers and duffel bags. Everything in, around, or about helicopters had to be done quickly; Charlie had no greater target than a landed bird.

"Lieutenants McGrath and Johnson?" said a short, bulkily built man in faded fatigues. "I'm Sergeant Alvarez. Follow me."

Frankie clamped her boonie hat onto her head and angled low beneath the whirring rotors. Red dust flew up, swirled, made its way into her eyes, her nose, her mouth.

He pointed to the Quonset hut nearest the helipad, yelled, "ER. That one's Pre-Op." He kept walking and talking and came to another Quonset hut, its entrance stacked in sandbags: "OR."

"There's a large air base nearby," he went on, "as well as the village of Pleiku. Don't go to either without an escort." He led them deeper into the camp, where personnel moved in a rush. There wasn't much here—some Quonset huts, a row of dilapidated wooden huts, tents. Everything was stained red and surrounded by barbed wire and protected by armed soldiers in guard towers.

"The morgue," he said, pointing left.

Frankie saw a tired-looking medic pushing a wheeled litter with a body-bagged soldier through a pair of double doors. Inside, she saw body bags stacked on tables and cots and a few even on the ground.

"I know it looks shitty compared to the Thirty-Sixth," Sarge said, not stopping. "And the rainy season lasts for nine months up here, but we have our benefits." He showed off an area he called "the Park," which was a stand of rotting brown banana trees, their giant fronds bent over and decayed, and an honest-to-God aboveground swimming pool full of brown water and leaves. Off to the side was a tiki-style bar, complete with torches and a sign that read HULA SPOKEN HERE. Beside it, a sandbagged bunker and a dozen portable chairs waited forlornly for partiers. "The officers have some kick-ass parties here at the Park, ma'am. You can find someone here most times if you're feeling angry or blue. Ain't much space between those emotions here in Rocket City."

He pointed out the commanding officers' trailers and walked past a row of unimpressive wooden huts. Up ahead were the latrines and showers. "By fifteen hundred hours, the water feels almost warm," he said. At the final wooden hut, built up on blocks and layered in sand-bags, he stopped and turned to them. "Home sweet home."

"Get settled in, Lieutenants," he said. "This quiet? It won't last. The fighting in Dak To has been brutal this week. Your duffels will be delivered ASAP. Shifts are oh-seven-hundred to nineteen hundred hours, six days a week, but if we're short on staff . . . and hell, we are always short . . . we work till we're done." He opened the door.

The smell made Frankie almost gag. Mildew. Mold.

Insects and dust motes thickened the air. Inside the small, stinky space were two empty cots, upon each of which sat folded woolen blankets and a pillow that she already knew neither of them would use, and two rickety chests of drawers. Red dust coated everything, even the ceiling. For the first time, she thought kindly—and nostalgically—about her hooch at the Thirty-Sixth.

Frankie turned back to thank the sergeant, but he was already gone.

She followed Barb into the hooch.

They stood there, shoulder to shoulder. "My mother would pass out," Frankie said at last.

"Spoiled white girl," Barb said.

Frankie tossed her purse and travel bag on the empty cot nearest her. They landed with a squeak of metal that did not inspire her confidence for a good night's rest. She felt insects feasting on her bare arms and legs. Slapping her own thigh, she unpacked a few belongings and carefully arranged her family photographs on the rickety dresser. Then she tacked up a picture of Jamie; in it, he was leaning against a post, holding a beer, giving her the kind of smile that lifted everyone's mood. She stared at it longer than she should have, then felt the start of tears and turned away.

Barb unpacked her posters. Unfurling them, she tacked them up on the wall, a trio of her idols: Martin Luther King, Jr., Malcolm X, and Muhammad Ali refusing to be drafted, with the words I AIN'T GOT NO QUARREL WITH THEM VIET CONG stamped across his body.

Frankie opened the creaking, makeshift dresser drawer, saw that it was full of rat droppings. "Shit," she said. "And I mean that literally. Shit." She started to laugh and then heard an incoming chopper.

Frankie slapped her thigh again. Her hand came back bloody.

"And here I was thinking we had time for a little gin rummy," Barb said.

"Or to do our nails," Frankie answered, stripping out of her shorts. She put on her fatigues and gathered her supplies: a lighter, a roll of bandages, scissors, a flashlight, chewing gum, and a felt-tipped pen. She looped a length of Penrose tubing through her belt loop, in case she needed to start an IV, and snapped a Kelly clamp on her bagging waistband. You never knew when supplies would be lacking, and being prepared could save a life.

Outside, the *whump-whump* of the helicopters was deafening.

Frankie and Barb ran past the helipad, where wounded were being offloaded from a Dust Off and coming in by ambulance. Men covered in mud and blood, working together, shouting at one another beneath the *thwomping* rotors. In the air, a row of helicopters hovered, waited their turn to touch down.

A grizzled-looking Black medic was running triage in the ER, determining who would be seen when. Sawhorses were being set up quickly, to hold the men on litters. A screen in the back corner shielded the expectants. "Lieutenants Johnson and McGrath," Barb said. "From the Thirty-Sixth. Surgical nurses."

He looked at their bloody, stained fatigues. It meant they'd been in the shit. "Thank Christ," he said, loudly enough to be heard over the din of yelling men and helicopters landing and taking off. He pointed to a Quonset hut. "OR 1. Report to Hap. If he doesn't need you yet, try Pre-Op."

Frankie and Barb were halfway there when the red alert siren sounded. Seconds later a shell exploded on the ground not far away from them. A sound like pelting gravel hit the Quonset hut. The air stank of smoke and something strangely acrid.

Something whistled over Frankie's head and thudded behind her. At OR 1, Frankie wrenched the door open.

Inside: Bright lights. Men waiting for surgery, lying on tables.

She and Barb washed their hands, then grabbed scrubs and caps and masks and gloves and found Harry "Hap" Dickerson, a lieutenant colonel, operating without assistance on a deep belly wound.

"Lieutenants McGrath and Johnson, sir. Reporting for duty."

"Thank God. Cart's there," Hap said to Frankie. "Johnson, that's Captain Winstead over there. He'll need you."

"Yes, sir." Barb ran toward the other doctor.

Another rocket blast, this one close enough to shake the Quonset hut. The lights dimmed and went out.

"Shit! Generators!" Hap yelled.

Frankie pulled out her flashlight and flicked it on, directing the narrow yellow beam on the wound.

Seconds later, the lights came back on, accompanied by the hum of the emergency generators.

The rounds kept falling, raining fire on the camp. *Thud. Whump.* The explosions were so close they rattled Frankie's teeth.

The noise was excruciating and heightened Frankie's sense that hell had broken loose here. Helicopters coming and going, the mortar attack that went on and on and on, the hum of suction machines, the drone of the generator, the snapping of lights on surging electricity, the hissing of respirators.

"Hap! It's Reddick. He's in trouble," someone shouted above the melee.

"Can you close?" Hap said to Frankie, stepping back from the patient.

"Yes," Frankie said, but her hands were shaking. Stitching up an incision was one thing; doing it with too few doctors and nurses, unreliable electricity, and *bombs* landing nearby was a whole other world.

She closed her eyes, brought Jamie to her mind, then Ethel. She felt them beside her.

No fear, McGrath.

She heard Jamie's voice in her head. *It's just like sewing, McGrath. Don't all you nice sorority girls know how to sew?*

Frankie closed out the chaos and the attack; when she felt calm, she closed the belly wound, then handed the patient off to a medic, washed her hands, put on new gloves, and followed Hap to another table.

"Hey, pretty," the patient said to her, his voice slurring, his eyes lowering heavily. He was a Marine, undergoing anesthesia. "Are you here to watch my game?"

She looked at his dog tag. "Hey, Private Waite." She kept her gaze on his face, careful not to glance down, where both of his legs had been severed mid-thigh. Thick yellow tubes were draining the blood from his chest wound, pumping it into a suction machine at Hap's blood-splattered boots.

Another rocket hit. Close.

"They're targeting us!" someone yelled. "Mandatory blackout in three . . . two . . . one."

The lights clicked off.

"Get down!"

"Lower the table," Hap said.

"Put me in, Coach," Private Waite mumbled. "I can score."

Frankie and Hap lowered the operating table as low as it would go. The nurse-anesthetist lay on the floor, monitoring the gauges with a flashlight.

Frankie knelt in the blood and turned on her flashlight, held it in her mouth.

For the next ten hours, she followed Hap from surgery to surgery in the blackout darkness; they peered at each other through flashlight beams.

The wounded kept coming, wave after wave of men brought in broken and in pieces after the fighting at Dak To.

There were South Vietnamese incoming, too: soldiers and civilians. Children. Filling the wards, the hallways, the morgue, overflowing outside.

Finally, Frankie noticed a lessening of the noise.

No Dust Offs landing or hovering, waiting to land. No bombing. No ambulances rumbling toward the OR.

The lights in the OR snapped back on, jarringly bright.

Hap pulled off his surgical cap and lowered his mask. He was older than she'd thought, fleshy, with large-pored skin and a dark shadow beard that had probably sprouted during the push. "Hey, McGrath, good job. First day at Pleiku and a mortar attack."

"Is this what it's always like here?"

Hap shrugged. It had been a stupid question: Frankie knew there was no always anything in 'Nam. Everything moved, changed, died; people and buildings came and went overnight, roads were built and abandoned. Hap tossed his surgical garb into an overflowing waste bin and left the OR.

Frankie stood there, unable for a moment to move; she felt people around her—nurses and medics, cleaning up, moving things around, rolling out gurneys.

Move, Frankie.

It took an act of will to simply lift her foot, to take a step. She felt dazed, overwhelmed.

She walked out of the Quonset hut. The squishing of her socks told her that—impossibly—there was blood inside her sneakers. Her feet hurt from standing for so long, and her knees ached from kneeling.

Outside of Post-Op, she saw dead men on litters, overflowing from the ER, out into the walkway. She'd never seen so many wounded in one MASCAL.

The morgue was worse. Black body bags stacked up like cordwood.

The darkness popped with noise and distant rocket fire. Here and there, beyond the glimmering silver of concertina wire, she saw blots of yellow light moving through the jungle. The enemy was just beyond the wire, barely out of machine gun range, watching them, planting bombs and trip wires.

Rounding the corner of the Quonset hut, she saw Barb sitting in the dirt, knees drawn up, back resting against the metal wall, her green canvas boonie hat drawn low on her forehead.

Frankie slid down the hut's wall to sit in the dirt beside her.

For a long moment, neither said anything. The distant *pop-thud* of the war raging in the mountain underscored their breathing.

"This is not the vacation we signed up for," Frankie finally said in an uneven voice. "I want my money back."

Barb's hands shook as she took a joint out of her pocket and lit it up. "We were promised champagne."

"Talk about out of the frying pan and into the fire. I feel like Frodo in Mordor," Frankie said.

"I have no idea what that means."

"It means give me that joint."

Barb looked at her. "You sure, good girl?"

Frankie took the joint from her friend and drew in a big lungful of smoke and immediately started coughing. She laughed for a second, said, "Look, Ma, I'm doing the drugs," and then she was crying.

"Jesus, what a night," Barb said.

Frankie could hear the trembling in Barb's voice and knew her friend needed her tonight, needed Frankie to be the strong one. She wiped the tears from her eyes and leaned sideways, put an arm around Barb. "I've got you, girlfriend."

"Thank God," Barb said quietly. And then, even more softly, under her breath, she said, "How will you do this alone?"

Frankie pretended not to hear.

Twelve

There were more than 450,000 American men in Vietnam now and God knew how many deaths and casualties. You certainly couldn't find that answer in the *Stars and Stripes*. Many of the new troops in-country had barely six weeks of training. Unlike in World War II, when soldiers had trained together in platoons and went to war alongside men with whom they'd trained, these new recruits came alone and were dropped in wherever they were needed, without the support of a platoon, without men they knew they could depend on. Army Basic Training had been shortened to get the men in combat sooner; Frankie wondered who in the hell decided that less training for war was a good idea, but no one had asked her opinion.

There were good days, though, when few wounded came in and the sound of helicopters was far away; days when the nurses played games and read novels and wrote letters home and organized MEDCAP trips to local villages to offer medical services. On bad days, Frankie heard the distinctive roar of the twin-engine Chinook helicopter, the workhorse behemoth that could hold more than two dozen injured, and knew trouble was on its way. Sometimes the pushes were so intense, the numbers of incoming and their injuries so bad, that Frankie and Barb and Hap and the rest of the doctors and nurses worked for eighteen hours straight on both soldiers and civilians, with barely a break for food or drink.

Frankie had learned to think fast and move faster. She could do more than she'd ever imagined; she could initiate a surgery or close a wound or put in a chest tube. Hap trusted her with morphine administration and talked her through all of his surgeries, teaching her every step of the way. And some of this took place under direct rocket attack and mandatory blackout conditions, in a pouring rain.

Now it was just past 0300 hours, and the last surgical patient had been wheeled to Post-Op.

No sound of incoming choppers. No mortar attack. No red alert siren.

Quiet. Not even a sprinkling rain.

She reached for a mop, began to clean blood off the cement floor. It wasn't her job, but she did it anyway. She was both dead on her feet and full of buzzing adrenaline.

She shoved the mop forward, through the blood, pushing it away. It slimed right back where it had been.

Hap entered the OR, nodded at the corpsman at the desk doing paperwork. He approached Frankie slowly, touched her shoulder. "You don't need to mop, McGrath."

He was giving her that look—she knew it now—sadness wrapped in compassion, wrapped in understanding. It was how they all looked at each other after a MASCAL, when all you could really count were the men you'd lost.

In the past ten days, most of them rainy, Frankie had spent well over a hundred hours across an operating table from this man. She knew that he never sweated, no matter how hot it was or how tough the surgery was; she knew that in easy moments, he hummed "Ain't That a Shame" under his breath, and in harder times, he made a clacking, angry sound in his jaw. She knew he wore a wedding ring, and that he loved his wife and worried about his oldest son. She also knew that he made the sign of the cross every time he finished a surgery, and that, like her, he wore a Saint Christopher medal next to his dog tags.

He smiled tiredly. "Get out of here, Frankie. I thought I heard dancing at the Park. Let off a little steam or you're going to blow."

Frankie knew he was right. She peeled off her gown and left the OR. At her hooch, she picked up clean clothes and a towel.

She took a shower in the dark, washed her hair, and dressed in a T-shirt and shorts. At her hooch, she traded her blood- and mud-stained sneakers for huaraches and headed to the Park, where the music of the Beatles greeted her.

She saw a trio of men standing over by the makeshift tiki bar, drinking and smoking. The stand of frayed banana trees rustled beside them. Tiki torches glowed yellow and sent a thread of black smoke into the night sky.

Barb sat in one of the beach chairs near the stereo setup, smoking a cigarette.

Frankie pulled up a chair, sat down beside her. A cardboard box, overturned and stained, created a coffee table that held a half-empty bottle of gin and an overflowing ashtray.

"You took a shower," Barb said. "I hate that about you."

"There was blood in my armpits. How the hell does that happen? And the water was cold. They should put that in the *So You Want to Go to Pleiku* brochure."

"Let's face it, you've got to be crazy to want to come here."

Frankie reached for the pack of cigarettes and lit one up.

"We got mail today. My brother, Will, sent this," Barb said, handing Frankie a Polaroid picture of thousands of people standing or seated on the ground, with the White House in the background. Someone held up an IMPEACH LBJ sign. Another sign read MY SON WAS KILLED IN VIETNAM. WHY?

"Why indeed?" Frankie said, leaning back, trying to work a kink out of her neck.

"My mom sent me a newspaper article about a march in D.C. A hundred thousand protesters gathered at the Lincoln Memorial."

Frankie didn't know what to say about that or, really, what to think about it. The world of hippies and protesters felt far, far away. It had nothing to do with the guys dying over here. Except that it did. The protests made them feel that their sacrifices meant nothing or, worse, that they were doing something wrong. "The world is upside down."

"Yeah. No shit. I heard that Canada is demanding the U.S. stop bombing North Vietnam. *Canada*. You know you're doing something wrong if you piss them off," Barb said, exhaling smoke.

"Yeah." The headline of the latest *Stars and Stripes* was IT'S ALMOST OVER. WINNING THE WAR.

But they'd been saying that since Finley had been killed. And look at all the deaths since then.

There was no winning in war. Not this war, anyway. There was just pain and death and destruction; good men coming home either broken beyond repair or in body bags, and bombs dropping on civilians, and a generation of children being orphaned.

How could all this death and destruction be the way to stop communism? How could America be doing the right thing, dropping all these bombs—many on villages full of the old and the young—and using napalm to burn whatever was left?

———

November 7, 1967

Dear Mom and Dad,
This is a bad night for me. I'm not even exactly sure why. Today was just another day at the 71st. Nothing particularly horrible.

God. I can't believe I even wrote those words.

*If I chose to describe a mass casualty, you'd be horrified. I'm hor-
rified, and I'm even more horrified that normally I can get through
it. Do I want to know how to see these things and still breathe and
eat and drink and laugh and dance? It feels obscene to have a life
and yet, given what these soldiers give up for their country, for us, it
feels obscene not to. The fighting near Dak To has been devastating.*

*And it is not just American soldiers who are being killed. The
Vietnamese people are suffering and dying, too. Men. Women. Children. Last week, an entire village was bombed and set on fire. Why?
Because no one really knows who the enemy is over here and our
boys are being killed by jungle snipers and they're jumpy as hell. It's
dangerous to be scared all the time.*

*What a waste of life and promise it all is. The only thing I know
is that the soldiers—I used to think of them as my "boys" because they
were so young. But they are men, fighting for their country. I want
to help them. I'm trying not to think of anything else. For a few, I'm
the last American girl they will ever see, and that means something.
You wouldn't believe how many want to take a picture with me
before they leave.*

*You keep writing about war protests and flag burnings. None of
that is in the* Stars and Stripes. *And Barb's mom said Martin Luther
King says this war is unjust. I'm starting to wonder about it myself. But
can't they support the warriors and hate the war? Our men are dying
every day in service of their country. Doesn't that matter anymore?*

Much love,

F

*PS. Send hand lotion, perfume, crème rinse, Polaroid film, and can-
dles. The damn electricity is constantly going out.*

A heat wave hit the Central Highlands in mid-November. The ever-present mud dried out, turned into a fine red dust that coated every-thing, filled every breath, turned their tears red. No matter how often Frankie placed a wet cloth across her brow, there was no getting rid of the dirt that stained the new creases in her forehead, settled in the lines that fanned out from her eyes, coated her teeth. Fat red drops of sweat slid down the sides of her face and along her spine. In its way, the heat was as demoralizing as the mud and the rain. There was no sleeping in this heat, and that meant the Park was packed after work with people listening to American music, trying anything to ease the sharp edges of their war.

"Go, Frankie," Hap said, taking her by the shoulders, turning her toward the doors of the OR. "Barb left an hour ago."

Frankie nodded. Had she fallen asleep on her feet for a second? Too tired to argue, she pulled off her mask, scrubs, cap, and gloves, and tossed them away.

Outside, daylight.

She blinked, confused for a moment. What time was it? What day?

Move, Frankie.

She left the OR and stepped outside, onto the walkway; there were pods of people about, looking tired, not much talking going on, drift-ing in and out of the mess hall.

In front of the morgue, she saw a single litter, positioned between two sawhorses. Beside it was a stack of body bags.

She headed slowly toward the litter, drawn to the loneliness of the man lying there, hoping he hadn't died alone out here. He was young—so young—and Black. He had one limb left—his right arm—and it hung limply over the side, his fingertips just inches above the bloody ground.

His youth upended her. She was twenty-one years old, and she felt ancient. All these young men who'd come here, most of them by choice, being shot at, ripped apart, broken into pieces. The majority were Black or Hispanic or poor, straight out of high school. They didn't have parents who could pull strings to get them out of service or into the National Guard, or college classes to keep them safe, or girls who would marry them. Some volunteered just to choose the branch of service, rather than be shipped out in whatever service when their number came up.

A generation gone. *Her* generation.

Dirt and blood streaked his face. She could see clumps of sweaty skin where his helmet had been. She couldn't help wondering who he was, what he had believed in. They all had stories, these guys, stories that they'd thought would go on for years, through marriages and jobs and children and grandchildren.

She saw a helmet nearby and bent over to pick it up. A Polaroid picture, splattered with mud, stuck up from it.

This young man in a white tuxedo coat and black pants, wearing horn-rimmed glasses with his arm bent at a crisp ninety degrees. Beside him was a Black girl in a long gown, wearing elbow-length white gloves, her hand tucked into the crook of his arm.

Senior Prom 1966 was scrawled on the white border of the print. On the back it read *Come home, Beez. We love you.*

Frankie gently wiped the Polaroid clean and put it in his pocket. "At least you'll be going home," she said quietly, touching his cheek. "That will mean something to your family."

In the distance, she heard a mortar thud and explode, and then nothing.

She was so tired of watching young men die. Instead of turning toward her hooch, she went to the Park, where people sat in chairs, watching a movie. The *rat-a-tat-tat* of the noisy projector garbled the dialogue.

Frankie knew that no movie would ease her loneliness or dim this new and acute sense of impending doom that had attached to her, but it was worse to be alone than to be among people. She sat down in the chair beside Barb, who handed her a drink.

"What are we watching?"

"*The Great Escape.*"

"Again?"

One drink, Frankie thought. *Just one.*

On their first day off in two weeks, Frankie and Barb sat in chairs in the Park, a cooler beside them, drinking lukewarm TaBs. Barb was reading a letter from home aloud.

November 17, 1967

Dear Barbara Sue,

Lord, I don't know who to worry more about these days, you in harm's way, or your brother in California. The letters coming from Will are worrisome, that's for sure. I sent you clippings about the riot in De-troit this summer, remember, when the Guard was called in? There were other riots, too. In Buffalo, Flint, New York City, Houston. Lots of cities. Cops clobbering on us negroes. Looting. I just found out that Will was in Detroit that day, rioting. 33 Black folks died.

I'm afraid. Ever since your brother got back from Vietnam, he's been angry in a way that will get him killed. Those college white boys might get away with violence at their protests, but it won't fly for Will and his Black Panther friends. I know you're busy, but maybe you could call him? He might listen to his big sister. Lord knows he won't listen to his mama. Thinks I oughta be mad as a hornet, but what good will that do? Me breaking a window or marching across a bridge won't change a thing. He forgets I saw your uncle Joey get lynched for looking wrong at a white lady. That wasn't all that long ago.

Anyway, we miss you plenty back here. Counting the days till you're home.

Love, Mama

"Lieutenant Johnson?"

Barb looked up.

Talkback, the camp's radio operator, stood beside them. He was a skinny kid from Nebraska with apple cheeks and a swizzle-stick neck. "Lieutenants Johnson and McGrath, I have a message for you both from Lieutenant Melvin Turner."

"Who's that?" Barb asked.

"Coyote, ma'am, of the Seawolves."

"Your water-ski buddy," Barb said to Frankie.

"He said to tell you there's gonna be a shit-kicking-good—his words, ma'ams—bon voyage party at a club in Saigon tonight and it sure would be sad to see the two purtiest nurses in 'Nam miss it. There's a C-7 at the airfield right now."

"That sounds like an order, Talkback. I usually prefer a printed party invitation," Frankie said.

"Engraved," Barb added.

Talkback looked nervous. "Coyote didn't make it sound like much of a question, ma'am. I reckon he figured you'd love to get off the compound for a while. That plane won't stick around for long. It's on a supply run."

Barb folded up her letter. "Thanks, Talkback."

"I do hate being told what to do," Frankie said.

"And being taken for granted," Barb added.

Then they both smiled and said, "Outta here!" at the same time.

The two women ran to the hooch and packed for an overnight trip.

Less than fifteen minutes later, packed and dressed in civilian clothes, with their military scrip converted into Vietnamese money, Frankie and Barb boarded the fixed-wing cargo plane and sat down.

At Tan Son Nhut, an MP escorted Frankie and Barb to a waiting jeep; they jumped in the backseat.

Amazingly, this was Frankie's first close-up view of Saigon in daylight. The city was a chaotic mess: Streets teeming with Army tanks and armed military men and MPs. Bicycles and pedestrians fighting to make their way around them. Whole families sat crowded on scooters that zipped in and out of traffic. They passed a skinny Vietnamese woman squatting on a corner, cutting vegetables on a wooden board.

Military vehicles jockeyed for position with motorbikes and bicycles. Horns honked. Bike bells clanged. People yelled at one another. Three-wheeled vehicles threaded aggressively in and around the motorbikes, belched out great plumes of black smoke. The Saigon police—called the White Mice by Americans because of their white uniforms—managed traffic where the lights didn't work or weren't being obeyed.

Barbed wire and oil drums and sandbags protected the government buildings. On one corner there was a floral memorial for one of the Buddhist monks who'd self-immolated to protest the South Vietnamese government's treatment of them. No doubt the police would take it all away, and the flowers would appear again tomorrow.

The jeep pulled up in front of the Caravelle Hotel, which dominated an entire street corner.

Frankie jumped out, slung her worn, faded overnight bag over her shoulder, and thanked the driver.

Barb came up beside her. "Damn, those flights make me thirsty."

Smiling, they headed for the hotel's glass double-door entrance.

They spent the day in the old French Quarter of Saigon, with its gorgeous, ornate buildings and tree-lined streets. It was like seeing a beautiful corner of Paris through a dirty window. You could sense what it once had been, this city, picture the French occupiers dining on foie gras and drinking fine wine, while the Vietnamese cooks and waiters struggled to feed their families on paltry pay.

At 1200 hours, they went to a small French-style bistro, with white tablecloths and uniformed waiters and fresh flowers; Frankie was struck by the incongruity of this place existing in a land torn apart by war. It was as if they'd crossed some magical portal that led back in time.

"Just go with it," Barb said, touching her arm. "We'll be back in the shit soon enough."

Trust Barb to know exactly what Frankie was feeling. She slipped her arm through Barb's and they followed the host to a table by a window, where they sat down and ordered lunch.

Inside, the roar and clatter of the city faded and the sweet fragrance of fish and broth replaced the outside odors of exhaust and diesel fuel. After lunch, they walked from shop to shop, buying new clothes and sneakers and candles and scented body lotion. Frankie bought a T-shirt that read SKI VIETNAM. They each ordered an *ao dai* to be made in soft, diaphanous silk, and Frankie bought a bolt of silver silk shantung for her mother and an ornate brass cigar cutter for her father.

At 1615 hours, they returned to their hotel and readied for the party at the club.

What a treat. Hot, hot water, and lots of it. Scented soaps and lotions.

Frankie put on a new purple dress with a white plastic hip belt and a pair of sandals. When she looked in the mirror, she saw herself for the first time in eight months. Eyes still a vibrant blue, pale skin freckled by the sun, lips so chapped lipstick didn't work, hair shaggy and grown out at different lengths.

Her face was thin; she'd lost so much weight that her upper arms were like pencils.

Barb came up beside her, put an arm around her. They stared at their reflections. Barb wore navy blue knit bell-bottom pants and a white shirt with a bold geometric silk tie around her neck. A headband accentuated how big her Afro was getting.

"I didn't know I'd lost so much weight," Frankie said. "And why did I buy this ridiculous dress today? Did I want to be Grace Kelly at war?"

"It made you think of home. Cookies coming out of the oven. Dad's martini. Or, in your case, your mother's."

Frankie smiled. Barb was right. Frankie *had* bought this dress because it made her think of home, of her mother, of the life that girls like her had been taught to want in the 1950s, when conformity was all important. No more.

Frankie might be a virgin, but she didn't want to be a "good girl" anymore. Life was too short to miss out on anything because of an older generation's rules.

She changed into the new blue-and-white gingham pants she'd bought and a white fitted tunic top with bell sleeves. At the last minute, she added the white plastic hip belt. "Come on. Let's go."

They went up to the rooftop bar and ate a delicious dinner, overlooking the chaos of the city below. At 2015 hours, they left the hotel and found an MP waiting for them. They drove through the hectic, busy streets and pulled up in front of a seedy-looking club, where a sign tacked up over the door read BON VOYAGE, HAWK! in bold black script. Inside the murky interior, a bar ran from end to end; in front of it, officers in fatigues and khakis and T-shirts and jeans stood shoulder to shoulder, clapping each other in challenges and congratulations, drinking cocktails that contained actual ice cubes. Vietnamese waitresses moved through the crowd, serving drinks and food; others cleared the tables. A dance floor had been created by pushing tables to the walls; several couples danced in the middle of the room. A three-piece band played unrecognizable music. Two ceiling fans whopped quietly overhead, pushing the hot air around, rather than cooling it.

At the bar, Coyote saw Frankie and waved. He approached Frankie with an endearing hesitation that reminded her of life back in the world, of first dates and school dances. Not the usual pilot's swagger at all. "You look beautiful, Frankie. May I have this dance?"

"You may," she said. It felt so ridiculously old-fashioned and otherworldly that she had to laugh.

He pulled her into his arms and onto the dance floor. She felt his hand settle on her hip.

She moved his hand back up to her waist. Apparently there was more good girl left in her than she'd thought. "I think you've confused me with a different kind of girl."

"No way, Frankie. You're the kind of girl a guy brings home to his ma. I knew that the minute I met you at the beach party."

"I sure used to be," she said. "Thanks for the invitation tonight, by the way."

"I've been thinking about you since we met," Coyote said.

The next song sped up in tempo and he twirled her around until she was out of breath and dizzy. For a beautiful moment, she was just a girl in the arms of a boy who thought she was special.

She was well past the "glowing" stage her mother had often warned her about. In this heat, she was sweating, and she loved it.

"Frankie. There's Riot. I want you to meet my new CO," Coyote said, taking her by the hand.

Frankie stumbled along, laughing at his quick change. One minute he was trying to touch her ass, and the next he was dragging her off the dance floor.

He stopped so abruptly, she bumped into him. Coyote's hand slid down her bare arm; his fingers took hold of hers.

"Riot?" Coyote said. "I'd like you to meet my girl."

"Your girl? I'm hardly . . ." Frankie laughed and looked up at Coyote's commanding officer, who was dressed in fatigues and wearing aviator sunglasses. He looked like a CIA agent. Or a rock star. His stance and demeanor screamed regulation.

"Well, well," he said, and slowly lowered the sunglasses. "Frankie McGrath."

Rye Walsh.

Frankie was momentarily plunged back in time, to the Fourth of July party when Finley had brought home his new best friend. "Rye, like the whiskey," she said, feeling a tightness in her throat. He made her think of Finley, of home, of innocent schoolgirl crushes.

He pulled her into his arms, gave her a hug so fierce she was lifted off her feet.

"Wait. You two know each other?" Coyote said, frowning, looking from one to the other.

"He went to the Naval Academy with my big brother," Frankie said, stepping back. "He was the one who told me that women could be heroes."

Coyote put his arm around Frankie, pulled her close. She pulled free.

Rye put his sunglasses back on. "Well. I don't want to intrude on your fun, kids. Carry on. Nice to see you again, Frankie." He turned on one heel, a parade-smooth gesture, and walked back to the bar.

Thirteen

"What do you know about your CO?" Frankie asked.

"He's tough as nails. Doesn't talk much about himself. I hear he's engaged to some admiral's daughter. You probably know him better than we do."

"No," Frankie said. "I didn't really know him well. An admiral's daughter, huh? Engaged. It's hardly surprising."

"Why?"

Frankie almost said, *Look at him,* but held her tongue.

Even with Coyote's arms around her, slow-dancing, Frankie found her gaze drawn again and again to Rye; she watched the way he laughed with his men, the way he stood apart from them sometimes. She could tell how much they respected him. Every glance took her back to Finley's going-away party, when she hadn't been able to look away, either, and their moment in her father's office.

Women can be heroes.

Those words—his words—to an impressionable twenty-year-old had led her inevitably to this room, this war. It felt like fate, them meeting here.

"I have my own room, Frankie," Coyote said, nuzzling her neck as they danced. "We could be alone . . ."

"Coyote," she said quietly.

He drew back, looked at her. "You're right. I should ask you out for a real date. I want to do this right with you, Frankie."

The music changed. There was a crash of furniture and a rise of laughter.

At the edge of the dance floor, Barb had missed the chair and fallen to the floor. Frankie pulled out of Coyote's arms and went to her friend.

Rye was there first, helping Barb to her feet. Barb threw her arms around Rye's neck and hung on. "My bones melted," she said. Her head lolled back, and she grinned drunkenly at Frankie. "Look a' this one, Frankie . . ."

Frankie turned to Rye. The way he looked at her was unnerving. Too intense. It made her feel strange, fluttery. "I should get her back to the Caravelle."

"I'll get an MP to drive you."

Rye helped maneuver Barb out of the O Club and to an MP jeep. Frankie climbed in beside her.

Coyote came out of the O Club. "Frankie, I'll come to see—"

"'Bye, Coyote!" Frankie said, waving as the jeep took off.

Back at the hotel, she helped Barb up the stairs and into their room.

While Barb was peeing, she looked up, bleary-eyed, and said, "Don't let me fall off the toilet. M'balance is for shit."

"Whiskey," Frankie said, and they both laughed.

Frankie helped Barb out of her clothes and into bed.

"D'ya see the cat in the sunglasses?" Barb said, flopping back into the clean white sheets. "Good-lookin' man."

"I saw him," Frankie said, pulling the covers up to Barb's chin.

With the lights out, and to the sound of Barb's snoring, Frankie tried to sleep. It should have been easy; she had drunk plenty tonight, and there was no fear of a mortar attack or a MASCAL to waken her in the middle of the night. She was on clean, fresh sheets. Still, sleep eluded her. She felt restless, anxious.

The phone rang. She answered before it wakened Barb. "Hello?"

"Miss McGrath," said a Vietnamese man in French-accented English. "There's a young man here to see you. He asks that you meet him at the top-floor bar."

Coyote.

Frankie didn't want to see him now, but she owed him the truth. He wasn't the man for her. And she couldn't sleep, anyway.

She threw back the covers and dressed in jeans and a T-shirt and went to the elevator, which was out of order. Sighing, she walked up four flights of stairs and emerged onto the hotel's dimly lit rooftop bar.

A three-piece band sent music out across an empty dance floor. She could see a small group of men and women huddled in one corner, all of them smoking and talking loudly, arguing. She could hear typewriters clacking.

Journalists. She'd heard that this bar was one of their hangouts, along with the bar at the Rex Hotel. She wondered what they were arguing about, if their perspectives on the war were as at odds as her own; if they were as divided as America seemed to be.

Frankie walked over to a quiet table by a window and sat down. In the moonlight, the Continental Hotel across the street was dark except for a few illuminated rooms. She couldn't help thinking of Jamie, who long ago had told her about this romantic rooftop bar. Sadness tainted the memory, left a sharp little bite, and then softened into regret. She tried instead to imagine him at home, with his family, but couldn't quite manage that kind of optimism.

A slim Vietnamese woman appeared quietly to take Frankie's drink order. Moments later, she returned with a glass of Sancerre.

Frankie took a sip of the wine as she stared out at the night lights of Saigon. Even with music playing, the noise of the war was ever-present: the whir of a helicopter flying over the city, the pop of gun-fire. Here and there, streaks of red arced through the night sky like fireworks; orange fires blossomed. From here, the war was almost beautiful. Maybe that was a fundamental truth: War looked one way for those who saw it from a safe distance. Close up, the view was different.

"Frankie."

Rye.

She looked up in surprise.

The Vietnamese waitress glided effortlessly into place beside Rye.

"Scotch. Neat," Rye said. When the waitress left, Rye sat down opposite Frankie, saying nothing until he had his drink in front of him and the waitress had gone. "Seeing you . . . was like going back in time."

"Yeah."

"Finley was the best friend I ever had."

"Me, too."

He sat back, studied her. "So. A combat nurse. I would have thought you'd be married to a millionaire's son by now."

"Some guy I met at a party told me that women could be heroes. No one had ever said anything like that to me before."

"I don't think you needed to hear it from me," he said, his gaze steady on hers. She couldn't help wondering what he saw when he looked at her. Finley's kid sister? Or did he see who she'd become?

"I did need to hear it," she said quietly.

The music changed to something unrecognizable.

He said, "Dance with me."

As a girl, she'd dreamed about this moment with him; as a woman, she knew how fragile dreams were and this war had taught her to dance while she could. She got to her feet.

He took her hand in his and led her to the dance floor. She fit up against him, felt his arms encircle her. They moved in time to the music, but they weren't really dancing. She would have sworn she could feel his heart beating against hers.

He looked down and she saw desire in his eyes. No man had ever looked at her like this, as if he wanted to devour her, bones and all.

When the song ended, she pulled free. "We probably shouldn't dance," she said, feeling shaky. "You're engaged, from what I hear."

"She's a long way away."

Frankie managed a smile, but only barely. They were not the words she wanted to hear from him. "I've already had my heart broken over here," she said quietly, taking another step back. "And I expect an officer to be a gentleman, Rye."

He locked his hands behind his back. Soldier's stance. A respectful distance. "Forgive me for coming here tonight." His voice had a rough edge to it. "It wasn't my place."

She nodded, tried again to smile. "Stay alive, Rye. I'm seeing too many bird pilots in my OR."

"Goodbye, Frankie."

"Goodbye."

———

Frankie tossed and turned all night, her sleep plagued by sharp, unfamiliar longings. When she woke, it was late morning and sunlight streamed through the clean glass windows.

Her first thought was of Rye.

That dance. And the way he'd looked at her.

She got out of bed, saw that Barb had left her a *Meet you at breakfast* note.

Downstairs, she found Barb already seated at the hotel restaurant, drinking a Bloody Mary. "Hair of the dog," she said. "What happened last night? How did I get back to the hotel?"

"I used my superhuman strength and carried you."

"Ugh. That's good for the reputation."

"You were dressed the whole time, if that helps. And there was no public vomiting. You may or may not have used the men's bathroom."

The waitress returned with a second Bloody Mary, which she handed to Frankie.

"I know I was drunk as shit last night, but you were acting weird," Barb said.

"Was I?"

Something about the casual response put Barb on alert. "So, now I know there's a story. Spill the beans, girl."

Frankie sighed. "Fin used to bring his Naval Academy friends home in the summer. They seemed like gods to me." She smiled, a little one, and thought maybe it was too sad to be real. "Rye Walsh was his best friend. The CO in the sunglasses last night? I had a huge crush on him."

"The guy who looks like Paul Newman? Wow. So, grab his hand and show him—"

"He's engaged."

"Shit. Not again." Barb took a drink. "And you're a damn good girl."

"When I danced with Jamie, I felt safe. Loved, I guess. It was like being home, but with Rye . . . when I was in his arms, I felt . . . I mean, the way he looked at me was . . . hungry. Almost scary."

"It's called lust, Frankie, and it can rock your good-girl world."

Back at the Seventy-First, the only thing that ever changed was the weather. By December, the days were uniformly hot and dry. Now, with the temperature rising to 110 degrees in the OR, Frankie was hot and headachy. She hadn't slept well since Saigon.

The OR doors opened and a pair of medics rolled a soldier in from Pre-Op; he was face down on the gurney, his naked, bloody butt stuck up in the air. One of the medics was laughing at something—a good sign. "Butt shot," he yelled to Frankie, who showed the medics to an empty table and snapped on a new set of gloves.

The kid on the stretcher craned his neck around to look at Frankie. "I got me a fine black ass, don't I?" he said with a glassy-eyed smile that revealed he'd been given some morphine for the pain. He was barely over eighteen, Frankie would guess. "I'm Albert Brown. Private first class."

"Hey, Private Brown. Yes, you do have one fine ass, I'd say. Too bad I'm going to have to pick shrapnel out of it." She waved over the male nurse-anesthetist—nicknamed Gasman—who injected a local anesthetic. When the patient's buttocks were numb, Frankie bent over his backside and went to work, tweezing out jagged bits of shrapnel. It would hurt like hell if he could feel it. And he would when the drugs wore off.

"Where are you from, Albert?"

"Kentucky, ma'am. Land of bourbon and good-lookin' men."

"With fine asses," Frankie said.

He laughed. "I'm glad to represent, ma'am."

When she had finished, cleaned him up, and bandaged his backside, she called for a medic to take him to Post-Op.

"Wait, ma'am," he said. "Can you take a picture with me for my mama, Shirley? She'd love that."

Frankie smiled tiredly. It was a common request. "Sure, Albert. But your ass looks like it's been chewed by wolves and so does my hair."

Albert grinned. "No way, ma'am. You're the prettiest girl who has ever touched my butt."

Frankie couldn't help but laugh. She leaned down and let the kid's friend snap a Polaroid picture of them. With a wave, she sent him off to recovery and peeled off her gloves, tossing them away and reaching for a new pair. She was thinking about going for a soda when she heard choppers.

Several of them.

She glanced across the OR, made eye contact with Barb, who looked as exhausted as Frankie felt.

The two nurses ran for the helipad, their feet lost in a cloud of red dirt. They helped offload the wounded and guided them back to triage. There, they moved through the wounded fast, barking out orders, prioritizing treatment.

They were almost done when Frankie heard, "Where do you want him, ma'am?"

Two medics appeared, with a wounded man on a litter between them. She took one look at this casualty's wound and said, "OR, STAT," and ran along beside the medics.

In the OR, she pointed to an empty table and called for Sharlene, the newest nurse at the Seventy-First; the poor thing was fresh off the plane from Kansas. This would be her first shift. "Sharlene," Frankie said, thrusting a pair of scissors at her. "Cut off his clothes."

The young blond woman stared down at the blood falling from the soldier's chest and onto her shiny black combat boots.

Frankie saw the woman's fear and thought, *Take a breath, Frankie.* She forced her voice to soften as she said, "Look at me . . . Sharlene."

Sharlene's eyes were full of tears. "Yes . . . ma'am . . ."

"It's scary, I know. But you can cut his clothes away and take off his boot. You're a registered nurse."

Sharlene took the scissors in shaking hands and went to the end of the table. Staring down at what was left of the soldier's left leg, she began to cut away the blood-and-mud-soaked pants leg.

The patient sat up suddenly, saw his mangled leg. "Where's my foot? Where's my foot?"

"Doc! Over here." Frankie reached for a shot of morphine and administered it. "This will help. You'll be okay, Corporal."

"I'm a bulldogger, ma'am," he said, starting to slur his words as the morphine took effect. "In Oklahoma. You smell mighty fine, ma'am, like my girl back home."

"It's Jean Naté perfume. What's a bulldogger, Marine?" Frankie said, looking for a surgeon.

"Rodeo, ma'am. I surely need that foot . . ."

Frankie yelled, "Is there a damn doc here, or am I going to do this kid's surgery myself?"

———

On her birthday, after a long shift in the OR, Frankie headed to the Park, where a party was in full swing. Barb and Slim were standing by the dirty, leaf-infested pool. A banner had been strung between two dying banana trees: HAPPY BIRTHDAY, FRANKIE! A small, tired-looking group of nurses and doctors whooped and clapped at her arrival.

Coyote saw Frankie. He leaned over the tiki bar, poured a drink, and brought it to her.

In the days since she'd seen him at the O Club in Saigon, he'd shaved his mustache. He looked younger.

"Happy birthday, Frankie. I'm glad I could be here. Dance with me?"

She started to say no, but when she looked in his eyes, and saw how hard he was working to smile, she realized that they were alike: just trying to conceal the pain of every day here, tired of being alone.

"Give me a chance, Frankie. I'm a good man."

He sounded so earnest, and she knew he meant it, knew that it made sense to do as he asked, so, she let herself be pulled forward. She wouldn't sleep with him, wouldn't even let him kiss her—that would be wrong, to lead him on that way—but just now, she was lonely and tired. It was the wrong song and the wrong man and the wrong hand in hers, but honestly, it felt good not to be alone. And it was just a dance, after all.

"Say you'll be my girl."

"I'm sorry, Coyote," she said softly. For a moment she almost hoped he hadn't heard her.

"Yeah," he whispered back, his breath hot against her ear. "I know. You're out of my league, Frankie McGrath."

She tightened her hold on him. "No, Coyote. You're everything a girl could want."

He drew back. "Just not you."

God, she hated this. "Just not me."

He pulled her close again, resumed their dance. "I love a challenge, Frankie. You should know that about me. But I'm going home soon. Short-timer. So don't lose your chance."

He threw his head back and howled, but for the first time, Frankie heard the loneliness in the sound, the sorrow and the heartbreak. She wondered if it had been there all along.

Fourteen

December had been a hell of a month in the Highlands. The NVA had killed hundreds of South Vietnamese civilians at Dak To. The OR and the wards had been filled with kids who'd lost their parents, old men who'd lost their daughters, mothers who'd lost their sons.

Now, on Christmas Eve, after hours on her feet in the OR, Frankie was exhausted. They were finally done treating the last of the casualties. Hopefully, the remainder of the night would be quiet.

"Go," Hap said. "This is the last one. Go have some eggnog."

"You sure?"

"Sure as gonorrhea itches. Go."

Frankie peeled off her gloves and tossed them, along with her cap and gown, into the barrel by the door. "Merry Christmas Eve," she said to the corpsman stationed at the desk by the door.

"Ain't it lovely?" he said. "You, too, ma'am."

She left the OR and emerged into unexpected sunlight. She found Barb in the triage staging area, standing beside a dead Black man on a stretcher. An exploding mortar shell had blown off most of his uniform. One side of his face was ripped and charred. It looked like both of his arms and legs were shattered.

"Explosion blew the dog tags right off him. No name," Barb said. "On Christmas Eve."

"Someone will know him. His platoon is in Post-Op."

"Yeah," Barb said, carefully placing the soldier's hand on his chest. She kept her hand atop his.

Frankie knew Barb was thinking of her brother, Will, who'd come home from Vietnam two years ago a different man. Angry. Radical. Bound for trouble.

Frankie found a white sheet and covered the dead soldier, whispering, "God bless and keep you, soldier."

Barb didn't look up. "The *Stars and Stripes* reported no American casualties yesterday. Seven men died in OR One alone."

Frankie nodded.

Whatever doubt—or hope—she'd once held was gone now: the American government was lying about the war. There was no way to avoid that simple truth anymore. LBJ and his generals were lying to the American people, to reporters, to everyone. Maybe even to each other.

The betrayal was as shocking as the assassination of Kennedy had been, an upheaval of right and wrong. The America Frankie believed in, the shining Camelot of her youth, was gone, or lost. Or maybe it had always been a lie. All she knew was that they were here in this faraway country, soldiers and sailors and airmen and Marines and volunteers, risking their lives, and their government could no longer be trusted to tell them the truth about why.

Men were still arriving in Vietnam by the thousands, and contrary to what the hippies and the protesters suggested, the majority of them were volunteers, believers in their country. How could the government—and, worse, how could the American people—not care about that?

Frankie and Barb walked past the morgue, where a pair of corpsmen were processing last night's corpses.

Frankie was the first to hear the chopper. She turned and tented a hand over her eyes. "Damn."

The sound of the rotors grew louder.

"Just one."

They rushed to the helipad to help offload the wounded and saw a Huey gunship touch down.

Coyote sat in the left seat; he leaned toward Frankie, grinning. "Just the nurses we hoped to see on Christmas Eve," he said. "Want to have some fun?"

"You don't have to ask us twice." Barb jumped up into the chopper, and Frankie followed.

Once inside, Frankie saw that Rye was in the right seat, wearing his comms helmet with RIOT written across the front. Mirrored aviator sunglasses hid his eyes. He gave her a smile; she answered with a thumbs-up.

Coyote handed them headsets.

Frankie put her headset on and sat on the floor, next to the gunner positioned at the open door, and behind Rye. She let her legs dangle over the side as they took off.

They flew over the flat, treeless red swath of the evac hospital, and over the leafless, empty jungle, where dead orange leaves lay on the ground beside dying trees.

Up. Up. High into the mountains, where the world was impossibly green.

A few minutes later, Rye said into his mic, "There," and the Huey descended sharply, lowered to about six feet above the ground. Hovered there. "Two minutes, Coyote. I don't like being a target."

Coyote grabbed a rifle and an ax and jumped to the ground. Weapon out, he ran for a stand of trees.

Frankie surveyed the open area. Charlie could be anywhere, hiding in the lush green jungle . . . they could have planted Bouncing Betties or punji stakes—sharpened sticks, stabbed deep in the ground and coated with human feces to assure both a deep wound and infection when stepped on.

"This is crazy," Frankie said. "What's he doing?"

Moments later (it felt like an eternity), Coyote came back, carrying a straggly tree. He tossed it into the back of the chopper and climbed up into the left seat.

"All that for a tree?" Frankie yelled into her microphone. "You two are crazy."

"A Christmas tree," Coyote said, laughing as the helicopter spun and arced back up toward the clouds.

Twenty minutes later, they landed back at the Seventy-First.

Coyote turned and pulled off his helmet and smiled. "Riot and I figured you gals needed a Christmas tree."

Barb laughed. Frankie thought it might be the truest laugh she'd ever heard from her friend.

"You Seawolves sure live up to your crazy-as-shit reputation, I gotta say," Barb said. "I just hope you have a turkey to go along with it or my mama would whoop your ass for playing with a girl's tender heart."

Coyote grinned. "And a pecan pie, all the way from my mama's kitchen in San Antonio."

They put the tree up in their hooch and decorated the scrawny branches with anything they could find. Paper clips, strips of aluminum foil, empty C-ration can lids, lengths of tubing, Kelly clamps. It stood in the corner in all its Charlie Brown glory. Barb made a tinfoil star for the top. Rye and Coyote sat on Frankie's cot, watching the decorations accumulate. "White Christmas" played through the speakers of Barb's transistor radio.

Frankie was on her knees in front of the tree, stringing a loop of paper clips from one branch to another, when Coyote said, "We need drinks."

"Hot damn, flyboy, you're right!" Barb said, and the two of them left the hooch.

Frankie heard the metal frame of her cot squeak as Rye got to his feet. She heard him coming closer, felt him standing behind her. Every cell in her body seemed attuned to his presence. Slowly, she stood up, but didn't turn around. "Thanks for this," she said. "It was crazy and stupid and dangerous . . . and lovely."

"I didn't want to think about you," he said.

She turned to him at last.

Their gazes met, held.

She felt her breathing speed up. *Lust,* Barb had said. Was it that simple?

There was no reason to pretend she didn't feel it. If she'd learned anything during her tour it was this: say what you meant while you could. "You're engaged," she said. "And I know it's old-fashioned, but I can't be the other woman. I couldn't live with myself."

"You do know we're at war," he said.

"Please tell me you aren't going to try the we-could-die-tomorrow line on me."

He stepped back. "You're right. I'm wrong. Merry Christmas Eve, Frankie. I won't bother you again."

"You don't need to go."

"Yes, I do. You . . . do something to me."

Long after he and Coyote had gone, while Barb and Frankie drank eggnog and listened to Christmas music and opened their gifts from home, the echo of those words remained.

You do something to me.

The Christmas cease-fire held, giving everyone at the Seventy-First time to enjoy a real holiday meal in the mess hall. Turkey, mashed potatoes and gravy, green beans, sausage stuffing, and sweet potato casserole.

Pecan and pumpkin pies. Afterward, a group walked over to the Park, where Frankie had hung up a banner: BON VOYAGE, LT JOHNSON. WE WILL MISS YOUR SORRY ASS.

Barb's send-off party.

Now Frankie and Barb sat in beach chairs tucked in close to the stand of banana trees. A party raged beside them; music blared. A sorry-looking tinsel tree, decorated with red bows, leaned brokenly against the tiki bar.

"I guess we'd better talk about it now, Frankie," Barb said, handing Frankie a lighter.

Frankie lit her cigarette. "About you leaving? I'd rather not."

"You're the only thing I don't want to leave behind."

Frankie turned to her friend. In this light, Barb's Afro looked like a dark halo. If you didn't look in her eyes, you might think she was an ordinary twenty-five-year-old. Frankie couldn't calculate all that her friendship with Barb had given her. Barb had shown Frankie glimpses of a world she'd not been exposed to or taught much about. Frankie had thought the passage of the Civil Rights Act was a triumphant end. Barb had shown her that it was a fragile beginning. She knew that Barb was scared for her brother, Will, and his Black Panther affiliation, but she was proud of it, too. She knew about fighting for things; even though she had a master's degree in nursing, she'd had to fight to get sent to Vietnam, and then she'd had to fight again to get assigned to an evac hospital. Black officers were few and far between over here, but Barb had been determined that Black soldiers should see a Black nurse in the hospital.

Barb leaned back, sighed. She took a drag, exhaled smoke slowly. "I can't take another tour," she said at last.

"I know that. I just . . ."

"I'll miss you, too, Frankie."

The next morning, when Frankie woke, the first thing she saw was Barb's empty cot. The posters above the bed—Malcolm X and Muhammad Ali and Martin Luther King, Jr.—had been removed; all that was left were tufts of paper on thumbtacks pushed into the wooden walls. Things ripped away, pieces left behind. A metaphor for life in Vietnam.

Frankie saw a folded-up note on the dresser beside her cot. She unfolded it slowly.

December 26, 1967

Dearest Frankie,

Call me a coward. I should have wakened you when my bird showed up, but you were actually sleeping, and we both know how rare that is over here. I didn't want you to see me crying.

I love you.

You know that, and I know that you love me, and when that's in place, we don't need a goodbye.

So, I'll say, "See you."

Come visit me in Georgia. I'll teach you about grits and collard greens and you can meet my mama. It's a whole different world from your little island, trust me.

Until then, sister. Keep your head down.

And now. I know losing Jamie hurt like hell, but you're still young. Don't let this damn war take that, too.

I saw the way your Mr. Cool looks at you. Lord, I'd kill for a man to look at me like that.

Life over here is short and regret lasts forever.

Maybe happy now, happy for a moment, is all we really get. Happy forever seems a shitload to ask in a world on fire.

Be cool.

B

Beside Frankie, on the dresser, was a Polaroid picture of Barb, Ethel, and Frankie, all of them in shorts and T-shirts and combat boots, arms around each other, smiles so big and bold it seemed impossible that this was a wartime photograph. The beaded door of the O Club was behind them. Frankie could almost hear the multicolor beads clattering together, pushed by rain or wind. For all of it, they'd had good times.

She hoped they remembered that.

Fifteen

January 5, 1968

Dear Frankie,

I promised to write when I landed back in the good ole U. S. of A. I am home with my mama (for now) and sitting on my porch, sipping some sweet tea. Kids are playing kick the can in the street out front. Their laughter is something.

I miss you. I miss us. I even miss the 71st. Speaking of that, you'll never guess who was on my Freedom bird. Coyote. Lordy, that boy has it bad for you. Showed me a picture of you two at the O Club in Saigon, but don't you worry. He'll find a sparkly little cowgirl in Texas.

Life here isn't what I expected. I took a job at my local hospital and honestly, I'm bored to tears.

I need to find a new path. I'm sick of being treated like a candy striper. There's not a lot of love for us veterans here.

I don't know what I'll do now. It's hard to go from red alert sirens and saving lives to pantyhose and heels. The world might be changing, but we women are still second-class citizens. And Black women. Well. You do the math.

Life isn't calm back here. Race riots. War protests. Dr. Spock was arrested for telling guys to resist the draft. The National Guard being called out. But it isn't war.

I'm kind of at loose ends. Mama recommends more food and dating. Last week she bought me a used sewing machine.

I guess she thinks perfecting a blind stitch hem will revive me. I'm thinking I need a change. Maybe this little town is just too small for me now. But where would I go?

Anyway, stay safe and keep your flak jacket close.

Save some lives for me.

B

On a quiet day in mid-January of 1968, Frankie's DEROS came in. She tacked the paper up on the plywood wall above her cot and drew a big red circle around March 15 and an *X* through today.

She was officially a short-timer.

At 0400 hours, on January 31, a rocket hit the Seventy-First.

Explosions ripped through the night.

The red alert siren blared.

Frankie scrambled out of bed, grabbed her flak jacket and steel pot helmet from underneath the bed, and dressed quickly.

Another rocket hit. The hooch shook. A rat ran across the floor, looking for shelter.

Frankie's new hooch mate, Margie Sloan, sat up in bed and screamed. "What's happening? Oh my God—"

The red alert siren sounded again, became continuous. Over the loudspeaker the words: *"Attention all personnel, take cover. Security alert condition red. We are under rocket attack. Repeat: Condition red. Take cover."*

"We've got to get to the hospital," Frankie yelled as she ran to the door, flung it open. Outside, the camp was filled with fire and smoke: buildings on fire, black smoke billowing, acrid-smelling. An oil drum behind the latrines burst into flames. One of the four-hundred-gallon water trailers positioned above the showers exploded; water geysered out. "Margie. Now!"

Margie moved in beside her. "We can't go out there."

Frankie grabbed Margie's hand, wished there was more time to ease the young nurse into a night like this. "I know it's scary, Margie, and I wish you weren't so green. But one thing at a time, okay? Put on your flak and steel pot—"

"My what?"

"Your helmet. Put it on and get to the ER. Help with triage."

"I can't—"

"You *can*."

It was all the time Frankie had. As she ran for the OR, something big exploded behind her. The Red Cross building, maybe.

Outside the OR, personnel in flak jackets and helmets, some still in pajamas or shorts and combat boots, were running to the different wards, readying for wounded, carrying sawhorses to triage. The alert warning continued to blare out.

In the OR, Frankie got the lights on, the tables ready, the supplies carted and at hand: dressing carts, crash carts, thoracostomy trays, oxygen tanks, a portable suction machine. She sure wished Hap were still here, but he'd shipped out two months ago. Their newest doc had been here a week. It was going to be a tough night for him.

She heard the first Dust Off arrive at 0430.

The first wave of casualties hit Pre-Op and the OR minutes later. Too many for the operating tables they had, for the nurses, for the medics. Wounded lay on litters set on sawhorses, prepped for surgery and waiting. She saw civilians, heard a child crying for her mother. Had the U.S. bombed another South Vietnamese village?

As Frankie scrubbed in and masked up, she could hear the constant whine and thump of shells ripping the camp apart. The Quonset hut shook, IVs rattled in their holders. Her helmet kept clanking down onto the bridge of her nose.

Another hit. *Close.*

In the OR, the wounded who were able rolled off their beds or litters and hit the floor, their IVs yanked out of their veins. Frankie grabbed pillows, blankets, whatever she could find to lay over the patients who were too wounded to move. It wouldn't save them from a direct hit, but it was all she could do.

The lights went out. Total darkness. Then the generators hummed to life and brought light back.

Frankie went to the nearest operating table, saw the soldier lying there. He was barely conscious, moaning for help. His uniform had been cut off in triage, exposing the devastation of his chest wound. He was bleeding everywhere; bits of shrapnel were embedded in his neck.

"I've got you," she said, putting her strength into applying pressure to the chest wound. The patient gasped, tried to breathe, panicked. He bucked up. "Calm down, soldier," Frankie said, looking for a doctor. "We need a trach here. Stat!"

All she saw was a sea of wounded men and medics rushing in and out.

She yanked a surgical cart close. The array of silver instruments lay ready. She'd never performed a tracheotomy before, but she'd watched and assisted on dozens. Hap had shown her how to do it step-by-step.

She looked around, called again for a doctor.

In the chaos, there was no answer.

She swabbed antiseptic on the anterior aspect of the man's throat and picked up a scalpel and made her incision, opening a direct airway in his trachea. Blood bubbled up; she blotted it away and inserted a tracheal tube.

He took a gasping breath and released it, calmed.

She taped the tube in place and grabbed some gauze and went back to his chest wound.

"Where's a goddamn doctor?" she yelled.

The noise in the OR was deafening. IVs and bottles and instruments and carts crashed to the cement floor. The lights flickered. Wounded streamed from triage into the OR.

The new doctor skidded into the OR, slipping on the bloody floor, almost falling. He wore his flak jacket and helmet.

"Captain Morse. *Mark.* I need you."

He stared at her, not seeming to comprehend.

"*Now,*" she yelled.

He looked down at the patient's sucking chest wound. "Holy shit."

Frankie knew what the doctor was feeling. Unfortunately, there was no time to let him know that. This wounded soldier needed the doctor's best, and *now.* "Look at his face, Doc. *See* him. See Specialist Glenn Short."

The young doctor's gaze moved slowly up to Frankie's face; his eyes were wide with fear. She nodded in understanding, said, "See him."

"Anesthesia," Frankie yelled, waving the nurse-anesthetist over.

"Go on, Doc," she said, as the patient was anesthetized. "Get scrubbed up, get your gloves on. You've got this," she said. "We make little holes out of big ones, right? Go on . . ."

The attack went on for so long that Frankie finally took off her unwieldy flak jacket and oversized helmet and stopped even flinching at the sound of explosions or shelling.

For hours, the evac hospital overflowed with casualties; Pre-Op, the ER, the OR, the ICU, and the Vietnamese ward were all wall-to-wall beds, and there was overflow, but at last, they were nearing the end of the push. All of the casualties had been operated on. Now Frankie stood in the middle of the OR, sopping the sweat from her brow, watching Dr. Morse finish the last surgery. She knew he would fall apart soon, start shaking and be unable to stop, but he was still going. That meant he had what it took.

"McGrath," a medic yelled from the doorway. "Someone wants you out here. STAT."

Frankie ran out of the OR, saw Rye standing outside, covered in blood and mud. "Are you hurt?"

"It's not my blood." He pulled her into his arms, held her tightly. "You're okay," he said shakily, and then, steadier: "You're okay." He drew back, stared down at her. "I heard about the direct hit here and all I could think about was you. I thought . . ." he began. "I wanted to make sure you were okay."

He let her go, but she didn't step back. It had felt so good to be in his arms, to be comforted, even for a moment. "Just another shit day at the Seventy-First," she said, trying to smile.

"Come on, Frankie," he said. "I'm taking you out of here."

"There is no out of here," she said tiredly.

He held her hand and led her away from the OR.

The compound was a stinking, smoldering mess. Something over by the Park was on fire, lighting up a sky that would soon be darkening again.

Rye said, "I've never seen a night like this."

Frankie started to say something—she had no idea what—when she heard a soldier moan in pain. She yelled, "Medic!" and ran toward the morgue overflow area, where there were rows of canvas-covered dead bodies. A pair of exhausted-looking corpsmen were managing it all, gathering the names of the dead, checking dog tags, zipping the bodies into bags.

Over to the left, there was a single litter left on a pair of sawhorses. She saw blood dripping down from the sides and through the canvas bottom; she heard the patient moan again.

"Westley, has this soldier been given morphine?" she asked one of the corpsmen.

"Yes, ma'am. Doc Morse saw him. Said he couldn't do any more."

Frankie nodded and went to the man on the litter. She felt Rye come up beside her.

There was almost nothing left of a man who had been whole minutes ago. Field dressings were blood-soaked on three missing limbs. Blood and mud covered what remained of his face.

She reached for his dog tags so that she could comfort him by name. "Hey, Pri—" Her voice broke.

Private Albert Brown.

"Hey, Albert," she said softly. "Did you come by to show me that fine ass of yours again?"

She leaned over the dying man, barely older than a boy, and placed a hand on his ruined chest.

His head lolled toward her. One eye looked at her. She knew he recognized her when his eye filled with tears.

"I'm here, Albert. You're not alone." She held his hand. It was all she could do for him in this moment, be the girl back home he'd never had. "I'll bet you're thinking about your family, Albert. In Kentucky, wasn't it? Land of bourbon and good-looking men. I'll write to your mama . . ." Frankie couldn't remember his mother's name. She knew it, but couldn't remember. It felt like another loss, her not remembering. Albert tried to speak. Whatever he wanted to say, it was too much. He closed his one eye; his breathing turned as clunky as an old motor. Frankie felt his last breath expand and empty through her own lungs.

And then he was gone.

Frankie let out a heavy breath and turned to Rye. "God, I'm tired of this."

Rye picked her up in his arms and carried her through the burning, smoking camp, past people drawn together in groups, grieving for what had been lost. The mess hall was half gone, as were the Red Cross offices. Giant smoking pits spat fire into the falling night.

The door to her hooch lay in pieces in the dirt.

Rye carried her inside and set her down on the narrow cot.

She slumped forward. "We have too many FNGs here. We needed Barb and Ethel and Hap and Jamie tonight . . ."

Rye sat on the cot's edge, stroked her back. "Go to sleep, Frankie."

She leaned against him. "His mama's name was Shirley," she whispered, remembering too late. "Shirley. I'll write to her . . ." As exhausted and lonely as she felt, it would have been easy to turn to Rye, to reach for him, to let him hold and soothe her. Longing came with the thought. She lay down and closed her eyes, almost whispered, *Stay until I'm asleep*. But what would be the point?

Hours later, when she woke, he was gone.

The *Stars and Stripes* called it the Tet Offensive: a massive coordinated attack across the country by the North Vietnamese in the early hours of January 31, 1968, the bloodiest day of the Vietnam War so far. The attack blew the doors off the secret side of the war. Apparently, when Walter Cronkite reported on the Tet carnage, he'd said—on air—"What the hell is going on? I thought we were winning the war."

Suddenly everyone in the media was asking the question: *What in the hell is going on in Vietnam?*

On February 2, LBJ used death as the success matrix of Tet, claiming that 10,000 North Vietnamese had died and only 249 Americans. "I can count," the President said, implying that hearts stopped were what mattered. (He didn't even mention the South Vietnamese casualties.)

Two hundred forty-nine American deaths.

A lie, Frankie was sure, given the number of deaths she'd witnessed at the Seventy-First alone, but who knew the truth?

———

The next morning, Frankie stood at the bedside of a young South Vietnamese woman who'd been brought in late the previous night, burned and in the throes of labor. The team had done everything they could to save the baby, but it hadn't been possible.

The woman was sitting up in bed, holding her dead newborn in bandaged arms. Beneath those white gauze bandages, the skin had been charred to black, but the woman hadn't even cried out when Frankie debrided the dead flesh. She'd made a sound only when she tried to take the baby.

Unbearable grief.

So many dead and dying and lost.

Her hooch mate, Margie, approached Frankie, offered her a hot coffee. The cup shook in her unsteady hand. "Are you okay?"

"How could any of us be okay?" Frankie answered.

"Well. You're on your way out. Just think. You're going home."

Frankie nodded. She'd been looking forward to going home, *longing* for it, dreaming about it, but suddenly she pictured it.

Coronado Island.

Mom and Dad and the country club.

What would it actually be like, being home, living with her parents?

How could she go from red alert sirens and saving lives to butter knives and champagne glasses?

"I don't know how we'll manage without you," Margie said.

Frankie turned to look at Margie, whose eyes were red from crying. The young nurse was nowhere near ready for what was to come. She would be someday—probably—but not yet.

There was no nurse here with the experience Frankie had.

How could she leave this hospital and the casualties—American and South Vietnamese—who needed her? She'd come here to make a difference, to save lives, and God knew lives still needed saving. As much as she sometimes hated the war, she loved nursing more.

February 3, 1968

Dear Mom and Dad,

This is a difficult letter to write, and I am sure it will be difficult to read. I apologize in advance. I wish I could just pick up the phone and call you, but believe me, the MARS phone is not our friend.

It sounds crazy and absurd, but I have found my calling here in Vietnam. I love what I do, and I make a real difference. As you know, the war is heating up. I know the media and the government are lying to the American people, but I'm sure you've heard of the Tet Offensive.

More troops arrive every day, and a lot of them end up wounded.

We do our best to save them, and if they can't be saved—like Finley—I sit with them and hold their hands and let them know they aren't alone. I write letters to their mothers, their sisters, their wives. Can you imagine what such a letter would have meant to us?

So.

I am not coming home next month. I have signed up for another one-year tour of duty. I simply can't leave my post when the men need me. We don't have enough experienced staff here.

There. I can hear you screaming. If you knew me now, you'd understand. I am a combat nurse.

I love you both.

                                        F

February 17, 1968

Dear Frances Grace,
NO. NO. NO.
    Change your mind. Come home. Be safe.
    You could get hurt over there. Enough. Come home NOW.
    Your father is extremely unhappy with this idea, I might add.
                Much love,
                Your mother

March 1, 1968

Dear Frank,
Of course you're staying. I never doubted it.
    You're as tough as dried-out rope and the men need you.
    God knows it's strange here, too. Nixon announced that he's running for president and state troopers used tear gas to stop a protest. Holy crap. Nothing makes sense.
    Still, strangely, life goes on. I'm in Veterinary School at long last and working my ass off. I've joined the local orchestra and am back to playing the violin. It helps a bit, although I still don't sleep well.
    Come visit me when you're back in the world. I'm waiting with open arms. We have a new mare that is a dream for beginners. Nothing soothes the soul like a gallop in the sunshine.
                Love,
                Ethel

On a blisteringly hot day in early March, Frankie began her shift, tired and jittery from a lack of sleep.

The OR hadn't been especially busy in the past week—there had been lots of time for games and movie nights and writing letters home. Frankie had even jumped on a slick ship—a Huey stripped down for transport—and gone to Qui Nhon for an afternoon of shopping. Even so, she was on edge, peevish, demanding too much from the people around her. It didn't help that they were short-staffed. Frankie knew she should reach out to the newer nurses, especially Margie, and mentor them, but she was worn out. And lonely.

"Lieutenant McGrath."

She turned, saw Captain Miniver, the new, by-the-book chief nurse of the Seventy-First, holding a clipboard close to her chest, her body stiffly upright. "Lieutenant McGrath?"

"Yes, Captain?"

"I've been informed that you have failed to take an R and R this tour. And your new tour starts in two weeks."

"Who ratted me out?"

"Someone who cares about you, obviously. A little bird."

"Barb."

"Barb who?" She smiled. "Anyway, I'm ordering you to go. I have your itinerary right here. A beach hotel on Kauai sounds ideal. It's a farther flight, but there will be fewer soldiers looking for boom-boom there."

"I'm needed—"

"None of us is irreplaceable, McGrath. I have been watching you. Getting reports on the level of bitchiness you've recently achieved. It's impressive." Her expression softened. In it, Frankie saw understanding. "You need a break."

"You think a little hula time will fix me?"

"It won't hurt. Either way, you leave tomorrow. Here's your itinerary. Go. Rest. Drink cocktails that come with umbrellas. Sleep. I could be saving your life, McGrath. Trust me. I've been where you are. We all can break."

Sixteen

After more than twenty-two hours of travel, Frankie stumbled into the lobby of the Coco Palms Hotel on the island of Kauai, and checked in. Once in her room, without bothering to shower, she yanked the curtains closed and collapsed onto the softest bed she'd ever felt and fell asleep.

When she woke, she heard birds singing.

Birds. Singing.

No mortars exploding or shells hammering the walls, no smell of blood or shit or smoke in the air, no screaming, no Dust Offs whirring overhead.

The captain had been right; Frankie needed this respite.

She lay in bed, feeling drowsy in a lovely way and listening to the unexpected birdsong, surprised to see that it was well past noon. Refreshed and revived, she got out of bed and pushed the heavy gardenia-print yellow-and-white drapes aside and saw Kauai for the first time.

"Wow."

The California beaches were magnificent, powerful, endless, and awe-inspiring, but this . . . this was an intimate kind of beauty, drenched in jewel tones—golden sand, vivid green grass, deep blue skies, vibrant purple bougainvilleas.

She opened the window and leaned out into the bright, beautiful day. The air smelled of a sweet floral fragrance mingled with the sharp tang of the sea. Palm trees grew on a flat patch of lawn, singly and in groups.

She took a long, hot, luxurious bath, using soap that smelled of coconut, and washed and dried her hair, seeing for the first time how long it had grown. She'd spent months pruning it as she would a runaway weed, cutting away whatever impaired her view, which left her with an uneven fringe of bangs. Thankfully, she had her boonie hat. It wasn't fashionable, in fact was the opposite, but the olive-drab hat had become a favorite possession in 'Nam, almost a companion, and it kept the sun out of her eyes. A dozen pins and patches decorated the crown, gifts she'd gotten from her patients. Each bore the insignia of some unit. The Screaming Eagles, the Seawolves, the Big Red One.

She put on her faded two-piece knit bathing suit and SKI VIETNAM T-shirt and shorts, noticing that everything bore the pink-red tint of the Vietnam soil. For the first time in months, she bothered with makeup—mascara and lipstick and blush. Slipping into sandals, she put on sunglasses, grabbed a hotel towel, and went down to the lobby.

Although she was hungry—her stomach was grumbling loudly—she needed fresh air more. Fresh air and the sound of the sea. A little sand between her toes, a little floating in salt water.

She left the hotel and walked through the manicured grounds, palm trees swaying all around her. She crossed the quiet street and stepped out onto the sand. Tomorrow she would bring her camera and take pictures of the beauty around her.

On this sunny day, locals and tourists filled the beach: families on blankets; parents keeping watchful eyes on their children, some of whom were naked, all of whom were smiling brightly. There were men with long hair, wearing peace symbol necklaces, and several men in khaki shorts, their hair buzzed to regulation length, standing at a lava-rock beach bar with a thatched roof. SEASHELL SNACK BAR AND COCK-TAILS read the sign.

Out in the ocean, she saw kids on surfboards, bobbing on the in-coming swells. It made her think of Finley, made her miss him acutely. *That's your wave, doll. Paddle harder.* She let out a long breath; it had become a kind of goodbye, her way of releasing her grief just enough to keep going.

She stripped down to her bathing suit and walked into the sea. The water was warmer than she was used to in California, but still cool. Sunshine sparkled on the surface. She swam beyond the low, incoming curl of surf and flipped onto her back in the calm swells.

Eyes closed, she felt almost young again, a girl floating on waves with the sun streaming down on her.

Finally, she left the water and staked out a patch of sand—all by herself, no one around—and laid out her towel.

Eyes shielded by her boonie hat and big round sunglasses, she drifted to sleep, slept deeply, and woke with the sun lowered in the sky. She sat up, brought her knees up, and stared out to sea. Treasured images came to her, of Finley paddling out on his surf-board, waving his hand, telling her to catch up. Of them on the beach, bouncing uncomfortably on the backs of their rental horses, Finley muttering something about the family jewels. And the sunsets they'd watched together as they spun out their childish dreams and talked about their future.

"Can I buy you a drink, ma'am?"

Frankie shook herself free of the memories and looked up. A young man stood in front of her, shirtless, wearing khaki shorts and a military belt. A SEMPER FI tattoo covered the top left quadrant of his chest. She could tell by his eyes that he'd been in-country, maybe in the bush. She wondered how long the men would wear that haunted, hunted look. She hated to let him down. "Sorry, Marine. I came here for the quiet. Stay safe."

He turned away, no doubt scouting the beach for another girl to approach.

Frankie began to feel the sting of a sunburn and noticed how pink her legs were. How long had she been out here?

She heard someone else coming her way. She should have gone farther down the beach, away from the snack bar. This time she didn't look up. "I'm fine alone, thanks."

"Are you?"

She slowly looked up, lowered her big round sunglasses.

Rye.

He stood at ease, his hands clasped behind him. He wore multi-colored shorts and a pale blue T-shirt that read LIVE TO SURF, but no one would mistake him for a surfer, not with his military posture and built-up muscles and unfashionably short hair.

"This is quite a coincidence," Frankie said.

"It's no coincidence. I worked hard to get you to take R and R."

"So you're the little bird who ratted me out. Why?"

"To see you."

"Rye, I told you—"

"I broke off my engagement."

That stopped her. "You did?"

"I couldn't pretend anymore, not after Tet. Life is short, and . . ." He paused. "There's something between us, Frankie. Tell me you don't feel it and I'll walk away."

Frankie stood up to face him.

"Say you don't want me." The way he said it revealed an unexpected vulnerability.

There was no way in the world she could flirt with him or lie. "I can't say that," she said evenly.

He finally released a breath. "Will you have dinner with me tonight?"

She knew it wasn't just dinner he wanted; she wanted more, too. Still, he was Rye Walsh, the rule-breaker who'd pushed her brother into trouble more than once (not that Finley needed much help in that regard), and she knew she wouldn't be safe with a man like him. But he was still an officer, and hopefully a gentleman. "You broke off your engagement? You swear it?"

"I swear I'm not engaged."

Frankie stared at him, felt a spark of excitement, like coming alive after a long hibernation. "Dinner sounds great."

———

Frankie stood in line at the pay phone for thirty minutes. In the past year, she'd called stateside only twice: on Christmas and her mother's birthday.

Barb answered on the second ring, sounded harried and distracted. "Hello?"

"Barb! It's me."

"Frankie! It is so good to hear your voice."

Frankie leaned her elbows on the cool metal shelf below the pay phone. A small stack of quarters stood at the ready. She hoped it would be enough. She could only imagine how expensive this call would be. "I'm in Kauai on my R and R."

"Wait! I'll join you!"

"Ordinarily I'd jump on that, but . . ." She glanced around, made sure no one could hear her. "Rye Walsh is here."

"Mr. Cool?"

"He broke off his engagement. Maybe for me. The point is: I need advice. What if he wants to have sex?"

"I guarantee you he wants to have sex. Call me telepathic. If you weren't such a damn Catholic-school girl, you would, too."

"I do. I mean, I might. But I need some . . . practical advice."

The operator came on to ask for more money. Frankie put in the rest of her quarters.

"Use birth control," Barb said. "It'll have to be condoms. Unless you have a fake wedding ring."

"What?"

"They won't give single women the pill. Don't even get me started on that shit, but if you pretend you're married, you can get it. Not that it will work by tonight. So, yeah. Condoms. Get lots."

"Seriously, Babs. I need, you know, step-by-step kind of stuff."

"They did have sex ed in your all-girls' school, didn't they? Did you sleep through it? And in nursing school—"

"Shut up. Help me. What do I—"

"Believe me, Frankie. That man has the sex part down. Just try not to tense up and don't expect too much the first time. It can hurt a bit."

"That's not very detailed."

"Okay, shave your legs and armpits. Wear sexy lingerie," Barb said, laughing. "Oh. And be bold. Not ladylike. And don't believe him if he says he loves you."

"What? Why—"

The connection ended.

Frankie left the lobby and hailed a cab, which took her into the small town of Lihue. There, she got her hair cut in a chin-length, side-parted bob, and bought a red-and-white hibiscus-print sheath dress with a matching headscarf and heeled white sandals.

Back at the hotel, she followed Barb's advice and shaved carefully and moisturized her sunburned skin.

As she stood in her hotel room bathroom and stared into the opal-escent shell-framed mirror that hung over a large clamshell sink, she hardly recognized herself. The beautician had brought back the shine in her black hair and the sleek haircut emphasized her blue eyes and the sharp line of her cheekbones. There was still an air of sadness about her—the sorrow she'd learned in Vietnam. She wondered if that would ever fade. But there was a youthful excitement in her look, too. *Hope.* Long since forgotten and never again to be taken for granted.

At 1830 hours, she left her room and went downstairs. The ceiling of the hotel lobby arched high overhead, soared up like the nave of a church.

She entered the open-air dining room. Beyond the half walls, she saw the shadowy lagoons where tiki torches blazed. Coconut palm fronds swayed and whispered, stark black trees against a violet sky. Somewhere, someone was playing a ukulele.

Most of the tables were full of vacationers, talking, laughing, smoking. It was a sharp reminder that while she'd been in Vietnam, the world had gone on. Kids had gone to school, parents had gone to work; not everyone lived and breathed the war. In 'Nam, it was easy to hear about the protests going on in America and think that everyone was burning the flag and protesting for peace; here, it was obvious that most people had quietly gone on with their lives, avoiding the dangerous shores on either side of the divide.

She saw Rye seated at a quiet table in the back corner.

A lovely Hawaiian woman, dressed in a floor-length bark-cloth print muumuu, wearing a fragrant lei, led her across the busy restaurant.

As she neared the table, Rye stood, waited for her to be seated before he sat back down.

He offered her a gorgeous lei made of small yellow-white flowers. "It's white ginger."

The fragrance was intoxicating.

"May I bring you a cocktail?" the hostess asked when Frankie was seated. "Perhaps a mai tai? The hotel's owner, Mrs. Guslander, believes it is the best cocktail in the world."

Frankie nodded. "Yes. Thank you."

"I'll have a Jameson on the rocks," Rye said.

The hostess left them alone.

The candle in the center of the table sent golden light upward.

The hostess returned with the two drinks and a pair of menus.

The mai tai was sweet and sour and strong. Frankie toyed with the pink umbrella, lifted it, ate the sweet, sweet maraschino cherry and chunk of pineapple. She knew this dinner with him meant something, maybe everything, but she felt awkward. She could reach into a man's chest and hold his heart in her hands, but she had forgotten how to make small talk.

Rye stared down into his glass, rattled his ice cubes around.

"Ice," Frankie said, just to be talking. "I'll never take that for granted again."

"Or a hot bath."

"Or dry sheets."

The waitress appeared, took their orders, and disappeared again.

Frankie could tell that he was uncertain, too. They knew each other only in the flimsiest of ways, and now he'd broken off an engagement for a chance that might come to nothing.

The waitress delivered two shrimp cocktails.

Frankie dipped a plump, pink shrimp in the spicy cocktail sauce and took a bite, chewing slowly. "You remember the night of Finley's going-away party?"

"A going-away party for Vietnam," he said. "Talk about another world."

"We didn't know."

He took a drink. "No," he said quietly. "We didn't."

"Did you ever talk to Fin about Vietnam, I mean really talk?"

Rye looked away just for a moment; in his hesitation, she saw regret. "We were at Annapolis," he said. "It was all rah-rah Navy. And he believed in it. He wanted to make your dad proud of him. I know that."

"Yeah," Frankie said. "My dad. The heroes' wall. We met there at the party."

Rye smiled at this shared memory. "Both of us hiding out."

"What were you hiding from?"

"I'm a poor kid from Compton. I didn't know how to act at your house, how to dress. Anything. And . . ."

"What?"

"Well. If we're telling all our secrets here, I followed you into the office."

"You're kidding."

"I wanted to ask you to the Ring Dance in '65. Did Fin ever tell you that?"

"No."

"He asked me not to, said you were too good for the likes of me. He was smiling when he said it, but I knew he meant it. We both ended up taking . . . a different kind of girl, shall we say?"

"The kind who didn't mind steaming up the windows of a parked car," Frankie said, smiling. "That sounds like Fin."

"I knew he was right. I had nothing in common with a woman like you. Still, I followed you into the office that night, thought I'd steal a kiss, but I could tell you weren't ready. And now . . ."

"Here we are," Frankie said in understanding. They had made it through hardship—death all around—to be here, sipping cocktails on a tropical island. Did it mean something?

How would they know unless they dared to begin?

They needed first to get to know each other. So she said, "Tell me about your family. Do you have siblings?"

"Ah. Twenty questions. Good choice. No siblings. My mom was an English teacher. Loved Yeats. The old man still lives in Compton. Bought the place in the thirties, thinks the city has gone to hell around him. He owns a car repair shop. Stanley and Mo's, although there's no Mo; no one could stand my old man for long, not even his brother."

The waitress appeared at their table, paused, then said, "I'm sorry to disturb you, sir, but there's a gentleman at the bar. He requests a moment of your time." Behind her, at the dark lava-rock bar area, an elderly man in an out-of-style suit and tie stood and waved.

"Of course," Rye answered.

The man who approached them walked in a slow, limping gait. He was tall and thin, wearing an expensive linen suit that seemed sized for a larger man. He had a thin mustache and neatly trimmed hair. "Edgar LaTour," he said in a lyrical Louisiana drawl. "Captain. U.S. Army. I'm guessing you're here on leave," he said to Rye.

"We both are, sir. This is Lieutenant Frances McGrath. Army nurse. I'm Navy."

Edgar grinned. "Well, I won't hold that against you, boy. I just want to say thank you for what you boys—and girls, I guess—are doing to fight communism. It's a tough world out there and you need to know that a lot of us still appreciate your sacrifice. I'd be honored to buy your meal."

"That isn't necess—"

"Necessary, no, but my honor. And, ma'am, a woman like you saved my life in France. Bless you."

Moments after the man left, the waitress brought their entrées—lamb roasted in a firepit, baby peas, and buttery potatoes rissole. Throughout the meal, they talked about their hopes for life after Vietnam, the friends they'd made over there, the protests going on back home.

When dinner was over—after a fabulous Baked Alaska—Rye picked up a picnic basket at his feet and offered Frankie his arm. They walked out of the restaurant, past a trio of women dancing the hula in the lobby to the sweet strains of the ukulele.

Outside, the hotel grounds were a wonderland of shadow and moonlight and tiki torches. The grounds enveloped them in fragrance and sound—sweet ginger and plumeria and a warm, salt-tinged breeze.

Flaming tiki torches stood amid elegant manicured landscaping. The lagoons lapped quietly against the shore as they walked over the arched bridge.

Rye led her to the beach, where he found a private, perfect spot, far from the closed-up snack shack, and unpacked the basket he'd brought. A blanket. Several votive candles in holders, a pack of matches, a bottle of champagne, and two glasses. He set it all out on the sand and poured her a glass of champagne.

"You're prepared," she said, not sure whether she felt romanced or manipulated.

Romanced won out.

"Always," he said with a smile. "I was an Eagle Scout."

"Really?"

"No." He laughed. "Scouting wasn't the sort of thing offered in my neighborhood."

They sat down on the blanket; each stared up at the white spray of the Milky Way. He pointed out constellations, told her the stories that went along with each one.

Halfway through one of those stories, Frankie turned to ask him something at the same time he turned to her.

They stared at each other, neither speaking for a moment, then Rye leaned forward slowly, his gaze questioning. "May I kiss you, Frankie?"

She nodded.

He leaned toward her; she met him more than halfway. It wasn't until the last second, when his lips touched hers, that she remembered to close her eyes. The kiss went on and on, until she felt his hand slide down her back, guide her body toward the sand. They stretched out on the blanket, moving together without a word.

She waited for him to reach under her dress or kiss down her throat, to push for more the way the boys she knew had always done,

but he didn't. He seemed content to kiss her deeply, bringing her closer
to some edge she hadn't known existed that left her dizzy with desire,
and still he was a gentleman.

For the first time, she was the one who wanted more.

In all the world, all the universe, they'd come together somehow,
halfway around the world, and it felt like destiny.

She drew back and looked at him. Since childhood, she'd been
taught that this kind of need was wrong, immoral, a sin, unless it happened in a marriage.

"We can wait," he said.

"In six days we'll be back in Vietnam." She thought about the helicopter pilots that had come through her OR. About Fin and Jamie
and the heartbreak of loss. "I don't want to wait."

"Are you sure?"

"I'm sure." She looked at him. "Scared, but sure. I don't know what
to do . . ."

"I do." He kissed her chin, along her throat, across the swell of her
breasts. He unzipped the back of her dress, eased it down her body,
leaving goose bumps along her skin.

Somehow, he'd released her bra without her knowing it and she felt
his mouth on her breasts.

"Oh my God," she whispered.

He kept kissing her, touching her, awakening her body. She fought
it for a moment, tried to hold herself together; it felt as if she were
unraveling.

"Relax, baby," he said, pulling her dress farther down, her panties,
until she lay naked in the starlight, shivering. Somewhere deep inside,
her body was pounding, aching.

"I want to touch you," she said.

He smiled down at her and pulled off his T-shirt. "I was hoping
you'd say that."

She reached for him, unsure of what to do and how to do it.

Be bold.

Dear Barb,

I only have time for a postcard.

    Sex was great. I was bold. And you were right.

    He knew what he was doing.

                      F

Frankie became a new version of herself in Rye's bed. They spent their days and nights exploring each other's bodies, learning cues, and listening. She discovered a passion so deep it stripped away her shyness, dissolved the once-important rules of propriety, redefined her. Her desire for him felt endless, boundless, desperate.

Now they lay on a deserted beach beneath a cliff that had taken resolve to descend. The locals called it Secret Beach, and the name was apt. They were the only people on this stunning white sand beach. Waves crashed along the shore, made a roaring sound, while shorebirds wheeled overhead, white specks against the cloudless blue sky. The water looked too rough to swim in, so they just lay near it.

They had fallen asleep in the shade for a while, holding hands, their bare feet touching. She already couldn't sleep without touching him.

Frankie didn't know how long she'd been asleep, but when she woke, the sun was beginning to set.

She rolled over, rested her chin on his chest.

Rye kissed her and they made love again, in the way that had already become familiar to Frankie, slowly at first, building desire to a fever pitch, and then in a pounding, gasping, shattering fury that left them both breathless and depleted.

Afterward, she stared at him, unable to look away, still a little breathless. Sand speckled his tanned cheeks, clung to his dark lashes. Every moment with him coalesced at once into this heaviness in her heart, and she realized suddenly, sharply, how much passion changed things. He could break her heart in ways she couldn't even imagine.

"Is this real, Rye?" she asked. "It happened so fast. I'm not experienced enough—"

"I've never felt this way before," he said. "Honest to God. You . . . destroy me, Frankie."

"Thank God," Frankie said softly.

True love. She hadn't known until now, this second, that she'd been waiting for it all her life, saving herself for it, believing in it even in the midst of war.

~

On their last day on island, Frankie and Rye stayed in bed all day. When night finally began to fall, they showered and dressed for dinner and went to the restaurant, where they tried to keep up a steady stream of conversation, but time and again, each lapsed into silence.

After dinner, they carried cocktails to the beach and sat down.

A half moon, draped in diaphanous gray clouds, shone silver light on the sand. A pale, foamy surf crashed up and back, whooshing toward them and retreating.

"I want to see you as much as I can before you go," Rye said.

"Go?" She looked at him.

"You're going home in a few weeks, right? On Christmas Eve, you told Coyote your DEROS was in March. I knew we wouldn't have long together."

"I re-upped," she said.

He drew back, let her go. "What? You're not going home? The war is escalating, Frankie. The U.S. can't admit it's losing, so it's going to get worse—"

"I know all of that, Rye. It's why I re-upped. They need me."

"No. *No.*" He actually looked angry.

She loved him for worrying about her. "That's not how this is going to work, Rye."

"Not how what is going to work?"

"Us. I was raised to do as I was told and it's bullshit. So, no telling each other what to do. Okay?"

He was clearly struggling with this. "Can I say it scares me? Does it make me a chauvinist to want you to be safe?"

"We'll be together."

"Together in Vietnam," he said harshly. "It's hardly Kauai."

"C'mon, Rye. This is who we are. We're believers, following our beliefs. I believe in you, your duty, your honor. Do you believe in me?"

She saw how the question crumpled his resistance. "Of course."

"Okay, then. We will be a great wartime love story, the pilot and the nurse, holding hands while dodging bullets."

"You've seen too many movies."

"Just tell me you love me. We'll make it through and go home together."

He stared at her, looking sad and afraid and proud and still a little angry. "There's no getting rid of me now, McGrath. I guess I'll have to re-up, too. I'm not leaving my girl over here without me."

Seventeen

On the way back to Pleiku, in a helicopter, flying over the Central Highlands, Frankie heard the familiar *pop-pop-pop* of gunfire. The chopper swooped and swerved, leaned so far to the left, she slid into Rye. He put an arm around her, held her close. "Hold on, baby. Charlie doesn't like our bird," he yelled to be heard over the noise. He took his helmet out of his bag and put it on her, tightening the straps beneath her chin.

She grinned at him. "Oh, that will save my life."

He laughed. "Let me be a hero, willya?"

Later, as the helicopter descended toward the helipad, Rye pulled Frankie close and kissed her.

Frankie unhooked his helmet and handed it back to him. With one last look that seared his smile into her memory, she grabbed her travel bag and jumped off the helicopter and stood on the helipad, looking up. "Be safe, Riot!"

Rye took a seat in the open door by the gunner, smiling at her as the helicopter lifted into the air.

He yelled something she couldn't hear. Waved goodbye.

The helicopter veered sharply sideways, headed north, and swooped down close to the jungle canopy.

Pop-pop-pop.

She saw sparks of light hit the Huey's broadside. The gunner shot back as the bird veered sharply away.

Another shot. Sparks. The *ra-ta-ta-tat* of the gunner shooting back. The Huey maneuvered swiftly. Orange bits streaked through the sky.

The shooting stopped, leaving silence in the jungle and the softening sound of the helicopter's rotors as it flew away.

Safe.

This time.

From now on, until she and Rye both landed safely back in the U.S., she knew there would always be a piece of her that was afraid.

———

April 10, 1968

Dear Frankie,

I don't know how to write this. My brother, Will, was killed by the Oakland police this week. A shoot-out with the Black Panthers. He was shot ten times, even though he'd surrendered.

I'm devastated.

Heartbroken.

Pissed off.

I need my best friend here with me to keep me steady.

Love you,

B

———

April 24, 1968

Dear Barb,

I know your grief. Losing a brother is losing a piece of yourself, your history.

I'm sorry is a shitty, useless, not-enough thing to say, but what else is there?

If I still believed in a benevolent God, I'd send you prayers.

Stay strong for your mom.

Find a way to honor and remember him.

Love,

F

June 16, 1968

Dear Mom and Dad,

I can't believe that another Kennedy has been assassinated. What is wrong with the world? Things are getting worse over here, too. Morale among the troops is the worst I've ever seen it. Between the assassination of MLK and Robert Kennedy and the protests back home, everyone is mad as hell. If you wonder how we can lose a war, imagine how the guys fighting it feel. And LBJ just sends more and more untrained kids to fight. The ORs here are always full. The sound of Dust Offs landing is becoming constant. We used to have days off, times the OR was quiet. Not so many anymore. Don't believe everything you read—our boys are dying every day. I see more and more soldiers stumbling in from the boonies, their minds broken, their nerves shot to hell. They walk through the bush, snipers everywhere, and step on hidden mines and blow up five feet away from their buddies. It's awful. And yeah, a few of them are high. Heroin is its own horror. So is the way they look when they find their way to the hospital. I can't fix them all. No one can. But I'm doing my best, I want you to know that. I am making a difference and helping to save lives.

Thanks for all the letters and for the care packages. I really

needed more film. And who knew you'd miss Twinkies and Pop-
Tarts in a war?

Love you,

F

On a still, sweltering evening on the Fourth of July of 1968, Frankie stood beneath the bright lights in the OR, stitching up a minor abdominal wound. Sweat dampened her mask and cap, slid down her back. The temperature today had gone past 102 degrees. When she finished, she peeled off her bloody gloves and dropped them into a garbage can.

Two soldiers stumbled into the OR on bare, bloody feet, carrying a man on a litter between them. The men looked sucked dry, hollowed-out. Sunken eyes, sunken cheeks, the thousand-mile death stare that Frankie had begun to recognize as the look of men who'd been out in the boonies too long, trekking, trying to avoid land mines, looking for Charlie in every shadow and bush. Constant fear turned a man inside out.

Frankie grabbed some masks and handed them to the men.

"We carried him thirty miles," one of the men said. "We broke out . . . too late."

So. Prisoners of war. No wonder they looked so beaten, both physically and mentally. Word was that the NVA kept American POWs in cages too small for them to stand up in. And that they tortured them. "How long were you prisoners?"

"Three months," the other one said. He was wearing a necklace made of amputated fingers and ears strung on a leather cord. Trophies, probably, taken from their North Vietnamese captors when they escaped. It was the kind of thing she'd seen more of in the past few months, as the fighting had heated up. It was profoundly disturbing. Sickening. A terrible sign that the soldiers' minds were being as broken by war as their bodies.

She couldn't imagine what they'd been through or what they'd done to escape, or how hard it had been to carry this wounded man for thirty miles through the booby-trapped jungle on bare feet.

The man on the litter had an infected bullet wound in his chest that oozed pus. Frankie didn't need to touch his forehead to diagnose a raging fever. She could see it in his eyes, smell it on him. Frag wounds had torn up his arms and neck. He could barely breathe, kept gasping. Something must be swollen or lodged in his airway.

He was going to die, and soon.

Frankie called out to Dr. Morse, who came over, took one look at the kid on the litter, and said, "Expectant, McGrath."

"Put a trach in, Doc," she said. "Let him breathe easy, at least."

"Waste of time, McGrath. Go find someone you can save."

One of the soldiers said, "Wait. We just humped through the boonies for a week with Fred—"

Frankie knew that the doc was right. This kid wasn't going to make it, and the OR was crowded with casualties they *could* save, but she couldn't turn her back on these men and what they'd suffered.

She pointed to an empty table. "Set him there, boys."

"What are you doing, McGrath?" Dr. Morse asked.

"Letting him say goodbye to his friends and die in peace."

"Be quick. I've got a sucking chest wound that needed you ten minutes ago."

The men set the wounded soldier on the table. Frankie cut off what was left of his fatigues. Yanking her cart close, she changed into clean gloves and wiped his neck with antiseptic solution. Holding her scalpel, she took a breath to steady herself, then made a small cut between the thyroid and cricoid cartilages and inserted a breathing tube.

The dying man took a deep, wheezing breath; Frankie saw relief come into his eyes. How long had he been fighting just to breathe?

"We got out, Fred," one of his buddies said. "Took five of those fuckers with us."

Frankie took hold of Fred's hand, held it in hers, and leaned close, whispering, "You must be a good man. Your friends are here."

His buddies kept talking—about his girl, the baby waiting for him back home, how he had saved their lives in that hellhole.

Frankie saw Fred take his last breath; felt the way he went still.

"He's gone," she said tiredly, looking at the two bloodied, dirtied men in front of her. "You gave him a chance, though."

She wouldn't be surprised if those death stares would be a part of them forever now. Men staring into a world they no longer were a part of, no longer comprehended, a world where the ground beneath your feet exploded. Another kind of casualty. She thought of other men who had grabbed her hand over the past few months, begged her to answer the question, *Who will want me like this?*, and it struck her that it wasn't just physical wounds that soldiers would take home from Vietnam. From now on, all of them would have a deep understanding of both man's cruelty and his heroism.

A medic shoved through the OR doors and yelled, "Forty-five Vietnamese villagers coming in. Napalm," and left again.

Napalm.

"Go to the mess," she said to the two soldiers as she stripped out of her gloves. "Get some chow. Take a shower. And get rid of that damned necklace."

She yelled for someone to take the dead man away. Then she found Margie and together they pushed the few OR patients to one side and gathered empty beds to turn the OR into an overflow burn unit.

Two minutes later, a flood of villagers hit the OR, most of whom had been burned beyond recognition. Frankie knew it was the same scene in the ICU and Pre-Op and on the wards.

Napalm—a jellied firebomb used in flamethrowers by the U.S. to clear out foxholes and trenches, and dropped in bombs by U.S. planes—had become common in these first few months of her second tour. More and more of its victims were coming into the OR; most of them were villagers.

Tomorrow they'd be flown to the Third Field—a real burn unit—but few would survive until then. The few who did would wish they'd died. These burns were like nothing else on earth. The gel-fueled firebomb mixture stuck to its target and didn't stop burning until nothing was left.

Frankie moved from bed to bed, applying topical ointments and debriding dead tissue, but there was so little she could do here to help them heal, and nothing to ease their tremendous pain.

By 1000 hours, she was exhausted, and the burn victims were still arriving. She could hear Margie and Dr. Morse and some medics talking to each other, rolling carts, yelling for ointment.

The next bed held a woman—impossible to tell if she was young or old; her body was burned from head to toe. The black, charred flesh still smoked.

Beside her, tucked protectively against her body, was a baby.

Frankie stopped. For a split second, the horror overwhelmed her. She had to take a deep, steadying breath.

The infant was still alive.

"Dear God," Frankie said under her breath. How could that be?

With care, she picked up the infant, who couldn't be much older than three months. "Hey, little one," Frankie said, her voice breaking. Thin white ribs shone through the gaping wounds and burns on her chest.

She found a chair and sat down. The OR was a cacophony of screaming, moaning, crying casualties, and shouting medics and nurses and doctors. The sound of wheels rolling on concrete, of new gloves being snapped on. But for a moment, Frankie heard nothing except this one infant's struggle to breathe.

"I'm so sorry, baby," Frankie said.

The baby drew in an uneven breath and exhaled slowly and then went still.

Frankie held the dead baby, overwhelmed by this loss, unable to move, unable to stand.

No one would ever know who this child was or even that she had lived and died. How could this be done, even in the name of war?

"McGrath! I need you."

It was Dr. Morse.

Ignoring him and the melee of the OR, she carried the infant to the morgue, where body bags lay stacked along the walls.

Private Juan Martinez, a kid from Chula Vista who'd been drafted right out of high school, stood in the center of the morgue. He looked as exhausted as she felt. "Rough night," he said.

She glanced down at the baby in her arms. "And now this."

Martinez stared down at the baby. "Jesus," he said softly, moving closer. He placed a black-gloved hand on the baby's body, covering the entire ruined rib cage. "He will hold you in heaven."

Frankie was surprised to hear that bit of faith from a man who stood in the morgue all day, cataloging the dead, zipping up body bags. Then again, maybe you couldn't do this job otherwise.

Martinez found a cardboard box and an old T-shirt. Frankie wrapped the baby in the soft khaki cotton and laid her in the box.

She and Martinez stood there for a moment, the box and the baby between them.

Neither spoke.

Then Frankie left the morgue. As she shut the door, she heard the incoming choppers and felt something ugly take root inside of her: a dark anger. She was so tired of pulling green canvas over young men's faces, and now this baby.

With a sigh, she headed back to the OR, grabbed a gown, and went back to work.

"Get out of here, McGrath," Dr. Morse said at 0200. "You're dead on your feet."

"We all are," she said. The OR was so full of burn victims that many lay three to a bed.

"Yeah, but you look it."

"Har har. A beauty joke. Perfect."

He touched her shoulder, gave it a squeeze. "Go. If you don't, I will."

Frankie pulled off her blue surgical cap. "Thanks, Doc. My tank really does feel empty."

"Get some sleep."

She looked around. "After this?"

He gave her a look of commiseration. They both knew sleep was unlikely. There wasn't enough pot or alcohol on-site to make her forget that baby dying in her arms.

She thanked Doc and headed for her hooch. As she passed the new admin building, she ducked in, found Talkback on the radio.

"Hey, Talkback, could I make a MARS call? Short, I promise."

He glanced left to right, looking for a superior who might disagree. The Military Auxiliary Radio System phones were not for personal use. "Short."

She settled into a chair and picked up the handset. "Call to Vung Tau HAL-3. Lieutenant Commander Joseph Ryerson Walsh. Over."

Frankie tapped her foot impatiently, listening to static.

"Who is calling? Over."

"Lieutenant McGrath. Seventy-First Evac. Over."

"Emergency, ma'am? Over."

"Yes. Emergency. Over."

"Hold. Over."

Frankie knew she shouldn't be doing this, calling him and saying it was an emergency. But they hadn't seen each other in more than a month, and she needed him.

"Frankie?" Rye's voice broke through the static. "Are you okay, over?"

"Hey," she said, her voice quaking. "Over."

"What happened? Over."

"Napalm. Over."

In the staticky silence, she knew they were both seeing the suffering of tonight.

"Sorry I woke you. I just needed to hear your voice. Over," she said.

"I get it, babe. I'm sorry. Over."

"I miss you. Over."

"Hang tough. Over."

"Copy that. Over and out." She hung up. "Thanks, Talkback."

She headed back to her hooch. The Park was empty now, but she knew that wouldn't last. When tonight's push was over, folks would need to unwind. A faint beat of music pulsed through the open door. She almost recognized the song, but not quite. Mostly, she heard the beat of American music, the soundtrack of home.

She took a quick shower, then passed a soldier tossing things into a burn barrel that gave off the stench of charred flesh and human excrement.

In her hooch, she peeled out of her fatigues, shoved them in the laundry bag hanging off the end of her cot. Laundering them wouldn't remove the blood, but it would soften the smell. She climbed into bed. Knowing she wouldn't sleep, she picked up her latest letter to Ethel and started to add to it.

Rough night in the OR. Could have used someone with your kick-ass skills, but Margie has really come into her own, and that young doc—Morse—is getting good.

   There was a baby, tonight.

   Napalm

She put down her pen, unable to write about it. She set the letter aside. Did Ethel need to read this? Turning off the lights, she stretched out, closed her eyes.

She was still awake at 0400 when Margie came home and climbed into bed.

She was still awake at 0524, listening to her hooch mate's snoring, when she heard the whine of a helicopter nearing the hospital.

Only one.

Releasing a breath, she closed her eyes again. *Please, God, let me sleep.*

A knock at the door surprised her.

She sat up.

The door opened.

Rye moved into the small hooch, seeming to take up a lot of space. Stepping carefully so as not to waken Margie, he moved to the cot, sat down, and took off his boots.

Frankie still hadn't spoken. She was afraid that if she did, she'd cry.

He took her in his arms and held her. They barely fit together on the narrow cot. She snuggled up against him, kissed his neck.

"I got here as soon as I could," he said.

She started to answer, but before she could speak, she was asleep.

───

For once, the Seventy-First was quiet. On this hot, dry early November day, not long after Nixon won the election back home, and eight months into her second tour, Frankie sat in a beach chair in the Park, wearing shorts and a T-shirt and her worn huarache sandals. A hot breeze ruffled the drying banana leaves. After a long, wet, muddy monsoon season, the dry air and dust were a welcome relief. At least she didn't smell like mildew anymore. She kept her boonie hat pulled low to shield her eyes from the sun and wore a pair of big round sunglasses. A warm TaB sat on the ground beside her. Behind her, "I Heard It

Through the Grapevine" blasted through the speakers at the tiki bar. She could hear people talking, laughing, singing along. It had been a particularly tough week, but at this moment in the late afternoon, while a bright sun shone down on them without baking them into submission, the Seventy-First wasn't a bad place to be.

Men played volleyball on the flat red pad of dirt. The Red Cross Donut Dollies were handing out mail and snacks from a cart. Frankie had also brought some letters to reread, while she ate the Pretzel Stix Ethel had sent in her latest care package. Barb and Ethel had both continued to write and send goodies every month. Margie sat in a chair beside Frankie, her hair in pink curlers, reading *Rosemary's Baby*.

Frankie took a drink of her warm TaB, then leaned back and closed her eyes.

"Ma'am?" someone said a few moments later.

Frankie sat up. The Park was empty; no men playing volleyball, no Donut Dollies. Had she actually fallen asleep?

The new radio operator—she couldn't remember the kid's name—stood there. "There's an emergency in the mess hall, ma'am. Dr. Morse needs you."

Frankie got up and followed the kid to the mess hall.

At the closed door, he stopped, allowed her to go in first.

Frankie opened the door and stepped into the mess. A banner hung over the bulletin board wall: CONGRATS 1ST LIEUTENANT MCGRATH!

"Congratulations!"

It took Frankie a second to process. No heart attack. No emergency. A party.

For her.

Major Goldstein from the Thirty-Sixth stepped forward, with Captain Miniver beside her. "This promotion is late in coming, but nothing happens on time in the Army," Major Goldstein said. "We all know that. Congratulations, Frankie. You've come a long way, baby."

Captain Miniver added, "Thank you for staying. There are men back home because of it."

"Toast! Toast!" someone yelled.

Ryan Dardis, the new surgeon they called Hollywood because of his good looks, stepped forward with a bottle of gin. "We know how much you love your gin, McGrath. What we wanted to make sure is that you know how much we dig you, too. Even though you can't dance for shit, and your dancing makes your singing look good." He held up a bottle of gin and there was a roar of approval.

Someone cranked up the music. Behind her, the doors banged open.

Frankie felt herself being picked up, spun around.

"Sorry I'm late, babe." Rye grinned, tilted back his black Seawolves cap. "Traffic was a bitch."

The music changed to "Born to Be Wild," and people started pushing chairs aside.

Frankie grabbed Rye's hand and pulled him onto the makeshift dance floor.

"You sure you want to dance with me in public?" he teased.

"I'm the one with two left feet," she said, smiling up at him.

Sometime later, Margie found them on the dance floor and hip-bumped Frankie. Her face was flushed and dewy from dancing. "I'm going to bunk with Helen tonight," she said breathlessly. "Or maybe with Jeff. He's looking better every second."

"Thanks, Margie," Frankie said.

Rye took Frankie by the hand and led her out of the party, which was in such full, chaotic swing that no one noticed them leave. They hadn't seen each other in almost a month.

"I really needed this," Frankie said, leaning against him as they walked through the compound.

He put an arm around her. "I've missed you, too. Another orphanage was bombed last week. St. Anne's in Saigon."

Frankie nodded. "I heard rumors of something bad up near My Lai, too," she said.

"There are a lot of bad stories coming through."

Outside her hooch, she turned to him, looked up into his eyes, saw his sadness; it was the same look she had seen in her own eyes. The last thing she wanted to talk about was the war. "Love me," she whispered, pressing up onto her toes.

The kiss was everything: coming home, taking flight, a dream for tomorrow.

When he drew back, she saw something in his eyes that frightened her. Then he said, "I'm afraid I'll love you till I die, Frankie."

Love.

How long had she wanted to hear that word from him? It felt like forever, because time in Vietnam moved in strange ways—sometimes too fast, sometimes too slow. "I love you, too, Rye."

It wasn't until hours later, when they lay pressed together on her narrow cot, exhausted by lovemaking, that Frankie realized what he'd said and how he'd said it—*I'm afraid I'll love you till I die*—and the promise planted a small and terrible seed in her heart.

I'm afraid.

Till I die.

They were the wrong words for wartime, a gauntlet thrown to an uncaring God.

She wanted to have the moment to do over, to make him say *I love you* in a different way.

Eighteen

On her last day in-country, March 14, 1969, Frankie woke up well before dawn, listening to Margie's quiet snores.

She turned on the light beside her bed, reached past the hot plate, picked up the photograph of her and Finley at Disneyland, and stared down at it, thinking of their youth.

Hey, Fin. I'm going home.

She'd joined the Army to find her brother and found herself instead; in war, she'd found out who she really was and who she wanted to be, and as tired as she was of all the death and destruction, she was also more than a little afraid to go home. What would life look like stateside?

She got out of her cot and pulled her footlocker out from underneath. Lifting the lid, she stared down at the belongings she'd be sending home: mementos she'd been given by soldiers, a leather-and-bead bracelet, a small gold elephant charm "for luck," some silk she'd bought in Saigon, a Kelly clamp and some rubber tubing, the gifts for her friends and family, and her treasured Vietnam photographs, both those she'd taken and others she'd been given, like the one of her and Barb and Ethel, dancing in shorts and T-shirts at the O Club, the one Barb had left her of the three of them standing together, one of Jamie giving her a bright smile and a thumbs-up in front of a deuce and a half, and another of her and Rye. There were at least a dozen photographs of her with soldiers who'd come through her OR. The lucky ones for whom she'd waved goodbye and posed for a picture.

Back in the real world, the so-called Summer of Love had come and gone; in its wake, the protests were getting louder, longer, angrier. Even here, there was anger about the war. Soldiers had begun to draw peace symbols on their helmets, in violation of Army regulations.

At 0600 hours, she packed up her duffel and travel bags and wrote Margie a goodbye note that said in part, *I know you'll wish I'd wakened you for a goodbye. It won't be long before you'll know how hard it is. We are professionals at goodbye, and still it hurts. Stay tough. Thanks for sending my footlocker home for me.*

She dressed in her Class As, complete with pantyhose and polished black pumps. She didn't have a full-length mirror, but she imagined she looked nothing like the wide-eyed girl who'd first landed in-country two years ago. And her uniform smelled like mildew.

When she opened her hooch door, she found Rye leaning against a pole, smoking a cigarette.

"Ready?" he said, taking the duffel from her, swinging the big, awkward bag easily over his shoulder.

"Not really."

They walked through the surprisingly quiet camp, boarded the Huey, and lifted up into the sky.

In Saigon, at the airport, she thanked the pilot, checked her duffel, and let Rye take her to the Freedom Bird that would take her home.

A steady stream of soldiers walked past her on the tarmac at Tan Son Nhut, climbed up the movable stairs, and ducked into the large Braniff jet. They were a quiet bunch; there was no joking or laughing. Not yet, not while they were still in-country.

"Twenty-seven days until you leave, too," Frankie said, looking up at him. She had to raise her voice to be heard above the rumble of the engines.

Twenty-seven days. An eternity in wartime.

No fear, McGrath.

A jeep rolled past them, full of soldiers with guns, looking for snipers.

More gunfire nearby. *Pop-pop-pop.* In the distance, a loud explosion. Something burst into flames on one of the runways.

Rye stared down at her. "Frankie . . . I don't know how to tell you . . . I . . . won't—"

"I know," she said, touching his rough, unshaven face. "I love you, too."

He let out a breath, gazed down at her. "God, I'll miss you."

He pulled her into a tight embrace, held her hard against him, and kissed her goodbye. She clung to him for as long as she dared, and then slowly pulled away.

Neither said goodbye. The word carried more than a hint of bad luck.

She straightened her shoulders and forced herself to walk away from him. At the top of the steps, she finally turned back.

Alone, he stood tall and straight in his worn fatigues, with a brimmed Seawolves cap pulled down low on his forehead. From here, he looked solid and steady, the perfect sailor, but she saw the clenched line of his jaw. He raised a single hand, fingers splayed, and held it there, then pressed it to his heart.

Frankie nodded, waved back one last time, and entered the jet. Most of the seats were already filled with men who kept glancing back at the door, as if Charlie might come breaking through any second, rifles drawn. They all knew they weren't safe in the air until they were out of Vietnamese airspace.

Frankie found a seat on the starboard side, put her travel bag in the overhead bin, and sat at the window, staring out at Rye. She pressed her hand to the glass.

She heard the aircraft door close, clank shut. Moments later, the jet rolled down the runway, bumping over the bomb-pocked ground, and slowly lifted off.

Frankie stared out the window, saw clouds as they flew over the war-torn land, toward the safety of home.

The passengers applauded; someone shouted, "We're outta there!"

Frankie was surprised to feel a version of sorrow.

As bad as it had been in 'Nam, as frightened and angry and betrayed as she'd often felt by her government and the war, she'd also felt alive. Competent and important. A woman who made a difference in the world.

This place would forever hold a piece of her heart. Here, she had found her place in the world, and she was afraid that "home" was no longer the place she wanted it to be.

Thirty-four hours later, after a six-hour layover at Travis Air Force Base in Northern California, Frankie stared out the oval window at the busy runways of Los Angeles International Airport.

Full daylight. A sun so bright it hurt one's eyes. A blue and cloudless sky.

California.

The Golden State.

Home.

She had intended to call her parents from Travis, but when she'd finally made it to her turn in the pay phone line, she had turned away. She didn't really know why.

The gate area at LAX was crowded. She saw military personnel sleeping on benches, sprawled on the dirty floor, using their duffel bags as pillows. Passing time on their way home. It didn't seem right: Men who'd been shot at, and in some cases been patched up and sent back into harm's way, sleeping on the floor between flights. The military paid your way to a base airport; once there, you had to buy your own ticket home. A real thank-you for serving your country.

As she neared baggage claim, she saw a group of protesters holding signs: END THE WAR BEFORE IT ENDS YOU! DROP ACID, NOT BOMBS! GET OUT OF VIETNAM NOW! BOMBING FOR PEACE IS LIKE SCREWING FOR VIRGINITY!

They saw her, coming their way in her skirted Army uniform, and thrust their signs at her, as if to convince her.

Someone spat at her.

"Nazi bitch," one of the protesters yelled.

Frankie stumbled to a halt in shock. "What the—"

A pair of Marines appeared and flanked Frankie, one on each side of her.

"Don't listen to those assholes," one of them said. Bookending her, they made their way to the carousel. "We got nothing to be ashamed of."

Frankie didn't understand. Why would someone spit at her?

"Go back to Vietnam!" someone yelled. "We don't want you baby killers here."

Baby killers?

Frankie's duffel bag thumped onto the carousel. She started to reach for it, but one of the Marines beat her to it. "I'll get that for you, Lieutenant."

"Let the bitch get her own bag," someone yelled. Others laughed.

"Thank you," Frankie said to the Marine. "I mean . . . I heard about the protests, but this?"

She looked at the people crowded around the carousel, men in suits and women in dresses, who'd said nothing to help her. Did they think it was okay to spit at an Army nurse coming home from war? She expected it from hippies and protesters, but from ordinary people?

"Ain't no World War Two victory parade," one of the Marines said.

"Guess losing a war isn't something people cheer for," said the other.

Frankie looked at the two men, saw the ghosts that lived behind their eyes. The ghosts that lived in her, too. "We're home," she said, needing to believe that was what mattered.

She saw that they needed to believe it, too.

Outside, she thanked the Marines for their help and looked for a cab. Alone out here, she saw the way people stared at her. First there was a widening of the eyes—surprise at seeing a woman in uniform—and then the narrowing of mistrust or outright disgust. A few looked right through her, as if she weren't there. She considered changing her clothes, but decided against it.

Screw them. She wasn't going to let them shame her.

At the curb, she put out one arm to hail a cab.

The nearest yellow taxi veered out of the middle lane, headed toward her, and slowed. She stepped off the curb and the cabbie yelled something and flipped her the bird and sped away, stopping not far away for a man in a suit.

One after another, taxis slowed for her just enough to get her hopes up and then sped away.

Finally, she gave up, bought a bus ticket, and ignored the veiled looks thrown her way as she lugged her heavy bags onto the bus.

What was wrong with the world?

It took four hours and three bus changes for her to reach Coronado Island. By then, she had been spat on four times, flipped off more times than she could count, and become used to—or at least immune to—the way people looked at her. No one had offered to help her carry her heavy duffel bag.

At the ferry terminal on Coronado, she was finally able to hail a cab. A dour-looking driver didn't make eye contact, but picked her up and stopped outside the gate at her house, for which she was extremely grateful.

She hauled her heavy duffel out of the vehicle and dropped it on the sidewalk and stood there, soaking in the sense of coming home. The air smelled of the sea, of lemons and oranges, of her childhood.

She looked over at the mighty Pacific Ocean. She could hear the surf from here; the familiar sound soothed her anxiety. A group of kids on bicycles, with playing cards in the spokes, sped past her, laughing. She couldn't help thinking of Finley, of the forts they'd once built among the eucalyptus, of the sandcastles they'd built, of the hours spent on bicycles. Come nightfall, the porch lights would start coming on up and down the street—beacons used by mothers to guide their children home for dinner.

A pair of Navy jets screamed overhead. She couldn't help wondering if they were piloted by men who would soon be flying combat missions on the other side of the world.

She opened the gate and stared at the home she'd grown up in, feeling a rush of emotion. She couldn't wait to be welcomed home at last, to be admired for her service instead of reviled.

How often had she dreamed of this moment, of safety and love and comfort, of hot baths and fresh coffee and long, slow walks along the beach without an armed guard standing by?

She stepped into the beautifully manicured backyard, drinking it all in: the whispering of the oak leaves, the scent of chlorine and ripening lemons, the soft clatter of her mother's wind chimes.

Struggling with her heavy duffel and her overnight bag, she walked around the pool and up to the glass-paned doors. Opening them, she stepped back in time. For a second, she was a girl again, following her wild brother wherever he went.

Home.

She dropped her duffel bag on the polished hardwood floor. "Hey, you guys!" she said at the same time her father came around the corner, dressed in a lime-green turtleneck with checkered slacks, holding a folded newspaper. His hair was a little longer, as were his sideburns, which held a few strands of gray.

At the sight of her, he stopped, frowned briefly. "Frankie. Did we know you were coming home?"

She couldn't hold back a smile. "I wanted to surprise you."

He moved forward woodenly, confusion on his face. She knew her father didn't like surprises; he liked to always be in control. He gave her a brief, hard hug.

He released her so quickly that Frankie stumbled back. "I . . . should have called," she said.

"No," he said, shook his head. "Of course not. We are glad you're home."

Frankie realized suddenly what she looked like after so many hours of travel—hair a mess, poorly cut, no makeup on, uniform wrinkled. No wonder her dad was frowning. She reached into her purse and pulled out her favorite picture of her and Ethel and Barb, arms around each other, standing in front of the O Club. "I brought this one just for you."

He glanced at the photograph. "Oh."

"For the heroes' wall," she said.

Mom came around the corner, dressed in bright red ankle pants and a white top, her hair covered by a silk scarf. "Frances!"

She rushed forward and pulled Frankie into a fierce hug. "My girl," she said, easing back, touching Frankie's face. "Why didn't you call?"

"She wanted to surprise us," Dad said. "Apparently it wasn't enough of a surprise when she joined the Army. I'm sorry, but I have a meeting."

Frankie watched her father leave the house, heard the door shut behind her. It unsettled her, his leaving so abruptly.

"Don't take it to heart," Mom said lightly. "Ever since Finley's . . . passing, and your leaving, he isn't himself."

"Oh," Frankie said. Had her mother just equated her war service to her brother's death?

"Frances, I . . ." Mom's hand slid down Frankie's arm, as if maybe she couldn't quite let her daughter go, couldn't quite believe that she was here again. "I've missed you so."

"Me, too," Frankie said.

"You must be exhausted," Mom said.

"I am."

"Why don't you take a nice, hot bath and perhaps a nap?"

Frankie nodded, confused; she felt battered by hours of travel and the way she'd been treated by strangers. And now by her parents. What was wrong?

She left her mother in the living room and headed for her childhood bedroom, with its canopy bed and pink ruffles. Most kids had posters in their rooms, but Mom hadn't allowed tacks to be stuck into her expensive wallpaper, so Frankie had framed art on her walls. A row of old stuffed animals sat along the top of her bookshelf. A pink ballerina jewelry box on the bedside table held junior and high school trinkets, probably a stack of senior pictures and prom memorabilia. You knew what was expected of a girl who slept in a room like this.

Only Frankie wasn't that girl anymore.

At the end of the bed stood a hope chest, which was filled with perfectly folded and pressed tablecloths and Italian linens, and embroidered sheets. Mom had started filling this chest when Frankie was eight years old. Every birthday and Christmas, Frankie had received something for her hope chest. The message then—and now—was clear: marriage made a woman whole and happy.

Again. It was for the girl who'd left for Vietnam, not for the woman who'd come home, whoever that woman turned out to be.

Frankie peeled out of her uniform and left it in a heap on the floor.

Crawling between the soft, lavender-scented sheets, she lay her head on the silk-cased pillow.

She shouldn't have surprised her parents. She'd caught them off guard.

Tomorrow would be better.

Nineteen

The smell of burning flesh. Someone is screaming.

I run forward, crying for help, trying to see through the smoke.

There's a baby in my arms, burning, her skin blackens and falls away. I am holding a pile of bones . . .

Choppers overhead. Incoming.

A scream. Mine? The red alert siren blares. Something explodes near my head.

I throw myself out of my cot, hit the floor, crawl for my flak jacket and helmet.

Quiet.

Frankie came out of the nightmare slowly, realized she was on the floor, in her bedroom.

Curling into a ball on the rug, she tried to go back to sleep.

———

The next time Frankie awoke, it was 2115 hours and the house was dark. She heard the faint ticking of her bedside clock. She had no idea how long she'd slept. A day? Two?

She got dressed and wandered through the house. At her father's office, she stared at the pictures on the heroes' wall, saw Finley smiling at her on his way to war.

Another world. Now no one welcomed you home, let alone celebrated your leaving. Suddenly she felt suffocated by the scent of lemon furniture polish and expectation. She'd been raised to be a lady, always, serene and calm, smiling, but that world, and those lessons, felt far, far away.

Outside, a full moon shone down on the waves. She felt drawn to the beach, as always, the stretch of sand that had been her playground as a child.

"Hey, Fin," she said, sitting close to the waterline. An occasional spray of water hit her cheek, felt like tears.

She closed her eyes. *Just breathe, McGrath.*

Gradually, the tightening in her chest eased. Much later, she went back to her frilly pink room and climbed into bed. In the glow of her bedside lamp, she opened her nightstand drawer and pulled out a piece of stationery with her full name written in elegant script across the top.

March 17

Dear Barb,

I'm home. No one told me how tough it was, this re-entry. Why didn't you warn me? People spat at me at the airport, called me a baby killer. What the hell? My parents haven't even asked about Vietnam. Mom acts as if I am home from band camp and my dad has barely said a word to me. Honest to God.

It's weird.

Tell me I'll be okay, will you?

And how about you? I've been thinking about you, sending good thoughts to you about your brother. Grief sucks.

Being home makes me miss Fin all over again. It's like staring down at a puzzle with one piece missing; it ruins the whole thing.

Now I'm back to bed. I'm more than tired. Too many hours of travel and despair and jet lag, I guess.

Love you, sis.
Stay cool,
F

Then she stripped down to her bra and underwear and climbed back into bed.

———

"Wake up, Frances."

Frankie opened her eyes slowly, feeling grit on her eyeballs.

She sat up, feeling bruised. Once again, she was on the floor.

"I'll meet you in the kitchen," Mom said, looking worriedly at Frankie before she turned and walked away.

"Okay," Frankie said, tasting something foul in her mouth. When had she last brushed her teeth?

She limped to her closet (how had she twisted her ankle?), pushed past her old pogo stick and shoved aside a hula hoop, and then slipped into her pink chenille robe and left the bedroom. Why was everything about her past so damned pink?

"Finally," Mom said from the kitchen table, smiling.

Frankie went to the coffeepot, poured herself a cup, and sat down at the table across from her mother.

"Where's Dad?"

"You look awful, Frances."

"I'm having nightmares."

"I've made reservations for lunch at the club. I thought it would feel good to get back to real life. Just us girls."

Frankie sipped her coffee, savoring the bitter, rich taste of it. Nightmare images clung like cobwebs to her mind. "Is that what you think the club is, real life?"

Mom frowned. "What's wrong with you?"

"People spat at me at the airport," Frankie said, surprised at the way her voice broke. "Called me a baby killer."

Mom's mouth opened in surprise, then slowly closed. "I've called Paul and made you an appointment for this morning. A nice new haircut always brightens my mood."

"Sure, Mom. I know how much appearances matter to you. Where's Dad?" she asked again.

"I bought you some new clothes. They're in your closet."

"Mom? You didn't answer me about Dad."

"Let me catch my breath, Frances, will you? A little warning that you were coming home would have helped."

"You've known the date for a year, Mom."

"You still should have called. Go take a shower and get dressed. You know I abhor being late."

Nodding, Frankie rose, took her coffee with her, and walked back to her bedroom. There she found the new clothes that Mom had bought.

Bell-bottom pants and plaid separates and tunic tops. All a size too big. None of it felt right. So she put on the red dress she'd bought on Kauai, and pantyhose, and sandals. So what if it was March and she was dressed for summer? The dress comforted her, reminded her that Rye was coming home to her in twenty-three days.

She found her mother waiting impatiently at the front door. At Frankie's appearance, one plucked eyebrow arched. As Frankie neared, Mom's nostrils flared.

"Yeah. The dress smells mildewed. I know."

Mom managed a smile. "Let's go."

Fifteen minutes later, she and her mother were at the island beauty salon, being fussed over by Paul. "Who has been cutting your hair, darling?" he said.

"Me," Frankie said. "Or a girlfriend."

"With a machete, it looks like."

Frankie smiled. "Pretty much. I just got home from Vietnam."

The distaste on Paul's face was unmistakable. He actually took a step back. "I think I can pull off a chin-length, sideswept bob. Okay?"

That look from him hurt, but she should have been ready for it. "Sure. Whatever."

Paul set to work, washing, combing, cutting, styling. When he began to tease the back of her hair, Frankie stopped him, said sharply, "None of that girlie shit for me, Paul."

She heard her mother's sharp intake of breath. "Language, Frances. You're not a longshoreman."

When Paul finished, Frankie stood up and looked at herself in the mirror. He'd made her black hair glossy again, teased it up in back, and cut it in a precise line along her jaw. Long bangs swept to one side. "It's nice," she said. "Thanks."

He nodded crisply and walked away.

At the Coronado Golf and Tennis Club, a uniformed Black attendant met the Cadillac, and opened Frankie's door. She stepped out, felt a strange sensation of collision. How could this cool, white, moneyed world exist in a bubble, while in Vietnam a war was raging, and here at home, people were protesting the violence and fighting for fundamental civil rights?

The main clubhouse was designed like an old-fashioned living room, centered around a stone fireplace. Here and there, groups of men were seated, drinking and smoking. Cocktail lunches were the norm here for the working men. A group of women wreathed in cigarette smoke played bridge in a room off to the right.

The waitress led them to her parents' favorite table, which overlooked the pool. White tablecloths, silver flatware, bone china plates, and a centerpiece of fragrant flowers.

Frankie sat down.

"How lovely to be out with my girl for lunch," Mom said, taking out her silver cigarette case, extracting a slim cigarette, lighting it up.

When the waitress appeared, Mom ordered two Bloody Marys.

"Kind of early, isn't it, Mom?"

"You, too, Frances?"

"What do you mean?"

"Your father keeps remarking upon my drinking. When he's home, that is."

Before Frankie could formulate a rejoinder, a man appeared at their table. An elderly man with walrus jowls and a gray military flattop, wearing a brown suit with a thin tie. "Bette," he said, smiling jovially. "How nice to see you out and about. My Millicent says you are favored to win the tournament again this year."

Mom smiled. "Millicent is too kind. Frances, you remember Dr. Brenner?"

"This can't be Frances, can it? Home from Florence already?"

"Florence?" Frankie was about to say more when she heard a loud crash.

Incoming.

She dove for the floor.

"Frankie? Frankie?"

What the hell?

The world righted. She wasn't in 'Nam. She was in the country club dining room, sprawled on the floor beside the table like a fool. Not far away, a waitress was kneeling on the floor, picking up broken glass.

Dr. Brenner took hold of her hand and helped her to her feet.

"Frankie?" Mom said, frowning. "Who falls out of a chair?"

Frankie didn't know what had just happened. The memory had felt so *real*. "I . . . don't . . ." She felt clammy, shaky. She pushed her hair out of her face, felt the sweat on her forehead. It took effort to smile. "I'm sorry. I just got home from Vietnam and . . ." And what?

Dr. Brenner let go of her hand. "There are no women in Vietnam, dear."

"There are, sir. I did two tours."

"Your father said you were studying abroad."

"*What?*" Frankie turned to her mother. "Are you fucking kidding me?"

Dr. Brenner left like a shot at the curse word.

Mom looked around to see if they were being observed. "Sit down, Frances."

"You lied about where I was?"

"Your father thought—"

"He was *ashamed* of me? Ashamed of my service, after all those stories, all that hero talk?"

"Sit down, Frances. You're making a scene."

"Am I *embarrassing* you?" she said. "And you think this is a scene? No, Mom. A scene is when a soldier comes in off the battlefield holding his own foot. It's when—"

"*Frances Grace*—"

Tears scalded Frankie's eyes. She ran out of the club, heard the whispers that would grow into rumors about "the McGrath girl," and she would have laughed if it didn't hurt so much.

Down the street, a stitch burning in her side, she hailed a cab.

It was easy now, just a hand in the air. No uniform to make people hate her.

The taxi pulled up alongside her, the driver rolled down the window. "Where to?"

Where to?

It felt as if there were nothing left for her here, in this place she'd always loved.

But where else?

She said, "Ocean Boulevard," with a sigh, and wiped her eyes.

She had nowhere else to go.

Once there, she pulled out a piece of the blue stationery. In a hand that wouldn't stop shaking, she wrote to Rye, tried to ease her hurt by sharing it.

March 22, 1969

My love,

I miss you so much I can't stand it. I'm counting the days until your return.

Things at home are terrible. I don't know what to do. My parents lied about my service in Vietnam. That's how ashamed they are of me. It makes me mad in a way I've never felt before. Furious. Pissed off. Today I caused a scene at the country club. I can't quite control this new fury that is eating me up. Maybe I just need sleep . . .

Everything is so weird and upside down, I haven't even told my parents about you. I'm not sure they'd care.

I can't wait for you to come home.

I love you,

F

———

Sometime later, Frankie woke up sprawled on her bedroom floor with a pounding headache and a sore throat. Probably because she had screamed in her sleep.

She got to her feet, held herself together by sheer force of will. Nightmares had left her shaken, and she was still angry at her parents' betrayal. The room was dark, no lights on to banish the night. How long had she slept?

In the hallway, decorated in rich wood and gleaming brass, she smelled cigarette smoke, lemon furniture polish, and a hint of Shalimar perfume.

Mom was in the living room, still dressed for the club, seated in a chair by the cold fireplace, sipping a martini, reading a *Life* magazine. A pair of table lamps illuminated the room; a fire in the fireplace sent out waves of heat.

Dad stood by the fire, dressed in a suit and tie, holding a drink and a lit cigarette. At the sight of Frankie in her robe, he frowned. No doubt she was not looking her best.

"Yeah. It's me, Dad, back from studying abroad in Florence. The food wasn't nearly as good as I expected," Frankie said, unable to keep the hurt out of her voice.

"No one likes a smart aleck, Frankie," he said.

She went to the bar, poured herself a large gin on the rocks, and took a seat by her mother.

The tension in the room felt heavy; she saw the wary, worried look in her mother's eyes.

Frankie reached over for one of her mother's cigarettes and lit up.

"When did you start to smoke?" Mom asked.

"I think it was after a red alert." At her mother's blank look, she added, "Rocket attack on the hospital. The explosions were deafening. Terrifying. Or maybe after a push in the hospital where men came in blown to shit. Who knows? One minute I wasn't a smoker, the next minute I was. It helped with the shaking in my hands."

"I see," her mother said tightly.

"No, you don't," Frankie said, desperate suddenly to explain. If they would just listen, everything might fall into place. "At the Thirty-Sixth—that's the evac hospital where I was assigned—my first shift in-country was a MASCAL—mass casualty—and, shit, was I a disaster," Frankie said. They were staring at her, listening. Thank God. "This soldier came in on a litter, all blown to shit. He'd stepped on a Bouncing Betty and his legs were gone. Just gone. I had no—"

"Enough." Dad slammed down his drink on the bar. He'd used such force the glass could have cracked. "No one wants to hear these stories, Frankie. Sweet God. Legs blown off."

"And the language," Mom said. "Cursing like a sailor. I couldn't believe the language you used at the club. And in front of Dr. Brenner. I had to call Millicent and apologize on your behalf."

"Apologize on my behalf?" Frankie said. "How can you not care about my war experience?"

"It's over, Frances," Mom said smoothly.

Calm down, Frankie. But she couldn't do it. Her heart was pounding and she felt a surge of fury so overwhelming she wanted to hit something.

For a moment she held back, but the effort it took felt toxic, as if the stories she wanted to share might turn to poison inside of her. She couldn't be here, pretending nothing had changed, that she'd been in Florence for two years instead of holding men's body parts together in her bare hands. She felt choked by her need to say, *I was there and this is how it was.* For them to welcome her home and say they were proud of her.

Frankie stood up abruptly. "I can't believe you're ashamed of me."

"I have no idea who you are anymore," Dad said.

"You don't want to know," Frankie said. "You think it means nothing when a woman, a nurse, goes to war. You think it's glorious that your son goes to war and embarrassing when your daughter does."

Her mother stood up, holding a now-empty martini glass, a little unsteady on her feet, tears in her eyes. "Frances, please," she said. "Connor. You both—"

"Shut up and drink," Dad said in almost a snarl.

Frankie saw how her mother sagged at that.

Had it always been like this? Had Mom always been a shadow woman, held together by vodka and hair spray? Had her dad always been this angry man who thought he had the right to dictate every action and emotion in this house?

Or had it been losing Finley that ruined them?

Frankie didn't know. She hadn't lived with them these past two years, and truthfully, she'd grieved alone and then she'd gone to Vietnam and learned a whole new kind of loss.

Frankie had to get out of here before she said something terrible.

She left them standing there, staring at her as if she were an intruder, and walked out of the house; she slammed the door shut behind her. It wasn't like her, that burst of fury and the wanting to display it, but she couldn't stop it. Out on the beach, with night darkening around her, she dropped to her knees, wanting to be calmed by the sound of the surf.

But it made her think of Vietnam, of Finley and Jamie and the fallen.

She screamed until she was hoarse. And the anger inside of her grew.

March 24, 1969

Dear Rye,
This time at home has been a shit show. Even as I write those words, I think, that isn't me, but it is me now.

I'm angry all of the time. And hurt. My parents hardly speak to me and rarely to each other. They don't want to hear anything about Vietnam.

That's not even the worst of it. I have these terrible nightmares of the war. I wake up feeling like I've been beaten up.

It's because you're not in bed with me. I could sleep in your arms. Dreaming of it, of you coming back, is holding me together.

I'm counting the days until you are here. With me. I think of us.
You. A house. In the country, maybe. I want to have horses, a dog.
A garden.

Things aren't as easy as I thought, coming home. But it doesn't
matter. All that matters is us.

I love you.

F

———

On a cool evening, two weeks after her homecoming, Frankie sat in a chair on the patio, her feet tucked up underneath her, a blanket wrapped around her shoulders. In her tattered Army-green T-shirt and baggy shorts, she smelled of mildew and mold and dust, but it was vaguely comforting. She sipped an ice-cold martini and glanced idly around.

She was home, in her own backyard, where soon the jacaranda tree would burst into full purple bloom, and the gardeners would spend hours raking up the fallen flowers. It was like a time capsule, this yard, where nothing ever changed. The outside world could be breaking apart, but inside these walls, all was calm, quiet, cocktails. Maybe that was why people built walls: to look away, to ignore anything they didn't want to see.

In the last few days, the family had fallen into an uneasy détente in which no one talked about the war. Frankie hated every moment of it, felt stripped bare by her parents' shame, but it wouldn't be for much longer. She just had to make it until Rye came home. She hadn't told them about Rye or their love affair; she hadn't talked to them about anything, really. Just the weather and food and the garden. Neutral topics, all. It was the only way to hold herself together in their presence.

"I'll call it the Shores, I think," Dad said, exhaling smoke as he poured himself a Manhattan. "Or maybe the Cliffs."

Frankie listened to her dad's business talk and pretended to be interested.

She was trying her best to be the girl they'd raised, the girl they
expected. She didn't fidget, didn't say much, never mentioned the war.
Played nice. They didn't seem bothered in the least by her silence.

It felt vaguely dangerous, this enforced calm. As if each word she
swallowed contained a venom that might someday kill her.

She focused on her martini. Her second. Thinking she would have
killed for this ice-cold drink in-country.

Dad went to the stereo system, changed albums, put on The Beach
Boys. "California Girls" started playing.

"Turn that shit off," Frankie snapped.

Both of her parents stopped what they were doing to stare at her.
"Who do you think you are?" Dad said.

Frankie stood up abruptly.

She almost screamed, *Look at me,* to him. *See me.*

"I'm right here, Dad," she said, her voice shaking. "Your daughter,
home from war."

He turned back to the stereo, busied himself with the stack of rec-
ords.

Frankie felt fury building again, filling her up, stretching her out
of shape.

She went to the bar, grabbed a bottle of gin, and walked back to her
bedroom, slamming the door behind her.

---

*St. Elizabeth's Orphanage. I'm kneeling on the cold stone floor, holding
Mai in my arms, stroking the child's soft hair. I hear the whir of incoming
helicopters from far away. The* pop-pop-pop *of gunfire.*

*A bomb rips into the stone walls, sends stone flying in a dozen directions.
I hear children screaming.*

Another bomb.

I look down; Mai is melting in my arms. Fire everywhere.

Frankie came awake with a scream, her heart pounding; she was drenched in sweat.

She stumbled out of her room, into the dark, quiet house.

0523 hours.

She went to the kitchen phone, picked it up, and dialed Barb's number. No doubt there would be hell to pay when the bill came in—long-distance calls were so expensive—but she needed to talk to her best friend.

Barb answered on the second ring. "Hello?"

"Hey," Frankie said quietly. Holding the receiver to her ear, she slid down the kitchen wall and sat on the linoleum floor. "I . . . just thought I'd check in on you. See how you're holding up? How's your mom?"

"Frankie?" Barb said. "How are you?"

"We don't have to talk about me. I know how much you miss your brother—"

"Frankie," Barb said. "Are you okay?"

Frankie shook her head, whispered, "No. Not okay."

"I got your letter. Your folks really told people you were studying abroad? That is brutal."

"Yeah." Frankie let out a breath.

"That's rough, man," Barb said.

"How was it when you came home? Bad?"

"Yeah, but my mama's block is full of vets coming home. Ain't no lying about it. All I know is you gotta push through, keep on going. Soldier on. It'll all settle out."

Frankie heard the hope in those words. "Rye's home soon. So, there's that. I swear, if he asks me to move in with him, I'm saying yes."

Barb laughed. "You, Miss I-Need-a-Ring-First?"

"That's not me anymore," Frankie said.

"Yeah. Life is short, and don't we know it? You having a party for him when he gets back? Maybe I could get Ethel to road-trip to la-la land."

"I hadn't thought about a party."

"You and I know how hard it is to come back. A little cake helps everything."

Frankie thought about it. A party. "His dad lives up in Compton. Maybe we could plan something together."

"That's the spirit."

"Thanks, Barb. I knew you'd haul me out of this funk I'm in."

"What are girlfriends for?"

They talked for a few more minutes, and by the time she hung up, Frankie had a plan.

It might be a bad idea.

Or a great idea.

She wasn't sure.

All she knew was that once Barb had suggested the idea of a party for Rye, Frankie was on a mission.

So she dressed in the new clothes her mother had purchased for her—baggy bell-bottom jeans and a tunic top with a hip belt—and called information to get an address for Stanley and Mo's Auto Repair in Compton.

By 0900 hours, without a word to her parents, she was dressed, with makeup on, and pulling out of the gated yard in the baby-blue Volkswagen Bug that had been her sixteenth birthday present.

On the ferry, she rolled down her window, let the air wash across her face. She heard the roar of heavy equipment and the clang of jackhammers being used to construct the bridge from San Diego to Coronado—an improvement her father had fought tirelessly for. She felt hopeful for the first time in days. Directed. She was—in the words of her favorite poem, "Desiderata"—advancing confidently in the direction of her dreams.

On the mainland, she cranked up the radio, heard Wolfman Jack's famous howl, and sang along with the music. Cream. Country Joe and the Fish. The Beatles. The music of Vietnam.

In Compton, she slowed down. It had been years since the Watts riots, but the remnant of that time of trouble was still visible in boarded-up windows, broken porches, and graffiti.

Spray-painted Black fists emblazoned the walls of empty store-fronts and closed-up restaurants. The poverty of the neighborhood was obvious.

She passed a junkyard, where heaps of metal and broken-down cars huddled behind chain-link fencing. A growling dog followed her moving car from one end of the fence to the other, straining at the end of big-linked chain.

Abandoned cars sat on untended lots, their tires missing, hubcaps gone, windshields cracked. Many of the houses were dilapidated, in need of paint. She saw groups of Black men ambling down the street, dressed in black, wearing black berets.

Stanley and Mo's Auto Repair was housed in a 1940s-era gas station with a large garage beside it. OUT OF BUSINESS had been spray-painted in red across the garage doors. Crushed beer cans littered the yard. A trash can erupted with garbage.

A trio of young Black men walked past the garage. One of them saw Frankie and stopped to stare for a moment, then walked quickly to catch up with his friends.

She pulled into the empty parking area and stepped out of the car.

Somewhere close by, a dog started barking. A car backfired, sounded like gunfire.

Calm down, Frankie. Breathe. It was just a car. Not a mortar attack.

She walked up to the shop's office, which looked abandoned. There was chicken wire and plywood over every window and someone had painted PANTHER POWER beneath one of them. The words were smeared, as if someone had tried to wash them away and given up.

She knocked on the door.

"Go 'way," someone yelled from inside.

Frankie opened the front door and was assailed by the odor of stale beer and cigarette smoke. "Hello?"

She pushed the door open all the way and stepped over the threshold.

It took her eyes a moment to adjust to the gloom inside.

A single lamp sat on a metal filing cabinet, which was covered with stacks of paper. Old calendars covered one wall, the pinup kind from another era. Betty Grable, Rita Hayworth.

A grizzled man sat hunched in a wheeled office chair, staring at a rabbit-eared TV on another filing cabinet. *As the World Turns* was on.

"We're closed," he said harshly, without even looking at her. "Been closed since the riots, but I ain't damn leaving. They won't run *me* out."

"Mr. Walsh?"

"Who wants to know?" the man said, taking the cigarette from his mouth. He turned slowly, saw her, and frowned. "Girlie, you are in the wrong part of town."

Frankie moved forward slowly. She saw the resemblance of Rye to his father—it was as if Rye's handsome face had been layered in fleshy gray modeling clay and left out in the sun to dry. The older man had cheeks that sagged into jowls, and a bulbous nose. Thick brown eyebrows contrasted sharply with his colorless face and graying blond hair. He had a mustache that was badly in need of tending. Gnarled hands curled around his drink glass. He wore a gray mechanic's jumpsuit that read STAN on the pocket.

Frankie saw the reality of Rye's childhood before her. No wonder he'd felt uncomfortable in the McGrath home, at Finley's going-away party. No wonder he'd joined the military and dreamed of flying faster than the speed of sound.

It made her even more determined to show him her love with a welcome-home party. "I wanted to talk about throwing Rye a coming-home party. I'm—"

"I know who you are, missy. And there ain't gonna be a damned party for my son. You should know that."

"Are you one of those people who are ashamed of the men and women in Vietnam?"

He snorted. "Women in Vietnam. You on drugs?"

"Mr. Walsh, I want you to know—"

"Let me stop you right there." He headed to the metal desk beneath the boarded-up window, which was covered with papers and ashtrays and dirty dishes. He rifled through a pile of envelopes and magazines and plucked out a piece of paper. "Here," he said, handing her a tele-gram. "Three days ago, two assholes in uniform showed up here to tell me my kid was dead. Shot down. Some place like Ankle. Ankee. Who the hell knows?"

Frankie stared down at the telegram. *We regret to inform you . . . Lieutenant Commander Joseph Ryerson Walsh has been killed in action.*

"Remains ain't *recoverable,* the shitheads said. He certainly won't need no welcome-home party," Mr. Walsh said.

Frankie couldn't draw a breath. "It . . . can't be true . . ."

"It is."

"But—"

"Go on, missy. Nothing for you here."

She turned away, stumbled out of the dirty office, and made it to the Bug and collapsed inside.

The telegram shook in her hand.

We regret to inform you.

Rye. She thought of him carrying her to her hooch . . . the night he'd shown up in her OR, worrying about her . . . their first kiss . . . that night on the beach on Kauai where he'd shown her what love felt like. *I'm afraid I'll love you till I die . . .*

Rye. Her love.

Gone.

Frankie didn't remember driving home. When she pulled into her parents' driveway and parked, she looked up through her tears and was vaguely surprised to see where she was.

She got out of the car, forgot to close the door or take her keys. She walked into the house and went directly to her bedroom. Music followed her—Pat Boone, her mom's favorite singer, tried to soothe and romance with his voice, but she barely heard it.

It had been only a few hours since she'd heard those words—*killed in action*—but already it felt like a lifetime of sorrow. Interminable.

She climbed into bed, shoes and all; she leaned back into the stacks of pillows against her headboard and stared up at the frilly pink canopy.

Grief blunted the world, put a thick, cottony veil between Frankie and everything else. She was so numb it took a moment to realize that someone was knocking on her bedroom door.

"Go away," she said.

The door opened. Her mother stood there, smiling uncertainly. It was how they looked at each other these days, but Frankie didn't care about that, either. "There you are—"

Frankie heard her own scream and knew it was a mistake, but she couldn't stop herself. She went from screaming in anger to sobbing in the time it took for her mother to get to the bed.

Frankie rolled away, tucked her legs up into the fetal position.

Mom edged up onto the bed beside her, stroked her hair. For a long time, she didn't say anything, just let Frankie cry.

Finally, Frankie rolled into her mother's embrace, instead of away from it.

"What is it?" Mom asked.

"I fell in love in Vietnam." Frankie drew in a shuddering breath.

"He was shot down. Killed in action." She looked at her mother. "How could I not have known?"

"You never said anything about a man over there . . ." Mom sighed heavily. "Oh, Frances . . ."

"You didn't want to hear anything about the war."

Frankie waited for words of wisdom, for something—anything—to remind her that she still had a reason for living.

Mom said nothing, just stroked her hair and held her close.

Frankie felt her heartbeat slow, felt vaguely that it might be physically breaking down and would be unable to beat in a world without Rye, in this body of hers that felt suddenly foreign.

Footsteps, coming down the hall.

Her father appeared in the open doorway, a briefcase in one hand, a handful of mail in the other.

"A friend of hers was shot down," Mom said.

"Oh," Dad said. He turned around and walked away, closing the door behind him.

Frankie curled into her mother's arms and cried.

<hr>

They're shooting at us.

Pop-pop-pop.

A spark of light hits the Huey broadside. The gunner shoots back, the chopper veers sharply to the left, then up to the right, does almost a pirouette.

Another shot. Sparks. The ra-ta-ta-tat of the gunner shooting back, and then a loud crack of an explosion. The tail of the helicopter bends, breaks, falls to the jungle. Another explosion; this one is the fuel tank. The chopper bursts into a ball of flame and smoke and crashes to the ground.

A thick black column of smoke and flames shoots up from the jungle; the trees catch fire.

Frankie woke up, still in the throes of the nightmare, thinking that she was in Vietnam again, that she'd seen Rye get shot down.

The world righted itself slowly.

She was in her bedroom, with the frilly pink tulle canopy overhead, and the ballerina jewelry box on her nightstand.

Last night had been brutal. Consecutive nightmares. She had a vague memory of wandering through the dark house, smoking, afraid to sleep.

Feeling numb, her body heavy, her heart heavier, she stood, but once she was up, she didn't know what to do.

She just stood there.

There was a knock at her door.

Frankie sighed. It had been only two days in a world without Rye; forty-eight hours of this grief, and already she couldn't stand being in this house. She hated the way her mom watched her, with sad, wary eyes, as if she were afraid Frankie might run out into traffic at any moment.

Mom opened the door. She was dressed in a lavender silk peignoir with pearl buttons and pom-pommed white slippers. A white turban covered her hair.

Frankie stared at her through bleary, bloodshot eyes. "How do I stop loving him?"

"You don't. You endure. You go on. I won't insult you by mentioning the supposed healing properties of time, but it will get better." Mom gave her a sad, compassionate look. "He would want you to live, wouldn't he?"

Frankie had lost track of the variations on life-goes-on that she'd already heard from her mother.

The words had become just clanging noises in the empty room inside of her.

"Sure, Mom. Right."

Twenty

"I'm worried about you, Frances," Mom said.

"Go away." Frankie rolled over, put her pillow over her head. How long had it been since she'd lost Rye? Three days? Four?

"Frankie . . ."

"GO AWAY."

A gentle touch on her shoulder. "Frances?"

Frankie played dead until Mom sighed heavily and left the room, closing the door behind her.

Frankie eased the pillow off of her face. Did Mom think that Frankie had moved on already?

At that, her grief expanded again; she let it submerge her. Strangely, there was peace in the nothingness, comfort in her pain. At least Rye was with her here in this darkness. She let herself imagine the life they would have had, the children who looked like them.

That hurt too much to bear. She drew back, tried to push the thought away. It wouldn't leave.

"Rye," she whispered, reaching for a man who wasn't there.

—⁓—

"Frances. *Frances.*"

Frankie heard her mother's voice coming at her from far away. "Leave."

"Frances. Open your eyes. You're scaring me."

Frankie rolled over, opened her eyes, stared blearily up at her mother, who was dressed for church.

"I'm not going to church," Frankie said. Her voice felt thick. Or maybe that was her tongue.

Mom picked up the empty glass on the nightstand. Beside it was an empty bottle of gin. "You're drinking too much."

"Takes one to know one," Frankie said.

"Dad said he saw you wandering in the living room. Sleepwalking, maybe."

"Who cares?"

Mom stepped closer. "You lost someone you think you loved. It hurts. I know. But life goes on."

"Think I loved?" Frankie rolled over and closed her eyes, thinking, *Rye, remember our first kiss?*

She was asleep before her mother left the room.

———

Frankie became aware of the music in stages. First the beat, then the rhythm, then at last, the words. The Doors. "Light My Fire."

She was in 'Nam, at the O Club, dancing with Rye. She felt his arms around her, felt his hips pressed against hers, his hand settling possessively in the curve at the base of her spine. He whispered something and it made her feel cold, afraid. *What?* she asked. *Say it again,* but he was pulling away, leaving her alone.

Suddenly the music blared, turned loud enough to hurt her ears, sounded like a red alert.

She sat up, groggy, headachy, pushed the damp hair out of her eyes.

Her lashes were stuck together. Grit itched at the corners of her eyes.

The music snapped off.

"Sleeping Beauty awakes."

"Not so much beauty, but plenty of sleeping."

Frankie turned her head, saw Ethel and Barb standing in her bedroom. Ethel was heavier than she'd been in Vietnam, with rounded curves that had filled out her tall frame. Her red hair was pulled into a low side ponytail. She wore bell-bottom jeans and a striped polyester tunic top.

Barb wore black corduroy pants and a black T-shirt and an olive-colored military-type jacket with the sleeves cut off. "Get out of bed, Frankie," Barb said.

"My mom called in reinforcements?" Frankie said.

"I called, actually," Barb said. "I hadn't heard from you since we talked about Rye's coming-home party. I got worried and called. Your mother answered the phone."

"Get out of bed, Frank, or I'll throw you over my shoulder," Ethel said. "Don't think I won't. I can lift a bale of hay."

Frankie knew there was no point arguing. She saw the way they looked at her, with a mixture of compassion and resolve. They were here to lift her out of despair; it was in the way they looked, the way they stood, the confident set to their chins.

They wanted her to just get up, stand, start to walk. As if grief were a pool you could simply step out of.

In reality, it was quicksand and heat. A rough entry, but warm and inviting once you let go.

She pushed the sour, sweat-smelling covers back and got out of bed. Without making eye contact—she couldn't look at them without thinking of Rye—she walked down the hall to her bathroom and took a shower, trying dully to remember when she'd last turned the water on or washed her hair.

She towel-dried her hair and put on the clothes she'd left hanging on a hook on the back of the door (clothes her mother had bought to cheer her up)—a blue tunic and pants set with a pointed white sailor collar and a white cinch belt. She felt like an actress dressing for the role of dutiful daughter.

Ridiculous. But the effort it took to choose something else was beyond her.

Barefoot, she walked back into her bedroom.

At the sight of her friends standing there, she knew how much she loved them. She could almost feel that love, but not quite. Grief had bludgeoned away every other emotion. "I'm fine, you know," Frankie said.

"Apparently you've been in bed for well over a week," Ethel said.

"Time flies when you're having fun."

"Come on, Frank," Ethel said, linking her arm through Frankie's. Barb grabbed the radio and moved to Frankie's other side. A flanking maneuver to make sure Frankie was hemmed in.

The trio walked down the hallway.

Frankie pulled them past her father's office. The last thing she wanted them to see was the heroes' wall, and her absence on it.

Frankie was surprised that they seemed to know the house and have a plan. They walked through the yard, across the street, and out to the beach, where three empty chairs and a portable ice chest waited for them. Barb set the radio on the ice chest and cranked up the music.

Frankie felt unsteady, listening to the surf roar toward her. The familiar music took her back to the best of Vietnam, and the worst.

"I loved him," she said out loud.

Barb handed her a gin and tonic, said, "Sit, Frankie."

Frankie didn't sit so much as she collapsed.

Ethel sat down beside her, held her hand.

Barb sat in the third chair.

The three of them held hands, stared out at the Pacific Ocean crashing beautifully onto the shore, the constant, ceaseless battering of water, the quiet retreat of each wave.

Frankie said, "How could I not know he was gone? How could I not *feel* his loss from the world?"

For that, there was no answer. The three of them knew death intimately, had stood side by side with it for years.

"You need to do something," Ethel said. "Start a life."

"There's this group," Barb said. "Vietnam Veterans Against the War. It started with six vets marching in a peaceful protest to end the war. Maybe you could take your anger and use it for something good."

Anger? That was a distant shadow on the horizon of her grief.

Barb had no idea how this felt, how debilitating it was to lose yourself along with your love. And Frankie couldn't explain it without sounding pathetic or worrying them more.

Best to just say, "Hmm."

"Life has to go on, Frank," Ethel said. "You're tough enough for Pleiku. You can survive this."

Ah.

Life goes on.

But does it really? Not the same life, that was for sure.

"I love you," she said, knowing that her friends wanted to help, but how could they, how could anyone? They were just telling her what she'd heard before: the only way out was through.

More platitudes.

The question was, *how?* How did you get through grief, how did you want to live again when you couldn't imagine what that life could be, how you could be happy again?

It was a question that hadn't occurred to her before. She'd done her best to exist (or not exist, really) in the safety of her bed, with the covers pulled up, but even she knew that couldn't go on forever.

What did she want?

Rye.

A wedding.

A baby to hold in her arms.

A home of her own.

"How has it been, coming home?" Barb asked.

"Besides finding out that the man I love is dead?" Frankie said.

"Before that," was Ethel's softly spoken answer.

"Tough," Frankie said. "No one wants to talk about the war. My father is ashamed of me even going." She looked at her friends. "So, what did you two do?"

Ethel shrugged. "You know my story: I started vet school and fell back in love with my high school boyfriend, Noah. He was in-country while I was, but we never saw each other. He knew how much I loved George. We have . . . history. When I'm feeling fragile, he has a way of holding me together."

Frankie nodded. "You have nightmares?"

"Not much. Anymore," Ethel said at the same time Barb said, "You've got to push it aside, Frankie. *Do* something."

"What do you have left, Frank?" Ethel asked after a while, when the music changed to something folky and soft. No anger in this music, just sadness and loss and sorrow.

"What do you mean?"

"You tell me."

"Well." Honestly, this was something Frankie had never thought about. She knew who she'd been raised to be, what was expected of her, but that was before, wasn't it?

Barb repeated the question: "What do you have left?"

Frankie thought about how she'd changed in the past two years, what she'd learned about herself and the world. About Jamie, and her certainty that she had to do the right thing, which meant that she'd never even kissed him; she thought about Rye and how their passion had transformed her, loosened her into a different, bolder version of herself. She thought about Fin and their idyllic childhood, the way he'd told her, *It's okay,* and she'd believed him.

All of them, the three men she'd loved, had awakened her, filled her heart, made her happy, but they couldn't be everything.

"Nursing," she said softly.

"Damn right," Ethel said. "You are a shit-kicking, take-no-prisoners-good nurse. You save lives, Frank. Think about that."

Frankie nodded. She sensed a glimmer of possibility, a way to move around her grief. In helping others, maybe she could find a way to help herself.

"You guys are the best," she said, her voice breaking. "And I love you. Truly." She got to her feet, turned, looked at them. They were here to help her, but she knew—as they knew—if she were to be saved, she'd have to do it herself.

In the next few days, Frankie showed Ethel and Barb all the places she'd loved as a child; the three friends spent long hours on the beach, just talking, listening to the music that made them laugh and cry and remember. By the time her best friends left, Frankie had a plan for going forward. She spent days scouring the want ads in the San Diego newspaper and making calls. When she finally scored an interview, she got up early to prepare. She typed up a résumé on the IBM Selectric on her father's desk that no one in this house ever used. Her mother believed, of course, in handwritten letters, and her father had secretaries to type for him. When she was happy with it, she zipped it off the roll, reread for typos, and then slid it into the lambskin-leather briefcase that had been her high school graduation gift. It was the first time she'd used it. Her initials—FGM—were stamped in gold on the black leather.

Grateful—for once—that her mother was an ardent shopper,

Frankie found a suitable two-piece striped dress with a funnel neck and a hip-hugging green belt hanging in her closet. Her top dresser drawer held an array of rolled-up panties, a few lacy bras, and some pantyhose in the cinnamon hue Frankie and all her high school friends had worn in the winter to look tan. She slipped her feet into a pair of low-heeled camel pumps.

From the ferry's car deck, she saw the almost-completed bridge; huge concrete stanchions rose out of the wavy blue water, curving from one shore toward the other.

On the mainland, the small hospital was housed in a Mission-style white building that took up a city block, its front and side yards studded with palm trees. Frankie parked in the visitors' lot and walked to the front door. The minute the doors opened and welcomed her in, she smelled the familiar scents of disinfectant, alcohol, bleach, and for the first time since coming home she felt like herself.

This was where she belonged, who she was. Here, she would find a path through her grief.

She went to the front desk, where a bouffant-haired young woman greeted her with a smile and pointed the way to the director of nursing's office on the second floor.

Frankie's hand on the briefcase's leather handle was damp. This was only her second real job interview. Military recruitment didn't count. She knew that she looked young—was young, at least chronologically.

She found the office she was looking for, two doors down from the elevator on the second floor. Outside of it, she stopped, took a breath.

No fear, McGrath.

Standing tall, shoulders back, chin up, as she'd been taught by her parents and the nuns at St. Bernadette's, she walked up to the door that read MRS. DELORES SMART, DIRECTOR OF NURSING, and knocked.

Mrs. Smart looked up from the work on her desk. She had a round face with bright red cheeks and wore her gray hair in old-fashioned pin curls that lay flat against her head.

Behind her, a large window overlooked the parking lot. "Mrs. Smart? I'm Frances McGrath. Here for an interview."

"Come in," the older woman said, indicating the empty chair in front of her desk. "Your résumé?"

Frankie sat down, took the folder out of her briefcase, and slid it across the desk.

Mrs. Smart read it. "St. Bernadette's," she said. "Good grades."

"I graduated at the top of my nursing school class at the San Diego College for Women."

"I see that. You worked for a couple of weeks at St. Barnabas. Night shift."

"Yes, but as you can see, I just returned from Vietnam, ma'am, where I was an Army nurse for two years. I worked my way up to surgical nurse, and—"

"You are hardly trained for surgical assistance," Mrs. Smart said crisply. She pushed her glasses up and stared at Frankie. "Can you follow instructions, Miss McGrath? Do as you're told?"

"Believe me, ma'am, the military demands it. And my Vietnam training has made me an exceptional nurse."

Mrs. Smart tapped her pen on the desk as she read and reread Frankie's résumé. Finally, she said, "Report to Mrs. Henderson at the first-floor nurses' station Wednesday at eleven P.M. for your first night of work. Tilda in the office next to mine will set you up with a uniform."

"You're hiring me?"

"I'm putting you on probation. Eleven P.M. to seven A.M."

"The night shift?"

"Of course. It's where all beginners start, Miss McGrath. You should know that."

"But—"

"No buts. Do you want to work here?"

"Yes, ma'am."

"Good. See you Wednesday."

―⁓―

On her first day of work, Frankie dressed in a starched white uniform with an apron, thick white stockings, and comfortable white shoes. The nurse's cap sat on her teased, precision-cut bob like a flag of surrender. In 'Nam, in the shit, it would have fallen into some patient's gaping ab wound, or been splattered with blood.

She arrived ready to work, was shown to her locker and given a key. At precisely 2300 hours, she reported to the night charge nurse, Mrs. Henderson, an elderly woman in white who had a face like a bull terrier's, complete with whiskers.

"Frances McGrath, ma'am, reporting for duty."

"It's not the Army, Miss McGrath. You can just say hello. I hear you have almost no hospital experience."

Frankie frowned. "Well. Civilian, maybe, but I was in Vietnam at a mobile—"

"Follow me. I'll get you started."

The charge nurse walked fast, her shoulders squared, her chin tucked in, her head on a swivel. "You are on probation, Miss McGrath. I assume Mrs. Smart relayed this information to you. Our patients are important to us and we strive to offer the highest caliber of care, which means, of course, that nurses who know next to nothing do next to nothing. I will tell you when you can treat actual patients. For now, you may help patients to the restroom, refill their water, change bedpans, and man the phone at the nurses' station."

"But I know how—"

Another hand held up for silence.

"Here's the emergency room. You'll see everything here—from a heart attack to marbles stuck up a kid's nostril."

"Yes, ma'am."

"Good sign. Politeness. Nowadays, most girls your age act like feral dogs. My granddaughter dresses like a vagrant. Follow me. Keep up. This is the surgical ward. Only highly trained surgical nurses work here." She kept going on her tour of the hospital.

Frankie followed her new boss down the hallway, past half a series of closed doors. She was shown the restrooms, the lab, the equipment room; they ended up back on the first floor at the nurses' station.

"Sit there," Mrs. Henderson said. "Answer the phone. If there's trouble, page me."

Frankie took a seat. *You may help patients to the restroom, refill their water, change bedpans.*

She took a deep breath and released it. Barb and Ethel had prepared her for this. She'd known it was coming. There was no point being angry. She simply needed to show them what she could do. Good things took time.

April 27, 1969

Dear Ethel,

I got a job as a nurse in a local hospital. Yay! I hope you can read the sarcasm in that word.

Barb was right. They're treating me like I'm a candy striper. Sometimes it makes me so mad I want to scream. They have me on the night shift, answering phones and changing bedpans and refilling water pitchers.

Me. On the night shift.

The only good thing is the anger sometimes makes me forget how sad I am.

I'll stick with it, though. Prove myself. I'll bet you're thinking of my first shift in-country.

I've got this. Thanks for reminding me, by the way. I still love nursing.

That's something.

So, how's life on the horse farm? Still kicking ass in your classes? How's that new mare coming along, what's her name? Silver Birch? After some book you read in junior high?

How's Noah?

Love,

F

Running, breathing hard.

The admin building blows up beside me.

A chopper overhead. I look up, see Rye in the pilot's seat.

A whistling sound.

I scream.

The helicopter explodes in the dark sky, blows into pieces. Ash rains down on me.

A helmet thuds to the ground at my feet, on fire. RIOT *melts off the metal.*

Frankie woke with a start, looked around.

At least she wasn't on the floor. That felt like a small victory.

She pushed the covers back and got out of bed, not surprised to find that she felt weak. Last night had been a bad one for nightmares. There was no rhyme or reason to it; she had nightmares and mood swings out of the blue. Sometimes she felt as if she were hanging on to the end of a giant undulating rope. It took all her strength not to let go.

Putting on her chenille bathrobe, she made her way out to the kitchen, which was empty at 1500 hours. She poured a cup of coffee and carried it out to the patio, where her mother sat at a table by the pool, doing a puzzle.

"There you are," her mom said, setting a puzzle piece aside. Her gaze narrowed, swept Frankie from head to toe. "You didn't sleep well again?"

Frankie shrugged.

"This vampire shift of yours isn't helping."

"Maybe not." Frankie sat down.

"How much longer will they have you working these ghoulish hours?"

"Who knows? It's only been two weeks."

"I don't like it."

"Me, either." She looked at her mother, who she knew saw the sorrow Frankie worked every day to overcome, and also worried about Frankie's unsettling anger, which could flare up without warning.

"We should go to dinner soon. At the club."

"Sure, Mom. Whatever."

———

At just past 2200 hours, Frankie drove toward the ferry terminal on Coronado. There were few cars out this late on a weeknight in mid-May; no tourists stumbling from bar to bar, no well-dressed couples walking to their cars after dinner out. The island was tucked in for the night already and Frankie was going to work. She intended to be early to start her shift, as usual; it was something she'd learned in Vietnam.

In San Diego, the hospital was brightly illuminated. She parked beneath a palm tree and headed inside, waving to colleagues on her way to the lockers.

She smiled tightly, hopeful that no one detected the rabid frustration she felt with every shift.

They *still* treated her like an FNG. They didn't even let her start an IV.

Still, she kept her mouth shut and soldiered on, as she had been taught to do. At her locker, she changed into her uniform and headed for the nurses' station, to take her place at the desk.

As usual, the halls were quiet; most of the patients were sleeping, their doors closed. Frankie's first chore was always to check each room, each patient. And to call for help if it was needed.

She poured herself a Styrofoam cup full of coffee and stood at the desk, sipping it.

An elderly man shuffled toward her, moving as if in pain, his shoulders hunched.

She put down her coffee.

He was dressed in an old-fashioned way: tan slacks and a crisply ironed white shirt. "Nurse?"

"Yes, sir?"

"I'm José Garcia. My wife, Elena, is having trouble breathing."

Frankie nodded. She knew she should call Mrs. Henderson, ask for reinforcements, but she didn't. Screw it. Whatever was happening with Mrs. Garcia, Frankie could handle it.

She followed Mr. Garcia to Room 111.

In the room's only bed, a woman lay still, her body covered in blankets, her head raised slightly on a mound of pillows. Her face was pallid; her mouth hung open. She breathed in and out slowly, making a terrible rattling sound.

"She just started breathing like that," José said quietly.

"How long has she been ill?"

"Six months. Cancer of the lungs. Her students come by almost every day, don't they, Elena?" He touched his wife's hand. "She is a high school teacher. Fierce," he added. He turned to Frankie. "You heard about the walkouts? Students and teachers protesting inequality in our schools? She was part of that, my Elena. Weren't you?" He gazed down at his wife. "She fought to get her students college preparation classes, instead of just training for domestic work. You changed lives, *mi amor.*" His voice caught.

Frankie took hold of the woman's gnarled, bony, dry-skinned hand and thought for a moment of all the hands she'd held in Vietnam, all the men and women she'd comforted and cared for. It steadied her, calmed the loud noises in her head.

"You're not alone, Elena," she said. "How about some lotion on your hands? I bet that would feel good . . ."

Twenty-One

On a hot June afternoon, three months after her return from Vietnam, Frankie woke from her first decent night's sleep.

Maybe she was getting better.

She was.

She *was* getting better.

She put a robe on over her SKI VIETNAM T-shirt and panties and headed down to the kitchen for coffee.

She found her mother at the kitchen table, dressed for the country club, smoking a cigarette, a cup of coffee beside her, reading the newspaper. Frankie saw the headline: FIRST LT. SHARON LANE KILLED IN ROCKET EXPLOSION IN VIETNAM.

Mom drew in a sharp breath, slammed the newspaper face down on the table. Then she looked up, tried to smile. "Good morning, dear. Well, good afternoon."

Frankie reached for the newspaper.

"No—" Mom said.

Frankie wrenched it away from her mother, turned it over to the article. *Army nurse Sharon Lane is the first—and so far only—nurse to be killed by enemy fire, although seven nurses have been killed or died during the conflict to date. First Lt. Lane died almost instantly when a rocket fragment struck her during an attack at Chu Lai.*

Frankie put down the paper. Enemy fire. A rocket fragment.

Almost instantly.

"Did you know her?" Mom asked quietly.

"No."

And yes. We were all the same in some ways. I could have been her.

Frankie closed her eyes, said a silent prayer.

"Maybe you should call in sick for work today."

Frankie opened her eyes. She felt jittery now, anxious. Angry. "If I called in sick every time I felt sad, I'd never go to work."

"I ran into Laura Gillihan yesterday at the Free Bros. Market. She mentioned that Rebecca would love to see you."

Frankie poured herself a cup of coffee, stirred in some heavy cream. She was breathing a little fast, felt almost light-headed.

Becky Gillihan. There was a name she hadn't heard in a long time. Once upon a time, they'd been friends. At St. Bernadette's Academy, they'd been inseparable.

"She's married. Still lives on the island. I could call. Tell her you'll stop by before work. What else will you do until your shift starts?"

Frankie wasn't really listening. She could feel her mother's worried gaze, felt how she was being watched. Frankie should say more, tell her mother that she was okay, *not to worry*, but the thought of Sharon Lane wouldn't let her go.

Almost instantly.

She walked down the hall, stripped out of her clothes in her bedroom, and took a long, hot shower, crying for the unknown nurse until her tears ran out.

Afterward, she re-dressed in the clothes she found on her bedroom floor—bell-bottom jeans and an embroidered peasant top—and realized she was shaky from a lack of food. She lit up a cigarette instead of eating.

On the kitchen table, she found a note from her mother.

Frances Grace,
I spoke to Laura. Rebecca was thrilled at the prospect of seeing you. She asked me to pass along that she is hosting a party for Dana Johnston today at 4:00 P.M. She invited you!
570 Second Avenue.
We are off to a charity auction in Carlsbad.
Home late.

Frankie glanced at the clock on the stove. The party had started fifteen minutes ago.

She didn't want to go to Becky's. In fact, the thought of going made her feel vaguely ill. Could she handle seeing old friends?

No.

But what was the alternative? Sit in this mausoleum of a house alone, waiting until long after dark to go to work? Or be here when her parents returned? Her mother eyed her nervously all the time, as if she feared Frankie was wired with explosives and one wrong word would set her off. And Dad seemed determined not to look at her at all.

She'd promised Barb and Ethel that she would do more than endure, that she would engage.

This was as good a place to start as any.

She ate a piece of Wonder Bread slathered with butter and sprinkled with sugar, and headed back to her room for her shoes and handbag. It occurred to her that she should expend a little effort with her hair and makeup. Maybe wear a dress. Several of her old high school friends would be there, after all, most of whom had grown up swimming at the country club and learning to play golf.

But Frankie couldn't do it. The Army nurse's death had stripped her defenses down to nothing. She was barely hanging on as it was. She started the Bug and backed out of the garage and headed across the island, drove up Orange Avenue, and turned left on Second, just a street from the park.

The house was a bungalow from the 1940s; small and perfectly kept up, gray paint, a bright red door. Flowers grew in neatly tended window boxes on either side of the stone path that led from the sidewalk to the front door.

Frankie got out of her car and walked very slowly to the gate, opening it—*click*—shutting it behind her—*click*.

The stone path was lined on either side with flowers in bright pink bloom.

She stopped at the front door, knocked, and immediately heard footsteps on the other side.

Becky answered the door. For a split second, Frankie didn't recognize the beautiful young woman with bouffant blond hair, who carried a plump, blue-eyed toddler in a sailor suit on her hip.

"Frankie's here, everyone!"

Becky shouted so loudly that the baby in her arms started to cry.

Frankie was pulled through a house cluttered with children's toys, out to the patio, where a dozen well-dressed women were sitting in folding chairs, drinking champagne. A silver coffee service sat on a slim wooden table; beside it, an array of hors d'oeuvres: pigs in a blanket, ants on a log, nut-covered balls of cheese encircled by Ritz crackers.

It felt strangely discordant to Frankie that this staid, unchanging world of flowers and champagne and women in summery dresses persevered while men—and women—were dying in Vietnam.

Frankie recognized several high school friends, girls she'd played volleyball with and gone on double dates with, a few of the cheerleaders, two or three older women—the mothers—and also saw some young women she didn't know. College friends of Dana's or relatives, perhaps.

The patio was decorated with balloons; a large table held beautifully decorated gifts. It was a birthday party, she supposed. Had her mother told her that?

"I . . . should have a gift," Frankie said, feeling out of place. She didn't belong in this party full of pretty housewives who wore pressed dresses and smoked Virginia Slims.

"Don't give it a thought," Becky said, taking her by the arm, leading her through the party to a chair near a fragrant, laden orange tree.

Dana began opening gifts.

Frankie tried to smile in admiration at appropriate times. She saw the way the other women oohed and aahed over household items. Silver candlesticks. Waterford glasses. Sheets from Italy.

Dana, whom Frankie barely remembered from grade school, smiled brightly at each present and said something special to the giver. Her mother sat beside her, making notes about each gift, so that short work could be made of the thank-you notes. A maid in a black-and-white uniform bustled from table to table, freshening drinks and delivering canapés.

A wedding shower, Frankie realized slowly. *Oh God.*

Frankie snagged a glass of champagne from a nearby tray.

She drank it quickly, put her empty glass down, and picked up another, and then lit up a cigarette, trying to smoke herself to calm. Then she remembered that she had to be at work at 2300 hours.

She shouldn't drink before her shift at the hospital.

It was just a party. Nothing dangerous or frightening, but she felt anxiety ripple through her. Panic rose up; she closed her eyes, thought, *You can leave soon.* But what was she so afraid of?

"Are you okay?"

She felt Becky come up beside her, smelled her floral perfume. Jean Naté. Their favorite from high school. It made Frankie think of 'Nam, and how her perfume had reminded the wounded men of their girls back home.

Frankie released a breath, let it out slowly, and opened her eyes.

Becky was there, tucked in close as she used to do a lifetime ago. Her smile was bright and untroubled. She seemed impossibly young, but she was Frankie's age.

Frankie tried to smile, but her anxiety was so high, she wasn't able to tell if she'd succeeded.

"Fine," Frankie said. How long ago had Becky asked? "Fine," she said again, trying to smile. "So. When's the wedding?"

"Two months," Becky said. "Dana is marrying Jeffrey Heller. You remember him? Football scholarship. We were all at USC together."

"Did he go to 'Nam?"

Becky laughed. A pretty, optimistic sound. "Course not. Most of the boys we know have ways out. A few have gotten married."

"How fortunate." Frankie got to her feet so quickly it must have looked like she wasn't in control of her body, and really, she wasn't. She was like an animal who had sensed danger and gone into full flight mode. If she didn't leave now she might scream. "I should go."

"Why, you just got here, silly!"

"I . . . have to work." Frankie sidled to the left to give herself a clear path.

Someone put a record on the stereo and turned up the volume.

"We gotta get out of this place . . ."

"Turn that shit off," Frankie snapped. She didn't realize that she'd yelled it until the record was scratched and the party fell quiet and everyone was staring at her.

She couldn't smile. "Sorry. I hate that song."

Becky looked frightened. "Uh. How was Florence? Chad and I are going for our anniversary."

"I wasn't in Florence, Bex," she said slowly, trying to calm down, pull back, be okay. Be normal.

But she wasn't okay.

She was standing with a bunch of debutantes and sorority girls who were planning a wedding with fresh flowers and honeymoons abroad while men their age were dying on foreign soil. Not *their* men, though, not their rich, pretty college boys. "I was in Vietnam."

Silence.

Then a titter of laughter. It broke the silence; the women all joined in.

Becky looked relieved. "Ah. Funny joke, Frankie. You always were a card."

Frankie took a step closer, went toe to toe with her best friend from ninth grade. All the while she was thinking, *Calm down, back off*, at the same time she thought, *Killed by enemy fire* and *almost instantly*.

"Believe me, Bex. It is not a joke. I've held men's severed legs in my hands and tried to hold their chests together just long enough to get them into the OR. What's happening in Vietnam is no joke. The joke is here. This." She looked around. "You."

She pushed past her friend and strode through the pod of silent, staring women, heard someone say, "What's wrong with her?," and before she made it outside to her car, she was screaming.

Frankie sat at a picnic table in Ski Beach Park, overlooking the ocean. As usual on a summer evening, the place was crowded with people out walking their dogs or jogging in brightly colored short shorts. Kids played in the grass and in the sand, their shrieks of joy sometimes startlingly loud.

She ignored all of it, or, more accurately, she didn't notice the commotion going on around her. She smoked one cigarette after another, only getting up to put her butts in the trash.

There was something wrong. With her. And she was unsure of how to fix it. Her behavior at the shower was unacceptable on any level. There was no doubt about that. Oh, Becky and the others had been offensive about Vietnam, but so was much of the country. That didn't give Frankie license to lash out. All she'd had to do was claim a need to leave and politely walk out of the party.

Instead . . .

Her anxiety and anger had surged, come out of nowhere, and suffocated her.

Even now, hours later, it was still there, lying in wait, ready to lash
out at a moment's notice. It made her feel weak, shaky. Fragile.

She'd never thought of herself as fragile, and yet here she was.
Alone and afraid.

She could handle a MASCAL in 'Nam with ease, but a long-
forgotten friend at a bridal shower could bring her to her emotional
knees with the flick of a word.

Vietnam.

That had to be at the root of her outburst. And how could it not?
She'd shown up at a *bridal* shower only months after Rye's death.
Wouldn't anyone be upended by grief at a time like that?

But what about the sudden anger? Was that part of grief?

She had to do better, be better. No more putting herself in upsetting situations. No more telling people she'd been to Vietnam.
They didn't want to hear it, anyway. The message was clear: *Don't talk
about it.*

She needed to do as everyone suggested and forget.

She knew that enforced silence added to her anxiety, increased
her anger, but it was undeniably true that even her own family was
ashamed of her service and expected her to be ashamed, too.

At 2245 hours, long after dark, she was still on the wooden picnic
table bench, worrying over all of it, gnawing on the bone of her failures.
When she stood up, she realized she hadn't eaten all day and the pack
of cigarettes she'd smoked had left her light-headed.

She got up and walked to her car, hearing the ocean purr behind
her. The park was mostly empty this late; just a few pairs of lovers out
here now.

She drove the short distance to the hospital and parked. Moving
cautiously—she was jittery, unsteady—she entered the brightly lit

halls, went to her locker, and put on her uniform. After brushing her teeth at the sink, she straightened and caught sight of herself in the mirror: a young face with old, tired eyes, black hair, and a stark white nursing cap.

She headed for the nurses' station, made herself a cup of coffee, ate something from a vending machine, and began her rounds.

The halls and rooms were quiet. Most of the patients were sleeping and there were no surgeries scheduled for tonight.

Four hours later, she sat at the station desk, tapping her pen. On her shift so far, she'd changed four bedpans, helped three patients to the bathroom, and replaced two pillows. She'd filled water pitchers and lowered a bed and helped one old woman sleep by reading to her.

As usual, she had pretty much just twiddled her thumbs.

Suddenly the elevator doors banged open. An ambulance attendant rolled a patient in on a wheeled gurney. "The ER is packed," he said. "Bus accident."

Frankie shot to her feet, felt instinctively for the Kelly clamp on her fatigue pocket. Not there.

"Gunshot wound," the attendant said.

Frankie felt a rush of adrenaline. "This way," she said and ran alongside the patient, who was a young man. Shot in the upper chest at close range. Blood gushed from the gaping wound, dripped onto the floor. He couldn't breathe, gasped, grabbed for her.

In OR 1, Frankie hit the intercom. "Code. Bay One. Code. Bay One."

To the attendant, Frankie said, "Get him on the table."

"There's no doc—"

"On the table," she shouted, washing her hands, looking for gloves. "*Now.*"

The attendant moved the kid onto the operating table. Frankie masked and scrubbed up and hurried back to the table. "You're going to be okay," she said to the young man.

He gurgled, gasped, clawed at his throat. Something was obstructing his breathing.

Frankie went to the intercom again, hit the button with her elbow, and called for help, this time saying, "Code blue. STAT. OR, Bay One."

"Hang on, kid," she said. "The doc will be here soon."

The patient gasped, started to turn blue.

Frankie glanced back at the door. Didn't these people *listen*? Did they not respond to calls?

She waited five more seconds, then found the surgical cart, grabbed some antiseptic ointment and a scalpel and a breathing tube.

He was dying.

She wiped his neck with antiseptic and picked up a scalpel. It took less than twenty seconds to do the tracheotomy and get the kid breathing.

"There," she said when he inhaled and exhaled through the tube. She cut off his shirt and vest, exposing the wound. It was *gushing* blood. She grabbed some gauze, applied pressure, and tried to stop the bleeding.

A short-haired man in scrubs rushed into the OR and stopped in his tracks. "What in the *hell*?"

Frankie threw him an irritated look. "There you are. What took you so long?"

The doctor stared at her, his mouth open. Mrs. Henderson appeared beside him. She looked at Frankie, her face no doubt streaked with the patient's blood, her white nurse uniform stained red in places, her cap thrown to the floor, applying pressure to a patient's wound.

"Who did the trach?" the doctor asked, looking around.

"He couldn't breathe," Frankie said.

"So you performed a trach? *You?*" the doctor said.

"I called. No one came," Frankie said.

"We have other emergencies," he said.

"Tell that to this kid."

The doctor turned, said, "Mrs. Henderson, get a team here. Now." He went to wash his hands.

Frankie felt flushed with pride. She had shown them her skills. Saved this young man, maybe.

Mrs. Henderson stood there, her arms crossed, her hair frizzed out around her white, starched cap, her forehead pleated, her mouth set in a grim line. "You could have killed that man."

"I saved him, ma'am."

"Who do you think you are?"

"I'm a combat nurse. A good one."

"That may be," Mrs. Henderson said, "but you're also a loose cannon. You have just exposed this hospital to liability. You're fired."

Twenty-Two

Headlights shone on the elaborately scrolled metal in front of her, illuminating the gold M in the center of the gates. When Frankie was young, this house had been neither gated nor walled, but open to the world, situated proudly on its large, ocean-facing lot. Back then, Ocean Boulevard had been a quiet street, mostly driven on by locals. The world had felt safe.

The assassination of President Kennedy had changed everything. She still sometimes thought of her childhood as Before and After. Following the death of the President, no one in America had felt safe from the Red Scare and up had gone the wall around the McGrath property. Not long after that, the gate had closed them in, created an oasis designed to shield the inhabitants from the ugliness of life.

As if bricks and mortar could protect a person.

Frankie drove through the open gate and followed the driveway into the four-car garage, where she parked beside her mother's Cadillac. Her father's silver gull-wing Mercedes was off to the left.

She realized too late—when she was nearly at the front door—that she'd forgotten her purse. Feeling unsteady, she walked back, retrieved her purse, got out her keys, and opened the front door.

It was 0400 hours. Quiet. Dark. A single lamp in the living room cast a little light, but otherwise the rooms lay in shadow. Frankie could have navigated this house blindfolded, so she didn't bother with any lights. She walked into the living room, grabbed a bottle of booze and a glass from the bar, and carried them out to the patio.

Fired.

For saving a young man's life.

What was going on in the world?

She needed to eat something. Why that came to mind, she had no idea.

She poured a glass of . . . vodka, apparently . . . and drank it fast and poured another.

She needed something to dim the pain, at least to give it a blunt edge.

She needed to get herself together. Her mind was a whirlwind: anger, fear, grief, sorrow. Every now and then she cried. Then she'd scream. Neither helped at all.

God help her, she missed Vietnam, missed who she'd been over there. She closed her eyes, tried to steady her breathing.

She heard footsteps. How long had she been out here, drinking and smoking and crying? And how could she still have tears to shed? It dawned on her suddenly that it was daylight. So she'd been out here for hours.

The lights flicked on.

Her father strode out onto the porch in his pajamas and mono-grammed robe. He saw her and stopped. "What in the Sam Hill . . . ?"

Mom came out behind him, still in her silk pajamas. "Frances? What happened? Are you okay?"

Frankie realized that she was still in her blood-splattered white nurse uniform. At some point, her cap had fallen off. There was blood all down her front, on her white pantyhose, on her shoes. "I saved a man's life in the hospital tonight. Performed a tracheotomy."

"You?" her father said, one eyebrow cocked in disbelief.

"Yes, Dad. *Me.*"

"We heard about the scene you caused at Becky's party," he said.

For a second, she didn't know what he was talking about; yesterday afternoon felt like a lifetime ago. At the suddenness of the topic change, she stumbled into confusion, lost her sweeping anger. She didn't want to disappoint them. Again. "I didn't mean to cause a scene. It's just—"

"Well, you did. No doubt the story will be all over the club by now. Connor McGrath's daughter went to Vietnam and came home crazy."

"Are you taking drugs?" Mom asked, twining her hands together.

"What? Drugs? No," Frankie said. "It's just the way people look at me when I say I was in 'Nam . . ."

"You exposed my fib about Florence," Dad said.

"Fib?" Frankie couldn't believe he'd said that. "*Fib?*"

She knew then what this was about, what it had always been about. His reputation. The man with his stupid heroes' wall who knew nothing about heroism and lived in fear of that embarrassing truth being exposed. "If you don't want to be seen as a liar, maybe you shouldn't lie, Dad. Maybe you should be *proud* of me."

"Proud? That you embarrass this family at every turn?"

"I went to *war*, Dad. War. I have been shot at in a Huey and lived through mortar attacks. I've had my ears ring for days when a bomb hit too close. But you don't know anything about that, do you?"

He paled at that, clenched his jaw.

"Enough," he said.

"You're right," she yelled back.

She pushed past him, headed to her bedroom before she could say something even worse.

The door to her father's office was open. She saw all those pictures and mementos on the heroes' wall, and without thinking, she went into the sacred space and started pulling the framed pictures off the wall, throwing them to the floor. She heard glass shatter.

"What the hell do you think you're doing?" Dad roared at her from the doorway.

"This," she said. "Your *heroes'* wall. It's a big fat lie, isn't it, Dad? You wouldn't know a hero if one bit you in the ass. Believe me, Dad. I've seen heroes."

"Your brother would be as ashamed of your behavior as we are," Dad said.

Mom appeared in the doorway, threw Dad a pleading look. "Connor, don't."

"How *dare* you mention Finley?" Frankie said, her anger swooping back in. "You who got him killed. He went over there for *you*, to make you proud. I could tell him now not to bother, couldn't I? Oh, but he's dead."

"Out," her father said in barely above a whisper. "Get out of this house and stay out."

"With pleasure," Frankie hissed. She snagged the photograph of her brother and stormed out of the office.

"Leave that picture," Dad said.

She turned around. "No way. He's not staying in this toxic house. You got him killed, Dad. How do you live with that?"

She ran down to her bedroom, stuffed a few things in her overnight travel bag, grabbed her purse, and left the house.

Outside, she felt the sting of regret, and tears blurred her vision. Dear God, she was sick to death of crying. And of these mammoth mood swings. She shouldn't have said that terrible thing to her father.

She threw her stuff in the backseat, along with the portrait of Finley, and climbed into the Bug, slamming the door shut behind her.

She knew she was driving on Ocean Boulevard too fast, but it couldn't be helped. She couldn't catch her breath. She felt like the last girl in a horror film, running for her life, but the danger wasn't behind her, trying to catch up, it was inside her, trying to break out. She thought, if it gets out, *something bad will happen*. All this rage and hurt could destroy her if she didn't bottle it up.

She reached over for her purse, felt around for her cigarettes in the mess inside.

The music blared through the small black speakers. "Light My Fire." For a second she felt it all, the missing of herself, of Vietnam, of her lost loves. Tears blurred her eyes; she couldn't lift her hand to wipe them away. She pressed her foot on the gas when she meant to ease off.

A flash of something.

Color.

A streetlight, a dog, darting in front of her.

She swerved and slammed on the brakes so hard, she was flung forward, cracked her head on the steering wheel.

Where was she?

She came to slowly, saw the crunched wreckage of the VW Bug's hood.

She'd hit a streetlamp, gone up onto the curb.

She could have killed someone.

"Jesus," she said, in both relief and prayer. Her whole body was shaking. She felt sick.

She couldn't go on like this. She needed help.

And she couldn't go back to her parents. Not yet, maybe not ever, after what she'd said to her father.

She put the Bug in reverse and backed up. The car clanged down onto the street.

A dog sat on the grass, watching her.

Frankie had never hated herself more than she did right now. She was hungry, brokenhearted, and drunk, and she'd gotten behind the wheel.

She parked the wrecked car on the side of the road and left her keys in it. In this neighborhood, the police would be alerted to its presence in no time. They'd call the registered owner, Connor McGrath, and he'd see it sitting here, broken.

She hoped it scared him. (Who had she become, that she wished pain on someone she loved?)

Slinging her bag and purse over her shoulder, she stumbled down the street.

It wasn't until she boarded the ferry and saw how people stared at her that she realized she was still in her bloody white uniform.

She went into the bathroom and changed into jeans and a T-shirt. She had forgotten to pack shoes, so she left her blood-splattered white nurse shoes on.

On the mainland, she walked to the bus station. Every step took something out of her, made her feel smaller, more worthless, more lost.

More alone.

Who could help her?

There was only one place she could think of.

She boarded a city bus and exited a few miles later, then walked to the Veterans Administration Outpatient Clinic.

The offices were closed when she arrived. She sat on a bench out front, smoking one cigarette after another, waiting impatiently, reliving the bad things she'd said and seen and done over and over.

At 0830 hours, the lights in the building came on. Cars began to drive into the parking lot.

Frankie walked inside. A wide lobby funneled into a beige hallway. Men sat slumped in chairs that lined either wall, some of them younger, long-haired, wearing ratty clothes—fatigues with the sleeves cut off, denim jackets, torn T-shirts—and some were older men, probably veterans from Korea or World War II. A few walked back and forth.

She stopped at the front desk. "I'm . . . I need some help," she said. "Something's wrong."

The woman behind the desk looked up. "What kind of help?"

Frankie touched her head, the new bruise that was forming. A headache made it hard to think. "I am . . ." *Crazy. Unraveling. What?* "My thoughts . . . I get angry and sad and . . . my boyfriend was just killed in action."

The woman stared at her a moment, clearly confused. "Well. I mean. This is the VA."

"Oh, right. I'm an Army Nurse Corps vet. Just back from 'Nam."

The woman gave her a skeptical look. "Dr. Durfee is in his office. He doesn't have an appointment until nine A.M. I guess you could—"

"Thanks."

She sighed. "Two doors down. On the left."

Frankie headed down the wide hallway, where more men sat on plastic seats beneath a framed portrait of Richard Nixon. Frankie saw posters and brochures offering different kinds of help to veterans: employment help, state benefits, education, and training.

At Dr. Durfee's door, she stopped, took a deep breath, and knocked.

"Come in."

She opened the door and stepped into a narrow, almost closet-small office. An old man—old enough to be her grandfather—sat behind a cluttered desk. Stacks of paper were on every surface in the room. A poster was tacked up on the wall behind him: a kitten hanging from one claw with the words HANG TOUGH.

The doctor peered at her through black-rimmed, Coke-bottle-thick glasses. What strands of hair he had left, he'd combed to one side and maybe sprayed in place. He wore a madras shirt, buttoned to his wattled neck. "Hello, young lady. Are you lost?"

Frankie smiled tiredly. It was such a relief to be here. To say, *I need help,* and receive it. "I am lost, but I'm in the right place. I probably should have come before now."

His gaze narrowed, moved from her face, down her rumpled blouse and wrinkled jeans, to the red-splattered white shoes.

"The woman at the front desk said you had until nine. I can make an appointment, but I really need some help now, if you don't mind."

"Help?"

She sank into the chair in front of his desk. "I was in-country for two years. And my boyfriend was supposed to come home in April, but he was KIA, so what came was a we-regret-to-inform-you telegram. And the way people treat us. We can't even say *Vietnam*. We went to serve our country and now they call us baby killers. My dad can't look at me. At my job, I was fired for being too good even though I might have saved a young man's life. And I, well, I can't seem to get a handle on my emotions since I got back. I'm always either banshee-angry or bursting into tears. My dad is so ashamed, he said I went to Florence." She said it all in a rush and felt exhausted afterward.

"Are you menstruating now?"

Frankie took a moment to process that. "I tell you that I'm having trouble after being in Vietnam, and *that's* your question?"

"You were in Vietnam? There were no women in Vietnam, dear. Do you have thoughts of hurting yourself? Hurting others?"

Frankie got slowly to her feet. It felt nearly impossible to do so. "You won't help me?"

"I'm here for veterans."

"I *am* a veteran."

"In combat?"

"Well. No. But—"

"See? So, you'll be fine. Trust me. Go home. Go out with friends. Fall in love again. You're young. Just forget about Vietnam."

Just forget. It was what everyone recommended.

Why couldn't she do it? The doctor was right. She hadn't seen combat, hadn't been wounded or tortured.

Why couldn't she forget?

She turned and walked out of the office, past the men sitting in chairs along the wall, under the watchful eyes of President Nixon. In the lobby, she saw a pay phone and thought, *Barb,* and stopped.

She needed her best friend to talk her down from this ledge of despair.

She went to the phone, made a collect call.

Barb answered on the second ring. "Hello?"

"This is the operator. Will you accept a collect call from Frankie McGrath?"

"Yes," Barb said quickly.

The operator clicked off the line.

"Frankie? What's wrong?"

"I'm sorry. I know it's expensive to call collect—"

"Frances. What's wrong?"

"I . . . don't know. But I'm in bad shape, Barb. I'm kind of falling apart here." She tried to make herself laugh, to lighten it, and couldn't. "My parents threw me out. I crashed my car. I was fired. And that was just the last twenty-four hours."

"Oh, Frankie."

The compassion in Barb's voice was Frankie's undoing. She started crying—*pathetic*—and couldn't stop. "I need help."

"Where are you?"

"At the useless VA."

"Is there somewhere you could go?"

She couldn't think. She was still crying.

"*Frankie.*"

She wiped her eyes. "The Crystal Pier Cottages aren't far away. Finley and I used to ride bikes on the pier . . ."

"Go. Get a room. Eat something. And don't leave, okay? I'm on my way. You hear me?"

"It's too expensive to fly, Barb—"

"Don't leave, Frankie. Get a room at the Crystal Pier and stay there. I mean it."

———

Someone was pounding on the door.

Frankie sat up, immediately felt sick to her stomach. An empty gin bottle lay on the carpet by the bed.

"Open the damn door, Frankie."

Barb.

Frankie looked blearily around the cottage she'd rented, saw the empty gin bottle, an overflowing ashtray, empty potato chip bags.

No wonder she felt like hell.

She climbed out of bed and went to the door, unlocking it, letting it swing open.

Barb and Ethel stood there, side by side, both with worried looks on their faces.

"I don't know what's wrong with me," Frankie said. Her voice was hoarse. She'd been screaming in her sleep again.

Barb was the first to take Frankie in her arms. Ethel moved in beside them, wrapped her strong arms around both of them.

"I'd rather be in Pleiku," Frankie said. "At least there I know when to put on my flak jacket. Here . . ."

"Yeah," Barb said.

"I don't know what to do, who I am now. Without the Army or Rye . . . my dad threw me out of the house. I just want . . . I don't know . . . for someone to care that I'm home. That I went."

"We care," Ethel said. "That's why we're here. And we came up with a plan on the way here."

Frankie pushed the damp, greasy bangs out of her face. "A plan for what?"

"Your future."

"Do I get a say in it?" she asked sarcastically, but really she didn't care. She just wanted her friends to save her.

"No," Ethel said. "That was our first decision."

"When your girl calls and says, *I need help*, you help. So don't think you can change your mind now."

Frankie nodded. Behind her friends, she saw a yellow cab idling at the curb.

"Get your stuff," Barb said.

Frankie felt too crappy to argue or question and more relieved than she could say. She went into the bathroom, brushed her teeth and put on pants, then tossed her bloody nurse shoes in the trash and walked out barefoot.

"So, what am I doing to fix my life?" Frankie asked as the three of them walked to the waiting cab. Her girlfriends bookended her, stayed close, as if they were afraid she'd bolt.

Frankie tossed her overnight bag into the car, then slid into the backseat, with Barb on one side and Ethel on the other.

"Train station," Ethel said to the driver. At the same time Barb said, "We checked you out of the motel, Frankie, so sit tight."

The taxi drove back down the pier, tires bumping over the rough wood.

"Where are we going?" Frankie asked.

"My dad's farm near Charlottesville," Ethel said. "You two are moving into the bunkhouse. We'll remodel it ourselves. Give us a legit reason to hit things. I'm going to finish school. Barb joined that new organization. Vietnam Veterans Against the War."

Frankie turned. "You're against the war now?"

"It's got to stop, Frankie. I don't know if this can help, and I sure as hell don't want to be a part of some privileged white kids picketing something they know nothing about. But this—the VVAW—is about *us* having a voice. The veterans. Don't you think someone should listen to us?"

Frankie didn't know how she felt about that. "And me. What have you two decided on for me?"

"That's what we're giving you," Ethel said, "time to figure it out."

If Frankie hadn't been so sick of crying, so emptied out, she would have cried. Thank God for girlfriends. In this crazy, chaotic, divided world that was run by men, you could count on the women.

"This bunkhouse," Frankie said. "Is there indoor plumbing?"

Ethel's face transformed with a smile, revealing how nervous she'd been that Frankie would say no to this bold plan. "Why? You too good for a latrine, Lieutenant?"

Frankie smiled for the first time in . . . how long? She didn't even know. "No, ma'am. With you two at my side, I can live in practically anything."

Barb held out her hand. The three put their hands together. "Enough bad memories," she said solemnly. "We won't ever forget, God knows, but we move forward. Away from Vietnam. Into the future."

It felt solemn and important and suddenly possible. Frankie thought: *I won't talk about it anymore. I will forget. Soldier on.*

"Away," they said in one voice.

They stopped only long enough to get Frankie a new pair of shoes.

PART TWO

In a country where youth is adored, we lost ours before we were out of our twenties. We learned to accept death there, and it erased our sense of immortality. We met our human frailties, the dark side of ourselves, face-to-face . . . The war destroyed our faith, betrayed our trust, and dropped us outside the mainstream of our society. We still don't fully belong. I wonder if we ever will.

—WINNIE SMITH
AMERICAN DAUGHTER GONE TO WAR

Twenty-Three

At twenty-five, Frankie moved with the kind of caution that came with age; she was constantly on guard, aware that something bad could happen at any moment. She trusted neither the ground beneath her feet nor the sky above her head. Since coming home from war, she had learned how fragile she was, how easily upended her emotions could be.

Still, she had learned to hide her outbursts, her crying jags, even from her two best friends, who, for most of their first year in Virginia, had watched her intently, trying constantly to divine her moods, assess her level of self-destruction, her grief and anger. In the beginning, it had been difficult, settling into the time-honored McGrath camouflage of *I'm okay.*

The nightmares had been terrible when she first arrived here, had still wrenched her out of sleep and sent her careening onto the floor.

But time—and friendship—had done exactly as promised: pain and grief had grown soft in her hands, almost pliable. She found she could form them into something kinder if she was deliberate in thought and action, if she lived a careful, cautious life, if she stayed away from anything that reminded her of the war, of loss, of death.

By Christmas of that first year, she'd felt strong enough to write to her mother, who had promptly written back. In their family's way, neither spoke of the terrible night that had precipitated Frankie's flight across the country. They simply merged back onto their familiar road, the ground a little bumpy between them, but both determined to stay the course. Frankie remembered, and often reread, that first letter from her mother: *I am so grateful to your Army girlfriends for being there for you when your father and I were not. We love you, and if we don't say it often enough, it is because we grew up in families where there was no such vocabulary. About your father and his . . . reticence about you and the war. All I can say is that something in him was broken by being unable to serve his country. All the men of his generation went to Europe, while he stayed home. Yes, he was proud of Finley and ashamed of you. But perhaps in truth he is ashamed of himself and worries that you judge him harshly, as he feared his friends had done . . .*

Frankie never spoke about her struggles, tried never to say *Vietnam* out loud. And when she felt a rise in her blood pressure, a flood of grief or anger, she smiled tautly and left whatever room she was in. She'd learned that people noticed a raised voice; quiet was the perfect camouflage for pain.

Initially, it had been almost impossible to sever Vietnam from her life story. The world, it seemed, had conspired against such a healing.

The war was constantly in conversation. In bars, in living rooms, on the television. Everyone had an opinion. Now the majority of Americans seemed to be against the war and the men who fought it. In 1969, the world had learned about the horrifying massacre at My Lai, where American soldiers had killed as many as five hundred un-armed South Vietnamese civilians—men, women, and children—in their village. It had intensified the baby-killer talk about vets, more and more of whom were turning to heroin in-country and coming home addicted.

America was losing the war; that was obvious to everyone except

Nixon, who kept lying to the people and sending soldiers off to war, too many of whom came home in body bags.

Each of the women had responded differently to the rising tide of violence that was ripping the country apart, dividing young from old, rich from poor, conservative from liberal. Ethel was in her third year of veterinary school and worked part-time with her father. She and Noah had begun to talk of marriage, kids. The two of them never missed a Sunday at church or a local high school football game. Their fondness for casseroles and cribbage had created long-standing jokes between the women. Ethel had grown up on this farm, among these people, and she intended to be buried here. So she kept her head down and did her job and said nothing controversial to her friends and neighbors. *This war will be over soon,* she always said, *but I'll always live here. My kids will be in 4-H, I'll probably run the damned PTA.*

Barb was the opposite in every way. She'd become a vocal, participatory member of the Vietnam Veterans Against the War. She went to meetings. She painted signs. She protested. And not just the war. She lobbied for passage of the Equal Rights Amendment. She marched for a woman's right to a safe abortion and basic health care. When she wasn't trying to change the world, she earned money by bartending. It was, she said, a great job for a woman who hadn't yet decided where she belonged.

Frankie, on the other hand, had found her way back through nursing. She'd put up with the initial prejudice and disregard for her Vietnam training and become determined to show her skills. She'd worked harder and longer than most of the other nurses, put in the hours, and had taken specialized classes. In time, she'd become a surgical nurse; now she was working toward a specialization in trauma surgery.

On this cool April morning, she woke well before the dawn and dressed for riding. It would be cold out, a spring crispness in the air.

She had come to love the sweet-smelling air of the South, the way mist clung to the grass in the morning. It calmed the tumult in her soul. Today, the cherry trees along the driveway were in full pink bloom. Ethel had been right, all those years ago, when she'd said that riding horses was restorative to one's sense of peace.

Frankie loved the undulating green fields, the black four-rail fencing, the trees that changed their color with the weather. Now the leaves were the bright lime hue of new growth, and full of pink blossoms. But mostly it was being around the horses that calmed Frankie. Ethel had been right about that. Riding had steadied Frankie as much as friendship had.

Frankie ducked through the empty space between fence rails and headed into the barn; she could barely see her boots, the mist was so thick and gray.

Inside, the barn smelled of manure and fresh bales of hay and the grain they stored in large metal garbage cans. The horses nickered at her as she passed.

At the last stall on the left, she paused and lifted the latch. Silver Birch walked toward her, lips moving, looking for treats, breath snorting.

"Hey, girl," Frankie said, holding out her gloved hand.

Silver ate the grain messily, more falling to the ground than getting in her mouth. Frankie led the mare out into the aisle and saddled her quickly, pressing a knee to the mare's belly to aid her in tightening the girth.

In no time, Frankie and Silver were out on the trails, galloping through the mist. When Silver started to sound winded, Frankie slowed the mare to a trot, then a walk. They walked home slowly, clomping at a steady, calming pace.

Back in the barn, she fed and watered the horses, turned Silver out, and headed back to the small bunkhouse. Early morning sunlight drenched the fields. Off to the left was the main house, with its steeply pitched roof, large and welcoming porch, and whitewashed wooden sides, where Ethel lived with her father. Well off to the right was the bunkhouse that had once boarded farmworkers. Over the past eighteen months, it had been remodeled into a two-bedroom cottage where Frankie and Barb lived. The three women had learned how to paint, demolish, rebuild, and do rudimentary plumbing. They'd spent hours haunting garage sales and hauling other people's junk to be their treasures. Many evenings were spent sitting around the sooty river-rock fireplace, talking. They never ran out of things to say.

Frankie climbed the few steps and went into the bunkhouse's only bathroom, where she showered, changed, and dressed for work.

She was out of the house and on her way to work before Barb was even out of bed.

At the end of a twelve-hour shift in the OR, Frankie waved goodbye to her coworkers and headed out to her car—a dented old Ford Falcon that she and Barb shared—and jumped in. On the way out of town, she popped a John Denver tape into the eight-track and sang along.

She drove to the tavern where Barb currently worked and parked among the battered old trucks of the regulars who were there this time of day. Barb's bicycle stood slanted against the rough exterior plank wall.

Inside, the place was dark and musty-smelling, with sawdust on the floors and barstools worn to a velvet feel by one hundred years of faithful customers.

Barb had worked here for the past few months; it was not a job she intended to keep much longer. Or so she often said. Soon she'd look for something higher-end, nearer to the city, where the tips were better. But this was close to the farm and gave her lots of time to volunteer for her causes.

Now she stood behind the bar, a soggy bar rag over one shoulder, a red-white-and-blue cotton kerchief over her Afro. Huge gold hoop earrings caught the light.

Frankie sidled up onto a barstool. "Hey, there."

"Jed! I'm taking a break," Barb called out. A moment later her boss, Jed, shuffled out from the office and took his place behind the bar.

Barb grabbed a pair of cold beers and led the way out back, to one of the picnic tables. Come summer, the bar would sell house-smoked barbecue on red plastic plates, but not till the weather warmed up.

Frankie took the beer, snapped the cap, and took a long drink, leaning back against the table, stretching her legs out. She glanced at Barb, frowned, and said, "What's wrong?"

"You can read my thoughts now?"

"This is not a new skill, Barbara. What's up?"

"Damn it, I was going to ease my way into it." She sighed. "I have a favor to ask."

"Anything. You know that."

"It's for all of them," Barb said. "Finley and Jamie and Rye, and all the fallen."

Frankie flinched. The names were rarely mentioned between them. Barb and Ethel still worried that Frankie was fragile and could slide too easily back into grief, and they were right to be concerned. Frankie still sometimes woke up and, for a split second, forgot that Rye was gone and reached for him.

"The VVAW are meeting in Washington next week to protest. Guerrilla theater, they're calling it."

Vietnam Veterans Against the War.

"You know I'm not interested. You've asked before," Frankie said. "I'm not a marcher."

"This is special. Trust me. We aren't the only group that will march. We want to create a media event so big Nixon has to notice." Barb looked at her. "Come with me."

"Barb, you know I try not to think about . . . over there."

"I know, and I respect the effort. I know how hard it's been for you, but they're still dying in the jungle, Frankie. Dying for a lost war. And, well . . . you told me to do something for Will. This is what I'm doing."

"Not fair, throwing my words back at me."

"I know, I know. It's shitty, but we're believers, you and me," Barb said. "As banged-around as we've been and as much as we've seen, we're patriots."

"No one wants patriots anymore," Frankie said. "I can't wear an Army T-shirt off the property or I'll be spit on. The country thinks we're monsters. But I won't disrespect the troops."

"It's not disrespectful to protest, Frankie. We had that wrong. It takes guts to stand up and demand a change. We're *vets*. Shouldn't our voices be heard in protest, too? Shouldn't they be *loud*?"

Barb pulled a folded-up magazine page out of her back pocket, smoothed out the wrinkles, and laid it out on the table. It was a full-page ad in *Playboy* for the Vietnam Veterans Against the War. The picture was of a solitary coffin, draped in an American flag. The headline read IN THE LAST TEN YEARS, OVER 335,000 OF OUR BUDDIES HAVE BEEN KILLED OR WOUNDED IN VIETNAM, AND MORE ARE BEING KILLED EVERY DAY. WE DON'T THINK IT'S WORTH IT. In the bottom corner of the ad was a plea to JOIN US.

Frankie stared at the advertisement. Since the tide of public opinion had turned so clearly against the war, more and more numbers of the wounded and fallen were being reported. It was tough to see in print. So many young men killed, while others were still being shipped over, spun up.

The press wasn't blindly reporting what Nixon wanted them to anymore. Journalists had been granted access to the troops; they witnessed the battles, reported on the dead. This week a female journalist from Australia had been among a group captured by the People's Army of Vietnam and taken prisoner. Kate Webb. Everyone should now know that women were in Vietnam, too. Frankie took a deep breath, exhaled.

Barb said, "Slim told me once that the average life expectancy of a helicopter pilot in Vietnam is thirty days."

"I know. I've heard that, too. I don't know if it's true."

"We have to stop it," Barb said. "Us. The ones who paid the price."

It was wrong. Criminal, the way the U.S. government was failing the military. But what could a handful of veterans do to stop a war? People like Barb had been marching for years, and what good had it done?

Protest seemed futile. Maybe even unpatriotic.

But men were dying over there, crashing in helicopters and stepping on land mines and getting shot by an enemy they never saw.

How could she *not* protest that, at least?

"We could be arrested," Frankie said.

"They could call in the National Guard. We could be tear-gassed or shot at," Barb said solemnly, then added, "Like at Kent State and Jackson."

"Way to look at the bright side."

"This isn't a joke," Barb said. "The old white men who run this country are scared. And people do stupid, ugly things when they're scared." She leaned close. "But they're counting on their power and our fear. And every minute, some woman's son is being killed over there. Some girl's brother."

Frankie didn't want to march. She didn't want to think about Vietnam and what it had cost her. She wanted to do what she'd been trying to do for more than two years: forget.

It was dangerous, what Barb was asking of Frankie, an upsetting of an already precariously balanced peace in Frankie's mind.

No fear, McGrath.

Jamie's voice in her head.

Barb was right.

Frankie needed to do this. As a veteran of Vietnam, and for Finley and Jamie and Rye; she had to add her voice to the rising scream of dissent. She had to say: *No more.*

"Just this once," Frankie said.

She regretted it almost instantly.

——

On the day before the march, Frankie had trouble concentrating at work. In between surgeries, she worried about what lay ahead, her mind obsessively scrolled through the violence that had marked so many rallies and protests. Nixon had sent the National Guard in to stop a peaceful protest at Kent State less than a year ago. When the smoke cleared, four students were dead and dozens wounded. Only eleven days later, the police had shot students at a Jackson State College war protest.

But the truth was that although she worried about violence at the march, she worried more about standing there with other veterans, saying, *I was there.* For the past two years, she'd hidden that fact at every opportunity, changed the conversation when Vietnam came up. Even Barb and Ethel rarely mentioned Vietnam; Frankie knew their silence was to protect her, and on good days, she knew it helped. On bad days, she worried that she couldn't forget because there was something wrong with her, something broken. In time, hiding her service and not talking about it had allowed shame to take root. She was never exactly sure what she was ashamed of, just that she was weak, or had somehow done something bad, been a part of something bad, something no one wanted to talk about. Maybe it was simply being a part of the apparent breakdown of American honor. She didn't know.

On the way home, she tried to figure out what the hell one should wear to a protest meeting. She decided on hip-hugger jeans with a wide western-style belt and a ribbed white turtleneck. She dried her hair down straight from a center part. At the last minute, she went in search of her ANC pin—a brass caduceus with its wings behind a bold N—and pinned it on her sweater.

Leaving her bedroom, she shut the door behind her.

In the kitchen, Barb and Ethel were talking quietly. Barb wore her old, stained fatigue pants with a black turtleneck and a Levi's jacket with the sleeves cut off. Dozens of the pins and patches she'd collected from friends and patients in Vietnam decorated the front of the vest. She'd drawn a big black peace symbol on the back. She'd painted a BRING THEM HOME! sign and stapled it to a yardstick.

Ethel, wearing her blue lab coat, poured herself a cup of coffee. "I don't know how Barb talked you into this, Frank. The VVAW is as sexist as the SDS," she added. "If you girls show up, they'll ask you to make coffee and do snack runs."

"Those who stay behind don't get to bitch," Barb said.

"Disappointingly," Frankie said glumly.

The three of them had spent at least an hour last night sitting around the firepit in the backyard, wrapped in woolen blankets, discussing today's march. Barb had said that more than a dozen anti-war groups were scheduled to arrive in D.C. in the next few days. The VVAW wanted to separate themselves by marching first. They had big plans to draw attention to themselves. Make the news broadcasts.

"Just be careful," Ethel said. "Be home on time, or I'm calling the police."

Barb laughed. "If we get into trouble, it will be with the police."

Frankie stared at her friend. "Comments like that are *not* helpful."

"Come on, kid," Barb said. "We're making like the wind and blowing."

Ethel hugged Frankie and said, "Go with God, girls. Change the world."

Frankie followed Barb out to the car and got into the passenger seat.

Barb started the car and cranked up the music on Creedence.

Barb turned, smiling. "You ready?"

Frankie sighed. Her nerves were strung taut. This whole thing was a mistake. "Just drive, Barbara."

It was nearing midnight when they pulled into D.C.

Their destination, Potomac Park, was a black expanse in the middle of the brightly lit city; in the darkness, Frankie could make out tents here and there. The VVAW had occupied the park, turned it into a campground.

"Let's find a spot off to ourselves," Frankie said.

Barb parked the car on the side of the street. "Get the tent out of the trunk."

Across the street, a long line of policemen in riot gear stood shoulder to shoulder.

"Don't say anything," Frankie warned as they passed the policemen on their way to the park. "I mean it. I am not getting arrested before the march."

Barb gave a curt nod. They came to the edge of the large park. Saying nothing—not to each other and not to the other VVAW campers—they pitched their tent, then set up two chairs out front. As they sat in the dark, listening to the din of tent spikes being pounded into the ground, more and more cars drove up, headlights spearing through the night. They heard music in the distance and the quiet buzz of conversations.

"I wonder if we are the only women," Frankie said, drinking coffee from a thermos.

Barb sighed. "Aren't we always?"

In the morning, when Frankie stepped out of the tent, she found herself standing amid a veritable sea of male veterans—thousands—most of them about her age, wearing worn, stained fatigues and jeans and boonie hats; some wore peace symbols and carried flags from their states, their units. Hundreds of cars were parked near the park, their doors emblazoned with slogans, convoys from California and Colorado. More had parked on the grass.

As she stood there, a battered, beaten-up school bus drove up onto the grass, stopped, and opened its doors. Veterans exited the bus, singing, "What's it good for? Absolutely nothing!"

In the center of the park, a bushy-haired man with a bullhorn jumped up into the back of a pickup truck onto which someone had spray-painted NO MORE! "My brothers-in-arms, it's time. We're marching to be heard today, we're raising our voices—but not our fists, not our guns—to say, *Enough. Bring our soldiers home!* Line up behind Ron in the wheelchair. A single, unbroken column. Be peaceful. Don't give the Man any reason to stop us. Let's go!"

The men slowly formed a column, led by several veterans in wheelchairs who held flags. Behind them were men on crutches, men with burned faces and missing arms, blind men being led by their friends.

Barb and Frankie were the only two women in the park that they could see. They held hands and joined their brothers on the march across the Lincoln Memorial Bridge.

Vietnam veterans: a river of them, marching and chanting, holding signs in the air.

More men joined them, rushed forward, yelling out slogans, signs raised.

Someone bumped into Frankie so hard that she stumbled sideways, lost her hold on Barb's hand, and fell to the ground. She yelled "Barb!" and heard "Frankie!" but men swarmed in between them.

Frankie couldn't see her friend in the crowd. "Meet back at the tent!" she yelled, hoping Barb could hear.

"You okay, ma'am?" A man helped her to her feet.

He was young, blond, with a scraggly reddish-blond beard and mustache. He held on to her upper arm, steadied her. He wore torn, stained jungle fatigues, with the sleeves cut off. He'd drawn a huge peace symbol on his helmet. In his other hand, he held a sign that read VIETNAM VETERANS AGAINST THE WAR.

The protesters kept moving, shoving the two of them forward.

"Stop the war! Bring them home! Stop the war! Bring them home!"

"You should move to the side, ma'am," he said.

Someone jostled Frankie again. She stumbled. "I'm here to march."

"Sorry, lady. This march is for vets. We're trying to make a statement. Hopefully that asshole in the White House will listen to us and stop lying to the country."

"I'm a veteran," she said.

"Of Vietnam," he said impatiently, looking ahead.

"I was there."

"There weren't women in 'Nam."

The chanting grew louder. "Stop the war! Bring them home."

"If you didn't meet someone like me, you were lucky. It means—"

"Just move to the side, ma'am. This is for the men who were fighting. In combat, you know?" He disappeared into the moving crowd full of military shirts and bare chests and fatigues. Long hair and Afros and helmets.

What the hell?

So she didn't belong here, either? "I WAS THERE," she screamed in frustration.

She muscled her way forward, melded into the throng of protesters as they crossed the bridge. "Stop the war!" she said, raising her fist. "Bring them home!" Her voice was nothing amid the yelling, but she kept shouting, saying it louder and louder until she was screaming it, screaming at Nixon, at the administration, at the North Vietnamese. The more she shouted, the angrier she became; by the time they reached Arlington National Cemetery with all those white crosses planted in the trimmed green grass, she was furious.

At Arlington Cemetery, policemen moved in to stop a group of black-clad women who carried wreaths.

"They're Gold Star Mothers," someone yelled. "Let them through."

"Let them through, let them through, let them through," the crowd chanted.

The Gold Star Mothers stood outside the entrance to the cemetery in a small clot, all in black, their movements blocked. It seemed they didn't know where to go. None dropped their floral wreaths.

Gold Star Mothers, women who had lost their sons in Vietnam, being denied the opportunity to put wreaths on their sons' graves. One of the mothers looked up, her cheeks lined with tears, and met Frankie's gaze.

It made her think of her mother and the loss of her brother. Losing Finley had destroyed their family.

How dare the cops haul Gold Star Mothers away from their sons' graves?

The mood of the marchers changed. Frankie felt the outrage, the anger. Frankie joined her voice in the chanting. "Let them in."

"Hell, no, we don't want your war!"

A helicopter flew threateningly over the crowd. Frankie heard the familiar *thwop-thwop-thwop* and thought of all the men who'd died. And she knew that helicopters had guns.

"Bring them home!" she screamed. "End the war!"

⸻

Two days later, Frankie and Barb were back in D.C. as hundreds of thousands of protesters poured into the city, coming together from side streets, from parks, from across the bridge; not just veterans anymore. College kids, professors, men and women from all across the country. Women pushing strollers, men with small children on their shoulders.

The denial of the Gold Star Mothers to mourn their sons on the day of the VVAW march had been shown on every news show across America. It had become the perfect visual reminder of how far wrong America had gone on Vietnam: Mothers not allowed to visit their sons' graves. Men decimated by the war, torn apart on the battlefield, and forgotten at home.

It was *wrong*.

Frankie had been told often enough by her girlfriends, by Finley, by Jamie, that she was unyielding in her morality, and it was true. Deep down, she was still the good Catholic girl she'd been in her youth. She believed in good and evil, right and wrong, the dream of America. Who would she be if she chose to look away from the wrongness of this war?

Today, she stood again with Barb on Constitution Avenue, a part of this larger, angrier crowd, two women in a vast sea of people carrying signs, veterans in wheelchairs, raising their fists in anger. This second march on Washington in a week had drawn dozens of anti-war groups; it was to be a massive protest, to last for days, a tidal wave of anti-war sentiment to flood the White House and the Capitol. All of it would be captured by news crews and broadcast into every living room in America.

Barb raised her sign. It read BRING THE TROOPS HOME NOW!

The Vietnam Veterans Against the War were easily recognizable in their fatigues and patched-up jean jackets and boonie hats, but there were thousands of other protesters: hippies and college kids stood with men in suits and women in dresses. Nuns, priests, doctors, teachers. Anyone with a voice who wanted to demand that Nixon stop the war.

Frankie and Barb held hands as they marched, but this time they understood the risks better and had agreed to meet at a local hotel if they got separated. Barb stuck her sign in the air, yelled, "Bring them home, bring them home!"

The marchers came to a stop at the Capitol steps, pressed in together, shoulder to shoulder. Men raised their voices and their signs, yelling, "Stop the war! Bring them home!" while television news crews filmed it all.

A man with long hair, wearing fatigues, stepped forward, stood alone for a moment. The crowd fell silent.

A wave of anticipation swept through the VVAW group, and then something flew through the air from the protest crowd, sailed over the barricade, and landed on the Capitol steps with a *clink,* glinted in a ray of sunlight.

A war medal.

One by one, veterans stepped forward, stood alone, ripped medals off of their chests, and threw them, clanging, onto the steps. Purple Hearts, Bronze Stars, Good Conduct Medals, dog tags. Some hit the steps and clanked against the sudden silence of the crowd. Barb let go of Frankie, pushed her way to the front of the crowd, and threw her first lieutenant's bars onto the steps.

Police in riot gear—helmeted, with plastic shields up—arrived in a blare of whistles. They charged the crowd, began hauling the protesters away.

The crowd broke up; pandemonium filled the streets.

Frankie was knocked off her feet, fell hard. In the confusion, she curled into a small ball and rolled away, trying to protect herself from both protesters and police. She edged toward the chain-link fence barricade and lay there, panting, feeling bruised. Tear gas floated through the air, stung Frankie's eyes, and blurred her vision until she could barely see.

How long did she lie there, blinking, her eyes on fire? She didn't know.

Slowly, she got to her feet, trying to focus. The street was full of police in riot gear, hauling protesters away, cars honking, driving away, news vans following.

Half-blind, Frankie stumbled forward, unable to quite comprehend everything she'd just seen, the deep and utter wrongness of it. The street was littered with cigarette butts, protest brochures, broken signs, ripped-up draft cards.

On the steps of the Capitol, behind the temporary chain-link fencing, hundreds of medals glittered in the sunlight. Medals that had cost each recipient so much, thrown away in protest.

A lone policeman began picking them up. What would happen to them, the medals men had sacrificed and bled for?

Frankie grabbed the chain-link fence, shook it hard. "Don't you touch those!"

A man grabbed her by the arm. "Don't," he said. "They'll arrest you."

She tried to pull free. "I don't care." Suddenly she was furious. How dare the American government do these things to her own citizens; stop mothers from honoring their fallen sons, ignore the meaning of a medal thrown through the air? She wiped her eyes again, tried to clear her vision. "They shouldn't be allowed to touch those medals."

"The vets made their point. A damn good one," the man said. "That image will stay with people: a vet in a wheelchair throwing his Purple Heart away? Powerful, man."

Frankie pulled back, wrenched her arm free. The man who'd stopped her wasn't what she expected. In the first place, he was older than most of the protesters, certainly older than most of the Vietnam vets. Long dark hair fell in feathery layers almost to his shoulders and was threaded through with gray. A thick mustache covered his upper lip. He wore round John Lennon sunglasses, but even so she could see how green his eyes were.

"You're a Vietnam vet?" she said, trying to find her calm again. All of this had upset her, dredged up emotions she didn't want to feel. She had to dial it back. And fast. Loosing her Vietnam emotions was never good.

"No. Just someone who's against the war. Henry Acevedo." He held out his hand.

She shook it distractedly. "Frankie McGrath. Did you have a son in Vietnam?"

He laughed. "I'm not *that* old. I'm here for the same reason you are: to say enough is goddamn enough."

"Yeah. Well. Thanks, Henry." Frankie walked away.

Henry fell into step beside her.

"Do you think these protests will do any good?" she asked.

"We have to try," was his answer.

Yeah, Frankie thought, *it's true.* She'd seen people hauled away by the police today, risking their freedom to protest a war many of them hadn't even fought. Civilians were being arrested for exercising the fundamental American right to protest their government; at Kent State and in Jackson, they'd been shot for it.

She didn't know if protesting and marching and making signs could actually effect change, but she damn sure knew that America wasn't preserving democracy or fighting communism in Vietnam, and it certainly wasn't winning. Ultimately too many lives would be lost in pursuit of nothing.

"Can I buy you a drink?" Henry asked.

Frankie had almost forgotten the older man was with her; she'd been lost in the wilds of her own past. They'd walked almost two blocks together. She stopped, looked at him.

Long, wild hair, bright green eyes, lines that hinted at sorrow, a nose that looked as if it had been broken more than once. Worn, faded Levi's, a Rolling Stones T-shirt. Sandals. He looked like a Berkeley philosophy professor.

"Why?"

He shrugged. "Why not? I feel . . . bereft, I guess. That was tough to watch."

What man used the word *bereft*?

"Are you a philosophy professor? Or a surfer, maybe?"

"Good guess. Psychiatrist. And yeah, I surf. Grew up in La Jolla. That's in Southern California."

Frankie smiled. "I'm a Coronado Island girl. My brother and I used to surf Trestles and Black's Beach."

"Small world."

Frankie felt a kinship with him. She liked that he was a surfer, that he knew Trestles, and that he was here, standing against a war he'd had no part in. "I could use a drink. I'm supposed to meet my girlfriend at the Hay Adams. We got separated."

They turned in tandem, heading toward the hotel.

Across the street, a small table had been positioned beneath a banner that read DON'T LET THEM BE FORGOTTEN.

At the table, behind stacks of anti-war flyers, two long-haired men with unruly sideburns sat in folding chairs. "Hey, lady, want to buy a bracelet and help bring a POW home?"

Frankie walked over to the table, looked down at a cardboard box full of silver metal bracelets.

"They're five bucks apiece," the guy behind the table said.

Frankie pulled one of the bracelets out. It was a thin silver cuff, with MAJ ROBERT WELCH 1–16–1967 engraved on it.

"We're a student organization," one of the kids said. "We're raising money. We work with the League of POW/MIA Families. It's a new organization."

"League of Families?" Frankie asked.

"Navy wives, mostly, fighting to bring their husbands home. There's a fundraiser in town next week, if you'd like to join the effort. Here's a flyer. They need donations."

Frankie took the flyer, handed the guy ten dollars, and put the bracelet on.

She and Henry walked to the hotel, passed a worried-looking doorman who seemed ready to stop them, but didn't. They went downstairs, into the sexy basement bar where it was rumored that much of the country's governing decisions were made by men drinking martinis.

They chose a booth in the back; he ordered a beer, she a gin martini. On the table in front of them, a pair of coasters showed a caricature of President Nixon. Frankie realized her hands were shaking so she lit up a cigarette.

The bartender brought over a small bowl full of homemade potato chips.

She sipped her drink, which helped to ease the slight tremor in her hands. Her eyes still stung, but her vision had cleared. Cigarette smoke wafted between them. Someone in here was smoking a cigar, too.

"Who did you lose to Vietnam?" Henry asked.

She put down her glass. There was something in the way he looked at her, a quiet compassion, maybe, a depth of caring she was unused to. "It's a long list."

"A brother?"

"He was the first. Yeah. But . . . there were . . . others."

He said nothing more but didn't look away. She had a feeling he saw more than most people. The silence became unnerving.

"I was there," she said in a soft voice, surprising herself with the admission.

"I see the pin," he said. "Your caduceus. Wings. You're a nurse. I've heard stories about women like you."

"How? No one talks about the war. No one who was there, anyway."

"I treat a few vets in my practice. Alcoholics, addicts, mostly. Do you have nightmares, Frankie? Trouble sleeping?"

Before Frankie could answer—deflect—Barb showed up, panting and out of breath. She slid into the booth, bumped Frankie hard. "Did you see us throw the medals? That will make the news." She raised a hand to the bartender, yelled, "Rum and Coke."

Henry was already sliding out of the booth, standing. He looked down at Frankie. "It was nice to meet you, Frankie. How do I find you?" he asked too quietly for Barb to hear.

"Sorry, Henry. I don't think I'm ready to be found."

He touched her shoulder gently. "Take care of yourself."

Did he give those words a weight?

"Who was that?" Barb asked, reaching for a potato chip. "One of your dad's friends?"

"He's not that old," Frankie said, staring down at the new silver bracelet she wore. With a fingertip, she traced the engraving. The major had gone missing three months before Frankie landed in Vietnam. While she was at Fort Sam Houston, not learning enough to deploy.

How many prisoners of war were there? And why were they never in the news?

"Frankie?" Barb said, finishing her drink. "What is it? Memories? Do you need to talk?"

Frankie looked up. "I'm glad we marched. You were right."

Barb smiled. "Girlfriend, I am always right. You know that by now."

"But I think we can do more."

Twenty-Four

"You owe me," Frankie said again.

Barb stood in their small pine-plank-walled living room, wearing only her underpants and a bra. Their old black-and-white television hummed quietly behind them; Hugh Downs saying that the Nixon administration had arrested thirteen thousand anti-war protesters in three days. The footage of the Gold Star Mothers and the medals being thrown filled the oval screen; after that came footage from Kent State, where the National Guard had killed unarmed students. "You're glad you went to the march."

"I am. And you'll be glad we went to a fundraiser to help bring POWs home. I followed your lead. Now you need to follow mine."

"Why do you even want to go? You're not a Navy wife."

"I was supposed to be," Frankie said gently. "And for Fin. I can't imagine him stuck in a cage somewhere, forgotten. Why don't you want to go?"

"Navy wives. And pantyhose. You know I haven't worn them in years."

"You can shimmy into pantyhose and eat lunch with other women. I'll buy you a rum and Coke after."

"I am going to need one."

Frankie dressed in a way that would have made her mother proud: in a navy blue knit pantsuit. Beneath the jacket, she wore a bold geometric print blouse with large, pointed lapels. She pulled her hair back from a severe center part and put it in a ponytail.

Frankie knew about Navy wives. Coronado was full of them. She knew they maintained a strict social hierarchy based on their husbands' rank. Frankie wouldn't be surprised to learn that they still gave out calling cards to each other. But she didn't share any of this with Barb.

At 11:50 A.M., she and Barb (who wore a black miniskirt and a black turtleneck and black knee boots) pulled up in front of the Hay Adams Hotel.

A stream of protesters passed the hotel, marching toward the Capitol. Thousands of them, intent on disrupting the government.

Police in riot gear stood behind barricades.

"We should be with them," Barb said.

"Not today," Frankie said. "Come on."

Once inside the hotel, they rode the elevator up to the rooftop, which overlooked the White House and the Washington Monument.

Inside the rooftop restaurant, a giant banner had been strung up: DON'T LET THEM BE FORGOTTEN.

Frankie felt a shiver of emotion. They *had* been forgotten. Even by her.

At the front entrance, two well-dressed women sold tickets for the luncheon and handed out donation envelopes.

Frankie bought two tickets and led Barb into the luncheon. The room reminded her of the Coronado Golf and Tennis Club: white tablecloths and bone china plates and sterling silverware. In the front of the room stood a podium with a microphone.

Women in dresses and pantsuits drifted into the room, talking to one another. Several moved from table to table. The officers' wives, probably. She and Barb found two empty seats and sat down. A waiter promptly poured them wine.

"See?" Frankie said. "Not all bad."

The room filled up slowly. Waiters moved from table to table, serving each guest tuna salad in a scooped-out red bell pepper.

A slim blond woman in a knit cornflower-blue dress took to the podium and said, "Hello, Navy wives and friends. Welcome to our nation's capital. I'm Anne Jenkins, from San Diego. My husband is Commander Mike Jenkins, who is currently a prisoner of war in Hoa Lo Prison in Hanoi. I am here, along with several of my fellow wives, to seek donations, in both time and money, to help bring our POWs home."

The room fell silent. Forks were set down.

"As some of you may know, many of us have been fighting this battle for years. The information coming from the Nixon administration is shoddy and incomplete at best. The military's *missing in action* and *killed in action* reports are unreliable. Jane Adon's husband was shot down in 1966. The government first told her he was killed in action and reported that his remains were 'unrecoverable.' She held a funeral for him. We all mourned for him. And then, six months ago, my husband included a mention in his letter of the perfect daylight he'd seen recently. Well, that was the name of Adon's boat. We think it *may* mean he is alive and at the Hanoi Hilton. But, I ask you, what is she supposed to tell her children now?

"This is unacceptable. And Jane is not alone. I spoke with Senator Bob Dole last year, who admitted that as of 1970, most senators didn't even know what MIA or POW meant. Think about that. Last year the people running our country—a country at war—didn't know what missing in action meant. Thankfully, Mr. Dole—a proud vet himself—is on our side, and we finally hope that the tide is turning our way. Enough of our silence, enough asking for information politely. Enough being ladylike. Being 'just' wives. It's time that we stand up, strong and proud as military families and wives, and *demand* answers. We've set up headquarters in an empty building here in D.C. And we are looking for space in San Diego, where most of us live. It is our goal to find the name of every American POW in Vietnam and put pressure on the government to bring them home. With help from our imprisoned husbands, we have been collecting a list of names. We believe we know all of the prisoners in Hoa Lo now. We intend to become a political machine with one purpose: make everyone in this country aware of the military men in cages in Vietnam."

"How?" someone asked.

"We start by writing letters and giving interviews. Make our missing husbands a story that needs telling. Who is willing to write letters to bring our brave boys home?"

Applause. Women stood up, clapping.

Anne waited for the noise to die down, then said, "Thank you. Bless you. And if you can't write letters, please donate generously to our cause. We will make this happen, ladies. No more silence on our watch. We won't let them be forgotten."

Anne nodded and left the podium, stopping at each table to say hello. She came at last to Frankie's table and paused there.

"That was wonderful, Anne," said one of the women at the table.

"Thank you. Lord, I hate public speaking." Anne looked at Barb, then at Frankie. "Welcome, ladies. Are you Navy wives?"

"We were Army nurses in Vietnam," Frankie said. "First Lieutenants Frankie McGrath and Barb Johnson."

"Bless you," the women at the table said in quiet tones.

Anne said, "We all know sailors who came home because of the medical aid they received. Are you ladies from D.C.?"

"Georgia," Barb answered.

"Coronado Island, ma'am," Frankie said.

"Coronado?" Anne said, looking at her. "Frankie McGrath. You're Bette and Connor's daughter?"

"Guilty as charged," Frankie said.

Anne smiled. "What a lovely woman your mother is. A tireless fundraiser even after . . . your brother's death. Bette and I chaired a beautification committee a few years ago. No one does a better event. I was sorry to hear about her stroke."

Frankie frowned. "Her what?"

"Her stroke. It's a reminder to all of us, isn't it? Tragedy can strike in an instant. And after all you've already suffered. Please tell your father she's in my prayers."

———

Beneath the bright glare of white light, Frankie sat in an uncomfortable chair, staring out at the busy runways of Dulles Airport. A series of recorded announcements blared through the speakers, but it was just noise to her. The mix of people in here was a microcosm of the sharp division in America—long-haired kids dressed in ragged jeans and bright T-shirts, soldiers coming home from war, ordinary folks trying not to make eye contact with either side.

Frankie had called the house a dozen times in the past twenty-four hours, but not once had anyone picked up the phone. She had no way of leaving a message, so she'd called her father's office for the first time in years and found out from her father's secretary that Mom was in the hospital. Ten minutes later, she was packed and ready to fly home.

At the gate for her flight, she dug through her macramé handbag for a cigarette and lit up.

How could her father not have called her and told her this terrible news?

Just more proof that he'd written her out of their family.

When they called her flight, she put out her cigarette, slung her old travel bag over one shoulder, and boarded the aircraft.

At her row, in the smoking section, she took her seat on the aisle.

When the stewardess came around in her pert red-and-blue mini-skirt uniform with matching hat and shoes, Frankie ordered a gin on the rocks. "Make it a double."

Frankie had never been to the medical center before. It was an impressive white building positioned at the top of a hill in San Diego: a glittering glass and stone architectural gem. They'd been building it the year Finley died.

It was nearing nighttime when her taxi pulled up in front of the hospital. She stepped into the brightly lit lobby, with its two-story wall of exterior windows and the curving wall of interior windows. Palm trees stood tall and vibrant, in contrast to the white walls and silver metal window frames.

The lobby held a collection of modern, comfortable-looking rust-colored chairs, most of which were empty on this Tuesday evening in May. A television in the corner stuttered out a canned laugh track on an episode of *The Beverly Hillbillies*.

Frankie walked up to the front desk, behind which sat a tall, bony-faced woman wearing round glasses and bright red lipstick. A name tag identified her as Karla.

"Hi, Karla," Frankie said. "I'm here to see Bette McGrath."

Karla consulted a set of papers. "Family only."

"I'm her daughter."

"Okay. She's in the ICU. Second floor. The nurses' station is to the left of the elevator."

"Thank you." Frankie headed to the bank of elevators and went up to the second floor.

The ICU was newer, brighter, than the SICU in the Virginia hospital where Frankie worked, but it was the same series of glassed rooms, with nurses moving from room to room, family members crowded at doorways, looking worried, offering each other brittle smiles.

At the nurses' station, she stopped, asked about her mother, and was directed to Room 245, where she found her mom lying in a bed in a glass-walled room, connected to a ventilator, which breathed for her.

A crisscross of white straps kept the breathing and feeding tubes in place. The bed's metal railings were up on either side, and the head of the bed was angled up slightly. A stark white pillow framed Mom's head.

Machines stood around her, whooshing, beeping, showing graphs of color.

Frankie drew in a sharp breath; Mom was fifty-two years old but looked ancient, gaunt, and drawn.

"Hey, Mom." She approached the bed slowly, pulled her mother's chart out of its sleeve, read it. *Intercranial hemorrhage. Respiratory failure.*

She put it back in the sleeve. "We don't care about statistics, do we, Mom? You're tough. I know you are."

She stared down at her mother's pale, bluish skin, her sunken cheeks and closed eyes.

Frankie wanted to shut out the sound of the ventilator and imagine the natural rise and fall of her mother's chest, but she had too much training to fool herself. She knew that stroke patients on ventilators often died within the first few weeks.

She brushed the back of her knuckles across Mom's soft, warm forehead.

She heard footsteps and knew without looking who was here.

Her dad. The man who'd once called her Peanut and carried her on his shoulders and tossed her playfully into the air until his arms must have ached from the effort. The man she'd gone to war to make proud.

He paused at the door.

Frankie looked up.

He stared at her for a long moment, as if deliberating what he should do, and then he walked slowly forward, took his place on the other side of the bed. His fingers curled tightly around the bed rail. She saw how tanned he was, even in May, from walking job sites, overseeing construction beneath the hot Southern California sun. He wore a bright blue polyester shirt, buttoned incorrectly, and beige polyester pants. A wide, tightened belt hinted at weight loss.

"You didn't call me," she said.

"I couldn't."

She heard the way his voice cracked and knew it had been fear that stopped him from calling, not anger. "When did it happen?"

"A few days ago. She had a headache," he said softly, in a voice she barely recognized. "I told her to quit complaining."

Pain filled his eyes when he looked at Frankie.

"She'll come out of this, Dad."

"You think? I mean, you're a nurse. You should know."

"She's tough," Frankie said.

"Yeah."

"It's just the three of us now, Dad," she said.

He looked up, tears in his eyes at the reminder that they'd lost Finley, that any one of them could be lost in a moment, while you looked away, took a breath, stayed angry.

"Will you stay?" he asked.

So, he felt it, too. They were family. As tattered and beaten-up as the connection might feel, it had a strong core, something you could hang on to. "Of course," Frankie said.

For the next two days, Frankie rarely left her mother's side. She made friends with the ICU nurses on all of the shifts and brought them donuts when she arrived in the morning. She sat at her mother's bedside hour after hour, reading books aloud, talking about anything she could think of, rubbing lotion onto her hands and feet. Dad stayed as much as he could, but she saw how difficult it was for him to be here. For a few hours every day, he went to work, just—Frankie thought—to escape the pain of waiting and watching, but then he came back, sat in the room with Frankie and Mom. He told Mom stories of their youth, retraced the steps of their love, laughed about the way her family had reacted. Frankie learned more about her dad, and the depth of his love for his family, than she'd learned in all the years before, but neither of them spoke to the other about it.

Today—finally—the ICU team was going to take Mom off the ventilator.

"What does that mean?" Dad asked for the third time as they rode up the elevator.

"If she does well on the readiness test—if her vitals are solid—they'll wean her off the sedation and wake her up and take out the breathing tube."

Frankie saw the change in her father's posture. His shoulders sank; he kind of caved in on himself and became smaller.

In an earlier version of their relationship, she might have slipped her hand in his, both giving and taking comfort, but they hadn't healed enough yet for so bold a move. Frankie had spent two nights in her frilly pink bedroom, had cooked him two dinners, and they'd spoken only about Mom. Perhaps nothing else mattered until she was better. The long silences didn't feel angry, didn't hurt Frankie's feelings. He was sad, and Frankie knew every nuance of sorrow; he just didn't know how to act without Mom, who to be, what to say. This locomotive of a man who'd rumbled so loudly through her childhood had derailed.

The elevator doors opened. Frankie and her father walked down the hall, stood outside the windows of her mother's room.

At six A.M., the ICU was relatively quiet. A team of nurses was in Mom's room, gathered around her bed, checking her readiness.

"What if she can't . . ." Dad said, unable to even voice the question. *Breathe on her own.*

"This would be a good time for you to pray." She stepped closer to the glass window, trying to hear what the nurses were saying inside the room.

Peak airway pressure . . . twenty-three.

That was good.

Vital signs.

She looked at the machines.

The nurses nodded to each other. One of them picked up the phone and relayed everything to the doctor.

Frankie saw the nurse nod and hang up. *Wean her off sedation.*

Frankie felt her father move closer to her. She almost leaned against him. They watched, waiting.

Through the window, Frankie saw her mother's eyelids flutter. Slowly, slowly, her eyes opened. The unit nurse extubated Mom, who immediately started coughing.

"She's breathing," Dad said.

As soon as they were allowed into the room, Frankie and her father took their places; one on either side of her bed.

Mom blinked slowly.

Dad touched her face. "Bette, you scared me."

"Yeah ..." she said with a lopsided half smile.

Mom's head lolled to the right. She stared up at Frankie. "My ... grl ..."

Frankie's eyes filled with tears. "Hey, Mom."

"Fran ..." she whispered, lifting one bony, shaking hand up to be touched. "What ... done ... to yr ... hair?"

Frankie could only laugh.

May 9, 1971

Dear Barb and Ethel,
Hello from the bubble world of Coronado Island.

Sorry it's taken a while to write, but it was kind of touch and go with my mom for a while. The good news is that she's out of the hospital. It will take some time for her to get full mobility, so I'm going to stay to help out. No idea how long. I've quit my job at the hospital in Charlottesville. Would you mind sending my few things here?

*I want you both to know how much you mean to me and that
my years with you—both in Vietnam and Virginia—have been the
best of times.*

I'll get back to see you when I can.

Until then, stay cool.

Love you both.

F

~~~

May 14, 1971

Dear Frankie,

*You're breaking up the band, girl, and I hate it, but I think it's time,
and this is the kick in the ass I needed. I've sent a résumé to Operation Breadbasket in Atlanta. Maybe I'll meet Jesse Jackson!*

I'll miss you!

Keep in touch.

Stay cool,

B

*PS: I'll bet Noah pops the question to Ethel now that we are out of
the way.*

~~~

Frankie rubbed lotion into her mother's dry hands.

"Tha feels . . . gd," Mom said, struggling for the words. Frankie
leaned down and kissed her mother's dry cheek.

Mom's eyes fluttered shut. She tired so easily. But that was to be
expected in the first few days after a stroke. She was at home, in a
hospital bed that had been set up in a downstairs guest room. She was
often frustrated. Sometimes she couldn't find a word, or chose the

wrong word, or slurred her speech. Every now and then a bout of vertigo made her sick to her stomach.

Frankie shut the door behind her and found her father sitting in the living room. He was hunched forward. Whatever it was that had once puffed him up had been lost with Mom's stroke.

"She's doing well," Frankie said.

"It's good you're here. Your mother missed you."

"And you?"

He looked up, surprising her with the directness of his gaze, as if maybe he'd been waiting for this question. "You were a different girl when you came home," he said.

"I . . . struggled for a while after Vietnam," she said.

"We all did. After Finley . . . I wasn't myself. I didn't know how to . . ." He shrugged, as unable to find the words as he'd been to process the grief.

"I'm sorry about that last night, before I went to Virginia . . . the things I said to you," Frankie said. In the silence that followed her apology, she got up, walked down the hall to her bedroom, and dug through her travel bag. Finding the photograph of Finley that she'd taken down in anger, she walked back to the living room and offered it to her father. "He belongs on the heroes' wall," she said quietly, putting the framed picture down on the table. "I'm so sorry, Dad."

He looked at her for a long moment, then stood. He was a little unsteady. Either he'd drunk too much or eaten too little or worry had upended him again. "Come with me." He went to the kitchen, grabbed some keys off the hook by the wall phone, and headed out to the patio.

Frankie followed him onto Ocean Boulevard. They walked down the wide cement sidewalk, side by side, not speaking.

"We fought about you after you left," he said at last.

Frankie didn't know what to say to that.

"She blamed me. Said I'd been unpleasant to you."

"I was kind of a bitch, too."

"I told her that."

Frankie surprised herself by smiling.

"She knew you'd be back," he said.

"Did she? I wonder how?"

"Life. Motherhood. She said something about spawning salmon."

After another half block, Dad stopped in front of a small gray one-story beach bungalow with a white-painted brick wishing well positioned out front on a patch of grass. An absurd bit of whimsy in this messy world. Larger, two-story houses bracketed the bungalow, made it look like a toy. A dark blue convertible Mustang was parked in the driveway.

"I was going to tear this cottage down and build something bigger. And then . . . when you went to Virginia, your mom wanted you to have a place to come home to. Someday. Told me in no uncertain terms that this cottage was to be your safe place. She put her foot down. I don't think she'd ever said such a thing to me before. Or to anyone. Anyway, she had this cottage painted inside and furnished it with the bare essentials. Well, bare essentials as defined by your mother. The car is my contribution."

He reached into his pocket and pulled out two sets of keys, handed them to her.

Frankie was too stunned to speak for a moment; she stared up at her father, seeing him in a way she never had before, seeing a ghost of the man who'd left Ireland as a kid and crossed an ocean alone, who'd been unable to go to war with the men of his generation, who'd fallen in love with a woman who was used to having it all. The man who'd lost a son to war and almost lost his wife, who'd sent his only daughter running off into the night because he didn't know how to welcome her home. She wondered if they would ever speak of these things, the two of them.

"Thank you, Dad," she said quietly. He looked uncomfortable with her gratitude, or maybe just with the history that came with it. He glanced down the street. "I should go. I don't like leaving your mom alone for long."

Frankie nodded, watched him head for home. When he turned the corner, she walked past the gray bungalow's white-painted brick wishing well.

She unlocked the door, opened it, and flipped the light switch. Inside, she found a quaint pine-paneled living room with a soot-stained river-rock fireplace and big windows with gingham curtains. Hardwood floors, an oval rag rug, a kitchen newly painted in a pale aqua, a floral overstuffed sofa, and a single chair. A vase full of silk flowers on the mantel.

She moved through the place, turning on lights as she went. There were two small bedrooms, the larger of which overlooked a fenced backyard with a live oak tree at its center. Mom had furnished the room with a queen bed, a fluffy white comforter, and a small bedside table with a shell-decorated lamp.

Frankie exhaled a long-held breath. Maybe this was what she'd needed all along. A place to call her own.

Twenty-Five

That night, Frankie slept well.

In the morning, she found a closet full of clothes in her bedroom. *Essentials.*

Smiling, she dressed in striped corduroy pants and a flowy, embroidered peasant blouse, and drove down to her parents' house, where Mom stood on the front step, holding on to a walker. "Y're . . . late," she said, looking agitated.

"I'm not late, Mom," Frankie said, helping her mother into the car.

Mom slid awkwardly into the seat.

"I love the house, Mom," Frankie said. "Everywhere I look, I see you. I know how hard you worked to make it homey. Thank you for letting me live there."

Mom nodded jerkily, not quite in control of her movement. Frankie could see how anxious her mother was, how she gripped the console between the seats to steady herself.

"Are you having a little vertigo?" Frankie asked.

Mom nodded, said, "Yes," in a way that stretched out the word, misshaped it. "Damn it."

Frankie could count on one hand the times she'd heard her mother

curse. "It will take time, Mom. Don't be too hard on yourself. The physical therapist will help, and the occupational therapist, too."

Mom gave a little snort that might have been agreement or disagreement; it was hard to tell.

In San Diego, Frankie turned into the medical center entrance and
parked. She helped Mom out of the car and steadied her. Using the
walker, with her knuckles white from effort, Mom limped slowly from
the car to the lobby. Frankie checked her mother in and got them both
seated in the waiting area.

"Scared," Mom muttered.

Frankie had never heard her mother even use that word before. "I'm
here, Mom. I've got you. You'll be okay. You're tough."

"Ha."

A nurse came out and called, "Elizabeth McGrath?"

Frankie helped her mother to her feet, steadied her as she used
the walker to cross the lobby. At the last minute, she turned, looked at
Frankie through frightened eyes.

"I'll be here when you're finished, Mom," Frankie said, giving her
a gentle smile.

Mom nodded awkwardly.

Frankie returned to her seat and sat down. Reaching sideways, she
picked through a stack of magazines, found an article about the POWs
still in Vietnam.

It reminded her of the League of Families and their quest to bring
the POWs home from Vietnam. They had been looking for an office
in San Diego when Frankie and Barb had attended that luncheon in
Washington, D.C.

Frankie went in search of a pay phone, found one, and called information. "Is there an office number for the League of Families in San
Diego?" she asked the operator.

A moment later, the operator said, "There's a National League of
Families of American Prisoners and Missing in Southeast Asia."

"That's it."

"I'll connect you."

"League of Families, this is Sabrina, how may I help you?" a woman said over the phone.

"Hi. Do you accept donations?" Frankie asked.

The woman laughed. "Boy, do we. Would you like to come by the office?"

"Sure. I have a little time." Frankie wrote down the office address and walked out to her car.

In the glove box, she found the *Thomas Guide* for the area, looked up the address, and started to drive.

Across town, on a pretty little side street, she parked in front of a small building that looked like it had once been a restaurant. A hand-painted sign over the door read THE LEAGUE OF POW/MIA FAMILIES.

She went to the front door, which was standing open.

The office was small, basically unfurnished except for a single desk that held stacks of flyers. A woman sat behind it. At Frankie's entrance, she looked up. "Welcome to the League of Families!"

Another woman was on her knees, her face covered by a cascade of blond curls, painting a sign that read DON'T LET THEM BE FORGOTTEN. She waved at Frankie, too. "Hi, there! Welcome."

The woman at the desk was beautiful in an exotic way, with long black hair and high cheekbones. Beside her, a toddler lay sleeping in a stroller. "I'm Rose Contreras. Come in. Are you a Navy wife?"

"No. I'm Frankie McGrath, former Army nurse."

"Bless you," Rose said softly. "Do you know a prisoner of war?"

"No. I'm just here to donate to the cause."

"We welcome all donations, of course," Rose said. "As you can see, we are pretty bare-bones at this point."

Frankie opened her handbag, reached in for her wallet.

"But Frankie . . ."

"Yes?"

"What we really need is help raising awareness. The older ladies—Anne and Melissa and Sheri, the gals married to the mucky-mucks—they do all the public speaking and testifying in front of the Senate. I'm chair of the Letter-Writing Committee. Our goal is to write letters to anyone and everyone we can think of who might be able to help. *Bury* them in letters. And the same with the newspapers. Would you like to help?"

Letter-writing. Something she could do while she sat with her mother and made the family dinner and waited for Mom to finish her various appointments.

Frankie smiled. "I would love to join that effort, Rose."

Writing letters on behalf of the League of Families and the Vietnam prisoners of war quickly became an obsession.

Frankie wrote when she felt lonely, when she couldn't sleep, when she felt anxious, when her mother was in physical or occupational therapy, while she sat in the waiting room at the medical center. She wrote sitting on the beach after dinner. She wrote to everyone she could think of—Henry Kissinger, Richard Nixon, Spiro Agnew, Bob Dole, Harry Reasoner, Gloria Steinem, Walter Cronkite, Barbara Walters. Anyone who might listen and help or talk to someone who might. *Dear Dr. Kissinger, I am writing on behalf of our American heroes, the men who have been left behind. As an Army nurse who served in Vietnam, I know the horrors these men will have endured. They went to war for their country, to do the right thing, and now our country must do the right thing in return. We cannot leave any man—or woman—behind . . .*

When she wasn't writing, she was with her mother, helping her to walk, encouraging her to eat enough to get her weight back up, driving her to and from appointments. It was slow going, recovery from a stroke, but her mother exerted her considerable will and pushed forward, sometimes to the point of exhaustion. The doctors were amazed at the speed of her recovery; Frankie and her father were not. Bette McGrath had always had a will of steel.

All in all, Frankie thought she was doing well; her mood swings had diminished and she hadn't suffered through a Vietnam nightmare in weeks, had never yet wakened on her bungalow's bedroom floor. Every other Sunday, she wrote to Barb and Ethel, and she received regular letters in return. With long-distance phone charges so exorbitant, they had to make do with letters.

It didn't bother her (although it bothered her mother) that she had no real social life and hadn't been on a date since ... well, before Vietnam. Love was the last thing on her mind. All she wanted was peace and quiet.

By late June 1971, nearly two months after she'd moved home, Frankie had settled into a steady routine. Helping her mother's recovery gave her satisfaction, and writing letters on behalf of the prisoners of war gave her purpose. But today—finally—she had been invited to do more than just write letters.

In midafternoon, she parked her car at the Chula Vista Outdoor Shopping Center and headed for the escalators. The shopping center was decorated in red, white, and blue bunting for the upcoming holiday weekend and most of the storefronts were advertising a SALE! of some kind.

In the courtyard, beneath a palm tree, a table had been set up. Behind it sat a pert, pretty young woman who wore her teased blond hair in two low ponytails; she was writing a letter. To her left was a crude bamboo cage, not nearly big enough for a man to stand upright in. A banner around the cage read DON'T LET THEM BE FORGOTTEN.

Frankie smiled and slid into the empty seat. "I'm Frankie," she said, extending her hand.

The woman shook it. "Joan."

"How is it going today?"

"Slow. People are getting ready for the holiday."

Frankie straightened the stack of flyers in front of her. In the center of the table was a box of POW bracelets that sold for five dollars apiece.

Joan went back to her letter. "Do you think *Live up to your damn promise, President Nixon* is too aggressive for the first sentence?" she asked Frankie, poising her pen tip just above the paper.

"I don't think you can be too aggressive," Frankie said, taking out a piece of paper and a pen.

A young man with long hair and a bushy beard walked past their table, muttered, "Warmongers," under his breath, and kept walking.

"Freedom isn't free, asshole," Frankie yelled. "How come you aren't in Canada?"

"We aren't supposed to yell at the peaceniks," Joan said, grinning. "But what a stupid rule."

"It's more of a guideline," Frankie said.

Joan laughed. "How long has your husband been a POW?"

"I'm not married. My brother and . . . several friends died over there. Your husband?"

"Shot down in '69. He's in Hoa Lo."

"I'm sorry, Joan. Kids?"

"Just one. A girl. Charlotte. She doesn't remember her dad."

Frankie touched the woman's hand. They were about the same age, living very different lives, but the war connected them. "He'll come home, Joan."

A dark-haired woman in a black-and-white plaid pantsuit neared the table. "They put our soldiers in cages like that? Really? Where they don't have enough room to stand up?"

"Yes, ma'am."

"What did they do?"

"Do?" Joan asked.

"To end up in cages. Are they like that Lieutenant Calley from My Lai?"

Stay calm. Educate, don't annihilate. "They served their country," Frankie said. "Just like their fathers and grandfathers, they did as the country asked in wartime, and they were taken prisoner by the enemy."

The woman frowned, picked a nickel-plated bracelet out of the box, read the name on it.

"That's someone's son, ma'am. Someone's husband," Frankie said. "And they're waiting for him to come home." She paused. "This woman's husband is in their prison."

The woman pulled a five-dollar bill out of her worn billfold and handed it to Frankie, and then put the bracelet back in the box.

"The idea is that you wear the bracelet until he comes home," Joan said. "To keep his memory alive."

The woman retrieved the bracelet, fit it on her wrist, stared down at it.

"Thank you," Frankie said.

The woman nodded and walked away.

For the next half an hour, Frankie and Joan handed out flyers, sold bracelets, and wrote letters. Frankie was halfway through her latest letter to Ben Bradlee when she felt Joan poke her elbow into her side.

"Incoming," Joan whispered.

Frankie looked up, saw two men walking toward their table.

No. Not two men, or not really. A man and a boy. Father and son, maybe; the man was tall and thin, with graying shoulder-length hair and a mustache. He wore a black Grateful Dead T-shirt and ragged jeans and sandals. The boy beside him—sixteen, maybe seventeen— was pumped up with muscles and wore an ANNAPOLIS sweatshirt. He was clean-shaven and his hair was 1950s-short. They stopped in front of the table, beneath the DON'T LET THEM BE FORGOTTEN banner.

The older man stepped closer. "Still fighting for the cause, I see. Frankie McGrath, right? Coronado girl?"

It took a moment for Frankie to recognize the man she'd met at the protest in Washington, D.C. "The surfer psychiatrist."

"Henry Acevedo," he said, smiling. "This is my nephew, Arturo."
He turned to the young man. "You see those cages, Art? Take a good,
long look."

Arturo rolled his eyes, gave his uncle a good-natured nudge in the
side. "My uncle is pissed I'm going to the Naval Academy in September. But my dad is thrilled."

"My brother went to the academy," Frankie said. "He loved it."

"My husband, too," Joan added. "It's a great school."

"I'm not in favor of a college that pumps out warriors and then
sends them into harm's way," Henry said.

"Just be proud of him, Henry," Frankie said quietly. "He's making
an honorable choice even if you don't agree with it." She pushed the
box of bracelets toward the young man. "Five dollars if you'd like to
help bring a hero home."

Arturo stepped forward, looked through the bracelets. "Groovy. Do
you know any POWs?" he asked Joan.

"My husband," she said, showing Arturo her bracelet. He leaned
in to read it.

"Nineteen sixty-nine," Arturo said. "Whoa. He's been there a long
time . . ."

Frankie felt Henry's gaze on her, but he didn't speak. After a moment, he put an arm around his nephew. "Come on, future flyboy. Let's
let these beautiful women save their husbands."

"I'm not married," Frankie said, surprised to hear herself say the words.

"Will wonders never cease?" Henry said as he tossed two twenty-
dollar bills on the table. "Keep up the good work, ladies. See you soon,
Frankie."

He led Arturo away, who pulled out from beneath his uncle's arm,
obviously thinking he was too old for it.

"Was that . . . you know, the guy who always plays a cowboy on
TV?"

Frankie shook her head. "He's a doctor."

"I don't know why you're still here," Joan said, pulling out a nail file, filing a broken nail.

"What do you mean?"

"If a man that foxy looked at me the way he just looked at you, I wouldn't let him walk away."

"What? You think . . . no. It's not . . . I mean, he's old."

"Time doesn't mean what it used to," she said.

Frankie couldn't disagree with that.

———

July 27, 1971

Dear Frank,
Greetings from blazingly hot Captiva Island. That's in Florida. Land of leathery people who drive yacht-sized cars and start cocktail hour at breakfast.

I know you are going to scream, as is Babs, who is getting the same letter. Noah and I eloped! I know you girls wanted to be at my wedding, but I just couldn't wait. We couldn't wait. When push came to shove, I didn't want a day that smelled like flowers and tasted like cake. When your mom isn't around . . . I don't know. I just didn't want that. But we will celebrate, and soon!

        Love you, girlfriend,
        Mrs. Noah Ellsworth

Twenty-Six

1972. And the war raged on.

More deaths, more grievous injuries on the battlefield, more helicopters shot down, more men sent to Hoa Lo Prison or missing in action.

Frankie, like most Americans, watched the nightly news in horror. Last year, the Winter Soldier Investigation, a media event sponsored by the Vietnam Veterans Against the War, had exposed the dark underside of the war—American atrocities in the jungles and villages and on the battlefield—and Lieutenant William Calley had been convicted and sentenced to life in prison for the My Lai massacre. America had invaded Cambodia. All of it increased the anger and disgust shown to returning veterans.

Sometimes, when she watched the news, Frankie couldn't stop crying.

It could be over nothing. Hell, sometimes she cried in her car when a song made her think of Finley, of Jamie, of Rye. Every tear reminded her that her stability was fragile at best.

No one believed America was winning the war anymore; even on Coronado Island, among the conservative, wealthy, Republican elite, doubt was expanding. "We need to be done with this," Frankie often heard her father say to his friends, as if the war were an expensive vacation gone bad.

When her mother was improved enough to drive and be alone, Frankie was forced to reach for a life of her own, at least a semblance of one. She took a job at the medical center hospital. Her education and experience landed her a surgical nurse job on the day shift, and once again nursing gave her life purpose and structure, both of which she desperately needed. She made sure to keep busy; she wrote endless letters and manned the League of Families booth when she could, and worked long, grueling shifts in the OR. Anything that would occupy her mind and make her tired enough to sleep.

But she knew that none of it would help tonight.

The Fourth of July.

Frankie dreaded the holiday. In the past few years, she'd remained cloistered inside on the Fourth of July, with the music cranked up loud, just trying to make it through the loudness of the night. Barb and Ethel had always allowed her to hide out in Virginia, and last year her mother hadn't felt well enough to host their annual party. This year was a different story.

A party at her parents' house was the last thing Frankie wanted to attend, but she had no choice. Following fifteen months of therapy and hard work, her mother was finally set to make her glorious return to Coronado's social life, and Frankie's attendance was mandatory.

I'm fine. I can do this.

She dressed in purple hot pants and a filmy white blouse, pulled down off her shoulders, then ironed her now-long hair down from a center part, and put on makeup. All of it a camouflage.

At dusk, she left the bungalow and walked on the beach toward her parents' house, toward the iconic red roof of the Hotel del Coronado. Lights twinkled from its eaves, lighting the way.

All around her, life went on. Families, kids, dogs. Shouting and screaming, people splashing in the waves.

She stayed on the sand for as long as possible, then crossed Ocean Boulevard, which was buzzing with activity on this warm evening: drivers looking for parking spaces, men unpacking trunks, women herding dogs and children to the beach, looking for a place to set up their chairs.

The Tudor house loomed above the brick privacy wall, its mullioned windows glittering with light. Lanterns hung from the branches of the live oak tree. Red, white, and blue bunting decorated the food table and outdoor bar. Frankie closed the gate behind her.

Independence Day had always been her father's favorite holiday. The family celebrated it in the way they did every social event. Full tilt. An "Americana" buffet was set up on the patio—trays of barbecued ribs and juicy hamburgers, buttered corn on the cob, potato salad, and, of course, a tricolor cake with ice cream for dessert. Everyone brought something to the party, and the women of Coronado sought to outdo one another.

The guests had obviously been here for a while; the volume of their voices hinted at copious alcohol consumption. She heard a man boom out, "Who does Jane Fonda think she is? Anti-American, I'd say."

Off to the left, a three-piece band was playing a bad version of "Little Deuce Coupe."

Taped to the patio walls was a sign that read GOD BLESS AMERICA AND OUR TROOPS.

"As long as they're men," Frankie muttered.

She released a slow breath, trying not to be mad. Or hurt.

If only Barb and Ethel were here. Frankie hadn't seen her friends in too long. Ethel and Noah had recently welcomed their daughter, Cecily, into the world, and Barb was marching somewhere this weekend, gearing up for some top-secret VVAW "event" that so far she'd only hinted about.

Frankie moved through the crowd, offering a fake smile to the people she knew. She heard snippets of conversation, well-dressed men talking about "soldiers, hopped up on heroin, bombing villages," and women in brightly hued dresses shivering at the thought of Charles Manson being kept alive: ". . . lock our doors now. They ought to have put him to death. Darn liberals."

Frankie concentrated on her breathing, trying to stay calm, until she reached the bar. "Gin on the rocks with a twist."

As she was handed her drink, her father peeled away from the crowd. He commanded attention with ease, as he always had. He flicked his wrist and the band stopped playing. Frankie saw his million-dollar smile, the one that had returned with his wife's recovery. But there was a new shadow in him, too, a realization that money couldn't buy good health or safety from its opposite. He wore striped pants with a wide belt and a polyester shirt with large lapels. In the past year he'd grown out his wide sideburns, which were coming in gray, and let his curly black hair grow long enough to comb over to one side. His new glasses were big and square. "I want to thank you all for coming. As you know, our Independence Day party is a tradition here on Coronado. We first invited our friends to celebrate America's independence in 1956, back when Elvis's moves were a scandal."

The crowd laughed at the sweet memory of a different world.

"I don't think my childr . . . my daughter remembers a life before the McGrath Fourth of July party." He paused, seemed to struggle. "But last year, we sent out no invitations. You all know why. And I thank you all for your letters and flowers. It was a difficult time for us, after Bette's stroke."

Mom appeared at the patio doors, her back straight, her chin held high. She had begun dyeing her hair to conceal the new white streaks in it, and that had led her to cut her hair short in perhaps the trendiest fashion choice of her life. With her flawless makeup and fashionable pantsuit, she looked as stunning as ever. She stepped cautiously over the threshold. Only someone who knew her well would see the slight frown in her forehead or the hesitation in her step.

Dad turned, reached back, took hold of her hand to steady her.

Mom smiled at her guests. "It's been a long road back, and I can't express how much you all encouraged me. Millicent, your casseroles were lifesavers. Joanne, I still don't understand mah-jongg, but the steadying sound of your voice stays with me. Dr. Kenworth, thank you for saving my life, pure and simple. And Connor." Here she looked at Dad, then looked out to the crowd again. "And Frances."

She saw Frankie and waved.

"You two were my rocks."

Frankie saw the way Dad tightened his hold on her hand, then kissed her cheek.

The guests applauded; someone yelled, "Hear, hear!"

"One last thing," Dad said. "Before we eat and drink and dance, I'd like to welcome home Lieutenant Commander Leo Stall. He's just home from Vietnam and Walter Reed." He lifted a glass. "To the men who serve! From a grateful nation."

Frankie slammed her empty glass on the bar. "Another one," she said as the band struck up again, playing "American Pie" so slowly it was barely recognizable.

The men who serve. A grateful nation.

She felt a surge of anger, downed her second drink, and looked back at the gate.

Could she leave yet?

Would anyone notice?

Her hand was shaking as she lit up a cigarette. *A grateful nation.*

"We've got to stop meeting this way," a voice said.

Frankie turned quickly, almost stumbled into the man who stood beside her.

He caught her.

"Henry Acevedo," she said, looking up at him.

His hair had changed: he still wore it long and layered, but the night's humidity had given it volume. He had obviously shaved for the party; there was no five o'clock shadow darkening his jawline. Long sideburns narrowed his face.

"What are you doing here?" she asked, easing a step back, trying to steady herself. "This is hardly your crowd."

"Your mother and her Junior League friends spearheaded a fund-raising effort for the hospital's new therapeutic drug and alcohol treatment center. She invited several of us board members tonight." He shrugged, smiled.

"You don't look like a board member of anything. And that's a compliment."

"It was either this party or my sister's out-of-control family in the suburbs."

"I would have chosen the suburbs."

Henry smiled. "You've clearly spent no time in the suburbs."

Frankie heard the distinctive whine of a mortar rocket and the crash of its explosion.

She screamed, "Incoming!," and dropped to the ground.

Silence.

Frankie blinked.

She was sprawled in the grass in her parents' backyard. *What the hell?* She crawled to her knees, feeling weak.

Someone had set off a firecracker. A bottle rocket, probably.

And she'd hit the ground. What was wrong with her? She knew the difference between a firecracker and a mortar round.

Oh my God.

Henry knelt down beside her, touched her shoulder with a gentleness that made her want to cry.

"Go away," she said, humiliated. This hadn't happened since the country club, years ago.

"I've got you," he said.

She let him help her to her feet but couldn't look at him.

"Those idiots who get their firecrackers and bottle rockets from Mexico should be in jail," he said.

Was he saying it was *normal* to hear that and hit the ground?

"Will you take me home?" she said. She heard the words and knew they sounded like an invitation, which wasn't what she meant. She didn't want *him*.

Or maybe she did.

She didn't want to be alone right now.

He slipped an arm around her waist to steady her. "My car—"

"We can walk."

She led him to the gate, opened it.

Ocean Boulevard was a madhouse of traffic and tourists. The wide swath of sand was crowded with families, kids, students, Navy personnel. All mingling together. Dogs barking. Kids laughing. Tired parents trying to keep their broods close. Soon they'd start setting off more of the fireworks they had bought just across the border in Mexico. Bottle rockets. M-80s. The sky would look and sound like they were under attack.

On the sidewalk, Frankie kept close to Henry, realizing at some point that she had forgotten to put her sandals on when she left the house tonight. She had walked here in her bare feet.

Frankie didn't know what to say to this man beside her, who kept his hand on her waist, a steadying pressure, as they walked the few blocks to her house.

There, she came to a stop.

The bungalow looked silver in the falling night. The shiny red door, the white-painted brick wishing well. All at once, she saw it for what it was: a home from another era, for a different kind of life. Kids. Dogs. Bikes.

It scoured her with sorrow, that realization.

"I'll bet you played on Coronado Beach when you were a kid, probably rode your bike on Ocean Boulevard with cards clothespinned to the spokes. What a childhood."

"With my brother," she said quietly. She turned, looked up at Henry. "Thank you."

He gave a dramatic bow. "At your service, milady."

Frankie felt a surprising spark of desire. The first in years. A desire to be touched, held. Not alone. "Are you married?"

"No. My wife—Susannah—died of breast cancer seven years ago."

She saw the sadness he'd been through with his wife, an understanding of loss that eased her loneliness, or shared it. "How old are you?" she asked, although right now she didn't care.

"Thirty-eight. And you?"

"Twenty-six."

He had nothing to say to that, and she was glad. This—they—weren't a thing that needed words. Words meant something; she wanted this—them—to mean nothing. "Come inside?" she said quietly.

He obviously understood the question, all of it, and nodded.

She opened the back gate, led him into her backyard, which she'd meant to fix up and never had. Grass ran wild, yellowing in places from the summer heat and her lackadaisical watering. The barbecue she'd bought secondhand had never been used and the oak tree branches longed for a tire swing. The backyard, like her life, was empty.

She closed the gate behind them, and the tinny *click* was like a starting bell. He drew her close, pulled her into an embrace. She felt the power in him, the desire for her, and it made her feel the same way—wanted. Something she hadn't felt in a long time.

He drew back, looked down at her.

She held on to his hand, led him into her bedroom. There, she let go, stood back, and faced him, wishing she had made her bed. There were clothes scattered on the floor. Empty glasses on the nightstand. Had she drunk too much last night and stumbled to bed? She couldn't remember.

He took her by the hand and led her to the bed.

She felt like a virgin again, uncertain, afraid. Slowly, she took off her hot pants and pulled off her top.

She wore a lacy white bra, white panties, and the gold Saint Christopher medal Mom had sent her in Vietnam.

"I've only . . . been with one man, and it's been a long time," she said, unsure of why she said it. "And I don't want . . . more than this. I don't have it in me."

"What don't you have in you, Frankie?"

"Love."

"Ah."

"I'm in love with someone else."

"Where is he?"

"Gone."

He pulled her close. She softened in his embrace; their lips touched, tentatively, the kiss of strangers.

At first she could think only of Rye, and what the kiss wasn't, who Henry wasn't, and then she lost her hold on that and felt herself falling into a new, slow building of passion.

"There," she said in a harsh, throaty voice when his hand moved down her bare skin, slipped inside her panties.

It wasn't love, but for a beautiful moment her body came alive, vibrated, hummed, and it was close enough.

―――

When she looked back on it, which she did often in that summer of 1972, she wondered how it was that she and Henry had begun actually dating.

In her mind, they had never really started a relationship. They'd simply merged somehow; two people walking on different paths that had somehow—inexplicably—become a single road. It started that first night in her bungalow. Henry knew about pain and loss; after the death of his wife, he said he'd fallen into darkness, drunk too much alcohol, and stumbled. Frankie knew about that kind of stumbling, how hard it could be to right oneself and how careful life needed to be thereafter. They were lonely, both of them, and brokenhearted. She saw the sorrow in his eyes when he mentioned his wife and she knew her voice broke when he asked about Rye, about Jamie, about Finley.

So they stopped saying the names, stopped talking about true love, and let almost-love—passion—into their lives. Frankie went to Planned Parenthood for birth control pills. She tried to feel modern and sure of herself when she walked into the clinic, but when the doctor asked if she was married, her cheeks flamed. She nodded quickly, then shook her head. The doctor had smiled kindly and told her she didn't need to lie anymore. It was finally legal for single women to get the pill. He wrote her a prescription.

She and Henry met after work for drinks and even sometimes for dinner. Henry was often busy with fundraising for the hospital and its proposed new clinic, and Frankie had no desire to join him at the events.

Neither was ready to merge so completely into the other's life. Or at least she wasn't, and so he didn't push it.

Frankie didn't tell her mother or her girlfriends about Henry because it felt vaguely wrong, immoral maybe, to touch a man you didn't love, to sleep in his arms for hours and watch him leave before dawn to go to work.

But she couldn't stop it. After so many years of loneliness and grief, Henry brought sunlight into her life. And she was afraid to go back to the dark.

August 1, 1972

Dear Frankie,
Enough is enough. Do you think I am an idiot?

In case you answer incorrectly, I'm not. Your mother called me last night. She tells me that you're acting even stranger than usual, and you're wearing perfume again. I know what this means, girlfriend.

Sex.

Who are you getting it from and how is it? Please tell a friend so she can live vicariously.

Life in Chicago is good. Not lonely, never lonely. I am in constant motion, but it's tough to be a woman in a man's world, even when you're working for change.

The next man who asks me to make coffee for the group or type up a flyer—because I know how—is going to get his ass kicked.

Ethel, on the other hand, tells me that all her clothes now smell like baby puke and she can't remember what sleep is like.

We all have our challenges, I guess.

I'm going with the VVAW to the Republican National Convention in a few weeks. I hope there's no violence, but good God, enough of this damn war.

Ok, I'm pouring myself a drink. The phone better ring the second you get this letter.

> *Stay cool, sister*
> *Luv ya*
> *B*

A hot morning in the third week of August. Sun shining through a dirty windshield, "Nights in White Satin" blaring through the speakers of Henry's Chevy Nova.

"I'm not sure about this," Frankie said, staring at the endless line of cars and trucks and motorcycles in front of them, seeing more in the rearview mirror.

Vietnam veterans, mostly, but not all.

They'd begun this caravan three days ago in Southern California, as one of about twenty cars, but more vehicles had joined the motorcade in a steady stream: VW buses with painted slogans and curtained windows, battered old trucks, souped-up Camaros, motorcycles with military flags flapping from the tail bars.

Now over a hundred vehicles strong, the group drove into Miami, honking their horns and flashing their lights, men leaning out of open windows to wave at one another.

Henry turned down the music. "Barb asked us to do this."

"Well. She asked me to do it. I thought I said no." Frankie crossed her arms, feeling mulish but trying to hide it. After a month and a half with him, she remained on her guard around Henry, concealed her irrational mood swings and inexplicable anger as much as she could. Otherwise, he'd ask probing questions that she refused to answer. He had no idea she still sometimes cried in the shower for no reason.

In a park, they found thousands of protesters already gathered—not just vets. Every conceivable protest group was here: hippies, college kids, feminists. The VVAW group followed the lead car to an unoccupied corner of the camp, where they set up their own domain, which was protected by veterans with walkie-talkies, who patrolled the perimeter. Frankie and Henry pitched a tent by their parked car.

By nightfall, the VVAW camp was a full-fledged party, where everyone was welcome—wives, girlfriends, supporters, former nurses, and Red Cross workers.

The leader seemed to be a man in a wheelchair—Ron Kovic, who'd been paralyzed from the chest down in 'Nam—and he called the upcoming march their "last patrol."

In the morning, Barb showed up, stood in the messy camp, and yelled, "Frankie McGrath, where are you?"

Frankie saw her best friend and ran for her, almost knocking her over with the exuberance of her hug.

"I can't believe you're here," Barb said. "Where is Henry? He promised to get you here, and here you are. He must be a magician."

"He is," Frankie admitted reluctantly.

Back at the pup tent, Henry was making coffee over an open flame. Frankie saw that he'd brought three coffee cups, and at that a feeling that was almost like love, at least a watery version of it, opened up in her.

He stood, smiling with the ease of a man who had a clear conscience. "Hey, Barb. Our girl has missed you."

Barb smiled, looked him up and down. "I've met you somewhere."

"Washington, D.C. At the bar in the—"

"Hay Adams," Barb said. "A fellow revolutionary."

"Time to go!" someone yelled out over a bullhorn. "Remember: Silence. We want those bastards to know we think there's nothing left to say."

The three of them moved forward, holding hands, merging into the crowd in the park. Leading the march were wounded veterans: men in wheelchairs, on crutches, blind men being led by brothers who could see.

They walked up Collins Avenue in silence, more than a thousand of them. Spectators lined the streets, witnessing the march, taking pictures.

Frankie felt Henry let go of her hand.

She turned.

"This is a veterans' march. I don't belong here, babe," he said quietly. "You do. You need this."

"So, you—"

"Just go, Frankie. Be with your best friend. I'll be at the car when you're done."

Frankie had no choice but to let him go and keep moving with the crowd, her fellow veterans, holding on to Barb's hand, toward the convention center, where the Republican National Convention was under way.

Frankie felt the power of it, their silence, as she had become silent about this war. They were the men and women who'd *been* there, and with their silence, they said, *Enough*.

Frankie was surprised at the pride she felt in being here, in marching, in seeing the fists raised but the voices still, the *thud-thud-thud* of their feet on the pavement, some, like Barb, in combat boots.

They stopped in front of the hall; the wheelchairs stilled.

Riot police stood in a straight line, blocking their entrance.

Within the marchers, platoon leaders gave hand-signal commands; the veterans fanned out, quietly blocked three lanes of traffic.

Someone—Ron Kovic, Frankie thought—yelled through a bullhorn: "We want to come inside."

They waited. Silent. Shoulder to shoulder.

Frankie saw photographers snapping pictures and a TV camera rolling film. National Guard helicopters whirred overhead.

The tension rose. Frankie felt a sense of danger; she thought all of them did. But surely the riot police wouldn't be set on military veterans?

"You might have taken our bodies, but you have not taken our minds!" someone yelled.

A congressman came out at last, to the cheers of the spectators.

Frankie pressed up onto her tiptoes, trying to see the front of the line.

The congressman escorted three vets in wheelchairs into the convention center.

The marchers couldn't get into the building without risking their lives and creating exactly the kind of scene they didn't want.

Frankie didn't know how long they stood there, packed in, blocking off traffic, but in time, the march that had begun in determination ended with more than a thousand vets walking back to the park, amid the cheers—and jeers—of the crowd, watching from the sidewalks.

"They won't hear us," Barb said. "Not if we scream, not if we're silent. They want to forget about us."

"I don't know," Frankie said. "Look at the troop withdrawals. Maybe something is working."

They kept walking.

"So, he's cool," Barb said. "Henry."

"Yeah."

"Why would you keep him secret? I tell you about every guy I even think about kissing."

"I have a flowchart of it, in fact."

Barb hip-bumped her. "Seriously."

"He's just . . . fun."

"Girl, you are hardly the princess of fun."

"He's helping with that."

"Do you love him?"

"I don't want that anymore. I don't think I can survive it again."

"Not all love goes bad."

"Uh-huh. This explains why you're married with kids."

"I don't want that life." Barb put an arm around Frankie. "I am pretty sure he loves you."

"Why?"

"Who drives a woman cross-country to make sure she marches in a protest and then says he doesn't belong? Kind of a kick-ass move, in my book."

"He's thirty-eight. Already been married."

"That's your answer to why not?"

Frankie hated to tell Barb the truth, but she knew her friend would keep digging until she did. "You're a damn wolverine, you know," she said, sighing. Quietly, she said, "Rye."

"Wouldn't he want you to be happy?"

"Yeah, sure." People said that all the time. All it did was make Frankie's loneliness worse. "That's what I'm doing," she said. "This is me happy."

———

The next day, the newspapers and news broadcasts were full of the story: three Vietnam veterans in wheelchairs had rolled into the National Convention just as Nixon was giving his acceptance speech. They'd shouted, *Stop the bombing.*

They'd been escorted out quickly, taken away by police, but the images made the news. The veterans had shouted so loudly that the President had had to stop his speech.

———

Medics run past me, carrying men on litters. Someone's screaming.

Frankie came awake with a startled cry and sat up, breathing hard.

It took a moment to remember that she was in her house on Coronado, in bed, with Henry sleeping beside her. She reached out a trembling hand, touched him, needing to know he was real.

"You okay?" he mumbled, not quite asleep, but not quite awake, either.

"Fine," she said, touching him until he went back to sleep.

Easing out of bed, she went down to the living room. On a top kitchen cupboard shelf, she found a pack of cigarettes and lit one up, standing at the sink. Images of Vietnam crowded in on her, demanded she remember.

It was the march.

All those veterans together, reminding each other of their shared past. All the pain, the loss, the lost, the shame.

She wasn't supposed to think about any of it anymore. She was supposed to soldier on.

Forget, Frankie.

Twenty-Seven

Nearly four months later, on her day off, Frankie pulled up to the Coronado Golf and Tennis Club and parked under the white portico. A valet rushed out to take the car from her.

"Thanks, Mike," she said, tossing him the keys to her Mustang.

Inside, the club was decorated for Christmas, from stem to stern, as the sailors in the club often said. Fake garlands lay across the mantel, studded here and there with white candles. A live Christmas tree shone with multicolored lights and golf-themed ornaments. Elvis's "Blue Christmas" wafted through the speakers. No doubt it was a scandalous music choice here.

Several men in polyester leisure suits stood near the fireplace, drinking Bloody Marys.

Mom was already seated in the dining room, which smelled of pine and vanilla. Behind her, the fairway stretched out in an undulating swath of emerald grass.

At the white-clothed table, Mom sat stiffly upright. She wore a cowl-collared jersey dress with a knit beret over her short black hair and long, dangling earrings.

Frankie slid into a chair across from her. "Sorry I'm late."

Mom flagged down the waiter and ordered two glasses of champagne.

"Are we celebrating?" Frankie asked.

"Always," Mom said, lighting a cigarette. "I'm walking and talking, aren't I?"

Frankie took a sip of the champagne and felt a spasm in her stomach, a rise of nausea.

Barely excusing herself, she ran to the restroom and vomited.

Twice.

She went to the sink and drank a handful of water.

She'd been sick yesterday morning, too.

No.

No.

She pressed a hand to her stomach. Was there a slight swelling? A little tenderness?

A *baby*?

But . . . she was on birth control. Could the pill have failed her? Had she been religious in taking it every morning? She might have forgotten once or twice . . .

She walked back to the table, didn't sit down.

Mom looked up. "You're pale, Frances."

"I just threw up. Twice."

Mom frowned. "Are you hungover? Do you have a fever?"

Frankie shook her head.

Mom's gaze remained steady. "Are you being . . . intimate with a man, Frances?"

Frankie nodded slowly, feeling her cheeks burn. "I've been seeing him for a few months."

"And didn't tell your parents. I see. And your last visit from Aunt Flo?"

"I'm not sure. Since I started on the pill, there's barely . . . anything."

"You need to see a doctor."

Frankie nodded numbly.

"Sit down. After lunch, we'll go to Arnold. He'll fit us in."

An hour and a half later, after an awkward luncheon full of things unsaid, they left the club and drove to the doctor's office on Orange Avenue. At the front desk, Mom said, "Hi, Lola. I need a pregnancy test."

The older woman looked up. "Are you—"

Mom waved her hand in irritation. "Not for me, Lola. For my daughter."

Lola pulled a pen out of her teased hair and said, "He'll make time. Nice to see you moving so well."

Frankie clasped her hands together and took a seat in the waiting room.

Moments later, a nurse came out, collected Frankie, and led her to an examination room. "Put on a robe. Ties in front. Doctor will be with you shortly."

Frankie took her clothes off and put on the robe, then climbed up onto the exam table.

Pregnant. The word kept repeating itself.

A quiet knock on the door, and then it opened.

Closing the door behind him, the doctor pushed the black horn-rimmed glasses higher on his bulbous nose. "Hello, Frankie. It's been a long time."

"Hi, Dr. Massie," she said. The last time she'd seen the doctor, she'd been seventeen, going off to college, and he'd given her a sex talk that was franker than the one she'd received from her mom, but still began with *On your wedding night,* and she'd been so nervous and uncomfortable hearing about penises and vaginas from an old man that she'd barely listened.

"I didn't know you'd married," he said.

Frankie swallowed hard, said nothing.

If Dr. Massie noticed her silence, he didn't remark upon it. "Climb on up to the table."

Frankie lay on the exam table and fit her stockinged feet in the metal stirrups. The doctor settled himself between her legs. She stared up at the brightly lit white wall, squeezing her eyes shut as he moved her legs farther apart, scooted closer, snapped on a pair of gloves.

"This will be a bit cold," he said apologetically, as he fit the speculum up inside of her. He followed the speculum with a digital exam. After that, he stood up, covered her legs with the gown, and came around to her side. Carefully opening the gown, he felt her abdomen, her breasts.

Then he covered her nakedness and stepped back. "When was your last period, Frankie?"

"I'm not exactly sure."

"Are you on the birth control pill?"

"Yes."

"They're not foolproof. Especially if you aren't conscientious in taking them." He stepped back. "I will run some tests to be certain, but physical indications tell me that you are indeed expecting. I'd say about two months."

Two months.

"Oh my God . . . I'm not ready . . . not married . . ."

He moved to her side, said softly, "Catholic Adoption Services do a good job of placing babies with upstanding families, Frankie. Your mother will know all about it."

Frankie remembered a few girls from high school who'd disappeared from class and returned months later, thinner and quieter. Everyone knew they'd gone to a home for unwed mothers, but the words weren't even whispered, it was considered so shameful. And there had been rumors—once—of a girl from St. Bernadette's who'd died from an illegal abortion.

Frankie couldn't imagine either path for her; not because they were wrong choices, but rather because she knew she wanted to be a mother, but not by herself, not as a single woman; she wanted the whole package: a husband, a baby, a family made from love.

She nodded, sat up, touched her abdomen. A *baby*.

She wasn't ready to be a mother, and yet, when she closed her eyes, just for a moment she pictured a whole different version of her life, one in which she loved unconditionally and was loved, where her present wasn't constantly shaded by images of the past, by shame and anxiety and anger. A version where she was *Mom*.

She dressed and walked out of the examination room.

Mom was in the waiting room, sitting in that stiffly upright way that was her new normal, as if she feared that poor posture could cause another stroke. She looked up, met Frankie's gaze.

Frankie felt the start of tears.

Mom limped toward Frankie and took her by the arm, maneuvering her out of the office, across the parking lot, and into the Cadillac, where Mom immediately lit up a cigarette.

"You shouldn't smoke, Mom," Frankie said dully. "You've had a stroke."

"Who is this boy you're seeing?"

Frankie almost laughed. "He's a man, Mom. Henry Acevedo."

"The doctor who wants to start that clinic for drug addicts?"

"Yeah, Mom."

"But . . . since when?"

"Your Fourth of July party."

She smiled a little. "A doctor. Okay, so you and Henry will get married. A quiet ceremony. The baby will be premature. It happens all the time."

"I don't have to get married, Mom. It's 1972, not 1942."

"Are you ready to raise a child by yourself, Frances? Or to give it away? And what will Henry say about that? He strikes me as a good man."

Frankie felt tears roll down her cheeks. If only this were a different life. If this were Rye's baby and they were married and ready for children.

What will Henry say?

The wrong man. The wrong time. "I don't know."

In the four days since Dr. Massie had called with confirmation of the pregnancy, Frankie's anxiety had increased daily. The phone in her kitchen rang often; Frankie didn't answer. She knew it was probably her mother, worrying about her, but she had no idea what to say in response.

Henry knew something was wrong, too; he kept asking her why she was so quiet.

She didn't know what to say to him, or to herself, or to anyone for that matter. So, she just kept moving, got up, went to work, did her job, and tried not to think about the future that was suddenly frightening. Now she was in OR 2, readying to assist on her last surgery of the shift. Christmas music pumped through the speakers.

"Happy birthday, Frankie," the anesthesiologist said. His long hair was barely concealed by his blue cap; across from the patient, on the opposite side of the table, stood the surgeon, who peered down at the brown-washed, blue-draped abdomen. Bright white lights shone down on them.

"Thanks, Dell." Frankie chose a scalpel from the instruments on her cart and handed it to the surgeon before he'd asked. The doctor made his incision.

Frankie blotted the blood that bubbled up.

"There it is," Dr. Mark Lundberg said. "Going in. Tumor. Clamp."

For the next two hours, Dr. Lundberg excised the tumor that grew in the patient's stomach. When the surgery was over and the incision sewn up, the doctor pulled his blue mask down and frowned.

"Is something wrong?" Frankie asked, lowering her mask.

"He's, what, Frankie, thirty years old? How the hell did he get gastric cancer?" He shook his head. "Send it to pathology."

Frankie peeled off her gloves and tossed them in the trash. Following the patient into recovery, she went over instructions for his care with the nurse there.

Afterward, she studied his chart. *Scott Peabody. Elementary school teacher. Honorable Discharge from the Army. 1966. Vietnam. Married. Two children.*

She made notes on his chart and dropped it back in the sleeve at the end of the bed. As she walked back to her locker, past the Christmas decorations on the walls, she realized for the first time how badly her feet hurt, and there was a dull ache at the base of her spine. She was, what, a little more than two months pregnant and already she was feeling it? After changing out of her uniform at her locker, she grabbed her handbag and left the hospital.

With the windows rolled down, she drove home, veering onto the new Coronado Bridge with Jim Croce serenading her about time in a bottle.

As she turned onto her street, she saw a column of smoke rising from the chimney of her house, and she remembered that Henry was here to celebrate her birthday.

Twenty-seven.

She wasn't so young anymore. Most of her friends from high school and college were already married, with children. Ethel sent so many baby pictures, Frankie had had to put them in an album.

She parked on the street and sat for a minute beneath a streetlamp, staring out at the black hump of the beach across the street.

It was time to tell Henry about the baby. She couldn't handle this on her own anymore. The secret was tearing her up. And the loneliness it caused.

She would walk into the house, open the door, and tell him. She considered how to say it, turned the words over and over in her mind, rearranging them, trying first to soften and then to obscure and even to harden what she had to say, but in the end, it was simple and she just needed the nerve.

She opened the door of the cottage.

The place smelled of roasting meat and browning potatoes. No doubt it was Henry's special recipe of chicken thighs, potatoes, and onion, browned in a cast-iron skillet and baked in the oven.

He was at the stove, wearing his favorite apron, which read LOVE MEANS ALWAYS HAVING TO SAY YOU'RE SORRY, over jeans and a long-sleeved California Angels sweatshirt.

"I'm home," she said.

He spun around. "Happy birthday, babe!" he said, untying the apron, laying it over the back of a chair. He pulled her into his arms for a kiss. When he drew back, she was crying.

"What's wrong, Frankie?"

"I'm pregnant," she said.

His gaze searched hers. She had no idea what she wanted him to say. Nothing could make this moment what she wanted it to be. He was the wrong man and it was the wrong time.

"Marry me," he said at last. "I'll move in here. Give up my lease in La Jolla. You'll want to be close to your parents."

He looked so serious, gazed at her as if she were the very center of the world. Exactly how a man in love should look at the woman he adored. "Henry . . ."

"Why not? You know I've always wanted to be a dad. And this—love—it's a thing I'm good at and you need it, Frankie, maybe more than anyone I've ever met."

"I don't . . ."—*love you*—"think I'm ready," she said.

"This is one of those times in life where it doesn't matter if you're ready. I hear it all the time from people: parenthood is a plunge into the deep end. Always." He looked so deeply, genuinely committed that it stirred her heart, gave her a glimpse of hope. People married for all kinds of reasons, in all types of situations. You never knew what the future might hold.

He was a good man. True. Honest. The kind of man who would stay, grow old with a woman, be there.

And she would need strength beside her for this. She wasn't strong anymore.

"We could be a family," he said.

She put a hand on her flat belly, thinking, *Our baby*. She had always imagined herself as a mother, a mom, but somehow her experience in Vietnam—that baby dying in her arms—had derailed her, planted fear where joy belonged.

She was surprised to find that the dream of motherhood was still there, wispy, uncertain, afraid, but there, tangled up with the hope she thought she'd lost.

It hadn't come the way she'd expected, or with the man she'd expected, but nonetheless, it was a miracle.

A new life.

"Okay," she said.

He pulled her close and kissed her so deeply, with such love and passion, she found herself believing in him. In them.

"We'll have to tell my parents—"

"No time like the present," he said. He turned and shut off the oven, covered the skillet on the stove.

Frankie didn't want to tell her dad this news, that she was "in trouble," and getting married, but what choice did she have? Pregnancy wasn't the kind of thing that could be hidden for long, and the clock was already ticking.

"I've got you," he said, taking her hand. "Trust me."

She nodded.

Even though it was cool by Southern California standards, Frankie and Henry walked down the street, holding hands, not bothering with sweaters or coats.

Cars rushed past them, headlights on. The beach was a vast, empty swath of black to their right, with a rising moon cut into the sky. The houses along Ocean Boulevard were decorated for Christmas, with Santas and reindeer and white lights wrapped around the palm trees.

At her parents' house, they crossed the backyard, which was aggressively decorated for the holidays, and went into the house, which boasted even more decorations. A huge tree dominated the living room.

Dad stood beside Mom at the bar, holding a silver martini shaker.

"Frances," Mom said. "Happy birthday, darling! We didn't expect you tonight."

Frankie couldn't let go of Henry's hand; he felt like her lifeline. "Dad. Mom. I think you know Henry Acevedo. We're . . . dating."

"Henry," Dad said, striding forward, smiling that big, inclusive smile of his, the one that made everyone feel welcome and important. "Good to see you again."

"Dr. Acevedo," Mom said, practically beaming.

Henry said, "Could I speak with you a moment, Connor? Privately."

Dad frowned briefly, then nodded. "Of course. Of course."

While the two men walked down the hallway, Mom sidled close to Frankie. "Is this what I hope it is?"

"Mom, I have never been able to divine your thoughts," Frankie said. It had never occurred to her that Henry would formally ask Dad for her hand in marriage. It felt so old-school, so *Ozzie and Harriet* in this *Bob & Carol & Ted & Alice* world.

Moments later, Henry and Dad walked back into the room. "Bette, we will have a son-in-law! Welcome to the family, Henry!"

Mom gave Frankie a fierce hug. When she drew back, there were tears in her eyes. "A wedding. A grandchild. Oh, Frances, your whole world will change when you hold your baby in your arms."

Henry moved in, put an arm around Frankie, held her so close she wondered if he thought she wanted to leave.

"Welcome to the family, Henry," Mom said. Then she looked up at Dad. "We need champagne!"

When her mother limped away, Frankie turned to Henry, put her arms around his neck, and stared up at him. "Are you sure we need an actual wedding? How about a quick zip in and out to the justice of the peace?"

"No way. This baby is a miracle, Frankie. Love in this screwed-up world is always worth celebrating. When Susannah died, I thought it was over for me."

She felt his love for her, for their child, felt his dream for them unfold and take flight. It filled her with hope.

"I want to see you walk down some aisle toward me and hear you say you love me in front of your family and friends. I want a baby girl who looks just like you."

"Or a boy who looks like Finley," she said, daring to dream it. "I guess that means there's a honeymoon in our future."

"Baby," he said, "our life is going to be one long honeymoon."

Twenty-Eight

December 20, 1972

Dear Barb,
Thanks for the birthday card!

I'm writing an identical letter to Ethel. Should I call? Yeah. Sure. Of course.

I just can't. Maybe I'm becoming a coward in my old age, I'm not sure.

Anyway, I'll cut to the chase. I'm pregnant.

Who saw that coming, right? Although I do recall you mentioning birth control a million years ago when I lost my virginity.

Henry and I are getting married. I know, it's a lot, and fast, and I'm a modern woman, I can raise a child on my own, but, well, there's something special about Henry. I think I'll learn to love him. More importantly, it seems impossible, but I'm already in love with the baby in my womb. How can that be? Sometimes I'm giddy and embarrassed by how much I want this. (Her, I think.)

The wedding won't be much, probably something small in our backyard or on the beach.

You'll come? Be my maid of honor? Ethel can be the matron of honor. She'll love how old that makes her sound.

Love ya—

F

———

Henry slipped his grandmother's diamond ring on Frankie's finger on Christmas morning, saying, "Forever, Frankie, and longer." They decided on Saturday, February 17, for the wedding, and sent out a small number of casual, handwritten invitations.

Henry taught Frankie how to spin a dream into something tangible: a nursery. They started with furniture—bought a crib and a changing table—and then went to the hardware store together early on a Saturday morning and picked out a sunny shade of yellow for the walls. They spent the next two weekends and several weekday evenings readying the small bedroom at the end of the hallway.

A yellow room, with big windows and new gingham drapes.

Henry was sitting on the floor now, with white crib pieces scattered all around, counting out screws, swearing under his breath. "Why in the hell do they give you more screws than there are holes?"

Smiling, Frankie left him with the incomprehensible instructions and headed to the kitchen. It took forever to wash the yellow paint off of her hands and cheeks. It was even in her hair, and she'd worn a kerchief. At last, she started dinner and made an apple pie for dessert.

"Something smells good," Henry said an hour later, when he walked into the kitchen.

"That's me," Frankie said.

He took her in his arms, pulled her close. "I love a woman who smells like apples and cinnamon. You made a pie?"

"From scratch, I might add. It's Ethel's family recipe." She smiled. Pregnancy had calmed her. For the first time in years, she was sleeping well. Her moods had evened out; finally, she thought, she was becoming herself again.

"I assume you'll start knitting booties. Or making your own baby food."

Frankie smiled. "Are you suggesting I'm going overboard on the whole nesting thing?"

"Never."

He kissed her, then led her down the hallway to the nursery. In the soft yellow room with bright white trim, the new crib stood against one wall.

She went to the crib, touched the rocket-and-stars mobile that hung over it, remembering the disagreement they'd had about this mobile: Should it be rockets or princess castles? *I want our daughter to know she can fly to the moon if she wants to,* had been Henry's winning argument.

A new rocker sat in the corner, next to an empty bookcase that she would soon fill with her favorite childhood stories. She sat down in it, pushed off with her feet. The chair made a creaking, clacking sound on the floor. She bumped the bookcase and a stuffed blue octopus fell into her lap. Idly, she stroked its soft fake fur.

Henry moved closer, gazed down at her, his clothes splattered with yellow, his graying hair a ragged mess.

"I love you," she said, and just then, as he pulled her up for a kiss, she thought it was true. Or at least that it could be true.

She wanted it to be true.

In the first week of the new year, 1973, they started a tradition of weekly dinners with Frankie's parents. Dad and Henry never seemed to run out of topics to talk about, even though their political views differed. The clinic Henry and his colleagues had worked so hard to create was months away from opening, and he could wax poetic about their big

plans to help addicts and alcoholics heal. Mom had offered to spear-
head another fundraising campaign with other Junior League wives.
She was already shopping for a gown for the opening.

Dad seemed thrilled that his daughter had finally stepped onto the
accepted female life path: marriage and motherhood. Mom talked ex-
citedly about the wedding, pressed for a small reception at the club
after the backyard ceremony, a request that Frankie politely denied.

Now they were in the living room, gathered in comfortable chairs
around the fireplace, with a fire roaring. The television in the corner
was on. Cronkite was reporting on the Watergate scandal. The aroma
of pot roast wafted in from the kitchen.

In the middle of the broadcast, Frankie got up from her chair and
headed to the bathroom. She was back in the hallway, heading for the
living room, when Henry appeared, looking worried.

"Are you okay? You look pale."

"I'm Irish," she said. "And I currently have a bladder the size of a
pea, which I'm pretty sure our daughter is sitting on."

He put a hand on her belly, leaned down to say, "Hey, baby. Daddy's
here."

Frankie's pregnancy was barely showing. There was just the tiniest
bump in her belly, which she touched often, stroked, imagining her
baby (a daughter, she still thought) like a little fish in there, swimming
around, doing effortless somersaults.

She had begun recently to touch her belly frequently, saying, *Come
on, baby, do a little twirl for Mama, let me feel you,* but she knew it was
too early.

"Mama wants a little attention, too," Frankie said, taking Henry by
the hand, leading him down the hallway. She opened her father's office
door, pulled him inside.

Henry kissed her, then said, "Okay, we've hidden out long enough.
Your mom's going to send a SWAT team in after us."

He pulled back.

Frankie realized her mistake; in the past few weeks—since the night of their engagement—she'd taken great care not to show Henry this room, to bypass the closed door. Now he'd seen the heroes' wall.

She tried to pull him away.

"Wow." He let go of her hand, moved toward the wall, staring at the photographs and mementos.

Frankie moved to his side, kept one arm around his narrow waist. She hadn't been in this room for years. The last thing she wanted to see was Finley's American flag, folded into a neat triangle, protected behind glass, framed in wood.

"Where's your picture?" Henry asked, and she loved him for noticing the absence and not being afraid to remark upon it. Before she could answer, the door behind them opened.

Dad strode into the room, moving as he always did, with authority.

"We are so proud of our family's service," Dad said.

"The men's service," Frankie remarked.

Mom arrived a second later, a martini in hand. "I hope you haven't told them without me," she said.

"Of course not," Dad said. He reached into his desk drawer and pulled out a fat, sealed manila envelope. "This is the deed to the cottage on Ocean Boulevard. It's our wedding gift to you."

"That's very generous," Henry said with a frown.

"I say a toast is in order," Mom said. "Henry, please, come help me choose a bottle of champagne."

Mom tucked her arm through Henry's and pulled him away.

That left Frankie alone at the heroes' wall with her father. They stood there a long moment, staring up at the pictures and memorabilia. "Why isn't there a picture of me up there, Dad?"

"We'll put your wedding photo up. That's what we do for the women in this family. You're a hero for putting up with the men."

How many times had he made that joke? "Nurses died in Vietnam, Dad."

"I'm uncomfortable with this conversation. Your fiancé is here. You're expecting a child. Your pride should come from caring for your husband and child. Women going to war . . ." He shook his head.

"If I'd been a son who went to Vietnam and came home in one piece, would my photograph be on the wall, Dad?"

"You're upsetting me with this jabble, Frankie. You're my daughter. You had no business going to war and I told you so at the time. Now we find out we shouldn't even have been fighting the damn war in the first place and we are *losing*. America. Losing a war. Who wants that reminder? Let it go, Frankie. Forget and move on."

He was right. She needed to forget it.

She was engaged to be married. Pregnant. Why should she care if no one—including her own family—valued her service to her country? Why should she care that no one remembered the women?

She remembered.

Why wasn't that enough?

Suddenly the door to the office banged open. Henry stood there, holding a bottle of champagne. "It's over," he said.

"Over?" Frankie said.

"The war," Henry said. "Nixon signed the Peace Accord."

———

Two weeks after President Nixon signed the Peace Accord, it was announced on the television news that the first wave of POWs would be coming home from Vietnam. Operation Homecoming, it was called, and, overnight, the League of Families' efforts changed from advocacy to preparing for the POWs' return, some of whom had been gone for nearly a decade. Letters and postcards began to arrive at the League of Families' San Diego and D.C. offices, letters from all over the country from people who had worn a POW bracelet; glowing welcome-home letters that thanked the men. Strangers sent gifts of gratitude, donations. A public that couldn't wait to get past the war embraced the return of the heroes released from the Hoa Lo Prison, a place that was just beginning to be written about as hell on earth, just beginning to be known by the public as the "Hanoi Hilton."

The wives launched their own Operation Homecoming by readying their homes, going to the beauty salon, gathering families close, painting welcome-home banners. Children were lined up and spit-polished; many were told stories of the fathers they'd never met.

———

On this February afternoon, the League of Families San Diego office was decorated for a party, with banners hung on the walls, painted with slogans like NEVER FORGOTTEN and WE DID IT. There was a buzzing, nervous energy in the room.

Frankie felt the women's pride and fear. She overheard several of them talking about the preparedness briefing the Navy had given the POW wives, who had been told not to expect too much from their husbands. They'd been given a flyer: *We don't know what shape the men will be in, physically or emotionally. As you know, there have been reports of torture. For these reasons, we suggest you plan your reunions carefully, keep your husband in a quiet setting until he tells you he's ready for more. No big parties, no magazine or television interviews, no loud noises or big expectations. Some of these men, as you well know, have lived in captivity, in harsh conditions, for up to eight years. This will have taken an extreme toll on their minds and bodies. Do not expect them to be themselves right away. We expect them to be sexually impotent and prone to hostility toward those they love.*

Torture. Captivity. Prone to hostility.

How could men come home after years of such treatment and be anything but hostile? Frankie listened to the wives as they expressed their nervousness—*I've gained weight, lost my spark, not as young*—and wondered aloud if the men they'd married would still love them. She listened to their plans to attend the return of the first group arriving in San Diego—on Valentine's Day—and felt a strong sense of pride.

But, as proud as she was of her service to the league, it was over now. She didn't belong in this room full of wives. She put down her empty cake plate and headed for the door.

"Frankie!"

She stopped, turned to see Joan moving toward her. The two women hadn't seen each other in months, but there was no mistaking the joy in the woman's eyes.

"I just wanted to say thank you," Joan said, touching her arm. "Your help meant so much."

Frankie smiled. "Thanks, Joanie. I'm glad your husband is coming home."

It was the perfect goodbye.

One chapter in her life closing—Vietnam—and another opening up. Marriage and motherhood.

On the day the first group of POWs was scheduled to land in Manila, Frankie poured herself an iced tea and sat on the sofa watching TV. Walter Cronkite was saying: *There have been stories of torture, as we know. The men in the Hanoi Hilton, mostly pilots, devised an ingenious way of communicating with each other. Today, one hundred and eight of them will land in Manila, the first stop on their way home . . .*

"Hey, babe," Henry said, scooting in beside her.

"It's starting." Frankie felt almost as anxious as the wives must be right now. This was really it, the end of the war.

Grainy color images of the war filled the screen, then changed to images of Navy wife Sybil Stockdale speaking to the Senate, to audiences, to Henry Kissinger. Walter Cronkite narrated it all: *The League of Families worked tirelessly to bring these American heroes home from their ordeal. Moments from now, a plane full of POWs will touch down at Clark Air Force Base. In two days, they will step on American soil for the first time in years.*

And then: *It's here. The jet has landed at Clark Air Force Base in the Philippines, ladies and gentlemen.*

Frankie leaned forward.

On-screen, a jet rolled down the runway. Lights blared on the scene. The jet came to a slow, bumping stop. Images of a cheering, jostling crowd: men and women, straining at a barricade to keep them back. The camera focused on a sign that read HOMECOMING 1973. WE LOVE YOU, JOHN!

The jet door opened.

All but one of these men who flew to freedom were shot down during some of the fiercest fighting of the war. Here is Navy Commander Benjamin E. Strahan, shot down in September of 1967 . . . and Air Force Major Jorge Alvarez, shot down in October 1968 . . .

Men emerged one at a time from the plane, saluted, and walked down the ramp. They looked skinny, but their hair was regulation-short and they stood tall. A few limped.

A man stepped out of the plane, saluted to the crowd gathered on the tarmac.

Navy Lieutenant Commander Joseph Ryerson Walsh, shot down in March of 1969, presumed dead until a year ago . . .

Frankie straightened.

Rye shuffled down the ramp, holding on tightly to the yellow railing. The way he walked was uneven, a limp maybe, and he held one arm in close to his body.

At the bottom of the ramp, he saluted again.

The camera closed in on Rye's gaunt, smiling face.

Frankie stood up, stared at the television, at Rye. The thudding of her heart was so loud she couldn't hear anything else.

"Babe?" Henry said. "Frankie? What's wrong?"

"I'm not feeling well. Nausea." An excuse that always worked for a pregnant woman. "I'm going to take a bath."

Henry stood. "I'll start it for—"

"No."

Had she shouted it? Was she crying? She wiped her eyes, felt tears. She looked at him. "No," she said more gently, as gently as she could, anyway, when all she wanted to do was get away. "Stay. Watch the broadcast. I'll go . . . calm down and relax in a nice hot bath." She gave him a quick peck on the cheek—almost a headbutt, because she was off-balance—and lurched toward the kitchen.

He's alive.

Those two words shifted the world off its axis, upset the precarious balance she'd found in the last year.

The phone on the kitchen counter rang.

"I'll get it," Henry said.

"I've got it," Frankie shouted, diving forward to pick up the phone. "Hello?"

Barb said, "Frankie?"

"You saw him?" Frankie whispered.

"I saw him," Barb said. "Are you okay?"

"Okay?" Frankie said, dragging the phone as far as she could, lowering her voice to a whisper. "I'm pregnant, my wedding is this weekend, and the love of my life just came back from the dead. How could I be okay?"

She heard Barb's sigh slip through the line. "What the hell are you supposed to do now? I mean, engaged is one thing. Pregnant is another."

"I know, but . . . it's Rye," she said quietly.

"I know."

"I have to see him, at least," Frankie said. As she said the words, she knew they were a half-truth. She wanted more than just to see him. She wanted the future that belonged to them. "I have to be on the airfield in San Diego when he lands."

There was a long silence. Then Barb said, "I'm calling Ethel. We'll catch a red-eye."

All the next day, Frankie was so nervous, she couldn't sit still, not even when Barb and Ethel showed up to rally around her. All she could think about was Rye . . . landing in San Diego . . . being alive.

"You should tell Henry," Barb said. They were in the bungalow's living room, she and Frankie and Ethel. Frankie's new wedding dress—a lacy white prairie-style gown—hung from a hanger on a kitchen cupboard hook, reminding them all of the wedding scheduled for Saturday.

"I can't," Frankie said. She knew it would break Henry's heart to learn that Joseph Ryerson Walsh, recently returned POW, was the Rye whom Frankie had loved.

Still loved.

She glanced nervously at the kitchen clock. It was 8:10 A.M. The plane full of POWs was scheduled to land in San Diego at 9:28. Frankie had called Anne Jenkins and gotten permission to be there. It had been easy to do on a day when Anne was busy with a thousand other details. "Sure," she'd said. "Of course. Thanks again for all your help, Frankie."

Frankie twirled her engagement ring on her finger, staring down at it, and then slowly took it off. She didn't want Rye to see it until she had time to explain.

"If we're going, we should go," Ethel said.

They piled into Frankie's Mustang and drove off the island and onto the mainland and arrived at the gates of the Air Station Miramar at 8:45.

There was already a crowd of people and reporters on the tarmac. Women, children, men, all holding up welcome-home signs. Wives and family and reporters were in front, friends and service personnel in the back.

"I forgot to make a sign," Frankie said. She was so nervous, she couldn't think straight, couldn't stand still. In the front of the line, reporters held out microphones, threw out questions. Barb and Ethel stood on either side of her like bodyguards, giving her time to collect herself.

Would Rye forgive her for Henry, for being weak enough to say yes? For carrying another man's child? While he'd been held and tortured, she'd been having a relationship with someone else. How could she make him believe she'd never stopped loving him?

"It's landing," Barb said.

Frankie glanced up, felt fear and joy in equal measure.

Would he still love her—a different version of him meeting a different version of her?

The C-141 medical evacuation jet descended, touched down on the runway, came to a stop.

Reporters ran forward, stretching out microphones and video cameras, clamoring with questions, but were stopped by a barrier from getting too close to the plane.

The three women were jostled by the crowd; a yellow line held all of the families back, but the wives and children strained against it, signs upheld, each jockeying to be in front.

At the plane, sailors moved the exit ramp into place. A naval officer stood at the bottom of the ramp, holding the reporters and families at bay.

The jet door opened and the first POW emerged, wearing khakis that were too big for him. Commander James, shot down in 1967. He paused at the top of the ramp, blinked in the harsh sunlight, and made his way down to the tarmac. At the bottom, he saluted the officer in front of him and was helped to a podium, set up in front of a phalanx of reporters.

He looked out at the crowd, searching for his family. "Thank you, America. We are grateful to have had the opportunity to serve our country, and grateful that our country has brought us home."

His wife broke free, pushed past the reporters, ducked under the yellow tape, and rushed toward her husband, throwing herself into his arms. The crowd spread out, families clumped together. Frankie saw Anne Jenkins, standing with her children, and Joan and her daughter, and several of the other wives she'd met along the way. They all looked anxious, didn't even wave to each other.

A commander emerged from the jet next. His wife and sons—and a man who was probably his father—moved forward to greet him.

And then there he was—Rye—standing at the top of the ramp, blinking as the others had, wearing freshly pressed khakis that were too big, a belt cinched tight at his waist. He limped down the ramp, clutching the rail with one hand.

Everything else fell away; the world around him blurred. Frankie saw the smear of camouflage-colored paint that was the jet, and a blob of reporters vying for comments, and heard the sound of sobbing all around her. She needed to push her way through the people in front of her, to get to the yellow tape, but she could hardly move. She was crying too hard to see. "Rye," she whispered.

He limped forward, searching the crowd. Not seeing her, he veered left, toward the group of waiting wives.

"Rye!" she yelled, but her voice was lost in the sound of cheering. "I'm here!"

He headed for a tall, curvy woman with a cascade of curly blond hair who stood to one side, holding on to a little girl's hand. The child held up a sign that read WELCOME HOME, DADDY!

He ran the last few steps forward, pulled the woman into his arms, and kissed her. Deeply.

Then he bent down to kiss the little girl with the WELCOME HOME, DADDY! sign. He swept her up into his arms. The woman wrapped her arms around both of them; all three were crying.

"He's married," Ethel said softly. "Son of a bitch."

"Oh my God," Frankie whispered, feeling everything inside of her start to crumble.

Twenty-Nine

Frankie became aware of the music: first the beat, then the words. "Hey Jude . . ."

She was in the O Club, dancing with Rye. She felt his arms around her, his hand at the curve of her spine; familiar, where it belonged, holding her close. He whispered something she couldn't hear. "What?" she said. "What?"

I'm married.

I was always married.

Suddenly the music blared, turned loud enough to break glass.

She opened her eyes. They were groggy with grit, wet with tears.

The music snapped off.

She was in her own house, in her bed.

She sat up, saw Barb and Ethel standing there, looking so sad that Frankie's wound opened again.

He lied.

She remembered asking him the wrong question in Kauai, and his answer: *I swear I'm not engaged.* The words played over and over in her head.

"You need to get up, honey," Ethel said. "Henry is on his way over."

Frankie couldn't respond. She'd come home from the air station and climbed into bed and cried herself first to a headache and then to sleep.

She knew her friends were ready to lift her up, buoy her, but this pain, this betrayal, was worse than her grief had been. She'd made her friends stop on the way home to buy a local newspaper. She'd read and reread the article about Joseph "Rye" Walsh, the local hero who had married his college sweetheart just before going off to war and never met the daughter who'd been born in his absence. Josephine, called Joey.

"Frankie?" Barb said gently, sitting on the bedside, pushing the damp hair back from Frankie's face.

Frankie pushed the sour-smelling covers back. Without making eye contact with her friends (she couldn't look at them without thinking of Rye), she got out of bed. Love and pain and humiliation almost toppled her again.

She felt so stupid. Hadn't Ethel warned her early on? *The men here, they lie and they die.*

She walked to the bathroom and ran a steaming-hot shower and stepped underneath the hot flow, let it pound her while she cried.

In the empty kitchen, her Gunne Sax dress hung limply from a high cupboard. She couldn't look at it, so she turned and went outside.

Barb and Ethel were in the backyard, which had been transformed for this weekend's ceremony. Folding chairs—eleven of them, for Frankie's parents, Barb and Ethel and Noah and Cecily, and Henry's small family—had been set up in front of a rented wooden arch, which Mom had insisted on festooning with white roses. As if Frankie were a naive debutante instead of a pregnant war veteran.

Two days ago, she'd been almost excited to marry Henry Acevedo and have his baby and start a new life.

Today she couldn't imagine any of that.

Barb got out of the chair and came toward her. Ethel followed suit.

"Henry loves you, Frank," Ethel said. "That's obvious."

"Do you love him?" Barb dared to ask.

The words submerged Frankie again, left her unable to straighten or breathe. She knew they would support her, these women, her best friends who had flown here at a moment's notice and were equally ready to stand at the altar with her or stand by her if she canceled the ceremony.

They loved her, were here for her.

But she didn't want them here now, didn't want to see their pity.

Away.

That was what she wanted. A place to hide.

"If you don't get married," Ethel said tentatively, "come back to Virginia with me. The bunkhouse is still empty. Noah will love you and Cecily needs an aunt to play with."

"Or to Chicago with me," Barb said.

They were offering her paths, lives. They had no idea how broken she felt by Rye's betrayal.

But her feelings weren't the most important anymore. She was going to be a mother.

"I'll marry Henry on Saturday," she said quietly. What choice did she have? "He'll be a great father. Our baby deserves that."

She knew what the right thing to do was. If there was one true thing in her life, it was that she always knew the right thing, and did it. Even when it hurt so much she couldn't breathe.

Rye had betrayed her. Didn't love her.

Henry loved her and their baby and wanted to create a family. The baby deserved that chance, and Frankie owed everything to her unborn baby.

"You sure?" Barb asked, reaching out to squeeze Frankie's upper arm.

Frankie looked at her two best friends. "I'm going to be a mom," Frankie said. "I guess my choices have to start there from now on."

"Then this is our bridal party. Let's get it on," Ethel said. She went back into the living room, cranked up the stereo, and opened the patio doors.

The familiar notes of "California Girls" drifted into the backyard.

"This song always reminds me of Frankie's first day at the Thirty-Sixth," Barb said to Ethel, pulling Frankie to dance with her on the patio. "Her eyes were so big they looked like burnt holes in my mama's best sheet."

"You guys stripped down to bloody bras and panties in front of me," Frankie said. "I thought I'd landed on the moon."

The music changed again. *Born to be w–i–i–i–ld . . .*

Halfway through the song, Frankie felt a cramp in her stomach. First a tightening, then a pain so sharp she gasped.

A rush of wetness dampened her underwear. She put a hand down her panties. When she brought her hand back up, it was covered in blood.

Someone knocked on the door. Before anyone could answer, the front door opened. Henry walked into the backyard. "Hey, gals, that's some good music, and—"

He saw the blood.

Frankie looked at him. "This can't be happening. I haven't done anything wrong."

Henry bounded into action, sweeping Frankie into his arms, carrying her out to the car, settling her in the passenger seat. He backed out of the driveway so fast, Frankie smelled burning rubber.

He sped up to the Coronado hospital emergency entrance and slammed on the brakes.

Lifting Frankie out of the car, carrying her into the bright white emergency room, he shouted, "We need help here. My fiancée is pregnant and something is wrong."

Frankie woke in a darkened room that smelled of disinfectant and bleach.

Hospital.

The previous night came back to her in a rush—blood running down her legs, a terrible cramping, a young doctor saying, "I'm sorry, Mrs. Acevedo. There's nothing I can do."

Her saying, ridiculously, "I'm Frankie McGrath."

She heard a chair creak beside her, saw Henry sitting there, slumped over.

"Hey," Frankie said; just the sight of him saddened her. He was such a good man and he deserved better.

She pressed a hand to her empty abdomen.

"Hey," Henry answered, rising, taking her hand in his. He leaned down to kiss her cheek.

"Was it—"

"A boy," Henry said.

Finley.

"The doctor said we can try again," Henry said.

There was a knock at the door.

It opened.

Mom stood there, dressed in a rust-colored suede skirt with a print vest over a blouse buttoned up to her throat, and knee-high boots. "How is she?"

Henry answered, "She's—"

"She's right here, Mom. And conscious."

Mom's smile turned brittle. "Henry, darling, would you go get me a coffee from the cafeteria? I've got a headache."

Henry kissed Frankie, whispered, "I love you," and left the room.

Mom approached the bed slowly.

Frankie thought her mother looked tired. Her makeup had been applied a little too heavily and she couldn't hold a smile. As usual, when she was tired or stressed, the effects of her stroke were more noticeable. There was the slightest downturn to one side of her mouth. "I am so sorry, Frances."

Tears scalded Frankie's eyes, blurred the image of her mother. "God is punishing me. But I was going to do the right thing."

"It's nothing you did." Mom reached behind her neck, unclasped her necklace, and handed it to Frankie.

As a child, Frankie had been obsessed with the necklace, wondering how that delicate gold chain could hold the obviously heavy heart.

Mom pulled out her silver cigarette case, lit an Eve cigarette.

"You're not supposed to smoke, you know," Frankie said.

Mom made a dismissive gesture. "Look on the back of the heart."

Frankie turned the necklace over, saw an inscription on the back. *Celine.* She frowned. "Who is Celine?"

"The daughter I lost," Mom said. "The baby I was carrying when I married your father."

"You never—"

"And I won't now, Frances," Mom said. "Some things don't bear the weight of words. That's the problem with your generation, you all want to talk, talk, talk. What is the point? I thought . . . you could give your . . . child a name and engrave it there, below your sister's, and wear it."

"He was a boy," Frankie said. "We would have named him Finley."

Mom blanched.

Some things don't bear the weight of words.

"I'm so sorry, Frances. Put the pain away, forget about it, and go on."

"Were you able to do that?"

"Most of the time."

Mom reached into her purse, pulled out two prescription bottles. "I know you're a nurse and all, but I swear by these pills. Cheryl Burnam calls them 'Mother's Little Helpers.' The white ones help you sleep and the yellow ones keep you awake."

"I *am* a nurse, Mom. And I read *Valley of the Dolls.*"

"Pooh. Those were bad girls. You just need something to take the edge off. These have hardly more kick than a gin martini."

"Thanks, Mom."

"I'll put them in your purse. Trust me, you and Henry will be married and expecting again in no time."

Frankie sighed. "Do you remember the man I fell in love with in Vietnam?"

"The pilot who was killed?"

"Yes, he—"

"Frances, enough Vietnam. For God's sake, that was years ago. Let it go. He's not coming back to you."

She closed her eyes in pain, unable to look at her mother anymore, unable to see pity and sorrow and know that it was for her.

———

Barb and Ethel stood at Frankie's bedside.

Their mission was obvious, to keep up a steady stream of banter, to talk about whatever they could think of: the commutation of Charles Manson's death sentence to life imprisonment, the rockiness of the Taylor-Burton marriage, the uproar over a movie called *Deep Throat*.

Frankie couldn't listen anymore. She raised a hand.

Ethel stopped talking—Frankie had no idea what she'd been talking about—and leaned in. "What is it?"

Frankie sat up, staring dry-eyed at the wall. "I'm not going to marry him," she said. "It wouldn't be fair."

"Give it some time," Ethel said. "Don't decide now, after . . ."

"Say it. After losing my son."

"Yeah," Barb said, holding Frankie's hand. "After losing your baby. I can't imagine your pain."

"Rye—"

"He lied to you, Frank," Ethel said. Her voice had a sharp edge, but the tears in her eyes were obvious. "He had his men lie to you. Or he lied to them. Either way, he's not good enough to lick shit off the floor, and if I ever see him . . ."

"I'll help you kick his ass," Barb said. "I'll pay people to help us."

"You can go home," Frankie said. "There's no wedding to stay for. Ethel, your husband and daughter need you, and Barb, I know Operation PUSH's convention is coming up and Jesse Jackson is probably counting on you."

"We don't want to leave you," Barb said.

"I'm fine," Frankie lied. She touched the golden heart necklace at her throat. All three of them knew the truth: that it would be a long time before Frankie was really fine, but whatever that journey looked like, however she healed, it would fall on her to do the heavy lifting. Her friends could be there for her, help her stand, but she had to walk alone.

They kissed her forehead, Ethel first, Barb next, her kiss a moment longer. "We will call you tomorrow," Barb said.

"And the day after that," Ethel added.

Frankie was relieved when they left. She lay back into the pillows, feeling exhausted. And afraid.

The hospital door opened and she winced.

Henry stepped into the room, closed the door behind him. He looked as tired and beaten as she felt.

He came to her bedside, held her hand. She couldn't find the strength to squeeze his hand back.

He smoothed the hair back from her face. She knew how badly he was hurting, how much he needed to share that with her, but she was a closed door.

She closed her eyes, hating that she would hurt him.

"Don't shut me out, Frankie," Henry said. "I need you . . . us. This happened to both of us. The doctor says we need to put it aside and try again. We can do that, can't we?"

Forget it, in other words. The same old advice, given for a brand-new pain.

God help her, she wasn't able to mourn with him. Even now, with loss all around her, in her own body, she couldn't help thinking of Rye. His was the touch she wanted.

"I'm sorry," he said, and his voice broke. "I should have been there earlier."

She looked at him, felt a hot rush of self-loathing. "It would have happened anyway," she said tonelessly.

"I know, but—"

"No buts, Henry. I don't want to talk about the baby." She took a deep breath. "I want to talk about the wedding. About us."

"Us? Oh, babe, don't worry about the wedding. We have time. Let's just get our feet under us."

She looked at him, seeing how deeply he loved her.

"Henry." She sighed, played with her engagement ring—his grandmother's. "You remember I told you about Rye? The man I loved in Vietnam, Finley's friend?"

He drew back, let go of her hand. "Sure. The pilot who was killed?"

"He didn't die over there. He's been in prison. He got back to the U.S. yesterday."

"Oh." He said it lightly, and then he frowned, said it again. "Oh. You saw him?"

"I did."

"And you still love him?"

"I do," Frankie said, starting to cry. She wanted to tell him about Rye's betrayal, about how the pain of it had somehow caused her miscarriage, and *still* she couldn't stop loving him. But Henry was too good a man for that. If she told him the truth, he'd stay with her, give her time, tell her she deserved better than a man who'd lied to her. She had no doubt that there was no future for her and Rye. She didn't fool herself about that. But just knowing that he was alive made it impossible for her to pretend to love Henry enough to marry him.

Slowly, she took the engagement ring off her finger, gave it back to him. "I can't marry you, Henry."

She saw his struggle with emotion. "You should talk to someone, Frankie. The new VA medical center offers therapy for vets. It can really help to talk to someone."

"I'm sorry," she said.

"I love you, Frankie," he said, his voice cracking on emotion.

"You'll find someone better."

"Jesus, Frankie. You break my heart."

"Henry—"

"And for a woman in love, you have the saddest eyes I've ever seen."

———

Frankie left the hospital in a wheelchair, like an ancient woman, wearing a pad to absorb the bleeding. Dad pushed the wheelchair and ordered the local nurses around as if they were employees under his charge.

Mom pulled up in front of the hospital and they both helped Frankie into the passenger seat of the new Cadillac.

At home, Frankie crawled into bed. Mom stayed in the bungalow, trying to distract her—as if such a thing were possible—until Frankie begged her to go home.

I'm fine, she kept saying, until at last there was nothing left for Mom to do but leave.

Alone, Frankie reached for the purse on her nightstand. She took a pill for pain and then two sleeping pills.

She closed her eyes, lay back. Drifted. Through a haze that captured her heartbeat, she heard the door open.

Frankie didn't open her eyes. She was hanging on by a thread here; the last thing she needed was an audience.

She could feel her mother watching her, worrying, but she didn't open her eyes. She was deeply, profoundly tired. Exhausted, actually.

Her last, terrible thought was, *He's alive.* And then: *It was all a lie.*

Thirty

For the first time in a long time, Frankie started to wake up on her bedroom floor again. She didn't know why the brutal nightmares of Vietnam had come back now. Maybe it was seeing Rye. Or maybe new trauma reawakened old trauma. All she knew was that there was no way for her to pretend she was okay and soldier on. Not this time.

The pills her mother had given her helped to take the edge off of her pain. She learned that two sleeping pills softened the nightmares and helped her fall asleep, but when she woke, she felt lethargic, unrested. One of the Mother's Little Helpers perked her right up, maybe even gave her too much energy. Enough so that she needed the pills again to calm down enough to sleep. It became a cycle, like the ebb and flow of the tide.

She stopped visiting her parents, stopped answering the phone, stopped writing letters to her friends. She didn't want to hear their pep talks, and no one wanted to listen to her despair.

To keep busy, she took extra shifts at the hospital. Most nights, she stayed in the hospital as long as she could, putting off the inevitability of having to go home.

Like now.

Long after her shift had ended, Frankie was still in her scrubs and cap, standing by the bedside of an elderly woman who was in the final stages of lung cancer, that terrible time when the body almost entirely shuts down, stops taking in food, stops any sort of intentional movement. The patient was frighteningly thin, her hands curled into claws, her chin tilted up. Her mouth was open. Her breath was that gasping death rattle that meant time was closing around her, but she hung on to life stubbornly. Frankie knew that four of her grown children and all of her grandchildren had been to see her today, all of them having been told that the end was near, but now, at 11:21, Madge had no visitors, and yet she hung on. Bright crayon drawings covered the window by the bed. Fresh flowers scented the hospital's disinfectant air.

Madge was waiting for her son. Everyone knew it. Her husband groused about it, while her daughters rolled their eyes. Lester, everyone seemed to think, was "too far gone to say goodbye to his mother."

Frankie applied some Vaseline to Madge's dry, colorless lips. "You still waiting for Les, huh?" she said.

Nothing from Madge, just that wheezing death rattle. Frankie gently took hold of the woman's hands and massaged lotion onto them.

She heard the door open and saw a young man with lots of frizzy hair and huge sideburns walk into the room. A mustache hid much of his mouth and a beard grew in tufts along his jawline. He wore a dirty PRO ROE T-shirt and baggy rust-colored corduroy pants.

But it was the tattoo on the inside of his forearm that caught her eye. The word AIRBORNE above a bald eagle head. She knew that insignia. The Screaming Eagles.

The family had called Lester a drug addict and a thief and said that he made candles at some commune in Oregon. No one had ever said he was a veteran. "Lester?" she said.

He nodded, looking lost, standing in the doorway. He might be high. Or just broken.

Frankie went to him, gently took him by the arm, led him to the bed. "She's been waiting for you."

"Hey, Ma." He reached slowly for his mother's hand, held it.

Madge took a great rattling breath.

Frankie moved to the other side of the bed, backed up to give him some privacy.

Lester leaned down. "I'm sorry, Ma."

Madge whispered, "Les," and took one last breath, released it, and slipped away.

Lester looked up, his dark eyes full of tears. "Is that it?"

Frankie nodded. "She waited for you."

He wiped his eyes, cleared his throat roughly. "I should have come sooner. I don't know what's wrong with me. I just . . . Vietnam, man . . ."

Frankie moved closer to the bed. "Yeah. I was at the Seventy-First. Central Highlands," she said. "From '67 to '69."

He looked at her. "So, we're both the walking dead."

Before Frankie could respond, he turned away from the bed and left the room, slamming the door shut behind him.

His presence—and his sudden absence—left Frankie feeling jittery, unsettled.

Without bothering to take off her scrubs or change her shoes, she left the hospital.

We're both the walking dead.

He'd seen her in a way that cut to the bone, saw what she was trying so hard to hide.

She was driving over the Coronado Bridge, listening to Janis belt out "Piece of My Heart," when she reached over into the passenger seat, felt around for her macramé handbag, and pulled out her sleeping pills.

There was no way she'd sleep tonight, and remaining awake—remembering—was worse.

She fumbled to open the cap at a stoplight on the island, and swallowed a pill dry, wincing at the taste.

At home, she parked and got out, a little shaky on her feet as she made her way into the house, where the phone was ringing. She ignored it.

She should eat something. When had she eaten last?

Instead, she poured herself a drink and took another sleeping pill, hoping two would be enough to get her through the night. If not, she might take a third. Just this once.

That spring, Tony Orlando and Dawn released "Tie a Yellow Ribbon Round the Ole Oak Tree" and reminded America that even though the war was over, there were still soldiers coming home from captivity in Vietnam. Overnight, yellow ribbons began to appear on tree trunks around the country, especially in military towns like San Diego and Coronado. Bits of yellow fluttering in the breeze to remind Americans of the POWs in captivity. Stories of heroes who'd been shot down and imprisoned for years filled the news. Frankie couldn't get away from the stories and the memories they raised.

She survived one day at a time, by keeping to herself, not saying much. She got a prescription for the pills she needed, worked as many hours as humanly possible, and visited her parents when they demanded it; she talked on the phone in short, expensive conversations with Barb and Ethel, most of which ended with Frankie's adamant (and dishonest) *I'm fine.* The letters she wrote to her girlfriends were long and chatty and filled with half-truths and pretense, not unlike the letters she'd written to her parents from Vietnam.

In May, her parents invited her to join them on the brand-new *Royal Viking Sky* cruise ship for a month at sea. Frankie declined easily and let out a deep breath when she saw them off.

Now there was no one to pretend for. She could be as alone and reclusive as she liked. Finally, she thought, she could mourn without anyone watching.

Despite her best intentions, Frankie couldn't seem to pull herself back from the edge of despair. If anything, the solitude and silence settled so heavily on her that sometimes she found it hard to breathe unless she took a pill, which she often did. By the end of May, she had refilled her prescriptions twice; it was easy to do for any woman these days, but certainly easy for a nurse.

In June, an unexpected weather front hit San Diego, a deluge that the local TV weatherman claimed came from the Hawaiian islands. In the middle of the night, Frankie was unexpectedly called in to work. Although she still felt a little lethargic from last night's sleeping pills, she popped another pill to wake her up and agreed. Without bothering to shower, she dressed in yesterday's clothes and headed for her car.

As she drove over the bridge, rain pounded on the convertible roof, sluiced across her windshield so hard the wiper blades could hardly keep up. On the radio, a story about the Watergate hearings droned on. Secret meetings. The president. Blah, blah, blah.

All she heard was the rain. Pounding. Rattling. Monsoon-hard.

—*blood washing across her boots, someone yelling, "Hit the generators"*—

She clung to the wheel.

In the hospital parking lot, she parked and ran into the bright building and went to her locker. Peeling off her damp clothes, she dressed in her scrubs and sneakers. She put on her surgical cap and coiled her long black ponytail up inside as she walked down the busy hallway toward the front desk.

Even inside the building, she could hear the rain, shuddering against glass, pounding on the roof.

At the nurses' station, she guzzled two cups of coffee, knowing it was a bad choice when she was this on edge.

It was the rain, reminding her of Vietnam.

She should eat, but the thought of food made her sick. Every time she closed her eyes, images of Vietnam assaulted her. Fighting them weakened her. Thank God it was a quiet shift. Just as she had that thought, the double doors at the end of the hall banged open. A pair of ambulance drivers rushed in, pushing a gurney into the bright white glare.

Blood.

"GSW," someone shouted.

The patient was wheeled past Frankie. She saw him in a blur—blood pumping from a chest wound, pale skin; he was screaming.

"Frankie!"

She ran after the gurney into the OR, but she felt dazed, untethered by memories, images. She was slow at scrubbing in, couldn't remember for a second where the gloves were kept.

When she turned around, a nurse was cutting off the kid's bloody jacket.

Silver blades snipped through the fabric.

And then: his bare chest. A gaping bullet wound, pumping blood.

Choppers incoming. Chinook. Thwop-thwop-thwop.

"Frankie. Frankie?"

Someone shook her, hard.

She looked up, realizing in a flash that she wasn't in Vietnam. She was at work, in OR 2.

"Get out of my OR, Frankie," Dr. Vreminsky yelled. "Ginni. You scrub in."

Shame overwhelmed Frankie. "But—"

"*Out,*" he yelled.

She backed out of the operating room and stood in the hallway, feeling lost.

The damnable rain.

Frankie woke on her bedroom floor, her head pounding, her mouth dry. Summer sunlight streamed through her window, hurt her eyes. The memory of last night's shame made her groan aloud. She stumbled to her nightstand, reached for her pills, and swallowed one with water.

She passed the closed nursery door on her way to the bathroom. She hadn't gone into the room in months, not even to clean. If she had the energy she'd gut it, paint over the cheery yellow walls, give away the furniture, but she wasn't strong enough to even open the door.

She took a hot shower, washed and dried her long hair and pulled it back into a loose ponytail, and then dressed in shorts and a T-shirt.

The phone rang.

She glanced at the wall clock. Twelve-twenty on a Saturday afternoon.

Barb.

Frankie knew her friend would keep calling until Frankie picked up, so she grabbed her beach hat and chair and left the house.

Carrying the chair across the street, she set it down in the sand.

As she stared out at the glittering blue waves, she remembered last night again, the way she'd frozen in the OR like some FNG fresh off the plane.

She couldn't go on like this. She needed to quit taking the pills and get her life back on track. But how?

She pulled the hat lower on her head and pulled her sunglasses and a tattered paperback copy of *Jonathan Livingston Seagull* out of the chair's side pocket. Maybe the bird could give her some much-needed advice on how to live.

The beach was a hive of activity on this hot June day. Kids running around, teenagers in packs, mothers running after their children. It soothed her, these familiar beach-day sounds, until she heard a man shout out, "Joey, come back from the water. Wait for me."

Frankie felt her skin tingle, even in the heat. She looked up slowly from beneath the wide brim of her sun hat.

Rye stood at the shoreline, facing this way, wearing shorts and a faded gray NAVY T-shirt.

The summer sun had darkened his skin and lightened his hair, which was long enough now that she knew he'd left the Navy. He moved in an awkward, limping way to keep up with his daughter—Joey—who giggled and tried to jump over the low roll of incoming surf.

His wife sat on a blanket not far away, wearing a billowy summer dress, one hand tented over her eyes, watching them, laughing easily. "Be careful, Jo-Jo!"

Frankie sank deeper into her chair, hunched her shoulders, trying to disappear, and pulled her hat down lower.

Look away.

She couldn't.

It was bad for her, maybe even dangerous, to watch Rye with his family, but she couldn't get up, couldn't stop looking at him and the easy, loving way he was with his daughter. It had been a day just like this when Rye had shown up in Kauai, standing over her, saying, *I swear I'm not engaged.*

God, how she loved him.

She heard his wife—Melissa, her name was Melissa, Frankie knew from reading about them in the newspaper. Melissa yelled something, and Rye and Joey moved toward her, him limping. They were close enough now that Frankie could see he was gritting his teeth. Ugly scarring encircled his wrists and ankles.

He knelt awkwardly in front of his wife, grimacing again in pain.

Help him, Frankie thought. *Melissa, help him.* But his wife just sat there, packing food back into a wicker picnic basket.

They look unhappy.

No.

He looked unhappy.

The thought was there before she could protect herself against it. And after all he'd suffered.

"Stop it," Frankie muttered. They were a family, the Walshes, and their happiness—his happiness—had nothing to do with her. She knew their true story now, how they'd met, how they'd married, the hardware store that her parents owned in Carlsbad, the managerial job that waited for him when he left the Navy.

Look away, Frankie.

This was wrong. Sick. Dangerous.

Frankie finally forced herself to get up. She turned her back on them, folded up her chair, and walked off the beach.

"Damn it, Melissa, slow down."

She heard Rye's voice behind her and froze. Then she gritted her teeth and kept walking, over the mound of greenery and down to the sidewalk and across Ocean Boulevard. On the other side, against her best intentions, she turned slowly, stared at them from beneath the brim of her hat.

He and his wife and daughter were leaving the beach, heading toward the street.

Frankie had to leave. Now. Before she called out to him. She clamped the chair to her side and walked resolutely down the block toward her house.

All the way there, she thought, *Don't look back, Frankie. Just let him go.*

But he knew she lived on Coronado, or at least that she'd been raised here. Did it mean something, that he'd brought his family here, to the beach she'd so often talked about?

She stopped at her car, which was parked in the driveway at her house, and looked back.

Now Rye was opening the trunk of a metallic midnight-blue Camaro, putting the picnic basket inside. Melissa opened the passenger door and helped Joey into the backseat.

Rye closed the trunk and limped toward the driver's-side door.

Frankie opened her car door, tossed her things in the backseat, and slid into the driver's seat. She plucked her keys from the visor, started the engine, and backed into the street. Slowly, her foot light on the accelerator, she drove forward, edged toward the stop sign on Ocean Boulevard.

Rye got into the Camaro. The engine started up with a roar.

She followed him. Them.

All the way across town, up Orange Avenue, over the bridge, she berated herself. This was stalking. Embarrassing. He didn't love her. He was a liar.

Still, she followed them, drawn by an obsessive need to see his life.

If he was unhappy . . .

No. That was something she couldn't think.

In San Diego, Rye turned onto A Street, which Frankie could see instantly was a street full of Navy families. American flags hung from many of the porches, a few lonely yellow ribbons still fluttered from the tree branches. Most of the POWs were home, but "Tie a Yellow Ribbon" was still a radio hit. On this summer afternoon, the street was full of kids and dogs and women walking side by side pushing strollers.

He pulled up in front of a pretty Craftsman-style bungalow. The yard was a scrabble of discarded toys and roller skates and doll clothes. The poorly cut grass was brown.

Frankie pulled over to the side of the road, the engine idling as if she might come to her senses soon and drive off.

But she didn't.

Melissa got out of the car. Holding Joey's hand, she walked up to the house, pulling Joey inside, leaving Rye to carry their stuff.

Rye moved slowly in his wife's wake, obviously in pain, carrying the basket and blanket. In the middle of the path to the front door, he stopped.

Frankie slunk down in her seat.

"I'll never do this again if he doesn't turn around," she promised herself, and maybe God. She peered up through the window, saw him start walking, limping in a hitching, painful way. He slowly climbed the porch steps, holding on to the handrail.

At the closed front door, he stopped again, as if he didn't want to go in, and then he opened the door and went into his house, back to his wife and child.

Frankie moved slowly back to an upright position, put the Mustang in gear, and drove forward. As she passed the house, she slowed, staring at the front door, feeling a toxic combination of longing and shame.

Rye opened the front door, stepped out onto the porch, and saw her. She hit the gas and sped past him.

Idiot.

What had she been thinking? She was still in turmoil when she got home. A gin on the rocks did nothing to lessen her anxiety. She kept looking at the phone, thinking he'd call, wanting him to, not wanting him to. Knowing all he had to do was call information to get her number. After all these years, she was still Frances McGrath on Coronado Island.

But the phone didn't ring.

Before the world even started to darken, she took two sleeping pills and climbed into bed.

What time did the phone ring? She wasn't sure. Bleary-eyed, lethargic, she climbed out of bed and stumbled into the kitchen and picked up the phone. "Hello?"

It was still daylight outside. The next day or the same day?

"Frankie? It's Geneva Stone."

Her boss. Shit. "Hi," she said. Was her voice slurry, were her words coming too slowly?

"You were supposed to cover Marlene Foley's shift tonight."

"Oh. Right," Frankie said. "Shorry. I don't feel well. I should have called in sick."

There was a long pause; in it, Frankie heard both displeasure and alarm. "Okay, Frankie. I will find someone else. Get better."

Frankie hung up, unsure the moment she heard the *click* of the line if she'd said goodbye.

She stumbled onto the sofa, fell sideways onto the cushions, pulled her legs up, and lay down.

Tomorrow she would get her act together. No more pills. And definitely no more stalking. She wouldn't even *think* of Rye Walsh.

No more.

—

Frankie sat in the director of nursing's office, stiffly upright, her hands clasped in her lap.

"So," Mrs. Stone said, her gaze steady on Frankie's face. "You froze in the OR. During surgery. And you missed a shift." She waited a beat. "Were sick."

"Yes, ma'am. But . . ." She stopped. What could she say?

"I know the trouble you're having," Mrs. Stone said gently. "I lost a child myself. As a woman, a mother, I understand, but . . ." She paused. "This isn't your first incident in the OR, Frankie. Last month—"

"I know."

"Perhaps you came back to work too quickly."

"I need to work," she said quietly.

Mrs. Stone nodded. "And I need to be able to count on my nurses."

Frankie drew in a shaky breath. Her life was falling apart. No, it was exploding. Without nursing, what would she have to hang on to? "I can't lose this."

"It's not lost, Frankie. You just need to take a break."

"I'll be more careful. I'll be better."

"It's not a conversation we're having," Mrs. Stone said. "You are on leave, Frankie. Starting now."

Frankie got to her feet, feeling shaky. "I'm sorry to have disappointed you."

"Oh, honey, I'm not disappointed. I'm worried about you."

"Yeah." Frankie was tired of hearing that. She meant to say more, maybe apologize again, but the sad and sorry truth was that she *should* be sidelined. She was unreliable.

How was she supposed to put the pieces of her life back together when she kept breaking apart?

⁓

Frankie slept fitfully, unable to get Rye off her mind. A terrible, dangerous obsession had taken hold of her. Every time she closed her eyes, she thought of him, remembered him, loved him. Over and over again, she saw him standing on his porch, staring at her. The more she imagined that moment, the more she thought he'd looked sad at her driving away. Or was she lying to herself? Manufacturing a dream from the shards of a nightmare?

At just after six P.M., the phone rang and she went down to the kitchen to answer it. "Hello," she said, picking the Princess phone off the counter, dragging the long cord over the counter so she could open the fridge.

"Hey, Frankie," Barb said. "You said you'd call on my birthday."

Shit. "Happy birthday, Barb. I'm sorry. Busy shift last night." She thought about pouring herself a glass of wine, and then closed the fridge instead.

Today, she vowed. Today she would do better. "Did you have a good one?"

"I did. Met a guy."

"A guy?" Frankie pulled the cord back over the counter. She turned on the stereo—Roberta Flack—and settled on the sofa, with the light blue phone beside her. "More, please. Salient facts."

"Thirty-four. ACLU lawyer. Divorced. He has two kids—twin boys. Five-year-olds."

"And?"

"We met standing in line for *Shaft in Africa,* if you can believe it. We sat together and then went out for drinks afterward, and, well, we haven't stopped talking since."

"Wow. That's a record for you, Babs. He must be—"

"Special," Barb said. "He is, Frankie. I was starting to think it wouldn't happen for me, you know? That I was too . . . militant, too angry, too everything. But this guy—his name is Jere, by the way—he likes all of that about me. He says lots of women have soft curves. He likes my sharp edges."

"Wow," Frankie said again. She was about to say more, ask a question about sex, actually, when the doorbell rang. "Just a sec, Barb. Someone's here." She kept the phone to her ear, carried the handset with her, and went to the door, opening it.

Rye stood there, wearing his aviator sunglasses and a Seawolves' cap pulled low over his eyes.

She started to shut the door.

He put a foot out to stop her. "Please," he said.

She couldn't look away. "I gotta go, Barb."

"Is everything okay?"

"Sure," she said evenly, surprised at how calm she sounded. "Happy birthday again. We'll talk soon." Frankie hung up, held the phone balanced in one hand. "You shouldn't be here."

"You shouldn't have followed me home yesterday."

"I know."

"I saw you on the beach," he said. "I was hoping to. It's why I picked Coronado. By the Del. You always talked about it."

"Did I?"

"Isn't that where you surfed with Fin?"

She swallowed the lump in her throat. "Why are you here?"

"I know why you followed me. It means you still—"

"Don't."

He pushed his way into her house, took the phone from her hand, set it on the counter. She felt robotic, confused. She couldn't let him stay but she couldn't seem to form the words to make him go.

He closed the door behind him and suddenly he was close, touching distance away, taking up too much space in her living room, just as he did in her heart. "You lied to me," she said, but the words didn't have the edge she intended. They sounded sad instead of angry.

"Frankie."

The way he said her name brought back so many memories, moments, promises. She shook her head. "Leave. *Please.*"

"You don't want me to go."

"I don't want you to stay."

"That's not the same thing. Come on, Frankie. I know you know it was real between us."

"Real and honest aren't the same thing, either. Are they?"

He reached for her. She wrenched out of his grasp, stepped back, putting distance between them. She needed a drink. "You want a drink? Just one. Then you'll go."

He nodded.

She went to the cabinet where she kept the liquor, realized she'd bought scotch for him at some point along the way. She poured two drinks, handed him one. "Outside," she said, afraid that in here, so close, he'd try to kiss her and she'd let him. She went to the patio door and stepped out into the backyard, noticing the changes Henry had made: a tire swing hanging from the tree, a firepit around which were four Adirondack chairs. An explosion of color along the fence: roses, bougainvillea, jasmine, gardenia. When had she let the grass die?

Rye limped over to the firepit area and sat in one of the chairs. Frankie sat across from him.

"Tell me the truth," she said.

He didn't pretend to misunderstand. She was grateful for that, at least. "I married Missy two months before I shipped out on my first tour. She—"

"Wait. Missy?"

"Melissa. I call her Missy."

I know who you are, missy, Rye's father had said to her, all those years ago. He'd thought she was his son's wife. "Go on."

"I was young, stupid. I wanted someone back home, waiting for me. And she was pregnant."

"So it was all an elaborate ruse, the engagement you supposedly broke off. You swore you weren't engaged. Swore it."

"And I wasn't."

"Did Coyote know the truth? Did all of your men? Were they laughing at me?"

"No. I never wore a wedding ring, never talked about a wife. I wasn't long in-country before I realized that I'd made a mistake getting married. I figured we'd get divorced when I got home. I never felt married . . . and then I saw you at the O Club, remember?"

"I remember."

"It hit me like a ton of bricks, the way I fell for you. It wasn't like anything I'd felt before. Maybe you can't understand how a baby can turn your head, make you do the wrong thing for the right reason. I told myself I'd learn to love Missy, and then I met you."

Frankie knew what he meant. She'd said the same thing about Henry, but it hadn't happened, had it? Intention couldn't force the heart.

"I knew it was wrong, but I couldn't tell you the truth and I couldn't let you go. I thought . . . after I got home, we'd work it all out and I'd find a way to leave Missy and be with you. Then I got shot down. For years, everyone thought I was dead. They held a funeral and buried an empty casket next to my mom. And then finally, Commander Stockdale got word out. After that, Missy was my lifeline. She wrote me religiously."

She believed him. Was it because she wanted to or because she was lonely or because she *felt* the truth in him? She didn't know, but it was dangerous, this loosening of anger. Without it, all she had was love.

"I can see that you suffered," she said quietly. "Your leg."

"Broke it jumping out of the Huey."

"What happened?"

"I hardly remember it, really." He didn't look at her. His voice went dead, became rote. She imagined she was being told the story he'd recited a dozen times in debrief.

"I came to when I hit the ground. I saw the Huey above me burst into flames and go down."

He drew in a ragged breath. "I landed hard ... saw the bone sticking out of my pants leg. Next thing I knew, I was being hauled to my feet. Charlie cut my clothes off me, dragged me, naked ... left me in the middle of some muddy road. I could hear them yelling at each other in their language. They kicked me, rolled me over, kicked me some more.

"I tried to crawl away, but my leg hurt like hell by then. And I kept bleeding from the bullet in my shoulder. They tell me it shattered the joint."

Frankie imagined him lying in mud, naked, his body broken and bruised.

Rye was quiet for a moment. "And then. The Hanoi Hilton," he finally said. "Four years and three months in a cell. Leg irons." Another deep breath, released slowly. "They had this ... rope they used to force my body to bend over. Kept me that way for hours of interrogation. Weeks of it. And then ... one day, when they were dragging me back to my cell, I heard other prisoners. American voices. That was my first moment of hope, you know?

"They finally moved me to another cell, one close to Commander Stockdale's. The other POWs had figured out a way to communicate." His voice broke. "I wasn't alone." He paused, collected himself. "We talked, sent messages. I learned about McCain and the others. I got my first letter from Missy, telling me she'd never given up on me, and I . . . needed her. Needed that. So, I tried to forget you, told myself it was for the best, thought you'd be married by the time I got home."

"If I'd known, I would have written. Your dad told me you'd been killed in action."

"You went to see the old man? What a treat." He looked at her. "I tried to let you go, Frankie. Told myself I'd been a cad and done you wrong and you deserved better. Told myself I could learn to love Missy. Again. Or maybe for the first time. But I saw you in San Diego, on the tarmac. One look at you, and it all came crashing down. I want *you*, Frankie. You."

He moved painfully to a standing position.

She rose at the same time, as if she were a planet in the orbit of his sun, drawn by an elemental force to follow him.

"Do you want me, Frankie?" The sadness in his voice ruined her resolve. She took his hand, felt the familiarity of his grasp.

"What you're asking . . . what you want," she said, wanting it, too. "It would destroy me. Us. Your family."

"I'll leave Missy. I can't even touch her without thinking of you. She knows something's wrong. I can't bear to kiss her."

"Don't ask this of me, Rye. I can't . . ."

"They grounded me, Frankie. I can't fly anymore."

She heard the loss in his voice, knew what flying meant to him. "Oh, Rye . . ."

"One kiss," he said. "A goodbye, then."

She would never forget this moment, the way he looked at her, the love that came roaring back into her soul, suffusing her with all the bright emotions she'd lost in his absence: hope, love, passion, need.

She whispered his name as he pulled her into his arms. At first, all she noticed were changes—he was so thin, it felt as if she could break his bones with her passion—and beneath the scent of his cologne, she smelled something almost like bleach. Even the way he hugged her was different, kind of one-sided, as if his left arm didn't quite heel to his command.

In his eyes, she saw the same awakening in him, a reanimation of life. She saw, too, all that he'd been through in captivity, a red scar that cut across his temple in a jagged line, the bags beneath his eyes. The gray in his blond hair that underscored their lost years.

At the first touch of his lips to hers, she knew she was doomed, damned. Whatever it was called, she knew it and didn't care, couldn't make herself care.

She had already given up everything for this man, this feeling, and she knew she'd do it again, whatever the cost.

She loved him.

It was that simple, that terrifying.

When he whispered, "Where's the bedroom?," she knew she should say, *Stop,* tell him to come back when he was divorced, but she couldn't.

He'd brought her back to life.

God help her.

Thirty-One

In love, Frankie learned to lie. It was one of two new constants in her life: lying and loving Rye throughout that long, lazy summer.

She didn't tell anyone she'd been suspended from nursing, and so she had hours when no one expected to hear from her. She lived frugally, on her savings.

Her life alternated between two worlds—one of passion and the other of guilt. Day after day, she promised herself, *No more.* No more pills, no more Rye. He was as much a drug as the others.

She swore each day she'd tell him to go away and not come back until he was divorced, but when he showed up at her door, wearing a smile just for her, she was lost, and as good as it felt to lose herself in his arms, the pleasure turned cold when he left her bed. Each day she was reminded of her weakness, her dishonesty, her immorality, her obsession. Over and over and over. At night, when she was alone, she agonized that he was in bed with his wife and she imagined the pain this affair would cause the innocent Joey. But as much as she despised herself, she couldn't deny him. She was like a starving person who was given two hours a day in a bakery, and in those hours, she came fully, gloriously alive, reveled in her appetite.

"Stay the night this time," she pleaded at last, hating the plaintive edge to her voice. She meant, *Choose me,* but she knew he couldn't do it. He and Melissa were talking to a lawyer; he was looking for his own place, but he couldn't do anything to upset his custody of Joey. He loved his daughter with abandon.

"You know I can't," he said, stroking her bare arm as they lay together in bed.

She couldn't help looking at the clock. Three P.M. She felt the incipient spark of panic, the sharp sting of regret. Regret that he was leaving, or that she'd let him stay?

"I can't wait for you to meet Joey. She'll love you," he said.

Frankie let herself be soothed by that. "I hope so. And we'll have children, too, right?"

"Of course. I want a daughter who looks just like you." He smiled. "Joey wants a brother or sister. She says it constantly."

"I love you," she said, rolling toward him. She traced the scars on his shoulder with her lips. Puckered burns covered his chest, created white patches of skin amid the graying blond hair.

She stretched out against his thin body, pressing into him. "I wish I'd been the one writing you letters."

"Me, too, babe. I care for Missy, but this . . . you . . . soon we can stop hiding."

His hand moved down her bare skin. Need pulled at her, made her move against him, made her breathing speed up.

She rolled onto her back, gave him full access to her body. His kisses awakened the part of her that belonged only to him.

By summer's end, Frankie was a knot of nerves; all of the waiting, the hoping, the hiding was tearing her to pieces. She was lying to everyone she knew and she hated it. She'd taken off her Saint Christopher medal and hidden it away, afraid it would burn her skin while she slept.

She needed more pills to sleep and more pills to stay awake. Still, she went on with the affair, waiting every day for the moment she could announce the truth to her friends and family and unpack this terrible, oppressive guilt.

She avoided answering the phone; lying to Barb or Ethel was impossible, but neither could she tell them the truth. She returned calls when she knew they'd be gone or hung up when one of them answered.

Never had she imagined herself to be the woman that she'd become; loving Rye had transformed her into a liar.

Every night, alone in her bed, she prayed that *tomorrow* he would say it was done, they could be together, walk hand in hand in the sunlight, spend the night together.

Each morning, she felt another piece of her soul fall away.

In August, when she got Barb's excited phone call that she was getting married, Frankie's first reaction was a searing, toxic jealousy that took all her will to suppress.

Now she was in a Chicago park, on a sweltering hot late summer day, standing in front of a few guests who sat in folding chairs, already drinking champagne. The aisle had been strewn with red rose petals.

Ethel and Frankie, both dressed in brightly colored, geometric print palazzo jumpsuits and white sandals, stood by a wooden arch that had been decorated with flowers and greenery.

Next to them, under the arch, was the groom, in a brown polyester sport coat with matching slacks. His twin boys were his groomsmen. A Baptist minister held on to a Bible.

A portable cassette player with not-great speakers played Jim Croce's "Time in a Bottle" as guests took their seats. Ethel swayed to the music, quietly singing along.

At the end of the aisle, Barb waited impatiently; she was dressed in a flowy white jersey halter dress, her hair decorated with flowers. She held on to her mother's arm.

When the last guest was seated, Barb gave the thumbs-up.

Ethel went to the portable tape deck, changed the music, and turned it up on "Here Comes the Bride."

Barb and her mother walked slowly down the aisle, past the smiling collection of friends and family who were here: a few of Barb's relatives from Georgia, some of her coworkers at Operation PUSH, Jere's ACLU colleagues, and Ethel's husband, Noah, and their daughter, Cecily. Barb was smiling so brightly it made Frankie's whole life look tawdry, sinful.

There, she thought, *that's love.* The way Barb kissed her mom and helped her into her chair in the front row; the way Jere looked at his bride.

Love. A thing to be shouted from the rooftops, celebrated, not cultivated in secret and clipped into shape in the dark.

"Dearly beloved," the minister said. The music snapped off.

Barb and Jere held hands, stared at each other. The minister's voice went on, saying the words she'd heard at other weddings and on television and in movies.

Old words. *Love. Honor. Commitment.*

And as much as Frankie wanted to celebrate with her friend, as much as she rejoiced in Barb's new love and new life, she felt that toxic shame growing in her, pushing kinder emotions aside.

She closed her eyes and imagined herself beneath the arch, with Rye at her side and Joey strewing flowers . . .

She heard Jere say, "From now on, Barbara Sue, I am here for you, standing beside you. To paraphrase Yeats, I love the pilgrim soul in you and love the sorrows of your changing face. Always and forever." He placed a ring on her finger.

"Barbara Sue Johnson," the minister said, "do you promise to love, honor, and obey Jeremiah Maine, as long as you both shall live?"

"I do," Barb said, beaming at him as she fit a plain gold band on his finger.

"You may kiss the bride," the minister said.

Jere pulled Barb into his arms. She clung to him, kissed him. When they drew apart, they were both laughing.

The music changed, turned up loudly: "Let's Get It On."

Ethel whooped and hollered. Frankie realized a moment too late that she was crying.

Ethel put an arm around her. "It'll happen for you, too," she said.

Frankie wiped the tears from her eyes. "I still think about . . ." It took pure strength to finish. "Rye." She looked up at Ethel, thought, *Tell me it's okay to love him. Release the shame.*

"Forget him, Frank. He's a liar. You're too good for him."

"But. I love him. I mean . . . he is my one."

Ethel gave her a look so hard and sad Frankie felt its impact in her bones. "No. He's *married*, Frank. He is a father. I know you. I know how much you cared for Jamie, but you wouldn't even *consider* dating a married man. You're a good woman. Honest. Moral to the point of ridiculousness. You couldn't survive an affair."

Each word felt like a nail, driving into her, breaking bones. *Honest. Moral. Good.*

No, she wanted to say. *That isn't me anymore.*

Frankie made her decision at the reception, while she danced to music she didn't recognize, holding Ethel's beautiful daughter in her arms.

No more.

Enough.

She wanted *this*. A wedding, a family, a baby.

How could she possibly be granted such grace after an affair? God and goodness and grace demanded change for redemption.

Every moment she spent at the reception, Frankie felt like a liar, a cheat. She drank too much and was unsteady on her feet when Barb and Jere drove off for their honeymoon.

"Are you okay?" Ethel asked, standing beside her, holding her hand, looking at her with love and worry in her eyes.

Frankie couldn't stand it. Suddenly she didn't want Ethel to love her, to care about her, to hold her hand. How could Frankie deserve such friendship? She mumbled an excuse, said she was tired, or too drunk, or just plain sad; she couldn't really remember her words. All she knew was that she needed to leave. Now, before she broke down in front of her friend.

She took a taxi back to the hotel, gathered up her things, and went to the airport, waiting hours for her flight, long enough to sober up, which only made her feel worse.

At home, she sat in her living room, chain-smoking, drinking gin, tapping her foot nervously, waiting for Rye, determined to tell him she'd had enough. She couldn't live like this anymore.

When he finally showed up, flowers in hand, she made him stay outside.

"I can't do it anymore," she said. "It's breaking me apart, Rye. I'm sorry. I can't be the other woman anymore. It's wrong."

She waited for him to answer; when he didn't, she took a step back, started to close the door.

Slowly, in the new and broken way he moved, he lowered himself to one knee. She could see how much it hurt him to do. "Will you marry me, Frankie?"

Frankie burst into tears, realizing just then how long she'd been waiting for this, how intensely she needed it. *This* would right them both, make everything okay, wash her of this sin. "Yes," she whispered. "Yes."

He climbed painfully back to his feet; she helped him. "I want us," he said in a gruff voice. "You. Me. A baby . . ."

"Thank God," Frankie said, pulling him into the house and back to her bedroom. Her whole body was shaking.

It would be okay. Finally.

He leaned toward her for a kiss. She met him more than halfway.

———

Autumn on Coronado Island came late this year, and gradually, a turning of the leaves, a need for sweaters at night, an emptying of the beaches. Once again, the restaurants on Orange Avenue were filled with locals instead of tourists. School buses had returned to their routes in the first week of September; to Frankie these were the things that would always mean fall.

On this cool late November day, almost ten months after Rye's return from Vietnam, Frankie put on a jacquard-patterned knit dress, parted her long, straight hair down the middle, pulled it back into a ponytail, and then drove to the hospital.

At the director of nursing's office, she was instructed to wait.

Frankie was ready for this meeting, more than ready. In the two months since Rye's proposal, she had started to become herself again. They had talked about wedding rings, and honeymoon plans, and a ceremony on the beach. Kauai for their honeymoon, for another week at the Coco Palms. He was ready to merge into her world, talk to her parents. She couldn't wait to tell her friends and family. Barb and Ethel. Oh, they would look askance at first, maybe wonder at her morality, but she would never tell them that she and Rye had slept together before his divorce. That shame she'd bear alone.

"Frankie? She'll see you now."

Frankie stood up. Holding her purse close, she walked into the office and took a seat when directed.

"Hello, Mrs. Stone," she said, sitting in the ladylike way she'd been taught a lifetime ago when the world had been softer, different. Back straight, chin up, legs crossed at the ankles. She knew she looked better than she had the last time she'd been here. This morning it had taken only one pill to rouse her spirits. In the past month she'd cut back. "I wanted to thank you for suspending me," she said. "I know that sounds odd, but you were right. I was underwater. I might have made a mistake in the OR, and I couldn't have lived with that."

"You're one of the best nurses I've ever worked with," Mrs. Stone said. "But the last time I called you for work, you sounded impaired."

Frankie hoped she didn't flinch. "Just before my first coffee. Moving a little slow. That's all."

"That's all?"

"That's all," she lied.

"I know about the pain of a miscarriage. And my husband served in Korea. He's told me that some . . . experiences settle in our bodies as well as our minds. Perhaps you need help dealing with some things?"

"I'm fine. Truly."

"Even if one's experience isn't as traumatic as combat, I'm told wartime can rather upend a man for a time."

A man.

"I'm ready to go back to work, ma'am," Frankie said. "I may soon even have some good news to share that will put your mind at ease."

Mrs. Stone studied her for a long moment. "All right, Frankie. In fact, Karen Ellis called in sick today. Can you finish out her shift?"

"Of course. I still have scrubs in my locker." Frankie stood up. "You won't regret it, ma'am."

"See that I don't."

Frankie left the office filled with hope.

This was the first step to recovery. She would be herself again in no time. Marry Rye and wear white. Not some off-the-rack prom dress this time. With Rye, she wanted it all: the gown, the veil, the church, the cake.

~

A week later, Frankie stared down at a display of wedding rings in the jeweler's case.

"May I help you, miss?" the clerk asked her.

Frankie glanced at her watch. Her shift at the hospital started soon. "No, thank you. I guess my fiancé has been detained," she lied. Next time she came to this store, she would bring Rye with her, see what kind of ring he wanted and show him her favorites. There was nothing wrong or weird with her looking by herself, was there?

Leaving the store, she drove across town to the medical center, which rose tall and white against the morning's cloudless cerulean sky. Inside, she changed into her teal-blue scrubs, covered her long hair with a cap, and headed to the surgical floor.

She assisted on one surgery after another for hours. At the end of her shift, she checked on her patients, and then headed down to the first floor.

In the lobby, she saw a crowd of men in suits gathered around the desk. Most were scribbling in open notepads.

Reporters.

Probably some famous local resident had given birth; like Raquel Welch, who had been Raquel Tejada back when she'd been crowned the Fairest of the Fair at the San Diego County Fair. Or maybe an actor had died.

Frankie headed for the door. As she passed the clot of reporters, she heard someone say, "Lieutenant Commander Walsh."

Frankie stopped, turned back. Pushing through the reporters, she got to the front of them just as the woman at the desk was saying, "We respect our patients' privacy. You know that. You may not speak to them yet. I've called security."

"But it isn't every day a former prisoner of war—"

Frankie edged around the reporters, ducked behind the front desk, and sidled up to one of the women seated there. "The reporters. They want to see—"

"Some famous guy's wife. A prisoner of war. Walsh."

His wife. "Is she okay?"

The woman shrugged.

"Where is she?"

"Four-ten B."

Frankie went to the elevator and pushed the button impatiently. It wasn't until she stepped inside that she realized where she was going.

The fourth floor.

Ping! The doors opened.

She walked slowly down the hallway, feeling suddenly sick; at the last door, she saw the patient's name and stopped: WALSH, MELISSA.

Frankie pushed the door open just enough to see Melissa Walsh, sitting up in bed, surrounded by balloons and flowers and baskets of candy. A soccer ball balloon said IT'S A BOY!

A bassinet was at her bedside; through the clear sides, Frankie could see a baby swaddled in blue.

Frankie backed away quickly, hit something, and turned around.

Rye stood there. "Frankie," he said, too softly for his wife to hear. "I meant to . . . it doesn't mean—"

She shoved him out of her way, ran out of the hospital, and got into her car, slammed the door shut. Her hands were shaking so hard she dropped the keys. She opened her purse, took out two Valium, and swallowed them dry, then bent down, tried to find her keys on the floor mat.

Someone banged on her window.

She couldn't look . . . had to look.

Rye stood there, looking as destroyed as she felt. "I'm sorry," he yelled.

She started the car, stomped on the gas.

She had no idea what to do, where to go. She'd fallen for his lies again. *Again.* Melissa must have gotten pregnant soon after Rye's return. With Frankie, he'd used condoms. Always. Never a mistake.

All these months, while he'd been sleeping with Frankie, his wife had been pregnant. When he'd proposed, Melissa had been nearing term. He'd dropped to a knee, said, "Marry me," and Frankie had believed him. She'd believed every smile, every touch, every promise. Believed blindly, believed when he said, *Soon, baby. Soon we will tell everyone we're together.*

Oh my God.

The only person she hated more than Rye was herself.

⁓

She needed a drink.

It was all she could think of. She couldn't go home, to the bungalow where he had clothes in the closet, where he'd dropped to one knee and proposed marriage.

She drove past the bar frequented by the hospital staff and drove to San Diego's Gaslamp Quarter and found a parking spot on the street in front of a tavern where she would be anonymous. She went inside, found it already half-full of patrons who looked like regulars.

She slipped up onto a barstool. "Gin on the rocks," she said. "And a pack of Virginia Slims."

When the bartender returned with her drink, she barely looked at him. Her hand was trembling as she reached for the glass.

It's a boy! crashed through her like a wrecking ball, destroying every fragile block of herself she'd tried to rebuild.

"I deserve this," she said.

"Huh?" the bartender said.

"Nothing. Another drink, please."

She took the second drink and downed it, then ordered a third. When a good-looking man sat beside her, said, "Hey, foxy lady," she snagged her purse and headed out again. In the car, she cranked up the music on "I Am Woman."

She drove out of the crowded quarter.

She should slow down; she was going too fast.

She sang along with the song, realized she was crying. Ahead was the bridge. She hit the gas, rocketed forward; a stanchion of concrete in front of her, a wall of gray to her right, and then nothing but water. She turned the wheel, just a fraction of an inch.

A man on a bicycle came out of nowhere. She slammed on the brakes, felt the car spiral out of control on the road, saw handlebars in her headlights. She yanked on the wheel, tried to turn the other way.

Too late.

Thirty-Two

Frankie woke in a hospital bed. Her entire body hurt, especially her left arm, and a headache pounded behind her eyes. For a split second she couldn't remember why she was here, and then . . .

The man on the bicycle. The bridge.

"Oh God."

She heard voices and footsteps coming down the hallway.

Her father walked into the room, looking grim and ashamed. Angry. Next to him was a policeman with short gray hair; the brass buttons on his khaki uniform strained over a big gut and a thin dark tie tried to hide the gaps that showed his undershirt.

"Did I kill him?" Frankie asked, unable to raise her voice above a whisper.

"No," the officer said. "But you came close. Kicked the shit out of his bicycle. Came close to killing yourself, too."

"You were drunk, Frankie," her father said. "You could have died." His voice breaking, he added, "Can you imagine me having to tell your mother that? Another lost child?"

Frankie's throat felt so tight she could barely swallow. She wished she *had* died. And then a terrible, terrible thought: Had she wanted to? Had she turned *into* the bridge wall, instead of away?

Dad looked at the policeman. "Can I take her home, Phil?"

The policeman nodded. "Yes. She's being charged with DUI. You'll be notified about her arraignment."

Frankie swung her feet to the side of the bed, slowly stood; she felt dizzy. Dad moved in close, steadied her as she limped out of the hospital, past her fellow nurses, who stared at her as she passed. They must have known what she'd done, that she'd almost killed a man. "The man I almost hit . . . you sure he's okay? You're not lying to me?"

"He's fine, Frankie. Bill Brightman. Coronado High principal."

Outside, the silver Mercedes gull-wing waited. Frankie refused her father's help and made her own way into the passenger seat.

Dad put the key in the ignition and started the car. It roared to life but didn't move.

After a long silence, he turned to her. "Do you want to die, Frankie? Your mother asked me that."

"I shouldn't have had that third drink," she said. "I'll do better. I promise."

"Enough," her father said sharply, and she saw it all on his face: the fear that he would lose her, the grief at their mutual loss, the anger that she couldn't seem to be the daughter he wanted.

She stared at him, knowing he was right. She could have killed a man tonight. She could have killed herself. Maybe she'd meant to.

"I love you, Frankie," he said in a sad voice. "I know we've had issues, but—"

"Dad—"

"You seem . . . broken."

Frankie couldn't meet his worried gaze. "I've been living this way for years," she said. "Ever since my time in Florence."

———

Enough.

Alone in her childhood bed, she lay awake, battling her need (addiction—had she ever thought of it in those terms before?) for a sleeping pill, and her overwhelming guilt, as well as this new and eviscerating fear that she had wanted to end her own life.

Who had she become?

A nothing woman, a ghost. No love, no child.

How could she survive? Each of the losses had derailed her, but this, now, the guilt and shame of last night, destroyed her.

She couldn't live like this.

She needed help.

Who?

How?

You should talk to someone, get help, Henry had said to her; it felt like a lifetime ago, when she'd thought she'd hit rock bottom but hadn't. *I treat a few vets in my practice . . . Do you have nightmares, Frankie? Trouble sleeping?*

Who else would understand the slow unraveling of her psyche since Vietnam, except her fellow veterans? She'd tried to get help before, once, long ago, and it hadn't worked. That didn't mean she should stop trying. The opposite was true, in fact.

She pushed the covers back and got out of bed. Weak on her feet, she went into her bathroom and took a hot shower and dried her hair, then dressed in jeans and a turtleneck.

She found her mother in the kitchen, looking tired. "Frances," she said softly.

"Can I take your car?" Frankie asked.

Mom stared at her so intently Frankie felt uncomfortable, but whatever words her mom needed to hear, Frankie couldn't say. No more promises. They both knew she shouldn't be driving.

"The keys are in my bag. When will you be home?"

"I don't know."

"Will you be home?"

"I will." She moved forward and touched her mother's thin shoulder, let her hand linger there. A stronger woman would have offered words to accompany the touch, maybe an apology or a promise; she said nothing and went to the garage, climbed into the Cadillac. She took the Coronado Bridge at a cautious speed and pulled up in front of the new VA medical center.

Frankie parked in the lot and sat there, afraid to move. Finally, she glanced at her black eyes in the rearview mirror. Digging a pair of big sunglasses out of her purse, she left the car and walked up into the building.

Inside, she went to the front desk, where a large woman in a floral-patterned polyester dress sat in front of an IBM Selectric, her scarlet nails clacking on the keys.

"Ma'am?" Frankie said.

The receptionist paused in her typing, but didn't move her hands away from the keyboard, then looked up. "You in trouble, darlin'? Is your husband . . . angry?"

Apparently the sunglasses weren't much of a camouflage.

"I've heard that you offer therapy for Vietnam vets."

"There's a rap session at ten. Why?"

"Where is it?"

The woman frowned, pulled a pencil out of her big hair, tapped it on the desk. "Down that hall. Second door to the left. But it's only for Vietnam vets."

"Thanks." Frankie walked down the hall, past several men sitting on molded plastic chairs. At Room 107, she saw a flyer taped to the textured, frosted glass panel in the top half of the door: VIETNAM VETERANS, SHARE YOUR STORIES WITH EACH OTHER. RAPPING HELPS! She took a seat, waiting, staring at the clock. Her whole body ached and her head hurt and she felt sick to her stomach, but she didn't move. Her left wrist throbbed. She looked down, saw a bruise blooming on her pale skin.

The door in front of her opened at 9:55. A few men walked into the room.

She paused, tried to calm herself, and then she got up, opened the door onto a small, windowless room, in which folding chairs had been set up in a circle. Several of the chairs were occupied by men, most of them Frankie's age or younger, with long, untended hair, big sideburns, and mustaches. A few older, grizzled-looking guys sat with crossed arms.

More men stood over by a table, eating donuts and pouring coffee from a tall silver urn.

Frankie had expected to be the only woman, but she still felt uncomfortable as, one by one, the men turned to look at her.

A man approached her. He wore a checkered shirt and cowboy jeans held up by a huge-buckled belt. His long, layered hair flipped back from a center part. A huge mustache covered most of his upper lip.

"Can I help you, foxy lady?" he said, smiling.

"I'm here for the Vietnam veterans rap therapy group."

"It's groovy that you want to understand your man, but this is for veterans only."

"I am a vet."

"Of Vietnam."

"I am a Vietnam vet."

"Oh. I ... uh ... there were no women in 'Nam."

"Wrong. ANC nurse. Two tours. The Thirty-Sixth and Seventy-First Evac Hospitals. If you never saw a woman, you were lucky. It meant you didn't end up in a hospital."

He frowned. "Oh. Well. You should talk to other chicks about ... whatever. I mean, you didn't see combat. The men would clam up with a woman in the room."

"Are you telling me I can't stay? I have nightmares. And I'm . . . scared. You won't help me?"

"You don't belong here, ma'am. This is for vets who saw action in 'Nam."

Frankie walked out of the room, slamming the door shut behind her. She strode down the hallway, saw a GET HELP HERE poster, and ripped it off the wall and stomped on it. *M*A*S*H* was a hit TV show this year; how could people still think there had been no women in Vietnam? Especially veterans, for God's sake?

Outside, she let out a howl of rage that she couldn't have held back if she'd wanted to—and she didn't want to. It felt good to finally scream.

Frankie had nowhere to go. No one to talk to. She knew something was deeply, terribly wrong with her, but not how to fix it.

She could call Barb and Ethel, but it was pathetic how often she'd called on them already. And when they heard about the affair with Rye and driving drunk into the Coronado Bridge, they would judge her as harshly as she judged herself.

Still, she had to do something.

She could go to the man she'd almost killed and beg for forgiveness.

She found a pay phone and asked the operator for the address for Mr. Bill Brightman.

He lived on Coronado, in a small house in the middle of the island. The perfectly tended yard was outlined by bright-red flowers and a white picket fence. A house someone loved.

She parked by his mailbox, sat outside for a long time, unable to get out of the car, unable to drive away. When she closed her eyes, she saw the accident again and again, in slow motion, saw his pale, terrified face in her headlights.

The door opened. A middle-aged man with sunken cheeks and

black hair stepped out of the house, wearing a brown suit. He was holding a folded-up newspaper in one hand and a battered leather briefcase in the other.

Frankie opened her car door, stepped out.

He looked at her, frowned slightly.

She opened the white picket gate, dared to step onto his property, slowly took off her sunglasses to reveal her black eyes. "I'm Frances McGrath," she said quietly. "The driver who almost hit you." She felt tears burn her eyes and wiped them away impatiently. This wasn't about her pain or guilt or shame. It was about his. "I am so sorry."

"Bring me my mail," he said, lighting up a cigarette.

Frankie nodded sharply, went to his mailbox, pulled out a stack of letters and magazines, and carried them up to the man. On the porch, she handed him his mail. "I'll replace your bike."

"My bike? Lady, you almost ended me," he said.

Frankie couldn't find her voice. She nodded.

"I have a daughter. A wife. A mother. A father. Do you know anything about losing people?"

"I do," she said.

"Remember that. Next time you get behind the wheel drunk."

"I'm sorry," she said again, knowing it wasn't enough, but what else was there?

He looked at her a long moment, saying nothing, then turned and took his mail back into the house, closing the door behind him.

She drove back to her parents' house and parked the car in the garage. Inside the house, she found her mother at the kitchen table. Frankie threw the keys on the table between them. "I'm back," she said dully.

"You're scaring me, Frances," Mom said.

"Yeah. Sorry."

"Go to your room. Rest. Things always look better in the morning."

Frankie turned slowly. "Do they?"

That night in her childhood bedroom, Frankie came awake reluctantly, fighting consciousness every step of the way. She didn't want to open her eyes and be in a world where she was this version of herself. Broken. A fallen woman. A liar. It was all so bad, an avalanche of bad.

She reached over to the nightstand, feeling blindly for her pills. She took two more. When had she taken them last? She couldn't remember, didn't care. She closed her eyes, drifted.

You almost ended me.

Do you want to die, Frankie?

It's a boy!

Frankie heard a creaking sound and tried to sit up. It was impossible. She drifted in and out, heard footsteps in the hallway. Or maybe it was her heartbeat slowing down to nothing.

One of her parents, checking up on her, probably. She closed her eyes again and heard someone whisper her name. And then a muffled laugh.

Finley.

She heard his voice out there, beyond the door. In the darkness, she could hear him breathing, could smell the Brylcreem he put in his hair and the spearmint gum he loved.

Come on, Frankie. Be with me.

They were kids again. *Summer.* She heard the ice-cream truck outside, bell jangling, kids laughing. She threw back the covers and stepped down onto the cold wooden floor, wondering what had happened to her rug.

Finley's laughter echoed in front of her. She followed it out of the house. She grabbed her old surfboard from the garage and stumbled into the pitch-black night.

No stars out.

No cars rolling on Ocean Boulevard. No house lights visible.

She crossed the empty street and stepped onto the cold sand. "Finley! Wait up!"

She tried to catch up with him, but her legs wouldn't cooperate. She felt weighed down, exhausted.

The water was so cold it shocked her, made her gasp; still, she splashed toward the incoming surf, jumped on her board, and paddled out.

She paddled weakly over the swells, made it out to the calm water, lay on her board, panting from exertion. She was shivering with cold, and confused. "Fin?"

He didn't answer. There was just the lapping sound of the incoming swell set, the smack of her board when it hit back down.

She wanted to sit up and look for Finley, but she was too weak. How many pills had she taken?

Cold embraced her, numbed her.

Was that why she had come out here?

A chance to feel nothing . . .

She closed her eyes.

She shouldn't be here. She should go back.

But she was tired. Bone-tired. And the cold began to feel good. She could just roll over, sink into the cold sea, and disappear.

———

Red lights, blinking on and off.

Incoming.

A siren, blaring.

Frankie blinked awake. She was in an ambulance, with her father sitting beside her. Water dripped from his hair and clothes.

It came back to her in a sickening rush, what she'd done. Shame compressed her into the smallest version of herself. All she'd wanted was to disappear, not . . . something else.

"I wasn't trying to . . . I didn't mean . . ." She couldn't say the words. "It was a dream. I thought Finley was here. I followed him."

"It's those pills," he said in a voice she barely recognized. "Your mother never should have given them to you. You took too many."

"I'll stop taking them."

"It's too late for that, Frankie. We're afraid . . ."

Of what you'll do.

"You tried to kill yourself."

"No. I just . . ."

What?

Had she tried to kill herself?

"We could have lost you."

She wanted to disagree, to tell him that he would never lose her, that she was *fine,* but for once, she couldn't say the words, couldn't soldier on.

"Why am I in an ambulance? I'm fine now. I'll be good. I promise."

Dad looked uncomfortable, embarrassed. Worse, he looked afraid.

"Dad?"

The ambulance came to a stop. The attendant jumped out, opened the back door. Frankie saw the words PSYCHIATRIC WARD.

She shook her head, tried to sit up, found that she was bound to the bed at her wrists and feet. "No, please . . ."

"Thirty-six hours," Dad said. "A mandatory hold after a suicide attempt. They promised it would help you."

Frankie felt herself and the gurney being lifted. Outside of the ambulance, the wheels snapped into place.

Her father was crying. Seeing that scared her more than anything ever had. "Daddy. No. Please . . ."

The next thing she saw was bright, bright lights and a team of men in white.

"I didn't try to kill myself," she screamed, struggling to be free.

One of the orderlies produced a hypodermic needle.

Screaming was the last thing she remembered.

Thirty-Three

Light. Blinding.

Where am I?

I lift my head to look around; it feels heavy. Someone else's head on my neck. Maybe I'm paralyzed. Someone says a word—detox—in a long, drawn-out kind of way. And then something about meds . . .

I hear noises that make no sense. I can't sort them out, isolate them, recognize them.

Bees buzzing. Boots on the ground. Humping in the boonies?

No.

I am not in 'Nam. Where am I?

Screaming.

Is that my voice?

No.

Yes.

It's too hard to think. My head is pounding. I close my eyes. Whatever's out there, I don't want to see.

Darkness.

Quiet.

—

"Frankie. Frankie McGrath, can you hear me?"

Frankie heard her name and tried to answer, but her mouth seemed to be stuffed with cotton and she still had a blinding headache.

"Frankie."

It took forever to open her eyes. Lifting her head was next: All she could see were her own hands. Red marks circled her wrists.

He came into focus slowly. Standing sideways, defying gravity.

Maybe her head was tilted to one side. She was blind in one eye. No. Her hair fell across her face, obscuring her vision. She raised her hand slowly, felt the tremor in it, pushed the hair back from her face.

He stood in front of her.

Henry.

She felt a rush of shame, and then a burst of relief.

"I'm going to get you out of here as soon as I can, okay?"

Frankie couldn't make her voice rise above a whisper. *Thank you* was too much. She got out, "Thaaaa."

He laid his hand on hers.

She looked down, wished she could feel his touch.

—

Frankie was having a heart attack. She became aware of the pain all at once, a blinding bolt of it in her chest.

She sat up, breathing hard.

A headache pounded behind her eyes. Tiny white stars danced across her field of sight.

The chest pain turned into a dull, thudding beat in her chest. She was sweating, trembling.

Where was she?

Dorm room, was her first thought.

Single bed, low to the ground, cheap blanket and sheets. A dresser with three drawers. No mirror. A closet.

She swung her legs around, saw her bare, skinny legs and the borrowed socks on her feet.

Headache.

Had they drugged her? She felt sluggish.

She got up and immediately felt dizzy, nauseated. She counted to ten and it passed.

What was she wearing? Cutoff shorts, socks, and an oversized tie-dyed T-shirt. Whose?

She walked to the door, half expecting it to be locked.

Psych ward.

That was where she was. She remembered now: the ocean, the ambulance ride, her father crying. She opened the door. Beyond it lay a hallway that looked like the elementary school she'd gone to: flyers on the wall, linoleum floor, windows that let in so much sunlight she blinked. Construction-paper turkeys and pilgrims decorated the walls.

Moving cautiously forward, she trailed her fingers along the top of the fake wood wainscoting, just for balance. The headache was bad and getting worse.

She passed what looked like a classroom, in which people sat in a circle, talking. "That was rock-bottom," one of them said.

"Frances McGrath?"

She looked up, saw a young woman coming toward her. A man walked past them, muttering to himself.

"Go back to your room, Cletus," the woman said.

The woman was beautiful, with doe-like eyes and a waterfall of brown hair. She wore a faded prairie-style dress that fell to her ankles, and brown suede Birkenstocks. Six or seven wooden bead bracelets encircled her fine wrist.

"I'm Jill Landis, one of the counselors here. I run group." She took

Frankie by the hand, led her down the hall, past a series of closed doors and a reception area that boasted a banner that read TODAY IS THE DAY!

"The director has been waiting for you. How do you feel?"

"Headache," Frankie said. "Weak."

"Of course." She stopped, got Frankie two aspirin and a glass of water.

Frankie forgot to say thank you, just took the aspirin and swallowed them with water.

Jill stopped at a closed door, squeezed Frankie's hand. "I'll schedule you for group at two. A rap session helps more than you'd think. Especially for vets."

"Group? Rap? I don't want—"

"It's just talking, Frankie. And it's mandatory." She knocked on the door.

"Come in."

Jill opened the door. "See ya, Frankie."

Frankie moved forward, one foot in front of the other. She was in her stockinged feet. Where were her shoes?

The door clicked shut behind her.

"Hey, Frankie."

She looked up just in time to see Henry open his arms for a hug. He wrapped her in an embrace that was as stunning as it was familiar.

She looked up. "You saved me."

He tucked her hair back behind one ear. "Not yet. And it won't be easy." He let her go. "Do you remember what happened?"

"Some of it," she said softly. The terrible images were there, waiting for her: running into the ocean, hoping to disappear, freezing, her teeth chattering . . . her dad pulling her off the surfboard, carrying her . . . an ambulance, her screaming, crying, being restrained . . .

She looked around his office. A window overlooked a park of some kind, a grassy area filled with picnic tables. Beneath the window was a cheap wooden credenza laden with framed pictures and a potted jade plant.

"Where am I?"

"Inpatient therapeutic drug and alcohol treatment facility. At the medical center. It opened about six months ago, remember? I run the place and see patients two days a week. I won't be your primary therapist, for obvious reasons, but I wanted to ease you into therapy."

"What obvious reasons?"

"I loved you."

"Past tense. Yeah." She looked away, unable to meet his gaze, remembered that she'd been in a psych ward for a suicide attempt. *Suicide.* She couldn't process that terrible word. "How did you get me out?"

"Your mom called me. She signed you up here for eight weeks. To start."

"Wow. Mom facing the problem head-on. That's new." Frankie pressed two fingertips to her throbbing temple.

"Your headache, by the way, it's withdrawal. You may experience other symptoms: anxiety, chest pains, sweats, tremors. Also, your cognitive abilities may have been impaired for a while now."

"No shit." Frankie sighed. Withdrawal. "So, in addition to everything else, I'm officially a drug addict and an alcoholic. Yay."

"The yellow pills you've been taking? Diazepam. More commonly called Valium, but I'm sure you know that. The Rolling Stones called them 'Mother's Little Helpers.'" He went to his desk, pulled out a magazine, opened it to an advertisement with the headline NOW SHE CAN COPE, which showed a woman in an apron, smiling broadly as she vacuumed. "Docs have been prescribing them like candy to women for years."

"Did I lose my nursing license?"

"You will. At least for a while, but that's not your biggest concern right now." He took her by the hand, led her to an antique fainting couch. "Sit."

She looked at it, and a bit of her old self rose up, made her laugh. "You're kidding."

"I'm a shrink," he said, smiling back. "It'll make you comfortable talking."

"I don't know if I want to be comfortable talking."

"Haven't you been uncomfortable and not talking for a long time?"

"I have a headache. No fair outthinking me."

She sat down, remained upright. Her hands were shaking. "Do you have a cigarette? I don't think I can stand you exploring the murky depths of my soul without *some* aid."

He found her a cigarette, a lighter, and pulled over a standing ashtray, then positioned his chair next to her.

Frankie stood up. She was afraid, agitated. She walked over to the credenza, studied the photographs displayed. Henry's life in images. It made her realize that she hadn't taken a picture in years. She picked up a framed photograph of him and a woman with long graying brown hair and round rose-colored glasses.

"That's Natalie," he said. "We're engaged. She loves me."

Had he meant to put the slightest emphasis on *she*?

Frankie felt both happiness for him and a sliver of pain for herself. Would she be sitting here, head pounding from withdrawal, if she'd married him?

Henry smiled. "She's an elementary school teacher and poet. But we'll talk about me later. Right now I want you to get better, Frankie. My colleague Dr. Alden specializes in Vietnam veterans. We're seeing too many addicted military personnel, especially after coming home from the war."

She drifted back toward him, sat down on the ridiculous couch. "No one gives a shit about the women." Frankie lit the cigarette, drew smoke into her lungs, and exhaled.

"Why do you say that?"

"I went to the VA for help. Twice. They brushed me off, told me to run along, that I wasn't a real vet, I guess."

"Why did you go to the VA for help?"

Frankie frowned. "I don't know. I just . . ."

"Just what?" Henry asked gently.

She felt his scrutiny. This was no idle question. He was asking a question Frankie had barely asked herself. She had never answered it aloud, not to anyone. She didn't really want to answer it now.

But she was in trouble here, disintegrating, losing pieces of herself. She needed to reach out to someone with her truth. "Well. It's been a rough patch. I almost killed a man because I drove drunk. Then there's the baby, the miscarriage . . . Rye coming back, lying to me. Our affair. And now I'll lose my nursing license. There's nothing of me left."

"That's all the middle, Frankie. You've had trouble sleeping for years, trouble with nightmares. You used to scream in your sleep," he said. "Before the baby, the miscarriage . . . before Rye."

Frankie nodded.

"What about surges of irrational anger? Irritation? Anxiety?"

Frankie couldn't look at him.

"Vietnam," he said. "That's why you went to the VA. You know Vietnam is the beginning of it all. Do you have memories that are more than memories, that feel like you're there again?"

"You mean, like . . ."

"Like a flashback in a film."

Frankie was stunned. She'd assumed it happened only to her, that she was crazy. "How do you know that?"

"The Fourth of July party, remember?"

She couldn't answer.

"It's called post-traumatic stress disorder. It's a bit controversial, they haven't added it to the APA manual yet, but we're seeing similar symptoms in your fellow vets. What you're experiencing is a familiar response to trauma."

"I didn't see combat."

"Frankie, you were a surgical nurse in the Central Highlands."

She nodded.

"And you think you didn't see combat?"

"My . . . Rye . . . was a POW. Tortured. Kept in the dark for years. He's fine."

Henry leaned forward. "War trauma isn't a competitive sport. Nor is it one-size-fits-all. The POWs are a particular group, as well. They came home to a different world than you did. They were treated like the World War II veterans. Like heroes. It's hard to underscore too much the impact of that on one's psyche."

Frankie thought about all the yellow ribbons on the tree branches in 1973. They hadn't been there when she came home. Hell, they'd had parades for the returning POWs. None of them had been spat on or flipped off or called a baby killer or a warmonger.

"And they were pilots, for the most part, so their war experience was different than the soldiers or Marines on the ground. In captivity, they banded together, held rank, communicated in secret, all of which strengthened their commitment to each other. We don't really understand PTSD yet, but we know it's highly personal. What about your friends, fellow nurses?"

"We don't really talk about it."

"The war no one wants to remember."

"Yeah."

"I talked to Barb this week," he said. "She told me about the fighting around Pleiku." He leaned toward her. "Nothing you feel is wrong or abnormal. It doesn't matter what your friends did or didn't experience. You're allowed to be uniquely affected by your wartime experience. Especially you, someone who was idealistic enough to volunteer. You have nothing to be ashamed of, Frankie."

Ashamed.

It hit Frankie hard, that word. She *had* let herself become ashamed;

maybe it had started when she'd been spat on in the airport, or when her mother asked her not to talk about the war, or maybe as news of the atrocities began coming out. Almost every civilian she'd met since coming home, including her own family, had subtly or overtly given her the message that what she'd done in Vietnam was shameful. She'd been a part of something bad. She'd tried not to believe it; but maybe she had. She'd gone to war a patriot and come home a pariah. "How do I get back to who I was?"

"There's no going back, Frankie. You have to find a way to go forward, become the new you. Fighting for who you were at twenty-one is a losing game. If that's what you've been trying for, no wonder you're struggling. The naive, idealistic girl who volunteered for war is gone. In a very real way, she died over there."

Frankie stared down at her hands. *Died over there.* The words resonated keenly. Hurt. She realized just now, sitting here, that she'd known that, felt it. Grieved for the innocence she'd lost in Vietnam.

"Now take my hand," he said, pulling her to her feet. "I'm going to introduce you to Dr. Alden."

Dr. Alden was a quiet, pale man with a thin neck and creased forehead and kind eyes. He gave off a Mr. Magoo vibe that was oddly comforting.

In his office, which featured dozens of inspirational photographs, he'd gotten her settled in a comfortable chair and begun to ask her questions. She'd wanted to talk about Rye, her heartbreak, her shame and anger, but Dr. Alden had a different idea.

"Memories," he'd said. "Vietnam. Let's start there."

At first it had been difficult to tell her story out loud, but once she said, *I remember the first time I saw a traumatic amputation . . .* the floodgates opened and her memories poured out. She realized the power they'd gained by being withheld.

In session after session, day after day, she exposed herself and her past, opening up her deepest wounds. She talked about the baby who'd died in her arms suffering from napalm burns, the expectants who'd died on sawhorses set in bloody mud, about the young men barely out of their teens who'd clung to her hand, about red alerts, and operations on the Quonset floor by flashlight during a mortar attack, about Mai, the little girl she still sometimes dreamed about. She talked about the terrible suffering of the Vietnamese people. The dark memories gradually gave way to others, also repressed until they'd been nearly forgotten. Like the way the soldiers had cared for each other. So many had refused treatment until a brother-in-arms was seen. They tried to hold each other together, literally, when horrific wounds had torn their insides out.

By the end of the first week, which was a rigidly scheduled combination of group and individual therapy, Frankie was emotionally drained. Dr. Alden had given her a journal to write down her feelings, and she'd started, slowly, writing about her shame at being here and how much she hated Rye and herself. By the end of the week, she was filling several pages a day.

On her third Saturday here, visitors' day, she drifted up one hallway and down another, too tense to talk with her fellow patients, too jittery to stop for long, smoking cigarettes one after another, trying to ignore the headache pounding behind her eyes.

Now she was at the vending machine, buying another Coke (her latest addiction), when her name blared through the speakers: "Visitor for Frankie McGrath."

Unsure whether she was ready to see anyone, she headed down to the visitors' area, a room near the entrance. It was painted a pretty, calming shade of blue and had pictures of rainbows and oceans and waterfalls on the walls. A corner table held children's toys and boxes of puzzles. A tea-colored poster of "Desiderata" gave advice for living: GO PLACIDLY AMID THE NOISE AND HASTE AND REMEMBER WHAT PEACE THERE MAY BE IN SILENCE.

She sat down in one of the empty chairs, tapping her foot on the floor. Her headache had dimmed but was still there; her mouth was dry. Sweat dampened her skin.

No doubt her parents were walking toward her now, feeling uncomfortable in a place like this. What would they say to her? If they'd been ashamed of her military service, what would they say about addiction? About driving drunk? Losing her nursing license? About all of her failures? What would she say to them?

Barb came around the corner, looking nervous. When she saw Frankie, she surged forward, yanked her into a hug. "You scared the *shit* out of me."

Barb held Frankie's hand, led her outside to a grassy area full of chairs and picnic tables, where families sat clustered together, talking.

Frankie sat down at a picnic table.

Barb sat down across from her. "What the hell, Frankie?"

"Rye," she said simply.

Barb looked confused. "Rye?"

"He . . . came to see me one night, and . . . no, that's not the start. I saw him at the beach with his family . . . it feels like a lifetime ago. I followed him. Like a crazy woman. Then he came to the house and . . ."

"And you believed him again?" She leaned forward. "You?"

"I thought he loved me."

"I could kill that son of a bitch."

"Yeah, I thought that, too. I hated him—and myself—so much, it . . . destroyed me. That's all I can say. When I first got here, I dreamed of confronting him. I thought I needed to hear, *I lied and I'm sorry.* But I don't. I know what he did and I know what I did. None of it is pretty, but he isn't the problem. My doctor and group are helping me understand that. I should have talked about things a long time ago, I should have told you . . ." Frankie drew in a steadying breath and looked at her friend. Her whole body felt shaky, fragile. Vulnerable. "I should have told you that I was struggling with memories of 'Nam, been honest, but you seemed so damn *okay*. I thought it was all me, that I was weak or broken."

"You think because I don't say anything about 'Nam that I don't think about it?" she said.

"How would I know? We almost never talked about it." She paused, took a deep breath, heard Dr. Alden's even voice saying, *Just begin, Frankie. Talk.* "I don't know why I can't let some things go, why I keep remembering when others can forget."

"I remember, too," Barb said. "I still sometimes have nightmares . . ."

"You do?"

Barb nodded. "Red alerts . . . napalm. There was this one night at the Thirty-Sixth. A kid from my hometown . . ."

Frankie held on to her best friend's hand and listened to her stories, her pain, which was like her own. They talked for hours, until night fell slowly around them; the stars came out. Frankie had never known before that words could heal, at least be the beginning of healing.

"You were a damn rock star in the OR," Barb said at last. "You know that, right? Men came home because of you, Frankie."

Frankie drew in a breath, exhaled. "I do."

"So, what's next for you?"

"It's one day at a time," Frankie said. Truthfully, she wasn't ready to think about her future yet, had no idea if she could believe in the idea of truly healing. She wasn't okay, wasn't even within striking distance of it, and that was something she would never lie about again.

But.

I will be, she thought. She could feel strength growing in her, gathering like sunlight in the distance, beginning to warm her. If she stayed the course, worked the steps, believed in herself, she could heal, be a better version of herself.

Someday, she thought.

Thirty-Four

It was remarkable how quickly a turbulent world could calm. In early 1974, with the war over, the country seemed to release a great exhalation of relief. The fight for rights went on, of course: Civil rights and women's rights were a constant battle and the Stonewall riots had put gay rights in the news, too. Equality was the goal, but no longer in that hold-a-sign-and-march kind of way.

The Vietnam veterans disappeared into the landscape, hiding in plain sight among a populace that either held them in contempt or considered them not at all. The hippies changed, too; they graduated from college and left their communes and cut their hair and began to look for jobs. Even the music changed. Gone was the angry protest music of the war. Now everyone sang along to John Denver and Linda Ronstadt and Elton John. The Beatles had broken up. Janis and Jimi were dead.

Frankie was fighting for a metamorphosis of her own. She had come to the inpatient center unwillingly, or maybe not that, exactly. Unconscious was more like it.

By February, although she felt stronger, she was well aware that she could relapse in an instant, fall again to her knees. Sometimes it felt overwhelming, to think of what her life would look like from now on. So much of what had filled her up in the past few years was dark—memories, love, nightmares. She didn't know who she was without the pain or the need to hide it.

But sobriety—and therapy—had given her the tools to heal. One day at a time. For the first time in years, she was sometimes able to imagine a future that didn't include pain or pretense. She didn't believe in "soldiering on" anymore and knew that trying to forget trauma only gave grim memories a fecund soil in which to grow. She accepted the loss of her nursing license and hoped to someday get it back, but she didn't take that future for granted.

She still had nightmares, still sometimes woke on the floor of her dorm-like room, especially following an emotional therapy or rap session. She still longed for people who were gone from her life and whom she'd lost, but as Henry and Dr. Alden each reminded her often, regrets were a waste of time. *If only* was the bend in a troubling road. She learned day by day how to navigate through life, keep going, keep moving forward.

Surprisingly, of all her pains and regrets, those that had driven her to drink too much and get hooked on pills and lose her nursing license, Rye had been the easiest to exorcise.

She'd begun her treatment devastated by her choice to have an affair with a married man and destroyed by her belief in him and his love. She'd learned that she was weak, a sinner, but at the bottom of it all, deep down, she'd believed that Rye loved her. Love had somehow given her latitude to recast her terrible choice in a prettier light.

Until the day Dr. Alden had asked, "When did Rye first tell you he loved you?"

The question brought Frankie upright on the sofa. Had Rye *ever* told her he loved her?

She scrolled through her memories; what she found was this: *I'm afraid I'll love you till I die.*

At the time, she'd seen it as romantic, sweeping, epic. Now she saw the sentiment for what it was. The dark side of love. What he'd really been saying was, *I don't want to love you.*

It had never been real love for him. Oh, he'd shown up in Kauai to romance her, thinking that she was leaving the military within weeks and their affair would be a bit of fun before she left. She'd believed every moment with him.

Worst of all, his lies had exposed an immorality in her that she could have sworn hadn't existed before him. She'd begun by believing she was stupid and learned slowly that she was just human.

From now on, she would always know there was a fragility in her and no matter how strong she became, she would have to guard against it. "I worry I don't believe in love anymore," she told Dr. Alden once.

"But lots of people love you, Frankie, don't they?" Dr. Alden had said.

She closed her eyes, thought of the best moments of her life—with her dad calling her Peanut and lifting her into the air, her mother holding her tightly while she cried, and Finley teaching her to surf, sharing his secrets, holding her hand. Jamie, teaching her to believe in herself, to try. *No fear, McGrath.* And Barb and Ethel, always there for her.

"Yeah," she said quietly, and let those memories be her shield, her strength, her hope.

In the end, the hardest aspect of her recovery wasn't Rye. Neither was it the pills or the drugs.

The thing she still grappled most violently with was Vietnam. Those were the nightmares that haunted her. She talked about it with her doctor, told him her stories, and hoped for a kind of resolution, and while talking helped, she knew that Dr. Alden didn't understand. Not really. She saw the way he sometimes grimaced at a memory, heard words like *napalm* and flinched. Those moments reminded her that he had never been in war, and no one who hadn't been in the shit could really understand it.

She knew, too, that when she left the safety of the inpatient center, she would be thrust back into a world where Vietnam veterans were supposed to be invisible, the women most of all.

Now, though, regardless of how she felt or how the world felt about her or whether she felt ready, it was time for her to leave the center. She had been here too long already, extended her original stay, and Henry had very gently told her that she was taking the spot from someone else who needed to be saved.

"You're ready," Henry said from across the desk.

Frankie stood up. She didn't feel ready. By any method or measure, she had failed in the world after Vietnam. "So you and Dr. Alden keep saying." She walked over to his bookcase, picked up a picture of his nephew, Arturo, in uniform.

"Look at that smile," she said. *So like Finley*.

"He learned discipline, that's for sure," Henry said. "My sister says she could never get him to make his bed or fold his clothes before Annapolis, now he likes everything just so."

"There's nothing wrong with a little discipline," Frankie said. She picked up a framed photograph of Henry and his fiancée, Natalie, who were soon to be married in some woodland retreat. They were a perfect match; they spent their weekends hiking and camping and never missed a political event. She hosted fundraisers for the clinic. "You'll invite me to your hippie-dippie wedding, right?"

"Of course. You're leaving the center, Frankie. Not leaving me. We are friends. You can *always* call me."

She turned to look at him.

He sat back in his tufted leather chair, his graying hair pulled back in a loose ponytail.

"Thank you," she said. "For all of it. And I'm—"

"Love means never having to say you're sorry."

Frankie laughed. "What a crock of shit. Then again, I'm hardly an expert on love."

"You know love, Frankie."

He moved toward her, pulled her into an embrace.

She held on more tightly than she should have, but in the last months, he'd become her lifeline, her anchor, her confidant. Not her doctor, but her friend, as important in a way as Barb and Ethel.

"I'll miss you," she said.

He touched her face. "Just don't come back here the way you did, okay? Ask for help when you need it. Count on the people who love you and, mostly, count on yourself. One day at a time. Get a sponsor. Find your passion. You've got this." He paused, didn't look away. "You deserve to be loved, Frankie. In that forever kind of way. Don't forget that."

Frankie stared at him for another long moment. She could tell him all of it again, how she'd learned to understand her own weakness, and her own strength, how she'd come to believe that Rye was not just a liar, but selfish and cruel as well. But none of that mattered anymore; Rye didn't matter. If she saw him on the street, she'd pass him by with nothing but a pang of sad remembrance, and Henry knew all of that. "It was a lucky day when I met you, Henry Acevedo."

"Lucky for me, too, Frankie."

She bent down and picked up the old, banged-up travel bag her mother had packed for her months ago, when Frankie's world had collapsed.

Down the hall, she saw that Jill Landis was conducting a group session: eight new people sat in a horseshoe in front of the therapist.

A young man with long hair and slumped shoulders was saying something about heroin.

Frankie paused, caught Jill's gaze, and waved. *Goodbye.*

Here, just like in 'Nam, people came, did their time, were changed in existential ways, and moved on. Some made it in the outside world, some didn't. It was especially bad with Vietnam vets. The statistics on their rates of suicide were becoming alarming.

Frankie didn't go back to her room, vaguely afraid that, once there, she would find a reason not to leave. She walked through the front doors, out into the cold day.

She saw her mother's black Cadillac, parked beneath a jacaranda tree.

The driver side door opened. Then the passenger side. Dad and Mom stepped out, stood at their respective sides of the car, looking at her.

Even from here, she saw their joy. And their anxiety.

She had given them so much to worry about in a few short years. Vietnam. Trauma. The miscarriage. Rye. The drunk driving. The pills. She knew how hard all of it was on two people for whom reputation and standing in the community were vital. She had no idea what they had told their friends this time. Maybe drug and alcohol treatment had become tagging penguins in Antarctica.

Either way, she wouldn't ask. Having discovered her own failings, she was less inclined to judge others.

Her parents didn't understand her, perhaps, and certainly they didn't condone most of her choices, but they were here.

You know love, Frankie.

Frankie walked across the gravel parking lot.

"Frances," Mom said at her approach.

A look passed between them, a sharing of emotion between mother and daughter. "You look good," Mom said. "Too thin."

"You, too," Frankie said, walking into her mother's arms, being held in the new, fierce way that Mom had developed. Like Frankie, Mom had learned how capricious life and one's own body could be.

When Mom finally let go—with tears in her eyes—Frankie turned, looked across the shiny black roof of the Cadillac at her dad.

She had aged him, she knew, taught him that success and money couldn't insulate a family from loss or hardship. Walls around a house were no guarantee of safety, not in a world that was constantly shifting. He'd changed with the times, in a way, grown out his sideburns, and traded in his custom suits for knit bowling-style shirts and double-knit pants, but there was no denying the wariness in his eyes when he looked at his daughter.

She remembered him carrying her out of the water that night. The memory of his crying would always be with her. What he'd learned about her that night, about them, could never be erased. She knew a part of him would worry about her forever. And that he would never say a word about it. He and her mother were of a quieter generation. They didn't believe in words as much as they believed in optimism and hard work.

"I think you look great, Frankie," he said.

"Thanks, Dad."

She opened the back door, tossed her bag in the backseat, and slid in next to it.

When Dad started the engine, Perry Como's voice sang through the speakers and pulled time away. Suddenly Frankie was ten years old again, sitting in the backseat of the car, sliding across at every turn in the road, bumping into her brother.

"That bag still smells mildewed," Mom said. "I don't see how that's possible."

"Monsoon season," Frankie said, staring down at the black, soft-sided bag that had gone around the world with her. "Everything was wet. Nothing ever dried."

"That must have been . . . unpleasant," Mom said.

The first real conversation they'd ever had about Vietnam.

Frankie couldn't help smiling. They were trying, hoping to change in small and meaningful ways. "Yeah, Mom," she said with a smile. "It was unpleasant."

They pulled up in front of the small gray beach bungalow, with its old-fashioned wishing well out front and the American flag hanging over the garage door.

"You could stay with us," Dad said in a gruff voice.

Frankie understood his worry. No one wanted to leave an addict alone for long, but she needed to stand on her own. Or fall. And if she fell, she needed to stand again. "I'll be okay here, Dad."

She saw the way he frowned. Nodded. He reached across for Mom's hand, held it.

Frankie nodded, grabbed her bag, and got out of the car and stood there for a moment.

Mom got out of the car and hugged Frankie.

"Don't scare me again," Mom whispered.

Frankie felt a surge of love for her mother, a kinship. She thought suddenly about what it meant to lose a child. When Frankie was young, it had bothered her, her mother's sturdy impassivity, her calm demeanor. But now Frankie knew better. You survived a day at a time, however you could.

Tomorrow Frankie would begin the work of day-at-a-time living: she'd find a local Alcoholics Anonymous meeting and get a sponsor. Then she'd send Mr. Brightman a check for a new bicycle—the first step in her lengthy reparation process. She would not seek to reinstate her nursing license until she was sure of her recovery.

Mom laid a hand on Frankie's cheek, looked deeply into her eyes. "I am so proud of you, Frances."

"Thank you, Mom."

Letting go of her mother, Frankie turned and headed for the cottage. The deed—in Frankie's name—lay on the kitchen counter. No doubt her father had put it there to remind her that she belonged here, on Coronado.

She went to her bedroom and tossed her bag on the floor, where it landed with a *thunk* and slid bumpily across the wooden planks.

Then she walked down the hallway to the nursery.

When had she last opened that door?

She opened it now and stood in the doorway, staring at the yellow room. For the first time, she let herself remember all of it, here, in this room where she'd once been filled with hope.

A different version of her.

A different world.

As she stood there, letting the pain in, remembering the whole of her life, she realized suddenly that she was young. Not even twenty-nine.

She'd made some of the most momentous choices in her life before she had any idea of consequences. Some had been thrust on her, some had been expected, some had been impetuous. She'd decided to become a nurse at seventeen. She'd joined the Army Nurse Corps and gone to war at twenty-one. She'd gone to Virginia with her friends to run away from home, and when her mother needed care, she'd come home.

In love, she'd been too cautious for years, and then too impetuous.

In retrospect, it all felt haphazard. Some good decisions, some bad. Some experiences that she would never trade. What she'd learned about herself in Vietnam and the friendships she'd made were indelible.

But now it was time to actually go in search of *her* life.

———

Summer, 1974.

The air smelled of childhood: of the sea, and sand baked by the sun, and lemon trees.

On Ocean Boulevard, Frankie tented a hand over her eyes and stared out at the wide blue Pacific. She imagined a pair of black-haired, blue-eyed kids running across the sand, carrying surfboards; kids who'd thought they had all the time in the world to grow up, who didn't know what it meant to be broken or afraid or lost.

Hey, Fin. I miss you.

She walked along the sidewalk, on her way home from an Alcoholics Anonymous meeting, with the long white beach on her left. A tuft of greenery capped the rise. In the distance, boats moved across the horizon. Tourists and locals filled the beach on this hot August day.

A jet roared overhead, probably a pilot from that new fighter jet school at Miramar. The roar of the engines was loud enough to shake the ground. She knew that no one on Coronado cared; they called it the sound of freedom.

At the gate to her parents' house, Frankie paused, steeled herself for what she was sure would be a battle, and opened the gate.

It had taken months of hard work to get to this place, and still it was just the beginning. Often, as she'd begun to contemplate her future, she'd panicked, felt weak, thought, *I can't do this.* On those hard days, she either went to a second—or third—meeting or called her sponsor and found just enough strength to keep going. Keep believing. One day at a time.

Today the yard was awash in summer color.

Dad was on the patio, smoking a cigarette.

She closed the gate behind her and walked around the pool to stand in front of him.

She fought the urge to say she was sorry. Again. She'd said it to him dozens of times in the past few months, and she knew how uncomfortable it made him.

At first she'd hoped her apology would be a beginning, the start of reparations, maybe, a healing that could only come through conversation. She longed to tell him he'd hurt her and understand why he'd been so cold and dismissive about her service in Vietnam.

But it was not to be. He had no interest in talking about it. He wanted to pretend the war had never torn this family apart. Dr. Alden had taught her to accept that, accept him. That was what family meant. Sometimes hurts didn't quite heal. That was life.

"I need to talk to you guys," she said.

"That doesn't sound good."

Frankie smiled. "I know how you love to talk." She took hold of his hand, squeezed it.

He squeezed back.

Mom came out onto the patio, a glass of iced tea in one hand.

"Our girl wants to talk to us," Dad said.

"That doesn't sound good," Mom said.

There was something to be said for consistency. Frankie led her parents into the living room, where a sofa and four chairs were gathered around a huge stone fireplace.

Frankie sat in one of the big wing chairs.

Her parents sat together on the sofa. Frankie saw her mother reach out to hold her father's hand.

Frankie thought—oddly—of that night, long ago, when she'd dressed with such care for Finley's going-away party, in a lavender sheath, with her hair teased to an improbable height. She'd done everything to make these two people proud of her. It was why her father's dismissal of Vietnam cut so deeply. But those were the needs of a child. She was a woman now.

"I love you guys," she said. That was the starting and ending point in life: love. The journey was everything in between.

Mom paled visibly. "Frances . . ."

"No fear," Frankie said, more to herself than to her mother, who was obviously imagining the worst. She took a deep breath, exhaled. "I've had plenty of time to think in the past few months. I've worked really hard to become honest with myself and to see my own life clearly, and maybe I still don't, maybe no one ever does until it's too late, but I've seen enough. I need to find out who I really am and who I want to be."

"You'll get your nursing license back. Henry says he'll write you a recommendation. You just have to start the process," Mom said. "And you've gotten your driver's license back."

"I know that. I hope to God I can be a nurse again, but I have to plan for the worst, too, that they deny me."

"What is it you're trying to say, Frankie?" Dad asked.

"I'm moving," she said.

"What?" Mom said. "Why? You have everything you need right here."

"Can you make it on your own?" Dad said. "Without your nursing license?"

Frankie had asked herself the same thing. She'd never paid rent or found her own place or lived alone. She'd gone from her parents' house straight to her hooch in Vietnam. The last time she'd lost her shit, Barb and Ethel had bailed her out and given her a place to live. While she'd been in recovery, her father had hired a lawyer and gotten her DUI downgraded to reckless driving and gotten her driver's license reinstated. She'd never even had her own credit card. "I don't know where I'm going or what I'm looking for, but you know what? That's okay. It's supposed to be frightening to make your way in the world, to leave your family."

"Oh," Mom said, looking hurt.

"I need quiet," Frankie said. "Everything has been . . . loud since Vietnam. Before that, maybe, since Finley's death. I need to live someplace where all I hear are leaves rustling and winds blowing and maybe a coyote howling at the moon, where I can focus on getting well. Strong. I want to have an animal, a dog, maybe. A horse." She paused. "I just want to breathe easily. Thanks to both of you, I have the cottage. I'd like to sell it and use the money to start over somewhere new."

Her parents stared at her for a long moment.

"We'll worry," Mom said at last.

Frankie loved her for that. "It's not like I'm going to war," she said with a smile. "I'll be back. And you'll visit, wherever I end up."

On a hot, late August day, Frankie packed up her repaired Mustang and went back into the bungalow, tossing her keys on the counter. She looked around at the empty room. She hoped a young family bought this place and raised their children here, letting them run as free as she and Finley had, that they loved the tree swing Henry had put up in the backyard and had birthday parties on the beach.

At last, she left the house, closed the door behind her for the last time.

Outside, Barb stood against Frankie's Mustang, with her arms crossed. In front of her was a FOR SALE sign stuck into the lawn. "Hey," she said.

Frankie laughed out loud. "Who called you? Mom? Henry? I'm surrounded by snitches."

"Uh-huh. You didn't think I'd let you go in search of your life alone, did you?"

"You're married. With stepkids. You don't have to sweep in and fill my empty life with your own, you know."

Barb rolled her eyes. "You're my best friend, Frankie," she said.

And that was it.

"Ethel wanted to come, but she's pregnant again. On bed rest. She said to tell you she's here in big, fat spirit."

An ice-cream truck drove past, bells jingling. The neighborhood children wouldn't be far behind. Frankie turned, tented her eyes; for a split second, she was ten years old again, running along behind her big brother, trying to keep up, both of them gilded in sunlight in her memory.

Frankie laughed and hugged Barb, then jumped in the driver's seat and started the car. The music came on loudly: "Hooked on a Feeling."

A few blocks later, Frankie eased her foot off the gas.

Her parents stood in front of the gate, arms around each other, hands in the air. How long had they been there, waiting to catch a glimpse of her as she left town? They'd said goodbye a dozen times and in a dozen ways in the last month.

Frankie waved and honked the horn in goodbye—to her parents, to Coronado, to her childhood, and to Finley. The Mustang rolled through town and onto the bridge, past the boats anchored in the harbor. Frankie saw the postcard beauty of Coronado Island in her rearview mirror.

With no destination in mind, Frankie and Barb drove north, listening to Creedence, Vanilla Fudge, Cream, Janis, the Beatles, the Animals, Dylan, the Doors.

The music of Vietnam.

The music of their generation.

At Dana Point, Frankie turned onto Highway 1 and stayed on the coast, with the endless blue Pacific to her left. In Long Beach there was an accident, so she turned onto a freeway, and then another one, just taking exits when it felt right.

She let the complex web of California freeways become her will; she let them lead her, this way and that. With the new fifty-five-mile-per-hour speed limit, she had to constantly check her speed.

She drove through downtown Los Angeles, with its graffiti and gangs and chain-link fences, and found herself on the glittering Sunset Strip, a world of lights and giant billboards and music clubs.

They drove up the magnificent California Coast, spent a few nights in the Santa Ynez Valley, staring out at the rolling golden hills, and Frankie said, "I like the open spaces, but I need more, and horses, maybe."

"Northward," Barb said.

This was how they made decisions; on the fly, by corners turned and roads taken and not taken.

In Carmel, the afternoon fog was too heavy; in San Francisco, there were too many people. The wildness of Mendocino called out to her, but the giant Sequoias hemmed her in somehow.

So, northward.

In Oregon, the green was vibrant and the air was clean, and still there were too many people, even though the towns were few and far between.

They bypassed busy Seattle, listened to radio reports of missing college girls, and turned east, passing through the empty endless wheat fields in the eastern half of Washington, which felt lonely to Frankie, desolate.

Montana.

When they drove into the town of Missoula, singing about time in a bottle, the sky was a vibrant, searing blue that explained the Big Sky Country moniker. A few miles out of town, and the view was stunning: hay fields that stretched toward jagged, snowcapped mountains, their peaks draped in snow, the wide blue Clark Fork river meandering by.

FOR SALE. 27 ACRES.

She and Barb saw the sign at the same time.

It was stuck on a slanted post, looked weathered by time. Behind it: an endless green field, the river running along it, a ragged barbed wire fence in need of tending, a dirt road that led to a stand of tall green trees.

Frankie looked at Barb. "It's beautiful."

"And remote," Barb said.

"A girl could breathe here," Frankie said. She turned onto the dirt road, followed it into a thicket of trees and out again. Beyond the trees lay another vibrant green field, with the mountains rising behind them into the blue sky.

Frankie stared through the dirty windshield at the peak-roofed farmhouse with a wraparound porch, at the fenced horse fields, at the big old once-red barn in need of a new roof. There were outbuildings, too, some of them collapsed, more barely standing.

"This is a shitload of work," Barb said.

"Fortunately, I know how to fix stuff." Frankie turned, smiled. "My friends and I spent almost two years rebuilding a bunkhouse."

"It's in the middle of nowhere."

"Look at the map. Missoula isn't far. Hospitals and a college, too. It's closer to Chicago than San Diego is. I know I can find an AA meeting here, get a new sponsor."

"You've made up your mind."

Frankie turned off the radio.

Quiet.

She looked at Barb, smiled. "I have."

Thirty-Five

WESTERN MONTANA
SEPTEMBER 1982

The invitation came in a smudged white envelope that was postmarked August 28 and stamped WASHINGTON, D.C. Someone had written across the back SAVE THE DATE.

You're invited to a reunion of the
36th Evac Hospital staff
following the unveiling of the new
Vietnam Veterans Memorial in Washington, D.C.,
on November 13, 1982

Frankie's first reaction surprised her.

Anger.

Now a memorial to the men who had died?

Now? More than a decade after they'd been unceremoniously buried and forgotten by their fellow Americans?

As hard as Frankie had worked in the last eight years, and she'd been dedicated to the endeavor, she'd never quite been able to completely dispel the shame her fellow Americans had made her feel over serving in Vietnam, nor her anger at how the government had treated the veterans who returned broken in body or mind or spirit. Even worse than that, in the late seventies she'd sat here in her living room and watched a fellow Vietnam vet claim on television that Agent Orange had given him—and thousands like him—cancer. *I died in Vietnam; I just didn't know it,* he'd said. Not long after that, the world had learned that the herbicide also caused miscarriages and birth defects. Most likely it had caused Frankie's miscarriage.

Her own government had done that to her. Maybe if the politicians in Washington, D.C., had built this memorial as an apology to a generation of servicemen and -women and their families, she might have felt differently, but no. The government hadn't moved to honor the veterans of Vietnam. The vets themselves had had to make this happen. Those who remained honoring those who had fallen.

She heard Donna come up behind her. Pause.

Donna had worked here at the ranch for more than seven years now. Frankie still remembered the cold day Donna had driven up to the front door, her fake black hair every which way, her skin pale from alcoholism, her voice barely above a whisper. *I'm a nurse,* she'd said. *Cu Chi, '68. I got your name from the VA. I can't . . .*

Sleep, Frankie remembered saying. That was all. Enough. Everything. She'd taken Donna by the hand and led her into the farmhouse. They'd sat in a pair of folding chairs in front of the fire and talked.

A rap session, Jill at the center had called it. *It helps sometimes to feel you're not alone.* They'd been there for each other, she and Donna, often held each other upright. Donna had urged Frankie to fight for the reinstatement of her nursing license, and the fight had proven to be healing. By the time she'd officially been granted the right to be a nurse again, Frankie felt strong enough to try.

That had been the beginning of the ranch. She and Donna had joined forces, using the money from the Coronado cottage sale to make improvements.

In Missoula, both of them took nursing jobs at a local hospital.

After work hours, Frankie attended night classes at the college toward a degree in clinical psychology, and a year later Donna did the same. When they weren't studying to become counselors or working shifts at the hospital, they remodeled the house and repaired the outbuildings and attended regular meetings.

That first summer, Frankie's friends and family had shown up to help. Mom and Dad, Barb and Jere and their growing boys, Ethel and Noah and their two kids, Henry and Natalie and their rowdy sons. They took over bedrooms and pitched tents in the grassy backyard. They worked together during the day and sat around a campfire at night, talking and laughing and remembering.

As soon as they got their master's degrees, Frankie and Donna put up flyers at the nearest Veterans Administration office that said: *To the women of Vietnam: We lived through it over there. We can live through it here. Join us.*

A year later, Janet had shown up, her face blackened by bruising, her quick laugh too sharp to be anything but a substitute for crying. Janet stayed for almost a year.

From then on, the ranch they called the Last Best Place became a haven for the women who'd served in Vietnam. They came, they stayed as long as they needed to, and they moved on. Each left an imprint somehow, a path for women like them to follow. They left art and easels and paints. Knitting needles and skeins of wool, short stories and memoir chapters and musical instruments. They worked during the day—hammering nails, painting walls, feeding horses, tending the garden. Whatever needed doing.

They learned to breathe, and then to talk, and then, if they were lucky, to hope. Frankie taught them the healing power of words and the joy of finding quiet. Peace, at least the beginning of it, was the goal. But it was never easy.

The beautiful, unexpected by-product of helping other women was that Frankie found her own passion again, her own pride. She loved this place fiercely, loved the life she'd forged in the wilderness, loved the women who came to her for help and helped her in return. She woke up each morning with hope. And each summer, her friends and family showed up to spend as much vacation time as possible on the ranch. It became a haven for them, too.

"Group is ready."

Frankie nodded, looking down at the silver POW bracelet she still wore for the major who'd never come home.

Donna came up beside her. In the years they'd worked together, both women had filled out, gotten physically strong by pounding fence posts and hauling hay bales and tossing saddles up on their horses' backs. Both routinely wore Levi's, cowboy boots, and flannel shirts; no shoulder pads or power suits in this part of Montana.

"There's a lot of talk about the memorial," Donna said. "Lots of reunions are happening."

"Yeah," Frankie said.

"It's a lot to think about."

They stood side by side, staring through the kitchen window, out at the autumn fields. Each knew what the other was thinking: they'd talked about it often enough.

Taking her cup of coffee, Frankie left the kitchen, heard Donna behind her, putting a pot of beans on to soak.

Outside, the world was awash in fall color; snow lay heavily on the jagged, distant mountains. Skiing would come early this year. The brilliant blue of the Clark Fork river meandered through the fields, swirled and bubbled over polished stones, made a sound like children laughing.

The Last Best Place Ranch now boasted a whitewashed farmhouse with three bedrooms and two bathrooms. The furniture was all second-hand, garage-sale finds, as well as the stuff Mom had shipped up years ago from the bungalow when it sold.

Here, women had painted through their pain and left images on the walls, a kind of graffiti. One wall—Frankie called it the heroes' wall—was filled with photographs of the women who'd served, those who'd come through the ranch, and others, their friends. Hundreds of photographs were tacked onto the pine planks. In the center was the picture of Barb, Ethel, and Frankie standing in front of the O Club at the Thirty-Sixth Evac. Across the top of it all, Frankie had painted in bold black script: THE WOMEN.

Three refurbished bunkhouses held bunk beds and writing desks. A fourth had been turned into a communal bathroom with showers and sinks and toilets.

The barn was still a little undone, but the roof was solid now and seven horses lived in the stalls. Frankie had learned how beneficial caring for animals and riding could be for women in crisis.

In the center aisle of the barn, six folding chairs had been set in a semicircle on the sawdust floor.

On this cool morning, four of the chairs were occupied by women. Frankie took her chair and pulled it closer and sat down.

The women looked at her; one in a shuttered, closed-off way, one in anger, one who seemed almost disinterested, and a fourth woman was already crying.

"I got an invitation to a reunion of the Thirty-Sixth Evac," Frankie said. "It's tied into the unveiling of the Vietnam Veterans Memorial. I suspect some of you may have gotten invitations, too."

"Ha," Gwyn said. She was older-looking, but not old, just worn out, her mouth flattened, her eyes dark with anger. "Like I *want* to remember," she said sharply. "I spend half my waking hours trying to forget."

"I'm going to go," the crying woman, Liz, said. "To pay my respects. This memorial matters, Gwyn."

"Too little, too late," said Marcy, who leaned forward in her seat, put her forearms on her thighs. It was her first full day at the ranch and she didn't believe in any of it yet.

"I am done with Vietnam, Liz," Gwyn said. "Everyone always tells me to forget. To let it go. And now I'm supposed to go running back? Nope. Not me. Not going."

"You'll disappoint the people you served with," said Ramona.

"What's new?" Gwyn said. "I've disappointed pretty much everyone since I got home."

Frankie had heard these words from every woman who'd come through the ranch, trying to right themselves after the war. She knew what they needed to hear. "You know, I wasn't afraid to go to war, and I should have been. I am afraid to go to the memorial, and I shouldn't be. People made us think we'd done something wrong, shameful, didn't they? We were forgotten; all of us Vietnam vets, but the women most of all."

The women nodded.

Frankie looked at the women, recognized their emotional wounds, and felt their pain. "I used to wonder if I would do it again, join up. Was there still a believer inside me, a last shred of the girl who wanted to make a difference?" She looked around. "And I would. In some ways, the war years were the best of my life."

"And the worst," Gwyn said.

Frankie looked at Gwyn, saw the woman's anger, remembered it. "And the worst," she agreed. "You're right, Gwyn, I don't think disappointing people is a reason to go to the memorial. Most of us have made too many decisions based on other people. We need to do what *we* need to do. But we've been silenced for too long, invisible for too many years."

"It's all about the men," Gwyn said. "Did I tell you I tried to join a Vietnam vets talk therapy session in Dallas? It's always the same thing. 'You don't belong. You're a woman. There were no women in Vietnam.'"

The women in the circle nodded at that.

"We don't have a memorial," Gwyn added.

"We share that pain, don't we?" Frankie said. "We've been dealing with the war for a decade, most of us, some even longer. Pushing through. I know how the Agent Orange news has brought it all back up," Frankie said. It was a topic that came up consistently in the circle.

"I had four miscarriages," Liz said, tears bright in her eyes. "A baby might have saved me, us, you know. And all that time, they were spraying that shit, killing us all slowly."

"Sometimes I think dying would be easier than living this way," Gwyn said. "We'll probably all get cancer."

Frankie looked at each woman in turn, saw the variations on pain. "Who here has considered suicide?" she asked.

A taboo question that she asked in each new group of women.

Gwyn said, "I've thought it might be a relief to . . . disappear."

"That's a brave thing to say, but we know you're brave, Gwyn. All of you are. And you're tough."

"I used to be," Liz said.

"You're here," Frankie said. "In the wilds of Montana, sitting in a barn that smells like manure, and saying the most frightening, intimate things out loud to strangers." She took a beat. "But we aren't strangers, are we? We are the women who went to war—the nurses of Vietnam—and many of us felt silenced at home. We lost who we were, who we wanted to be. But I'm living proof that it can get better. *You* can get better. It starts here. In these chairs, reminding ourselves and each other that we are not alone."

~~~

In Washington, D.C., on the morning of November 13, 1982, Frankie woke well before dawn.

She'd hardly slept last night. If she'd still been a drinking woman, she would have poured herself something strong. She almost wished she was still a smoker; she needed something to do with her hands. As it was, she got up at five A.M. and pulled her old black overnight bag out of the closet of her cheap motel room. She could have brought a new suitcase on this trip, but the travel bag just felt right. It had been with her in the beginning, in Vietnam. It should be with her now at the end.

It landed on the cheap shag carpet floor with a *thunk*. She clicked on the bedside lamp, knelt in the pool of light, and unzipped the bag.

The smells assailed her: sweat and mud and blood and smoke and fish. Vietnam.

Don't drink the water.

I'm new in-country.

No shit.

That's us, giving it back to them.

On top of her belongings was a Polaroid picture taken at the O Club. In it, Ethel, Barb, and Frankie all wore shorts and T-shirts and combat boots. Jamie had an arm around Frankie's waist and held up a beer in a toast. There was a picture of her dancing with Jamie, both of them sweaty and laughing, and another one of the guys playing volleyball in the sunlight while the women watched, and one of Hap playing his guitar.

Look at those smiles.

Good times. They'd had those, too.

Frankie pulled out her battered old boonie hat and felt a wave of nostalgia thinking of all the places where she'd worn this hat, all the times she'd had to hold it down so rotor wash didn't whip it off her head. A dozen pins and patches decorated it, mementos her patients had given her, both from platoons and squadrons, even a happy-face pin and a peace symbol. When had she written MAKE LOVE NOT WAR across the brim in magic marker? She didn't remember.

She'd worn this hat on her MEDCAP trips into the villages and on her supply flights to Long Binh, on the beach, and even on her R and R to Kauai. She'd worn it handing out candy to kids at the orphanages and sitting in the back of a deuce and a half, bumping over red dirt roads and splashing through rivers of mud.

Kristin Hannah

And she would wear it today.

No more hiding this treasured memento away in her closet, trying to forget the woman who'd worn it. No more hiding at all.

She pulled out her dog tags, held them in her hand for the first time in years, surprised by how light they actually were. They'd taken on a weight in her mind. She thought of all the bloody dog tags she'd held in her life as she looked for a wounded man's name, blood type, religion.

Some women had worn love beads in the sixties; others had worn dog tags.

She pulled out the stack of Polaroid pictures of Vietnam she'd brought, remembering the night, years ago now, at the ranch, when her mother had asked to see them, when they'd sat outside by a fire, a spray of stars overhead, and looked at these faded photographs of nurses and doctors, soldiers, Vietnamese children herding water buffalo along the banks of a river, green jungles, white beaches, old men in rice paddies. Mom hadn't said much, but she'd sat there, listening, for hours.

Frankie pulled out the latest of her journals. She'd first begun journaling in rehab, at Henry's urging. Her first sentence, written all those years ago, in angry black marker, was, *How did I end up here? I am so ashamed.*

In the years between then and now, she'd written hundreds of pages. They initially chronicled her pain and then her recovery, and finally her coming-of-age in Montana, on the land where she had found herself, her calling, and her passion. She didn't have children, imagined now that she would never have children, but she had her ranch, and the women who came to her. She had friends and family and a purpose. She had the big, full life she and her brother had once dreamed of.

She opened up the first blank page, dated it, and wrote:

I can't stop thinking about Finley today. Of course.
Mom and Dad chose not to come to the unveiling of the memorial.

I wish they were here, I need them here, but I understand. Some grief is too deep to reveal in public.

We were the last believers, my generation. We trusted what our parents taught us about right and wrong, good and evil, the American myth of equality and justice and honor.

I wonder if any generation will ever believe again. People will say it was the war that shattered our lives and laid bare the beautiful lie we'd been taught. And they'd be right. And wrong.

There was so much more. It's hard to see clearly when the world is angry and divided and you're being lied to.

God, I wish we

There was a knock at the door. Frankie wasn't surprised. Who could sleep? She got up, went to the door, opened it.

Barb and Ethel stood outside, beneath a feeble overhead light. A sputtering neon sign in the parking lot behind them read NO VACANCY.

"Smells like 'Nam," Ethel said. "I wish you'd let me pay for nicer rooms."

"It's her damn overnight bag," Barb said.

"I have to be careful with money these days," Frankie said.

The three of them left the room, each wearing whatever they'd worn to sleep in, and walked down the stairs to a kidney-shaped pool that needed cleaning. Lights in the water created an aqua glow, as did the few lights on the exterior of the motel. The neon sign gave off a faint beelike buzzing sound.

"Six bucks and you get a pool," Barb said, sitting in a creaky lounge chair.

"For seven, they might clean the pool," Ethel said, sitting beside her.

"I'd rather they wash the sheets," Barb said.

"Quit complaining, you two. We're here, aren't we?" Frankie said, stretching out on the chair between them.

"Last night, I dreamt about our first night in the Seventy-First," Barb said, lighting a cigarette. "Haven't thought about that in years."

Ethel said, "For me, it was my first napalm-orphanage shift."

Frankie stared out at the water in the dirty pool with the chain-link fence around it all. She'd had those nightmares, too, and they'd wakened her, too, gotten her heart pumping, but she'd also dreamt of waterskiing on the Saigon River, of Coyote's howl, of Jamie's smile, and dancing to the Doors with her girlfriends. She'd surprised herself by thinking about Rye—for the first time in years—and found there was nothing left in her that cared about him; all that remained was a patched and faded regret.

"It's going to be crazy today," Ethel said. "A huge crowd."

"We hope," Barb said.

They all considered that, feared it. The unveiling of a memorial to a war—and warriors—that no one seemed eager to remember.

"We're here," Frankie said. "That's enough for me."

<hr />

In a way, even with as far as she'd come, Frankie feared that the vein of fragility in her would open up when confronted again with Vietnam and all that had been lost there.

This morning, she stared at herself in the mirror, dressed in her fatigues, seeing the young version of herself staring back. She attached her ANC pin to her collar.

Outside the motel, in full daylight, she met up with Barb and Ethel; their husbands and children would be meeting them at the memorial. This, the beginning, was just for the girlfriends.

Each was wearing her fatigues and boonie hat and combat boots.

Barb smiled. "Don't tell me there were no women in Vietnam."

A ceiling of white clouds lay over the city. The air smelled crisp and cold, of the coming winter.

Here on the cordoned-off street, Vietnam veterans gathered; thousands of men, dressed in uniforms and fatigues, leather jackets with military patches on the sleeves, and torn jeans. There were veterans in wheelchairs and on crutches, some blinded and being helped along by friends. Thousands and thousands of Vietnam veterans, coming together for the first time in a decade or more. There was a feeling of reunion, joy. Men clapping each other on the back, laughing, hugging.

Someone with a bullhorn yelled out, "Brothers! Let's go pay our respects!" and the crowd began to form itself into a parade line.

Frankie and Ethel and Barb joined the line of men.

Someone started to sing "America the Beautiful," and others joined in, hesitantly, and then boldly. Their voices swelled in song. *And crown thy good with brotherhood, from sea to shining sea.* Frankie heard her friends and fellow veterans singing beside her. Spectators applauded from the sidewalks; car horns honked.

As they neared the National Mall, the vets fell quiet, all at once, with no one urging the sudden stillness. No more singing. No talking. No clearing of throats, even. They walked together, shoulder to shoulder, these men who'd fought in a hated war and come home to animosity and still didn't know how to feel about what they'd lived through. Helicopters flew in formation overhead. As far as Frankie could see, the three of them were the only women, although they searched the crowd for nurses or Donut Dollies or other military women with whom they'd served.

At the Mall, an American flag fluttered in the cool breeze above a trio of bright red fire trucks. Supporters filled the grassy area, lined the Reflecting Pool, waited for the parade of veterans: children on their parents' shoulders, families huddled together, mothers holding framed pictures of their lost sons, dogs barking, babies screaming. Five jets flew overhead; one peeled off from the rest. The missing man formation.

The welcome home these veterans had never received.

Veterans dispersed into the waiting crowd, joined their families, gathered in pods of old friends who hadn't seen each other in years.

"Come with me," Barb said, tugging on Frankie's hand.

Frankie shook her head. "Go, girls. Be with your families. We'll meet up."

"You want to be alone?" Ethel said.

Frankie bit back her instinctive response. *I am alone.* "Go," she said again, quietly.

Frankie moved forward on her own, through the crowd.

And then, there it was: The Wall. Gleaming black granite rising up from the green grass, the shiny surface alive with reflected movement. Honor Guards stood stationed at intervals along it.

Frankie was overwhelmed by the sight of it. Even from here, she could see the endless etchings on the stone. More than fifty-eight thousand names.

A generation of men.

And eight women. Nurses, all of them.

Names of the fallen.

In the distance, somewhere, someone tapped on a microphone, made a scratching, squealing sound that drew the attention of the crowd.

A man's voice rang out. "No one can debate the sacrifice and the service of those who fell while serving . . . Standing before this monument, we see reflected in a dark mirror dimly a chance now to let go of the pain, the grief, the resentment, the bitterness, the guilt . . ."

As the speech went on, the speaker remarked on the world the veterans had come home to and the shame now felt by Americans who hadn't welcomed their soldiers home. At last, the speaker said the words that Frankie and her fellow veterans had waited for all these years: "Welcome home and thank you." The soldier next to Frankie began to cry.

The veterans sang "God Bless America."

Their family and the visitors joined in.

At the end of the song, with the last notes echoing across the Mall, the speaker said, "Ladies and gentlemen, the Vietnam Veterans Memorial is now dedicated."

A cheer rose up from the crowd, a thunderous applause.

Someone else stepped up to the podium. A grizzled, old-before-his-time vet in stained fatigues. "Thank you for finally remembering us."

Reporters and cameramen pushed through the crowd, seeking statements for the nightly news.

Frankie drifted down the sloping grass, drawn to the Wall. She saw women holding framed photographs of the men they'd lost, and a teenager wearing his father's too-big dress uniform.

As she neared the mirror of black granite, she saw her own reflection—a skinny, long-haired woman in fatigues and a boonie hat—superimposed over the names of the fallen. She glanced down the black line, saw men in uniform standing tall in front of it, while women knelt before it, children and parents at their sides.

"Frances."

She turned and saw her parents moving toward her.

"You came," Frankie said, overwhelmed with emotion.

Her mother held a framed photograph of Finley to her chest. Dad held tightly on to Mom's other hand. "I wanted to see his name," Mom said quietly. "My son. He would want me here."

The three of them moved as one to the Wall, searched the names and dates.

There he was.

Finley O. McGrath.

Frankie reached out to touch the stone; to her surprise, it was warm. She traced the etching of her brother's name, remembering the sound of his laughter, the way he teased her, the stories he read her before bed. *I'm going to be a great American novelist . . . Here, Frankie, that's your wave. Paddle hard. You got it.*

"Hey, Fin," she said.

It felt good, to think of him as he was, as he'd been. Not just as a casualty of war, but as a beloved brother. For too many years, all she'd thought of was his death; now, at the Wall, she remembered his life.

She heard her mother crying, and the soft, wrenching sound of it brought tears to Frankie's eyes, too, blurred her vision.

"He's here," Frankie said. "I feel him."

"I always feel him," her mother said in a voice that held on to sorrow. Beside her, Dad stood rigid, his jaw clenched, afraid even here to show his grief.

"Ma'am?"

Frankie felt someone tap on her shoulder and say again, "Ma'am?" She turned.

The man who'd tapped her shoulder was maybe her age, with long sideburns and a straggly beard. He wore torn and stained fatigues. He pulled off his boonie hat, which held patches from the 101st. "Ma'am, were you a nurse over there?"

Frankie almost asked how he knew; then she remembered that she was wearing her fatigues and boonie hat, and her winged ANC pin.

"I was," she said, studying the man, trying to remember him. Had she held his hand or written a letter for him, or taken a picture with him or brought him a glass of water? If she had, she didn't recall it.

She felt her father step closer to her. "Frankie, do you—"

Frankie held up a hand for silence. For once, her father complied.

The soldier reached out to hold her hand, stared into her eyes. In that moment, on the Mall ground, with the Wall shining beside them, the two of them shared it all—the horror, the grief, the pain, the pride, the guilt, the camaraderie. She thought, *Here we are, for the first time since the war, all of us together.*

"Thank you, ma'am," he said, and she nodded and let him go.

Frankie felt her father's gaze on her.

She turned, looked up at him, saw the tears in his eyes. "Finley loved his service, Dad. We wrote letters all the time. He found himself over there. You don't need to feel guilty."

"You think I feel guilty for urging my son to go to war? I do. It's a thing I live with." He swallowed hard. "But I feel more guilt about how I treated my daughter when she came home."

Frankie drew in a sharp breath. How long had she waited to hear those words from him?

"You're the hero, aren't you, Frankie?"

Tears blurred her vision. "I don't know about a hero, Dad, but I served my country. Yeah."

"I love you, Peanut," he said in a rough voice. "And I'm sorry."

Peanut. God, he hadn't called her that in years.

Frankie saw him crying and wished she knew the perfect words to say, but nothing came to her. Life was like that, she guessed; it was all wrong until suddenly it was right, and you didn't really know how to react in either instance. But she knew love when she saw it, and it filled her. "I don't know about heroism," she said. "But I saw a lot of it. And . . ." She drew in a deep breath. "I'm proud of my service, Dad. It's taken me a long time to say that. I'm proud, even if the war never should have happened, even if it went to hell."

Her father nodded. She could see that he wanted more from her, absolution maybe, but there was time ahead for that.

This. Here. Was *her* time. Her moment. Her memories.

She left her parents standing in front of Finley's name, and walked along the Wall, looking for 1967–1969, seeing the flowers and pictures and yearbooks that were being set up at the base of the black granite. She saw a Gold Star Mother standing beside a pair of confused-looking teenagers trying to construct their lost father from letters carved into granite.

She followed the line of names, looking for Jameson Callahan—

"McGrath."

Frankie stopped.

He stood in front of her. Tall and gray-haired, with a jagged scar along one side of his face and a pants leg that ruffled against a prosthetic.

"Jamie."

He pulled her into his arms, whispering, "McGrath," again, into her ear.

Just that, being called McGrath again, hearing his voice, feeling his breath on her neck, sent her back to the O Club, beaded curtain clattering, the Beatles singing, Jamie asking her to dance. "Jamie," she whispered. "How—"

He reached into his pocket and pulled out a small gray stone that read:

YOU FIGHT

MCGRATH.

The stone she'd been given by the young Vietnamese boy in the orphanage, and which she'd slipped into Jamie's duffel bag. "It was a hellhole over there and worse when we got home," he said quietly, "but you got me through it, McGrath. Remembering you got me through."

"I saw you die."

"I died lots of times," he said. "They kept dragging me back. I was in bad shape for a long time. My injuries . . . Christ, look at me . . ."

"You are still as handsome as ever," Frankie said, unable to look away.

"My ex-wife would disagree."

"You're not—"

"It's a long, sad story with a happy ending for both of us. I stayed with her for years. We had another baby. A girl. She's nine, and a real spitfire." He stared down at her. "Her name is Frances."

Frankie didn't know how to respond; it was hard to draw a breath.

"How about you?" he said, trying to smile. "Married, with kids?"

"No," Frankie said. "Never married. No kids."

"I'm sorry," he said quietly; he of all people knew how much she'd wanted that life.

"It's okay. I'm happy."

She gazed up at him. On his face, she saw all that he'd been through:

the jagged jawline scar, the pucker of skin along one ear, the sadness in his eyes. His blond hair was long now, threaded with gray, a reminder that they'd been young once together, but weren't anymore, that there were scars on both of them. Wounds that remained, seen and unseen.

"God, I've missed you," he said in a cracked, scratchy voice.

"I've missed you, too," Frankie said. "You could have found me."

"I wasn't ready. It's been rough. Healing."

"Yeah," Frankie said. "For me, too."

"But we're here now," he said. "You and me, McGrath. Finally."

He gave her a smile that made her feel young again. For a moment, time fell away; they were Frankie and Jamie again, walking through camp, keeping each other upright, sharing their lives, laughing and crying together, loving each other.

She felt the start of tears, felt them on her face as she stood there, surrounded by her fellow Vietnam veterans, the wall of black granite blurring behind them.

Jamie moved toward her, stumbled; she reached out to steady him. "I've got you," she said, her words echoing his from long ago. There was so much to say to him, words she'd gathered and stored in her memories, dreamed of saying, but there would be time for that, time for them. Today, just being here, holding his hand, was enough. More than enough.

Miraculous.

After all these years, so much pain and regret and loss, they were here, she and Jamie and thousands of others. Battered and limping and in wheelchairs, some of them, but still here. *All of us.* Together again. In a group, at a wall that held the names of the fallen.

Together.

Survivors, all.

They'd been silenced, forgotten for too long, especially the women.

Remembering you got me through.

And there it was: remembrance mattered. She knew that now;

there was no looking away from war or from the past, no soldiering on through pain.

Somehow Frankie would find a way to tell the country about her sisters—the women with whom she'd served. For the nurses who had died, for their children, for the women who would follow in the years to come.

It started here. Now. By speaking up, standing in the sunlight, coming together, demanding honesty and truth. Taking pride.

The women had a story to tell, even if the world wasn't quite yet ready to hear it, and their story began with three simple words.

We were there.

Vietnam Women's Memorial, Washington, D.C.
© 1993, Eastern National, Glenna Goodacre, Sculptor.
Photo Credit: Greg Staley.

Author's Note

This book has been a true labor of love, years in the making. I first conceived of it in 1997, but as a young writer, I wasn't ready to tackle such an important and complex subject. I didn't feel I had the skill or the maturity to achieve my vision. It has taken me decades to circle back to the Vietnam War era.

I was young, in elementary or middle school, for the majority of the war, but I remember it vividly: the protests, the darkening tone of the nightly news, the arc of the story told by the media, more and more young men dying, and most of all, how the veterans—many of them my friends' fathers—were treated when they came home. All of it made a lasting impression.

Reading the firsthand accounts of the women who served in Vietnam was incredibly inspiring. I was also saddened to realize that these women's heroic stories have too often been forgotten or overlooked.

Not enough has been made or recorded or remembered about their service. It is even difficult to get certain agreed-upon numbers of the women who served in Vietnam. According to the Vietnam Women's Memorial Foundation statement, approximately 10,000 American military women were stationed in Vietnam during the war. Most were nurses in the Army, Air Force, and Navy, but women also served as physicians and medical personnel, and in air traffic control and military intelligence. Civilian women also served in Vietnam as news correspondents and workers for the Red Cross, Donut Dollies, the USO, Special Services, the American Friends Service Committee, Catholic Relief Services, and other humanitarian organizations.

Talking to these remarkable women, listening to their stories, and reading their firsthand accounts of both being in Vietnam during the war and their treatment upon coming home to the United States has been a revelation. Many of the women keenly remembered being told often that there "were no women in Vietnam." I am honored to tell this story.

Acknowledgments

This book would not have been possible if not for the help, guidance, honesty, and support of Captain Diane Carlson Evans, a former Army nurse who served in Vietnam. As the founder of the Vietnam Women's Memorial Foundation, she has dedicated much of her postwar life to remembering her sister-veterans who served in the war. Her own story, told in *Healing Wounds*, written with Bob Welch, is a stunning and revelatory look at how she saw her wartime experiences, and was a great help in writing this novel. My gratitude is boundless, Diane. You are truly an inspiration.

I'd also like to thank retired Army Colonel Douglas Moore, Dust Off helicopter pilot and recipient of the Distinguished Service Cross, awarded to him for actions during the Vietnam War. Doug flew 1,847 combat missions, evacuated nearly 3,000 wounded, and was inducted into the Dust Off Hall of Fame in 2004. Thank you for taking the time to read and critique an early draft of *The Women*, and for answering an endless series of follow-up questions.

Thanks to Debby Alexander Moore, Army Special Services recreation director, Vietnam 1968–70, for her help and recollections.

Thanks to Dr. Beth Parks, who served as an Army operating

room nurse at the Seventh Surgical (MASH) and Twelfth Evacuation Hospitals at Cu Chi, Vietnam, in 1966–67. Dr. Parks is now a retired professor and an adventurer, writer, and photographer. She read the manuscript in record time, shared her personal photographs and memories, and added her experience and expertise throughout. I am eternally grateful for her help.

For those who would like to read more about the remarkable women who served in Vietnam and about their return from the war, I can recommend a few outstanding resource books:

Healing Wounds, Diane Carlson Evans, with Bob Welch, Permuted Press, 2020; *American Daughter Gone to War,* Winnie Smith, William Morrow, 1992; *Home Before Morning,* Lynda Van Devanter, University of Massachusetts Press, 2001 (originally published 1983); *Women in Vietnam: The Oral History,* Ron Steinman, TV Books, 2000; *A Piece of My Heart,* Keith Walker, Presidio Press, 1986.

See also: *After the Hero's Welcome,* Dorothy H. McDaniel, WND Books, 2014; *The League of Wives,* Heath Hardage Lee, St. Martin's Press, 2019; *In Love and War,* Jim and Sybil Stockdale, Naval Institute Press, 1990; and *The Turning: A History of Vietnam Veterans Against the War,* Andrew E. Hunt, New York University Press, 1999.

In writing this novel, I have tried to be as historically accurate as possible. Originally I created fictional towns and evacuation hospitals to give myself the greatest possible fictional latitude in telling this story, but my Vietnam veteran readers felt strongly that I should name the places accurately. Therefore, the hospitals and towns mentioned in the novel are all real; the logistics and descriptions and timeline in a few places have been altered to support my narrative. Any errors or mistakes are, of course, my own.

I'd also like to thank Jackie Dolat for her candid remembrances of Alcoholics Anonymous and rehab programs in Southern California in the seventies.

I am grateful for the many people who work with me to make me a better writer. I am especially grateful to my early readers, who speak their minds with sharp honesty (sometimes loudly): Jill Marie Landis, Megan Chance, Ann Patty, and Kim Fisk. And as always, my thanks to Jennifer Enderlin, whose passion for publishing and eagle-eyed editing mean the world to me. Her insightful critique truly made this book what it is. Thanks to the stellar team at St. Martin's; I love working with all of you. And to Andrea Cirillo, Rebecca Scherer, and the gang at Jane Rotrosen Agency; we have been partners in this crazy world of publishing for more than two decades and I can't imagine my life without you all.

As always, I thank my family for continual support and encouragement, especially my husband, Ben, who gamely travels and listens and bears with an author-wife who is sometimes sitting right at the dinner table but is far, far away in her thoughts. To my mother: the memory of you during the war years is indelible; thank you for believing so strongly in what was right. And to my dad, thank you for your adventurous spirit and for opening my eyes to the world beyond my own backyard. To Debbie Edwards John, thank you more than I can possibly say for all that you do. To my son, Tucker, I am proud of you and I adore you, and to Mackenzie, Logan, Lucas, Katie, Kaylee, and Braden: may you love, read, and learn about history. You are the future.

Finally, I'd like to mention a man I've never met: Colonel Robert John Welch, Air Force pilot, who was shot down and lost in Vietnam on January 16, 1967. He never came home. I first got his POW bracelet when I was in elementary school and I wore it for many, many years. My thoughts and prayers have stayed with his family for all of these years.

About the Author

Kevin Lynch

KRISTIN HANNAH is the #1 *New York Times* bestselling author of more than twenty novels, including *The Nightingale*, *The Great Alone*, and *The Four Winds*. A former lawyer turned writer, she lives with her husband in the Pacific Northwest.